DEIRDRE SINNOTT is an author, researcher, and activist for social change. She grew up in the region of Utica, New York, and graduated from Syracuse University. Sinnott speaks nationally about the role of Central New York's residents in the abolition of slavery. She was the originator of Utica's Abolition History Day Celebration and has directed two award-winning documentaries on mass incarceration/prison issues. She facilitated the program "Resisting the New Jim Crow" at the National Abolition Hall of Fame and Museum. Sinnott's writing has appeared in newspapers, two anthologies, literary journals, and in various online resources. *The Third Mrs. Galway* is her first novel. She is a historical consultant for the Fort Stanwix Underground Railroad History Project, funded by the National Park Service.

The
Third
Mrs. Galway

The
Third
Mrs. Galway

deirdre sinnott

KAYLIE JONES BOOKS

Published by Kaylie Jones Books
©2021 Deirdre Sinnott

Paperback ISBN: 978-1-61775-842-3
Library of Congress Control Number: 2020948164

Kaylie Jones Books
www.kayliejonesbooks.com

Akashic Books
Brooklyn, New York
Twitter: @AkashicBooks
Facebook: AkashicBooks
E-mail: info@akashicbooks.com
Website: www.akashicbooks.com

Also Available from Kaylie Jones Books

Cornelius Sky by Timothy Brandoff
The Schrödinger Girl by Laurel Brett
Starve the Vulture by Jason Carney
City Mouse by Stacey Lender
Death of a Rainmaker by Laurie Loewenstein
Unmentionables by Laurie Loewenstein
Like This Afternoon Forever by Jaime Manrique
Little Beasts by Matthew McGevna
Some Go Hungry by J. Patrick Redmond
The Year of Needy Girls by Patricia A. Smith
The Love Book by Nina Solomon
The Devil's Song by Lauren Stahl
All Waiting Is Long by Barbara J. Taylor
Sing in the Morning, Cry at Night by Barbara J. Taylor
Flying Jenny by Theasa Tuohy

From Oddities/Kaylie Jones Books

Angel of the Underground by David Andreas
Foamers by Justin Kassab
Strays by Justin Kassab
We Are All Crew by Bill Landauer
The Underdog Parade by Michael Mihaley
The Kaleidoscope Sisters by Ronnie K. Stephens

To the fighters for justice past, present, and future

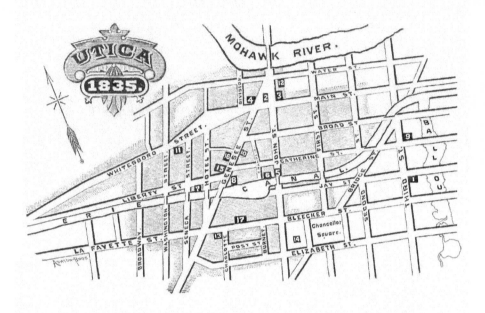

1. Galway House

2. Bagg's Square

3. Bagg's Hotel

4. City Hall

5. John Street Bridge

6. King's Victualing House

7. Canal Buildings

8. National Hotel

9. Sylvanus Bakery

10. Clarke's Temperance House

11. Miller's Hall

12. Horace's Home

13. Bleecker St. Presbyterian Church

14. Courthouse

15. Alvan Stewart's Office

16. Judge Chester Hayden's Court

17. Watchhouse

PART ONE

Utica, New York
October 1835

C HAPTER ONE

THE STINGING OCTOBER RAIN found the small opening between Imari's bonnet and the shawl bundled around her neck. Water slid down her skin, soaking her blouse all the way to the waistband of her skirt, and inched across her protruding belly. She felt heavy, weighted down by the miles and the baby inside her. It kicked and stretched in seeming complaint. Poor mite gotta be feeling bad as me, she thought. Her son looked miserable too, but he kept on. It was a lot to put on a boy of ten.

During the night, when she and Joe had started on this last leg of the journey, she figured that they had plenty of time to get from Frankfort to Utica before the sun came up. At least that was the way it looked on the map. All these months, she had carried herself and the infant inside her through muddy swamps, over mountains, and into the thickest woods. By this point, Joe had grown used to being silent on his feet—and watchful. Last night's miles shouldn't have been a problem, five or six hours of keeping to the Erie Canal's flat towpath and hiding when they passed mule teams pulling boats. But her legs felt weak and the baby wouldn't settle. Now there was a new pain in her abdomen that prickled her worry. They had to get inside, and soon. The day had brought purple-black clouds and cold showers. As they reached the outskirts of the town, the wind picked up. They got off the towpath to look for the wide creek that led to the place they had been seeking.

Only a few dozen steps off the canal, she noticed the last inch of a burning candle in the back window of a small two-story building. That must be the place the Frankfort man said to go, she thought. She pressed her hand down on the new ache. Feel like I only got one more stop in me. Once I set down, I won't be getting up. She decided it would be better to risk it and be at the place where she and her husband, Elymas, had agreed to meet if they got separated. The thought of him made her heart feel like a rope had been drawn around it. Nothing to do now but get to the Galways' property.

Joe bent to pull his boot out of the mud. She stepped between him and the window. "The Ballou Creek," she said, pointing back toward the water. "Ain't that a peculiar name?" He looked grim.

A gust of wind pushed her back on her heels. She grabbed her son to steady herself. Just a week ago she wouldn't have faltered, but now everything felt hard. They trudged on, leaning into the wind, finally stopping four streets up from the canal. Flying leaves swirled around them.

"This be where we going," she said, pointing to a group of buildings near a fine clapboard house.

"The man told us said we was going to a store," Joe said, looking skeptically at the group of buildings nestled in the corner of the block. "That ain't no store."

"Last night the man changed his mind," she said, gripping him. She surveyed the place. "Said go here instead." She knew she shouldn't lie to the boy, but it was easier, he wouldn't know the difference. Besides, Elymas had to be just a few days behind them. She prayed first that this was the right place, then asked God to not abandon her. To please, please let him come.

Lightning flashed, and for a moment the house, barn, and outbuildings looked like they were standing in the noonday sun. A deafening clap of thunder made her cry out. A horse whinnied nearby.

"That storm on top a us!" she shouted, anger and fear raising her voice. "We gotta get inside." They struggled to the corner of the barn. She peeked around.

Another bolt of lightning flashed overhead, its bony fingers disappearing quickly.

"That shed," she said, pointing. "Go!" In a few painful steps, they were inside. She leaned on a table, trying to stay on her feet. Her knees buckled. As she tried to right herself, she swept clay pots and gardening tools to the floor.

"Momma," Joe cried. He went to his knees, catching her and easing her to the ground.

"Good boy," she said, panting in relief as thunder rattled the dusty windows. "Pull that door closed tight. Careful now. Don't get seen." When his back was turned, she shivered.

He sat beside her. "You sick?"

She patted his hand and managed to smile. Even though the baby still squirmed, even though the shed was damp and gloomy, even though her heart ached over her missing husband, they had made it.

"Just need to rest is all," she said, leaning her back against a low wooden cabinet. Her eyes blinked closed and she allowed herself some moments of exhausted rest.

The next thing she knew, the door opened.

CHAPTER TWO

JUST ONE MONTH AFTER HER WEDDING, on the first morning of her first full day in her husband's house, Helen Galway descended the grand staircase, sliding her hand down the smooth cherry banister. She liked how the polished wood felt warm under her fingertips and how her pale hand contrasted with the rich maroon stain. At the bottom of the stairs hung a portrait of the first Mrs. Galway. She knew about her husband's late wife, of course. Augustin had spoken about her in the highest of terms during their monthlong courtship. Every time he did so, Helen had secretly winced.

She studied the painting, trying to dislike her. But Emma Galway's intelligent blue eyes seemed to gaze at her kindly and her golden ringlets framed her face perfectly and her creamy shoulders disappeared so discreetly into a handsome emerald dress that all Helen could do was envy her. Apologies, my dear lady, she thought. Today I begin to push you out of his thoughts.

The previous night, after the arduous journey back to Utica from their honeymoon in New York City, Augustin had gotten word that he must attend an emergency meeting of the American Colonization Society. The group had something to do with relocating slaves to Africa, but she had not followed the details when he explained it to her. He instructed her not to wait up, but instead to meet him in the library first thing in the morning. So strange, he seemed to love to keep her in suspense—testing her rather than simply saying what he wanted.

A burst of conversation came from the room to her right. Startled, she moved away from the painting and knocked on the door before remembering that Miss Manahan had taught students to "compose yourselves before entering a room so as not to bring any excited emotion inside."

"Come," her husband's voice commanded. She yanked the door open and stood on her tiptoes at its threshold. On the far wall, rows and rows of books stood neatly arranged on shelves that ran the entire length and height of the room. She had never expected to see so many hundreds of volumes in one place.

"They will never be comfortable here," Augustin was saying to a handsome stranger who nodded in agreement. "Africa is their natural homeland. Once the Negroes understand what the Colonization Society offers in Liberia, they'll be glad to go."

The other man rose, his fingers stroking an exquisitely trimmed blond beard. He smiled at her, his eyebrow rising in apparent approval. A shiver of nerves rattled through her and she quickly refocused her attention to the floor. When she looked at him again, his eyes traveled over her as if she were a confection in a shop window. Her stomach tightened, and the sting of a blush made her snap her eyes down again. It's not proper to stare like that, she thought. Why is Augustin letting this happen?

"My dear, what are you wearing?" her husband asked. She noticed that his right leg was wrapped in bandages and elevated on a pillow-covered footstool.

"What happened?" She rushed to his side and reached out to touch his leg.

"Leave that alone, Mrs. Galway," said the blond man.

Helen obediently pulled her hand back. She turned to Augustin. Surely it would be rude to demand to know who the man was, but wasn't it up to the husband to make the introductions?

"Dr. Corliss McCooke," Augustin said, remembering himself, "Mrs. Galway, and so on." He waved his hand through the air. "Don't worry about the leg. It's only a simple break. Dr. McCooke happened by and helped me home."

"You must be in terrible pain," she said, touching his arm.

"Don't trouble yourself." He patted her hand. "It's nothing and the doctor is seeing to it."

Helen's eyes met the doctor's, but again she found his gaze so penetrating that she quickly looked away. "If you say so."

"Now, my little one, don't you like your new clothes? You picked out some beautiful gowns in New York. Why wear that old school dress when you could be so lovely?"

Her hand rose to the collar and touched her own stitching. "I was not expecting any company."

"Company? I didn't buy those dresses for company. I bought them because you're now my wife." His voice softened. "You're the lady of the house. Your appearance reflects on me."

"Of course," she said. "I'll go change. If you'll excuse me."

"And see Maggie. She's readying the spare room for the doctor and needs help with the shopping. She'll tell you where to go."

"Is the doctor staying here?" she asked, noticing the contrast between his mild features and appraising eye.

"Dr. McCooke has graciously agreed to lodge with us until I'm well."

"I am at your service," said the doctor, bowing slightly, a smile rising on his lips. "You see, I found him after he had fallen off his horse. Luckily, I arrived a few minutes before the three a.m. coach made a meat pie out of him."

"Never mind that," said Augustin. "Dearest, as Mrs. Galway, you have new duties. I expect you to take charge of managing the house. Make sure things run smoothly. I want you to familiarize yourself with the property and Maggie's work."

Helen bowed her head.

"Now go about your business, my dear."

She took one last look at the rows of books, many more than the meager supply at Miss Manahan's Female Institute, her old school. As she closed the door, she heard her husband remark, "Doctor, open that bottle of brandy. Imported from Paris. I got an entire case of it."

Helen made her way past the serene face of Mrs. Galway, who now seemed to look at her with pity. After a frustrated sigh, she ran up to her chambers. At the closet, she examined the array of dresses that had been chosen for her by her husband and whatever seamstress happened to be staffing the various shops they visited. The clothing seemed far too fancy for shopping or simply sitting around the house. And what if she ran into one of the girls from the school? They might think that she now put herself above them.

She removed the gray frock and buried it deep in the closet. A sliver of her mind still believed that her husband might find her unsuitable and send her back to Miss Manahan like a bandy-legged horse.

Standing before the mirror on her boudoir table, she held up an ocher-colored gown. It was a fine dress, lovely, soft, with fashionably puffy sleeves. The earthy tone complemented her pale skin and dark hair. A woman should be proud to have such a gown. Mrs. Galway certainly would have been proud. Helen decided to wear it, as if she always dressed this way.

As she changed, a rumble of thunder brought her to the window. Rain beat against the pane, distorting her view. Past the shed and the barn, the line of trees at the back of the property bent in the wind. There'd be no leaves left after this storm. Already the waving branches were bare enough that she could see all the way out to the Ballou. The creek's swift waters often kept the basin from freezing over until mid-January. More than one restless child had tested the ice before New Year's, only to find himself falling through to the freezing water. Miss Manahan kept equipment handy in case a rescue was necessary. The fire volunteers had hooks and ropes for those unlucky enough to fall through and never surface again.

Lightning flashed and a crack of thunder sounded as if someone were pounding on the roof. The storm was strong, but there was a sharp line of bright sky in the distance. I'll wait for the rain to pass, she thought, turning back to the room.

Apparently, even to go shopping, a married woman had to be exquisitely dressed, so she continued pulling and tying drawstrings and adding the necessary decorative items until she again stood before the mirror. Her gown was accompanied by a dark-violet shawl, high-brimmed bonnet, and white gloves—the outfit of a proper lady. I can't . . . I have no business wearing a dress so nice, she thought, as a flush of shame climbed up her long neck, crept over her too-round cheeks, clamored past her brown eyes and dark brows, and brightened her face all the way to her widow's peak.

The next flash of lightning was blindingly close and followed immediately by a clap of thunder. She ran to the window to see if the barn had been hit. There seemed to be no damage to anything in the circle of outbuildings. Everything was the same, except that the shed door was open. It had been closed just a moment ago. She supposed that this was the sort of thing that Augustin expected her to care about when he said she should take charge. Oh, why wasn't there a manservant to send out to close it? Perhaps she could ask the cook to check.

She found Maggie, a middle-aged black woman, across the hall in the guest room, snapping a pillow cover and surrounded by bedsheets.

"Don't you look nice," said Maggie. Helen smiled, looking down at the dress. A clap of thunder made both women jump. "Oh, that's some storm. If you ask me, it's that darn Halley comet Mr. Augustin's been on about."

"That doesn't affect the weather, does it?"

"It's messing with everything," said Maggie. "We're in for it. Mr. Augustin say no, but to me everything's just different."

"I'm sure we'll be all right," said Helen. "You have a shopping list?"

"You ain't going out now, are you? That rain will be the devil on that nice dress."

Lightning flickered outside. Helen counted, "One . . . two . . . three . . . four—" The thunder stopped her. "I saw the edge of the storm. It will end soon, I think."

Maggie dug deep in the pocket of her dress and pulled out a carefully lettered list. As Helen held it, Maggie came up behind her.

"You read my writing?"

"It's perfect," said the younger woman.

Maggie pointed to one item. "Mr. Augustin said for me to tell you to find Mr. Horace down by Bagg's Hotel for that there." She leaned in. "He don't eat no fish but Mr. Horace's fish."

"Very well. Oh, by the way, the shed door is open," said Helen. "I'm afraid rain's getting in there."

"Now the shed's broke? As if I ain't busy enough." Maggie began stretching the sheet over the bed. "I swear, this whole place gonna fall apart 'cause a that comet."

"I'll check on the door before I go," said Helen quickly. "Is there a shopping basket?"

"Kitchen," said Maggie, nodding toward the back. She returned to the sheets.

Helen went down the tight servants' stairs into the warm kitchen and lingered at the back window, peering at the shed. All seemed perfectly normal now, door closed, nothing wrong. No reason to bother Augustin with this. He and the doctor seemed to be settling into drinking brandy this morning. She supposed that despite his denial, he must be in pain. Now was not the time to trouble him with something she could see to herself. And to ask McCooke? No. No. She wanted to make sure to have little to do with him. Besides, management of the house now fell to her.

Lightning flickered. She counted one . . . two . . . three . . . four . . . five . . . six . . . thunder. The clatter of rain on the roof slowed as if God had simply moved his water jug to some other spot. The storm was moving off.

She took a deep breath before plunging into the backyard. Light rain landed on her face as she marched to the shed. The iron handle was in place, but still she swung the door wide and stepped inside.

A woman's voice cried out from the dark. A metal bowl crashed to the ground and Helen heard scrambling as if she had startled a sleeping fox. Out of the gloom, a skinny black boy leaped before her, a hayfork in his hands. Helen gasped and backed up to the frame of the door, her muscles twitching in fear.

"Stop, Joe," came a sharp female voice from the floor. The boy neither dropped the long wooden fork nor backed away. "Sorry, miss," said the voice.

"Keep away from me," cried Helen, stepping back.

"Joe, I told you," said the voice sternly. "Get back here." The boy lowered the weapon, but did not withdraw. "Sit down," the voice commanded.

He kept his eyes on Helen. As he kneeled he revealed a woman sitting on the dirt floor, her legs straight out in front of her. She leaned against a sturdy built-in cabinet, a very large pregnant belly resting between her legs.

"What are you doing here?" demanded Helen, thinking that she should run and get . . . who? Her husband? No. He had a broken leg. The doctor? Heavens, not *him*. Maggie. She would get the cook out here—

"We sorry, miss. Just getting outta the rain," said the woman, talking very quickly. "Just getting outta the storm. Don't worry. Joe here got surprised, is all."

"You can't be here," said Helen, calming a little, stepping back into the shed. Looking at the woman more closely, she noticed that her tan blouse drooped with dampness. Her skin, the color of newspaper left too long in the sun, was heavily freckled and her face was as round as a casserole dish. Her hair disappeared under a dirty gray cap. A shawl was pulled tight across her shoulders as if she were freezing. Suddenly the woman clutched her stomach and groaned.

"Momma," the boy cried.

"Is the baby coming? Now?" said Helen, her voice strangled with new fear.

The last time she had been around a woman this close to lying-in was during her mother's labor. Poor Momma had screamed and ranted when the baby had tried to come out too early. She had pulled off her own britches and groped at a tiny foot dangling between her thighs. The ordeal had all ended finally, but the time spent waiting for her father to get a doctor had been full of blood and panic, leaving Helen helpless and her mother and her new brother quite dead. All the doctor had done was hold a mirror to her mother's mouth and declare that she was at peace.

"I'm getting a doctor," Helen said, looking back at the house.

"No, no," cried the woman. "Don't. The baby ain't coming. Don't bring no one else out here."

"You can't have a baby here. I'm getting someone."

"No, no, no," the woman pleaded in a loud desperate voice, her hands skyward, fingers knotted together as if in prayer.

The boy jumped to his feet again and grabbed Helen's arm.

"Let me go!" she yelled, and jerked backward.

"No. Please. Don't be scared. He just a boy," begged the woman. With her next breath she began to sing the first few trembling words of a lullaby. "*Dear baba, ah yaw, ah yaw, who momma is right here . . .*"

Helen froze, stunned by the thin reedy voice as it followed the simple course of a slow rhythmic melody.

"*Nice dry straw, ah yaw, ah yaw, lay you down so near, ah yaw . . .*"

Something inside Helen shifted. She stared back at the woman, who drew her hands around her pregnant belly, hugging the unborn babe. The tune, so plain and soothing, pierced Helen to her very marrow. For a moment, she had a vision of her mother, alive and young, her face close. She too was singing.

The woman's voice cracked as tears coursed down her face. "*Now you go to dream, ah yaw, sleep the night away . . .*"

Helen felt tears gathering in her own eyes.

"*Momma near, all is clear, ah yaw. Baba in the hay, ah yaw, ah yaw, baba sleep away.*"

All was silent. Together, as if on cue, all three released a breathy sigh.

Helen wiped at her eyes and closed the shed door. She pulled an overturned bucket to the center of the entranceway and sat quietly for a moment. "Who are you?"

"Imari, miss. My son, Joe."

The room darkened and brightened as clouds streaked across the sky.

"I believe you need a doctor," Helen said calmly.

"The baby ain't coming," said Imari. "I just need to rest awhile. Please, don't bring no doctor or no one else out here. You so very nice. I don't mean to trouble you." She took a few quick breaths as if to calm the pain. "Sorry, miss. What can I call you?"

"Helen—I mean Mrs. Galway."

"Yes, Mrs. Galway, ma'am." Imari closed her eyes as she gathered herself, pulling her shawl around her shoulders again. "Sorry we scared you. But you be doing a kindness to just let me sit a spell, Mrs. Galway. We gonna get through it. This ain't the baby's first fit." Imari tried to relax. Nothing was going to come right unless she was still. That's how it had worked with her other pregnancies and she prayed that it would work that way again. She moved her hands over her belly, making tiny circles with her fingers. If she could settle, the baby might settle too. She looked up at the woman. Gotta be a way to stay, she thought. Can't be sent back outside in wet clothing to spend hours in the open. The monster, Hickox, might be searching the town right now. They had to stay out of sight. She glanced at her son. He hugged his knees, his body absolutely still, watching the white woman. Her boy had almost gone crazy trying to protect her. The loss of Elymas had changed him and now he seemed like an oar bobbing away. Why had she been so stupid as to bypass the place she was supposed to have gone? Risky and foolish. She studied the white woman's face. Mrs. Galway. At least this was the right place.

"I'm sorry, but you can't stay," said Helen.

"See, me and Joe just walking along on the creek back there when that wind start blowing," Imari said. "Them clouds roll across the sky and rain got to falling and I know we gotta find shelter, missus. And the baby, he putting up some kinda fuss, kicking and twisting. He scared a getting killed by that lightning. So, I don't want to disturb nobody. I seen that don't nobody come in here. Figure we stay till this storm be over. Just a few hours a rest is all, missus. Please. We supposed to meet a man. He gonna take care a us."

Helen's mouth hung open, shock apparent on her face. She looked around as if something unimaginable had befallen her. "I don't know," she finally managed to say.

"Joe, my boy," Imari said, putting her hand on his arm, "he cold. He soaked through." She turned back to Helen. "He scared."

"Him? Scared of me?" asked Helen. "I didn't do anything."

"And you don't gotta do nothing, missus." Imari took her time, trying to talk calmly, the way one might speak to a wild creature. "Just close that there door and we be quiet as mice."

Helen drew back and glanced toward the door. She looked again at Imari, who nodded.

"We be quiet, missus," Imari whispered. "A few hours, then we be gone."

Helen looked again at the door. "Very well." After a quick glance back at the other two, she stood and left, closing the door behind her.

Imari patted her son's shoulder. "We gonna be all right," she said, and tried to make herself believe it.

C HAPTER THREE

HELEN LOITERED ON THE EDGE of Utica's Bagg's Square, her uneasy mind focused on the people in the shed. If they were still there next time she checked, she should order them to leave. But the woman was with child and Helen could not imagine herself being that cruel. The easiest thing was to do nothing, just as Imari had urged. Later they'd be gone as promised.

A young black boy passed hauling a stack of kindling on his back. How awful to be born a Negro, she thought. But they were a sturdy people. The stack of wood this boy carried looked quite heavy and yet he managed. Then again, the boy in the shed had been too skinny. Where had the pair come from? Vagrants, no doubt. They were so poorly dressed for October's unpredictable weather. She didn't believe for a moment that there was some man who would solve whatever their problem was.

Genesee Street bustled. Passengers loaded themselves onto a westbound stagecoach. An open carriage breezed by carrying several giggling ladies enjoying the respite from the rain. One woman protected her shining peach face with a tall leghorn hat that had a high shell-like brim and a large rose fashioned out of ribbons. What would it be like to be so carefree?

Helen shook her head and studied the shopping list. It was time to start, so she moved toward Williams & Hollister Grocers. A man in long pants with suspenders stretching over his corpulent form set to rights bushels of produce in front of the establishment. While Helen took in a deep calming breath, she noticed a tall, twig-thin man removing a handbill that had been nailed on the doorframe.

"Alvan Stewart's at it again," called the thin one to the thick. In bold black letters the notice read, *Come to New York Anti-Slavery Society's Founding Convention.* "Them abolitionists gonna tear this city apart. Heck, they's ready to burn up the whole nation."

"I told you—leave it alone," said the heavy one. "Meetings and conventions? That's too heady for the likes of us."

"Oh? You're for Stewart bringing them traitors into our city?"

"You're impossible," said the first man as he shifted his generous weight onto his right heel and swung into the store. The thin man's gaze followed his partner and he seemed about to prolong the argument when he noticed Helen fanning herself with a piece of paper.

"Is that meeting today?" she asked, alarmed.

The grocer lit up with attentiveness. "No it ain't, pretty miss. Say, you ain't gonna faint, is you? You fashionable gals always looking for a place to keel over."

The list quivered in her gloved hand. "I'm shopping," Helen said, squaring her shoulders, "for Mr. Galway." She poked the paper in his direction.

"So, Galway finally broke down and got him a housekeep," he said. "Good. He got laid low real bad when Mrs. Galway passed."

"*I'm* Mrs. Galway," she said firmly, surprising herself.

The man opened his mouth as if he wanted to add an additional comment, but had the good sense to refrain. He took the list and began reading Maggie's careful handwriting, gathering eggs, apples, autumn lettuce, tomatoes, carrots, parsnips, acorn squash, and cabbage, and methodically packed Helen's basket.

"Excuse me, miss . . . I mean, ma'am, it don't say what color beans." He held up his hands, right fist filled with yellow beans, the left with green.

Helen froze. Which was correct? She looked from right to left and back again. That Augustin had a preference, she had no doubt. He had a preference about everything. Why had Maggie not written it down? She thought back but could remember no instance of seeing him eat beans while they had honeymooned. She liked her green beans snapped short, blanched, and swimming in melted butter, but that might be the wrong choice. She should never have allowed herself to be instructed by him to go shopping. Wasn't that what a cook was for?

The grocer dropped his left hand and the green beans fell back into their bushel.

"Maggie usually gets the yellow," he said. "I'll just pack them."

When she left the store, her basket overflowed with the groceries. Her last errand required her to find the fishmonger, "Mr. Horace."

On the street, she watched as children darted between horses and oxcarts. It had all seemed quite easy before the wedding. Her days at school had been structured with classes, piano practice, needlework, reading, and drawing. She knew where to sit in church and which of the dormitory beds was hers. She thought she understood Utica's streets from her outings to the lending library at Mechanics Hall, but now everything seemed different.

Just a few feet away, two men tied their horses to a post in front of City Hall. One, his clothing dusty and stained, was thick with muscles. His face had a beaten look; nose flattened and ears rippled with strange lumps. The other, a sinewy man in his fifties, had a bullwhip hanging from his belt. Dangling from his saddle, iron chains clinked as the beast shifted. She heard someone mutter, "Slave catchers," and noticed shackles the size of wrists and necks dangling at the ends of the chains. How horrible, she thought.

As she turned, she saw a black woman and young boy hurrying through the intersection. With a jolt, she realized that the two people in the shed might be escaped slaves. A shiver went through her.

Miss Manahan had explained during her lectures on the "evidences of Christianity" that slavery had been common in the Bible. She said that only the worst types of men tried to escape their Christian duty and run away from their rightful, God-given masters. It could be compared to running away from one's own father. Perhaps a strict father, Miss Manahan allowed, but strictness was often called for when trying to civilize the Negroes. But, to Helen, these two men didn't seem to be the type to be on God's business. Helen supposed that the roughest lawmen would be the ones to chase down escaped slaves.

She dismissed the slave idea about the two in the shed. Here, in Utica? How ridiculous. But it was strange that the pair appeared on the same day as these slave catchers. If they were really runaways she supposed that turning them in was the right and lawful thing to do and would perhaps even earn Mr. Galway's approval. But then she remembered how desperate Imari had been—and how far gone with child. When Helen looked up, the older slave catcher met her gaze. Dirt had collected in the wrinkles around his blue eyes. He winked. She bristled. Good men didn't take such liberties. Quick as a breath, she decided that she would not turn the Negroes over to these men. With determination, she turned away and plunged into the bustle of the square. The situation is impossible, she thought. I can't decide the fate of another human being. She wished fervently that she had never opened that shed door. Well, they will be gone by the time I get back. I did what I was asked. Nothing more I can do. Still, she worried about them. It might be that they had already been discovered and that she might be in trouble. At least if she were home she would know one way or the other.

Once in front of Bagg's Hotel, she began looking urgently for Mr. Horace. The sharp smell of fish, hours out of their natural element, drew her attention to the northeast corner of John and Main Streets. There stood a fish cart, but seemingly attended only by a scruffy Negro in a floppy hat talking to another black man wearing spectacles and a suit. The scruffy one wore his pants rolled up at the bottoms, as if they had initially belonged to someone taller. He had dark skin and a smooth face. She watched as he caught sight of the two slave catchers walking into City Hall and signaled to the fellow in the suit. The man in the suit handed the scruffy one a newspaper and hurried away.

Approaching the cart, Helen opened her mouth to speak. The man leaned toward her. Her lips swiftly closed.

"Can I help you, miss?" he asked. "Got all kinda fish here."

"Please," Helen swallowed, "I'd like to speak to Mr. Horace?"

"I'm Horace, miss." He smiled and bowed with a flourish. "Horace Wilberforce, at your service."

"Oh." Maggie should have mentioned that she'd be looking for a black fellow. Flustered and anxious to be back at Augustin's . . . or, she supposed, her own home, she tried to ignore the darkness of the man and the stench of the cart, instead concentrating on her final task— picking out the right fish for her husband's supper.

"Is that a good type of fish?" she finally asked, after staring into the eyes of a spiny twitching specimen. She watched Horace's brown hand wave off flies.

"That's a popular fish, miss," he said. "Many folks swear by the sweet meat of the bullhead. And he a smart kinda fish, living off what others too proud to eat. You gotta watch that spine right there when you gut him, miss. That'll cut you quick, if he wriggles." Horace reached under the cart and produced a recent edition of the *Oneida Whig* newspaper. With a high degree of showmanship, he chose a fat bullhead and placed it in the center of the paper. "I tell you what. I can clean him right out. Save you the trouble."

"Wait. I want to be certain that Mr. Galway likes this type. He is very particular."

"Mr. Augustin Galway? He your uncle, miss?"

"No. Certainly not," she said, her finger twisting her bonnet ribbon around itself. "He's my husband."

"Excuse me." Horace lowered his eyes, removed the bullhead from the *Whig*, and selected a sturdy brook trout. Its sleek brown body wriggled, revealing a rouge-red belly and tan spots running across its back and tail. "Mr. Galway like his trout nice and fresh. The one here was swimming in the Mohawk just this morning, miss . . . I mean ma'am. Swimming and eating flies like that the only thing to do." In a flash, he had his knife out and split the poor trout's belly.

Wind suddenly streamed down John Street.

Horace looked to the sky. "That storm ain't done with us yet," he said. "Warm for this time a year."

Helen did not answer, instead peering up John Street toward the approaching clouds. Horace cleaned out the stomach cavity before closing the paper around the trout. Helen produced a few coins from a small crocheted bag tied to her wrist like a child's mitten.

"Coming from the south. That sort of wind never bring nobody no good." He pocketed the money. "You better get home, little missus."

Helen set the fish in her shopping basket and stalked up John Street in a temper. To think that people in Utica didn't even know Augustin had remarried. There had hardly been time to announce the banns at church, but was there no advertisement about it in the papers? Why had word not traveled beyond St. John's parish?

She had first noticed her future husband one summer morning, just when the bee balm opened their shaggy red heads and attracted hummingbirds to the garden of Miss Manahan's Female Institute. Helen surprised the younger students by lifting her arms over her head and doing a perfect cartwheel, ending with hands raised again. The girls cheered. After a moment of dizziness, she saw a man in the upper window of the house next door, looking at her, a pipe in one hand, the other smoothing his pointed brown beard. There was softness around his waist, but on the whole, his thin face and noble forehead reminded her of a scholar. The girls circled Helen, demanding to know how she managed the tumble. She set about teaching them, all the while secretly checking to see if the man was still watching. He was.

After several days of catching his eye, she began to build a story around him. He was a duke, or a count, or a marquis, exiled from his home country, sad and lonely and in need of company. She imagined that she would speak to him in his native language, charming him in French, or maybe Italian. She saw him kissing her hand, his mustache tickling her fingertips. Once, he even invaded her dreams, beard prickling her cheek and neck, a delightful soft brush that seemed to expand throughout her body. She awoke to her heart vibrating like a rabbit's in an open field.

July 31, the morning of her nineteenth birthday, he was not in his regular spot. Miss Manahan appeared on the threshold of the school building and beckoned her inside. She sat Helen down in the straight-backed pupil's chair of her austere office.

"I have never been a matchmaker for my girls," Miss Manahan began, "but since your mother and father are with God, I have little choice. There is a man who would like to meet you."

Helen drew in a sharp breath. Could it be her secret count? She felt heat rising up her neck and face. Had she won him with her cartwheels?

"He is a wealthy man. This would be a good match for you," said Miss Manahan. "Now, take a few minutes to make your toilet and don't neglect your hair."

Helen started up the stairs.

Miss Manahan called to her, "Use the mirror in my room, child. You look like Goliath has been holding you upside down."

When Helen opened the French doors of the parlor and saw the schoolmistress sitting on the divan with the man from next door, a sheen of glittery blackness blocked her vision. She gripped the door handles, afraid that she might swoon.

"Don't linger at the doorway like an indecisive cat, Helen. Enter the room," Miss Manahan said.

All Helen had learned about the proper way to comport herself flew out of her mind.

"Mr. Augustin Galway, this is Miss Helen O'Connell."

Augustin moved toward her, the warm smile from previous days absent. It had been replaced by a frozen critical look. Behind him, Miss Manahan mimed a curtsy. Helen, taking the cue, bent her knee, looked at the carpet, and bowed low.

"Miss O'Connell," said Galway.

She kept her eyes on a spot of carpet that had been worn through. A bit of the walnut planking could be seen through the hole. "Mr. Galway," she said.

"I must return to my office," said Miss Manahan. "I'll order tea brought in."

Alarmed, Helen watched her. The teacher gave her shoulder an encouraging squeeze and left.

"I understand you are alone in this world," the man said. "I, too, am alone. Mrs. Galway has been gone from this earth for a twelvemonth. A man could ask for no better than she. I have no children. I have my business." He shook his head, turning swiftly back to the divan and with a sweeping gesture indicating that she should sit. Helen obeyed.

He was no count, nor a French aristocrat, but he was attractive, if a bit older, with gray hairs interspersed among his curls. She had no idea how many years separated them. He might be thirty-five, or perhaps older. But he was no old man. His shoulders were square, though not as broad as her father's. He appeared to be in possession of his teeth. The gray eyes that studied her seemed chilly, but then again, they had never met before.

"It's your birthday?"

She nodded.

"If you'll permit me, I brought you this token."

A small package, neatly tied with a piece of dyed string, lay in his outstretched palm. Helen's hands remained in her lap. What did it mean to take the gift? Miss Manahan said he was a good match. Did this one package seal the matter? He seemed to see her hesitation and his hand dropped. He bent his head.

Alarmed that she had caused him pain, she spoke: "Please, let me see it."

Augustin again offered the gift. Helen felt its weight and took a deep breath before opening the box. Inside, nestled in lamb's wool, sat a necklace with a pendant. It was about the size of a sugar cookie and had a depiction of a Roman ruin with two figures seated on one of the fallen stones. Each element was made of small colored pieces of enameled glass that formed a mosaic. She flipped it over. On the back, there was an engraving: *For Emma, my love.*

"Happy birthday," said Augustin.

She met his eye. "It's lovely. Thank you." Later, she retreated to her bed and cried bitter tears. She was simply to be a replacement.

The courtship consisted of three additional parlor visits—with several of the older girls listening at the keyhole—and a few more presents: earrings, a bracelet, and finally a ring.

The wedding took place one month later, a simple affair at the Roman Catholic church. After the service, the hired carriage had bumped across Bleecker Street. At the front entranceway of the house, Miss Manahan herself stood in her charcoal dress and white cap, her face pale, spine straight, and carrying a look of satisfaction. Waiting behind her stood Maggie, with an expression of curiosity. It struck Helen that the black woman was now *her* servant. She let the carriage curtain drop and closed her eyes. *Please, God,* she prayed, *show me the way.*

Augustin slipped his arm around her waist. "Don't linger, my dear," he said. "The stagecoach will not wait for us." He leaned in and kissed her cheek, his salt-and-pepper beard soft against her skin. His lips touched her ear. "I want to be in Albany by nightfall."

A spasm of fear and anticipation streaked through her.

At the door, he pulled Miss Manahan aside. The words "instruct her" reached her ear and she saw Miss Manahan nod.

"Mr. Augustin said I gotta help you get ready," said Maggie, smiling and nodding.

"I'm sure I can manage."

"Mr. Augustin says help," said the cook, winking, "so I'm gonna help."

I am a wife now, Helen thought. The idea still didn't feel right, even though she had been repeating the sentence since the marriage service.

In the bedchamber, Maggie assisted her out of her frock and into a new auburn silk dress—a gift from Mr. Galway. Miss Manahan paced the length of the rug.

"Of course," the schoolteacher began, "normally your mother

would . . . ready you for what is to come. But it has fallen to me to tell you." The older woman looked up to the ceiling as if for divine inspiration. "A woman's happiness depends entirely on her husband. That means it is your job to be pleasing, to care for him, and to prepare for children."

Helen opened her mouth, but Miss Manahan stopped her.

"Mr. Galway is a man of worldly experience. He will guide you in the particulars."

Maggie caught her mistress's eye. "Don't you worry," she murmured, "every bride gotta go through it."

C HAPTER FOUR

As HELEN PROCEEDED UP JOHN STREET with her full shopping basket, the humid wind seemed to flatten the puffy melon-shaped sleeves of her dress around the down cushions that bolstered them. Her skirt, stylishly full with four wide pleats—front, back, and sides, like the points on a weather vane—clung to her petticoats and pantalets. She was certain that every man now had his own private view of her legs. Her carefully arranged dark hair began to curl in the damp air, pulling loose of its pins and showing itself under her hat. All manner of folk pressed around her.

Before her stood the John Street Bridge spanning the forty-foot-wide Erie Canal. As she stepped up onto the weather-darkened timbers, she thought back to being plain old Helen O'Connell and coming here to sketch and dream as the long narrow boats were pulled by mule teams. Young boys used switches to keep the animals moving on the towpath. Raw materials like lumber and quarry stone traveled east toward the big cities; finished goods, like huge bundles of pretty calicos that the girls at Miss Manahan's sighed over in the stores, traveled west. She had once sketched a load of freshly dug potatoes overtopping the hold of a freight vessel. In her drawing, the ship looked like a floating rock garden. The packet boats, crowded with passengers, interested her the most. They had raised sleeping compartments with windows and pretty curtains. On their roofs, chairs were filled with people taking the air. Sometimes she was lucky and saw fancy ladies whose dresses she could sketch. But the packet boats traveling west always gave her some heartache. That was the direction Uncle Bill had gone. When he'd dropped her off at Miss Manahan's she sobbed and he drew her to his chest. "I'll send for you," he had promised. The money he gave to Miss

Manahan for her board and education had dried up more than a year ago. He'd sent just one letter, from Buffalo, where he joked that he "ran out of canal." She knew at the time that he had to leave her behind. What could Uncle have done with a fourteen-year-old girl? For five years, she dreamed of joining him, but the invitation never came.

She climbed to the center of the bridge and looked east over the water. Her eye was drawn to a pair of mules slowly pulling a long packet boat. One of the animals, a handsome white, was dotted with large gray splotches that looked like ink stains. Quickly she put down the shopping basket, stripped off her glove, and pulled a small sketch pad and piece of charcoal from a sack hanging around her waist. The wind pulled at the pages and she had to press them flat with her palm. Her other hand danced across the paper marking the mule's spots. The team grew closer and she moved to the mule's brown and white face and tall forward-facing ears.

Just as the animal disappeared under the bridge, a voice called to her from the packet: "Forget about those old mules."

Her eyes rose.

"You can draw me." A smiling young man standing on the top of the ship's sleeping compartment plopped his top hat onto his head and struck a pompous pose, as if in a painter's studio. She brought her hand to her mouth to hide her amusement.

"What's that mule got that I haven't?" he said, coming closer as the boat continued its leisurely pace on the canal.

"At least," she began, struggling to think of something clever, "he has honest work to do." The man was near to her now. A lock of flyaway blond hair waved under his hat, and his eyes matched his hunter-green tailcoat.

"What kind of scoundrel do you take me for?" he said, keeping close to her by walking toward the back of the boat.

"The kind who has the . . ." she paused, fully engaged in the repartee, "*effrontery* to speak to ladies to whom he has not been introduced."

"What about you? What kind of girl talks to strange gentlemen?"

"The kind who must go home," she said, snapping her notebook shut and jamming it into her sack.

"Wait. I'm sorry. Pryce Anwell, of Little Falls, at your service," he said before bowing. His top hat flipped off his head, but he managed to catch it in midair.

"Careful, Mr. Anwell," she said, trying not to smile, "you're running out of boat."

Pryce saw that he had indeed come to the edge of the raised platform and leaped down to the deck of the vessel, surprising two men who had stationed themselves there to smoke cigars. He pressed between them to lean on the railing. "Favor me with your name, miss," he called, arching his back to keep her in view.

The packet disappeared beneath the bridge.

"Please!" His voice bounced off the stone walls of the tunnel. A delighted panic took hold of her. Impulsively, she picked up her skirts and ran across John Street. At the other side of the bridge, she saw him racing up the deck to meet her.

"You crossed the street, now you've got to tell me your name," he said merrily.

She laughed a little, surprised at her own boldness. "I'm Helen."

"Ah, fair Helen," he replied, his voice overly serious, "is this the face that launch'd a thousand packet boats?" He climbed again to the raised part of the ship and moved close to her. "Don't omit your family name."

She opened her mouth, but what to say? O'Connell? Galway?

"Helen is enough for a presumptuous man like you," she said finally, pulling her violet shawl close around her shoulders.

"Beauteous Helen," he said, striding as close as he could and speaking low so that only she could hear, "shall a thousand poets bleed?"

"You really are too much." She covered her pleasure with an outraged tone.

"Now I've offended you." A look of genuine concern crossed his face. He slowed his pace and the ship moved him away.

A pall of disappointment overcame her. "It's O'Connell," she called to him, immediately wishing she could take the answer back.

"What?" he said as he raced back toward her. Just as he got near enough for them to touch, he reached the end of the sleeping compartment and only saved himself by leaping onto the railing of the ship. There he teetered for a moment, his arms whipping through the air like Dutch windmills. The two cigar smokers tried to support his legs, but momentum had already carried him too far over the water and he splashed into the canal.

Helen screamed and started back. She saw him rise from the shallow water, unhurt, but dripping wet.

"He your sweetie?" someone said too close to her ear. A passing clerk wearing a striped waistcoat raised his left eyebrow in a knowing gesture.

"No," insisted Helen, reaching down for her shopping basket. It wasn't there. A sickening feeling came to her throat. All the food . . . it was lost. She saw the full basket on the other side of the bridge and ran across, sweeping it into her arms. When she looked longingly back, passersby appeared to be discussing her. Not daring to check any further on Mr. Anwell's condition, she drew in a sharp breath, bent her head low so that the brim of her bonnet hid most of her blushing face, and hurried away toward Bleecker Street and home.

A new thunderhead appeared over the New Hartford hills.

C HAPTER FIVE

DR. MCCOOKE REFILLED TWO SNIFTERS with generous portions of brandy.

The permanent crease between Augustin's eyebrows deepened. McCooke, feeling the heat of disapproval on his back, put the brandy in its spot on the maple tea table among the bottles of Holland gin, St. Croix rum, and Jamaican spirits. He applied a smile and turned. "Here is a second dose of tonic for the pain. Doctor's orders."

"That is why I am drinking it, Doctor. Why are you?"

"We share the same medical man," McCooke joked, as he took a quick and deep snort from his glass. "Really fine stuff."

"You won't find real French brandy at Williams & Hollister no matter what label they paste on," said Augustin, sipping.

McCooke turned toward the front window and swirled the brandy in his glass. Augustin's broken leg could not have come at a better time. In McCooke's present situation, he might have had to sleep in a barn. Never in his life had he dealt with such a discourteous landlord as Clarke. He had known that if you lodged in a temperance house you were supposed to be some kind of saint and never even have a glass of ale—even outside the establishment. Of course, drinking a few brandies inside would be frowned upon. That's why one had to keep it quiet, but the idea that they could demand total sobriety, well, that was inhuman.

Clarke hadn't said as much when he confronted the doctor about his small stash of alcohol, but McCooke suspected that he also disapproved of his examining a few patients in his rooms. It was proper enough. One had to be kind to the lower classes. What if an unaccompanied lady or two arrived for treatment? That sort of thing was done all the time in the hospitals of New York City. How else was he to procure the money to pay the bill? And if there was a little *jeu d'amour*, who was hurt by that? What a dullard Clarke turned out to be.

Last night, the doctor had been staring into Chancellor Square Park, his valise at one side and his medical bag on the other, considering the best spot to rest a bit. He knew that his proximity to Post Street and the Negro neighborhood promised a bed at a house of ill repute, where he could slumber between the legs of some striking Negress. His body had warmed thinking about one specimen in particular. Exotic. A lynx in need of taming. If only he had money. He had picked up his bags and started into the park, the dreams of warmth and eroticism receding like a vapor when he heard a strangled cry. Some damnable simpleton in trouble, no doubt. I've got troubles aplenty, the doctor had thought, I do not need fresh ones. In the flickering light of a streetlamp, he noticed a horse with no rider. It stood in the park chewing grass. At its feet lay a lump. McCooke exhaled through his nose. If it be a man with a horse, he might be able to offer help and earn enough for that whore and her bed.

He recognized the unconscious man lying flat on his back as Augustin Galway, legs and arms wide, but still gripping the nag's reins. The doctor kneeled and shook Galway's shoulder. Drunk, that's what. Augustin pushed McCooke's hand away and tried to curl up on the ground, but when he moved his legs, he woke with a start and cried out. Dr. McCooke sighed in relief. This time, the fates had seen fit to look upon him favorably. Money, he thought, flies from men like Galway the way seeds blow off a dandelion. One just had to be close enough to catch it.

After several rough hours spent getting the man to his home and setting the bone, McCooke's circumstances had changed. Now he anticipated six weeks in the guest room and three meals a day from Galway's kitchen, as well as access to an unlimited supply of alcohol without the shadow of Clarke's brand of temperance looming over him. Why, this situation might go on indefinitely if he cured Galway. He might even become the man's personal physician.

Now he stood at the window and peered up at the sky. A black cloud rose above the houses, tree limbs whipped in the wind, and red and golden leaves skittered across the yard.

Augustin turned in his overstuffed reading chair to reach for his pipe and tobacco. His right leg, bound in two splints and wrapped in bandages, slipped from its position on the ottoman and thudded to the rug. He cried out.

McCooke set his drink on the casement and rushed to Augustin's side. "You started with a simple fractured fibula, but if you keep moving you'll graduate to a compound." The doctor inspected the bandages and looked directly into his patient's eyes. "If you're too big a mule not to follow my orders to stay in bed, then at least sit still."

"How long am I expected to live like this? If I don't attend to my business—"

"Sir, you may have just purchased yourself another week's healing." McCooke supported Augustin's lower leg and, with exacting care, moved it back onto the ottoman. "Where is that little wife of yours, eh?" He returned to his drink and refocused his gaze out the window. "Why, if I wasn't here, you'd be helpless as a mewing kitten."

"And you'd be dry as Clarke," said Augustin with irritation.

McCooke spotted Helen scurrying across Bleecker Street toward Third.

"Your honeymoon, eh?" said McCooke, turning to Augustin. "Did your bride prove ready?"

"That girl," Augustin responded. "It's like trying to train a pup to run with the pack. Now, Mrs. Galway would have found a way to have all of New York at her command."

"There really can't be any comparison," said McCooke, lowering his voice, "in some areas." He raised a well-shaped eyebrow. Augustin's eyes narrowed. McCooke turned back to the window. "You must now hire some help, even if it's only temporary. Such a fine young wife can't be equal to running a house, nursing you properly, and maintaining your social position."

"I would not be in my position if I threw money away, lining the pockets of some scheming man or light-fingered girl. One plump cook is enough of a drain on this house."

McCooke watched Galway's new wife running in the wind like a schoolgirl, her hair in knots. She looks like she needs rescuing—from the storm and, he thought, perhaps from the boredom of an old husband. He trotted to the entrance hall and swung open the door. Leaves and rain flew in with her. He closed the door, pressing against it with his shoulder.

"Are you unharmed, Mrs. Galway?" he asked, his eyes sympathetic. He moved to relieve her of the basket, but let his knuckles linger momentarily against her wet bosom. She twisted away, knocking several eggs to the wood floor, but did not cry out.

He set the basket down, brought his index finger to his lips in a shushing motion, and winked. He departed with a grateful smile on his lips. Fate was suddenly very kind.

CHAPTER SIX

"WHY NOT GET HORACE TO DELIVER me the fish, missus?" asked Maggie as she inspected the basket. She was thick and strong from almost five decades of working for the Galway family. Although she tasted each dish to make certain nothing left her kitchen that was not up to her own standards—and Mr. Galway's—she never went to flab. Her face was wide and open with an indent between her eyes, as if a lifetime of worry had made its mark. In 1827, when slavery in New York State was abolished and freedom had finally come, she'd stayed put in the kitchen where her mother had lived out her life and where she herself had been brought as a child to help snap the yellow beans. She had been a slave for forty-three years and a free woman for eight, but her feet still pounded the same floorboards and her hands continued to prepare the Galways' food.

"That's Horace's usual way." She peeled the sodden *Whig* off of the trout in strips. "Always coming by to drop off fish and grab a bite outta Mr. Augustin's kitchen. He's no end a trouble, that boy. Oughta get hisself a wife, that's what I say."

Helen stood in the kitchen window, watching the storm lash the backyard. Sudden flashes of lightning brightened the area behind the house. Were the two still in the shed? It looked like the wind might just blow the small building away. Maybe Imari was at this moment giving birth.

"It ain't fit for nobody to be outside," said Maggie. "You best move away from that window. Never can tell what might happen."

Helen couldn't move. She felt miserable. If the boy and his mother had left, they were getting soaked. If they had stayed, the shed might just collapse on top of them. Perhaps she should confess to Maggie and let her handle them.

"At least," Maggie continued, "Horace give you a decent fish. Oh, yes. She'll do fine. Mr. Augustin likes his fish done just so. I saved some buttermilk. A bit of flour and meal is all you need. But you gotta have the oil right. Too cool and you got no brown, no crunch. Too hot and it ain't cooked through. You gotta make that water dance on the oil before you put her in. Take a look here, missus."

Helen turned, the word *shed* on her lips. Maggie put the fish on the wooden block and flicked some water into the black fry pan on the iron cookstove. It sizzled and snapped, gliding across the hot oil like a may-fly on the surface of a pond. "You seen how that water dances, missus?" She looked up at Helen, smiling.

Helen withered. If Imari was in distress, she thought, she would have showed herself by now. "Yes, I see." She could not yet get out to the shed, so without betraying their trust, she tried to put them out of her mind. "Did you teach your daughters to cook?" she asked. Maggie was silent. "I mean, if you had any daughters. I don't even know if you have children."

The cook focused intently on dropping cornmeal batter into the oil. "*Do* you have any children?"

"That's a hard question, missus," said Maggie. "Real hard." She watched the corn cakes sizzle. Her lips tightened into a straight line.

Helen wished she had never asked. She drew in a breath to apologize.

"Now," the black woman said, stopping Helen from saying more. She moved balls of cornmeal around in the sizzling oil. "Last year, when Mr. Augustin got me this here stove? You shoulda seen them other neighborhood cooks here clucking and fussing. 'Why a fireplace not good enough for you?' and, 'That iron cookstove gonna blow up and kill you.' They was just jealous, that's all. They seen he treats me right. None a them hens would know what to do with this here stove. That's why you gotta learn. I ain't gonna last forever, and Mr. Augustin, he ain't likely to hire nobody strange to cook for him. Somebody's gotta take care a that man. He sure ain't doing it."

Helen looked again out the window. The rain had eased. After a deep breath, she decided that the woman and the boy were fine. The shed was still standing. If she just stayed patient, the problem would fix itself. "I'm sorry," she said. "I'm quite tired."

"A course, missus. We got plenty a time. You go lay down. I'll call you and make sure you don't miss no supper."

* * *

Maggie was still thinking about who would cook for Mr. Augustin after she passed when the call bell jingled in a high corner of the kitchen and bounced on its springy coil of tin. Each bell on the panel had a brass plaque under it indicating which room the call had come from, but even without the identification, the summons could only be from the library, where Mr. Augustin was convalescing. *What's he got in his head now?* she wondered. *Couldn't be more liquor, unless that dirty doctor had drunk it all up.* She pulled the cornmeal balls out of the oil and threw a tea towel over them. At the dry sink, she poured a bit of water over her batter-covered hands. She wiped her fingers on her apron, massaged her sore lower back, and decided that if Mr. Augustin was going to ask her to do one extra task—more than the cooking, and the cleaning, and the clothes washing, and the ironing, and the sweeping, and the meal planning, and the bed making, and the mending, and the larder stocking, and the water toting, and the fire starting, and the ash hauling, and the chamber pot cleaning, and the keeping his whole house from sinking into Ballou Creek—she would fight him. Since the day Mrs. Galway died, she had done everything but feed him like a baby. *He got a new wife now, he gotta get himself new help too.*

At the library, she knocked and entered. Augustin sat on his chair, his curly hair lying flat and pasted to his forehead. The doctor gazed into the street, his back to the room.

"Mr. Augustin?" said Maggie as she approached. She studied his face for a moment. It was pale and dotted with sweat. *He look tired,* she thought. *Must be trying to keep up with a girl too young—that either make a man puff up or drain him.*

"Dr. McCooke may need the horse," said Augustin. "Can you see to it?"

Maggie narrowed her eyes at the thought of being at the doctor's command. She steered her gaze around to a gilt mirror at the side of the door and leaned toward it.

"What are you doing?" asked Augustin.

"I'm looking to see when I turned into a stable boy," Maggie replied, turning back to him. The doctor's head swung sharply around. Augustin remained placid. "I don't never tell you your business," she added.

"Certainly not," he said, his mouth rising at the corners.

Maggie focused on him. "I gotta run this house. I gotta keep you fed. Now, I gotta slop out the horse? You better be ready to go on one meal a day and no cakes."

"Careful," said Augustin.

McCooke looked on with undisguised outrage.

"Mr. Augustin," continued Maggie, more softly now, "all you gotta do is put up your little pinkie and some smart boy gonna come running. We find one who's gonna take care a that horse for a few pieces a bread and a bit a bacon, you'll see. Horace musta gotta have a nephew somewhere, dying to work. I'll ask him. I'm gonna take care a everything." She turned to leave.

"Is that all?" asked Augustin.

Maggie snorted and swept toward the door.

"I see some visitors arriving," said McCooke. "Do you answer the door? Or is that too much to ask?"

Maggie flicked her eyes to the doctor and strode out of the room.

McCooke put his hands behind his back. "There is competition for mistress of this house."

"You be careful too," said Galway, the amusement dropping from his face.

A door slammed and Maggie reentered the room. "It's that slave-catching devil, Hickox," she murmured. "You don't gotta see him. I can say you're laid up."

"Hickox?" Augustin said, glancing toward McCooke. "Unfortunately, I have to. Send him in."

"Why you *have to*? I'll go get the musket and you ain't *have to* do nothing. Why don't he give up coming here?" Maggie asked.

"Please just send him in," said Augustin firmly.

"You don't owe him. And you keep him away from me." Maggie turned on her heel, moved to the front door, opened it, and walked away.

Two men stepped into the foyer.

The tall, thin slave catcher entered the library first. Rainwater dripped off his wide-brimmed felt hat and onto the Oriental rug. Under his black leather vest, his shirt was darkened halfway down his body.

"Mr. Hickox," said Augustin.

"Mr. Galway," replied Hickox, removing his hat. His companion entered, his boots leaving a damp trail. "This gentleman is my new partner, Sam Swift."

"You and Mr. Colby have dissolved your arrangement?" asked Augustin tersely.

"I'm afraid Mr. Colby has departed this world," said Hickox. "Suddenly, and during the execution of his duties. Too soon. Too soon. May his lot be better in the next."

The muscles on the side of Swift's jaw twitched.

"Mr. Swift here is a good Southern boy. Got mixed up in pugilist circles." Hickox turned to Swift. "You could punch him in the head all night long and he'd never fall. Betrayed by a weakness in his stomach. Sometimes a man has to accept abject failure before he finds his true calling."

"I doubt you came all the way to Utica and to our quiet corner of town—in a punishing storm, no less—to talk about Mr. Swift," said Augustin, trying to shift in his chair. Pain crossed his face. "Forgive me for being short. As you can see, I am indisposed. State your business, sir."

"We have, once again, been charged with the highest duty," said Hickox, "to find some valuable property. I hope you'll assist us in spreading the word among your considerable contacts." He leaned in and passed Augustin a handbill.

$150 Reward. Escaped from the Barnwell Plantation, Virginia, July of this year, 1835, a Yellow Wench, 30 years old, bright, named Suzy. With her is a Negro Boy of 10 years named Joey. She is 8 months with child. They may be receiving help. Suzy is of light complexion, freckled, WELL-SPOKEN, CAN READ, and may be trying to work as a seamstress. DANGEROUS. The boy is of dark complexion, bushy red hair, skinny limbed. Originally ran with a Mulatto Man called Elymas, aged 30, since recaptured. From the best information, Suzy and Joey are in the neighborhood of Frankfort, New Hartford, Utica, or Whitesboro. Any intelligence about the pair should be directed to Abel Hickox care of the National Hotel at Utica on Genesee Street north of the Canal.

Augustin blanched as he read. He looked up and saw Hickox studying him. He crumpled the handbill and tossed it to his side table.

McCooke picked it up, read it, and whistled. "One hundred and fifty, that's substantial, isn't it? How much you get out of a deal like that?"

Smirking, Hickox kept his eyes on Augustin. "Doctor, the risk is all mine. I bought these two after we recovered the man and returned him to Arnold Barnwell. The capture was so costly that Mr. Barnwell no longer had the stomach for it." He turned his steady gaze to the doctor. "If they slip away again, as they have over these last five hundred miles, then I get nothing and I lose my whole investment. If I catch them, and I *will* catch them, I can sell each separately. That's three for the price of two."

"Three?" said McCooke.

"The wench, the boy—and the babe. That's three by my mathematics."

"You are a day too late for my assistance, sir," said Augustin, scowling. "With this injury, the doctor here has advised that I remain immobile. I have friends, but I don't expect them to appear on my doorstep. Doctor, show the gentlemen out." He looked at Hickox. "You will forgive me. My pain grows."

"I understand," said Hickox. "We shall not trouble you further, but may we call again, just to check on your healing?"

Augustin nodded curtly.

McCooke followed Hickox and Swift into the hallway. Augustin heard Hickox say, "Pleasure to meet you, sir."

Augustin snorted. The impudence of the dog, he thought, to sniff *here* for his prey. In a moment of pique, he shifted sharply, setting off waves of pain.

"Slave catching?" remarked the doctor. "You called it 'the highest duty.' Sounds like unpleasant business."

"That is an understatement, sir. But someone must right the wrong. These niggers are ruthless," said Hickox. "If you find you have information for me, do contact us at the hotel."

"Doctor," Augustin called, "get back in here and give me something for this pain."

Helen stood at the top of the stairs peering down at the slavers. Her mind spun. They must know that there were two Negroes in the shed, she thought. When they find them I can say I had nothing to do with it. She rushed out of the hallway, through her sitting room, and to her bedroom window. Her heart thumped. She dared to draw the lace curtains open a bit and stare into the yard. Nothing looked disturbed.

She waited a quarter of an hour. Nothing stirred. Nobody searched the shed. Nobody dragged Imari and Joe out of their hiding place in chains. She relaxed. Those poor people must be gone, she thought, calming herself.

She kneeled by the bed, her hands clasped. "God," she prayed, "let their journey be easy. I don't say what You should do with them but keep the babe and the child safe. God, even if she really is a slave and wicked for running away from her master, children need their mother."

She pushed her mind past the horrible last hours of her own mother's life, back to the day she learned she would be a sister. The sun had been shining through the kitchen window. Her mother was busy checking the bread dough. Saturdays were baking days, so several loaves were rising on the dough board, ready to be cooked and parceled out during the week. Helen resupplied the kindling in the stand on the hearth and went to check the fire in the oven chamber next to the fireplace. The brick walls and slate cooking stone were hot enough to begin the baking. Her mother was so pretty that day, brown hair pulled back, a few ringlets showing from under her mobcap, hazel eyes bright. Her apron was worn from everyday use, but she seemed happier than she had all winter. They worked quickly, performing each step in their bread waltz with the perfection of studied dancers. Her mother used a long-handled circular flat peel to remove the burning wood. Helen swept the embers and the ashes into a shuttle while her mother dusted the peel with cornmeal and placed the loaves one by one onto the oven's floor.

Once it was done, Helen's mother pulled her over to the chair near the window. The sun heated the top of her head, seeming to promise bright days to come. "Our family is going to grow," her mother had said, as she patted her stomach. How wrong Momma had been.

Helen wept, tears wetting the bed's quilt.

CHAPTER SEVEN

PRYCE ANWELL STOOD IN THE ERIE CANAL. His new beaver-skin hat floated nearby. Several men ran to the towpath and hoisted him out of the water. His clothing dripped with the mud that sluiced through the waterway. The packet boat he had been on continued west, as if the moment he flew into the water, he was no longer its concern.

He glanced at the retreating vessel and instead of running along the towpath to catch up, he fought his way past his rescuers and leaped up the embankment. Where was that adorable Miss O'Connell? He rushed to the apex of the John Street Bridge and looked among the crowd lining the side. There he inquired about her, but the idiots seemed to have no idea what he was talking about. She couldn't have simply disappeared. He ran down into Bagg's Square, saw nothing, turned around, and charged up John Street. Still nothing. How could she just be gone?

Lightning flashed, thunder rumbled, and a sudden downpour obscured everything. Out of the south, the wind shook shop signs, rattled windows, and drove water into his face. He held on to his hat and trudged back over the bridge. Once down on the towpath, he resigned himself to catching up with his vessel, but the normally calm waters of the canal had transformed into a boiling, splashing monster trying to break free of its confines. He fought his way half a block, but the weather was too severe. A battered sign caught his eye: *King's Victualing House.*

Inside the dark establishment, he was comforted by a wall of blazing heat emanating from a six-foot-wide brick fireplace. Several cauldrons of food hung on swinging cranes above the fire. A boy added logs into the flames. Lines of ruddy men sat on benches at a series of long tables. Some ate quietly, staring at the rain and likely contemplating the wet hours that must still be spent at their work. Others guzzled steins of grog and seemed to be enjoying the warmth of the fire and the spirits. Those who had emptied their bowls hollered to the King's staff for more. A heated debate between two canal boys erupted in the corner. Some shouted for the boys to stop, others urged them on, laughing merrily. Deciding that the victualing house was too common and commodious, he turned to go, but the wind-driven rain was too much to bear.

The fragrance of stewing beef and roasting potatoes stirred Pryce's hunger. Surprising himself, he took the nearest empty seat. Once he was settled, he noticed a new odor—rotting fish and moss. This is a filthy crowd, he thought. While turning to look about him, he noticed that the smell grew stronger.

"I know that Erie stink," laughed a gap-toothed man seated next to him, waving his hand to clear the air around Pryce. "Ya don't go takin a bath in a 360-mile-long chamber pot." Cackles and snickers surrounded the man as he tried to look dignified.

A tubby boy, with the self-satisfied look of a person whose belly would always be full, dropped a wooden bowl of food before Pryce. The boy waddled back to the cook, collecting empties at every turn. Pryce's stomach rumbled. He realized that he hadn't eaten since morning. While he dug hungrily into the stew, the noise of the establishment and the rude conversation of patrons receded. How did that tricky Miss O'Connell just disappear? Of course, there was nothing that special about her—except the intensity of her sketching, and the quickness of her wit, and her heart-shaped face, and those giant brown-black eyes. A couple of girls in his village were just as pretty and a few just as sharp, but they didn't interest him quite like this one had.

He had been on the boat since early morning, ducking at each low bridge and studying the workings of the seven locks that he had to pass through between his father's house in Little Falls and Utica. He had tried to draw the mechanisms of the sluice gates that allowed water into the docking area to raise the ship to the level of the upstream end of the lock. They seemed simple enough; for the most part they were small doors at the bottom of the main gate. One type swung around a central pivot, allowing water to wash in on both sides when open. A second model was a flat plate that could be pulled up to allow water to flood in or out beneath it. His sketches looked like the work of a four-year-old.

And who really cared which was superior? He supposed his father expected him to have opinions. Nothing disappointed the old fellow more than Pryce's lack of interest in the workings of all things mechanical.

"I suppose I should have known you'd be a greater man than me," his father had said modestly, his voice hinting at his sadness at the idea that his son wouldn't carry on his work. "You'll be a great success, you will. But *first* you should learn a practical trade." With nothing else to employ him—except reading, of course—Pryce had agreed to go on this time-consuming voyage and make an effort at becoming an engineer.

He looked at his half-eaten brown stew and lost his appetite just as the tubby boy returned and demanded payment. Clearly, the imbecile didn't know a gentleman from a thief. Pryce reached confidently into his overcoat. His purse was missing. He felt around his person. Had it fallen into the canal? Had his pocket been picked? With a swiftness that surprised him, the lad grabbed his collar and dragged him to the proprietor. Mr. King sat on a stately wooden chair elevated on a platform and held a heavy oak cudgel with a mean-looking knot at one end.

"He ain't got no money," reported the youth.

"What do ya call a man who eats, but refuses to pay a honest price for the grub?" demanded Mr. King, with the raggedy remains of an English accent.

"I assure you that I *had* money," said Pryce, tugging at his damp clothing. "May I sign a note? My father will pay, I simply have to write to him."

"A note?" King turned to the diners. "He assures me that he *had* money. That means he thinks one of my paying customers stole it." King shouted, "Come on now, boys—who stole this fellow's money?" He put his hand to his ear. "I don't hear no one admitting nothing." King stepped off the platform and bent close to Pryce, his breath fruity with the rum. He tapped the cudgel on his open palm. "I could go easy on ya, my man. But what would the rest of these boys learn from that?"

"If you strike me, I'll have the sheriff after you," said Pryce, trying to back up.

"Yes," agreed King. He turned to the tubby boy. "Fetch Sheriff Osborn and see if he knows who's an honest merchant and who floated in on a wave of canal sludge."

* * *

Pryce stood before Judge Chester Hayden, a conservative-looking man with cutting steely eyes, whose high desk resembled a squirrel's nest of papers and books. The judge looked him up and down, his nose twitching as if catching an overpowering whiff of Pryce's soaking-wet overcoat. He sentenced the young man to jail, until such time that he could make full restitution to Mr. King and pay a fine.

Pryce was delivered to the jail cell at the watchhouse under the Clinton Market. He sank onto the bed and in despair covered his face with his hands. How could a simple journey to look at a bunch of stupid locks have gone so wrong? He had only been out of his father's home for a few hours. Sheriff Osborn's wife, a sweet-faced old lady with pudgy hands and a flour-covered apron, arrived with a basket of food. "I'll not have you suffer, no matter what your crime," she said as she pushed the meal into his cell.

When darkness quieted the city, Pryce tried to sleep. But each time his mind replayed the scene at the bridge, embarrassment at his own foolishness causing him to twist on the cot like a plucked pheasant roasting on a spit jack. Finally, he gave up and climbed onto a wooden stool, trying to get a look out of a high window that faced north. Raccoons foraged through the refuse from the market above him. Nearby, church bells rang the hour. If he did not win his release, he would have to confess to his father that his "great man" fell off the boat while chasing after a girl, of all things, and got himself arrested. He imagined the look of disappointment on the old man's face. When they parted it was as if all of his father's hopes were nestled in his son's bosom. Even as he stood on the packet boat's deck saying one more goodbye, Pryce knew that this journey was just an appeasement. He would be able to say he tried, but had found nothing in engineering that captivated him. Father won't regret it when I'm representing Little Falls in the legislature, or when I go on to Washington to become a congressman or even a senator, he thought.

A whiff of rotting garbage brought him back from the heights of power to the cell he occupied. I can't tell him. It's too ridiculous. He collapsed onto the blanket, curling up into a ball, when he suddenly remembered that there was a man named Galway in Utica with whom his father had partnered on the construction of the canal.

Pryce leaped to his feet. Outside the cell a small writing table with quill, ink, paper, and candle had been left for him to contact home. He pulled up the stool, reached his hands through the bars, and began to write. Father doesn't have to know anything about this mishap, he thought. If Mr. Galway would cooperate, he could get out of jail, take a coach west to catch up with the packet boat, and act as if he had never stepped foot on dry land.

When the morning came, Sheriff Osborn found a letter addressed to *Mister Augustin Galway, Utica* and Pryce snoring in the bunk.

CHAPTER EIGHT

MAGGIE BROUGHT AUGUSTIN HIS SUPPER in the library, but at his insistence, McCooke and Helen ate together in the formal dining room. Both were seated at the polished oak table, McCooke at the head, Helen to his right. Maggie came in with plates already laid with food. The doctor sniffed in her direction. Ignoring him, she returned to the kitchen through a swinging door.

"Have you," asked McCooke, "found the house to your satisfaction?" Helen did not look up, instead staring at her china plate, her brow wrinkled. "Don't let the cook's impertinence distress you, Mrs. Galway. These Negroes are such trouble and they are everywhere—trust me, the country is crawling with them."

"What?" said Helen, looking up. "No, I . . . excuse me. Yes, I'm satisfied." She began to push her potatoes, beans, and fish around her plate. The china's pattern, a pretty one of blue, red, and gold depicting a showy arrangement of flowers in an Oriental vase, reminded her of something from the honeymoon. At the first of several proper dinner parties she and Augustin had attended, they had used a similar set of fine china. The hostess, a wrinkled old-fashioned woman who spoke with an upper-class British accent, had explained that England's porcelain makers often copied the Japanese patterns. The original china from Japan had been shipped out of the port city of Imari, and the name had been adopted for their wares.

"Do you not feel well?" asked McCooke, studying her.

"I am perfectly well," said Helen, straightening.

"It looks like you and I will be much thrown together," he said, smiling brightly. "We might as well have some fun, eh? Let's toast your new situation." He held up his glass. "To you, Mrs. Galway. May your marriage be fruitful." He drained the wine and reached for the bottle.

Helen looked at him, lips parted in surprise.

"We can't let things get too grim around here." He dug into his food. "I imagine soon enough, soon enough there will be children to attend to—but not yet, as the saints say."

He chewed his food looking off, apparently into Helen's own future.

"You must promise to let me know when you are in need of a medical opinion. Now that I am to be the physician of the house, I should know everything about my patients."

Had Augustin gone as far as arranging for the doctor to question her about personal matters? During the honeymoon, her husband had started by being patient about her ignorance and fear of performing her wifely duties. But after that dinner with the fine china, an event which bubbled over with wine and rum, Augustin had waited no longer. He went at the task as if he must complete it or die. No punishment at Miss Manahan's had ever come close to the pain she had felt. Though she never drew much pleasure from their coupling, she came to anticipate his advances while accepting that she was now fully a woman.

"The sooner we confirm the breeding symptoms," said the doctor, "the more measures we can take to insure the child's well-being. I'll be there every step of the way. And don't you worry a bit. I have a letter from Mrs. Elizabeth Preston McDowell Benton, wife of Senator Benton, an aide-de-camp to General—well now—*President* Jackson. Her husband was very close to Jackson in 1812. Benton had a falling out with him in 1813 and shot Jackson, but regardless, *she* gives me the highest recommendation. The letter is upstairs, if you'd like to see it. Praises me to the sky."

Helen said nothing. As a new wife, she knew that children had to be her highest priority, but she hoped there was a way to have them without McCooke's assistance. Her mind traveled back to the shed. She had left the two people so abruptly that she did not even know if Imari's spell had subsided. They must be gone by now. The woman said they'd only stay a few hours.

"Excuse me," she said, standing. "I'm afraid I'm exhausted. It's time for me to retire." She picked up her plate and went through the swinging door to the kitchen, leaving the doctor quite alone and too startled to object.

Maggie sat on a stool, her food in a wooden bowl on the chopping block.

"You want more? You coulda rung me," she said as she wiped her mouth. "You didn't touch nothing."

"Don't get up," said Helen, edging to the window and looking into the yard. "I'm going to dine in my room." The sun had set a few minutes earlier and twilight darkened the eastern sky. It was as if the shed had grown in size, it so dominated her view. They couldn't still be there, she thought. Later, she'd make certain that they'd left no trace.

"Eating with the doctor don't suit you?" Maggie said in a low voice. Helen made no comment. Maggie pursed her lips. "You go get you some rest. Things look brighter in the mornings anyhow."

In her sitting room, with an oil lamp on the table beside her and her sewing kit at her feet, Helen tried to concentrate on needlework. After a few hours, she heard Augustin being taken by McCooke and Maggie from his chair to a daybed that had been set up for him in the library. One anguished cry, when his leg must have collided with something, rattled her. Now would be the time to be at his side. Emma Galway would surely have been a constant and dutiful wife in such circumstances. She went to the door and waited for them to call. No one summoned her. Eventually the doctor tripped up the steps, lingering on the landing until finally shutting his door. She heard Maggie closing up the kitchen. After that, the night took hold. The iron cookstove clicked as the metal cooled and shrank. The pine-board floors seemed to ease and shift, creaking now and then.

Helen rose and looked out to the yard. The moon was high and almost full. Whatever had carried the storm through town had gathered up all the clouds and pulled them north. No one appeared to be about. Imari and Joe must have already moved on, she decided. They had to. It was the perfect time for her to sneak out and clean up after them.

Halfway out the side door, she hesitated. Some movement in the brush beyond the chicken coop froze her to the spot. Could it be those awful slave catchers? She strained her eyes, trying to make out the silhouette of Hickox's wide-brimmed hat. She saw nothing. As she cleared the corner of the house, careful to be silent, the yard was suddenly filled with a group of panicking white-tailed deer. Hooves thundered around her. In the moonlight, she saw sharp antlers and the whites of their terrified eyes as they ran past. In moments they were gone. It was all she could do not to rush back to safety. The smell of grass and damp fur filled her nostrils. Excited by the brush with disaster, her hands shook. She filled her lungs with cool air. As her heart raced, she found that the encounter had somehow thrilled her.

At the shed, she listened before opening the door. It seemed absolutely silent inside. Instead of relief, she felt a pang of disappointment.

"Are you still here?" she whispered, poking her head inside.

"Yes ma'am," Imari answered. Joe, appearing blue in the moonlight, came out from behind a stack of baskets that seemed to have been arranged to shield them from view. She felt his small hand rest on her arm. His heat transferred through her sleeve and warmed her.

"This way," the boy whispered. He guided her to his mother. She was seated on a box and leaned on the heavy wooden cabinet. Joe squatted beside her.

Helen tried to hide her shock, stammering, "You were s-supposed to leave. A few hours, you said."

"We meant to, missus," said Imari.

"Meant to?"

"Guess I was more tired than I thought."

Helen tuned her back on the pair and pressed her hand against her stomach, trying to calm the eruption of nervousness within. "Tell me the truth," she said, turning, her fists on her hips with her head leaning forward. "Where are you coming from?"

"We from Frankfort, just down the road," said Imari, holding up the palms of her hands. "Yes, yes."

Helen pressed her lips together, thinking that it might be the truth. Just then, she noticed that Joe's eyes dropped from her face and focused intently on the dirt floor. He seemed stiff, but a tiny tremor shook the fingers of his right hand. Had that been there before?

"There's two slave catchers in town," said Helen, shifting her attention back to the pregnant woman.

"Ain't got nothing to do with us," said Imari, her gaze unwavering.

Helen thought she saw Joe's focus shift, just slightly, to his mother's foot. She concentrated on him. "They were in my home this afternoon."

She heard Joe open his mouth. His breaths came faster. Though he remained still, he seemed ready to spring to his feet.

"Joe," Imari said sharply, "go get some water outta that well."

The boy was immediately upright. Helen flinched, in spite of herself.

"Wait." Imari turned her head to the frightened woman. "That be, if a little water for two tired and thirsty souls be all right by you." She paused for a moment. "Don't the Bible say to open your door to travelers?"

Helen drew back, blinking, remembering a line from Samuel. *For they are hungry, and weary, and thirsty, in the wilderness.* She realized with shock that, no matter where they came from, and even if they were Negroes, she could at least have brought them some food. That was the right thing to do. Whoever they were, they had to go, but Christian charity demanded at least food, a blanket, and a place to sleep for the night.

"One night," Helen said. "I'll be right back with some food." She shrank back to the door and was gone, leaving Imari and Joe alone.

"You go on and get that water," said Imari.

"Should we tell her?"

"No."

"But what if that was Mr. Hickox?" said Joe. "We gotta go."

"If it was, he ain't been back at the house. That mean maybe he weren't allowed. I ain't told you this 'cause I don't know if it gonna happen, but we need to be here so your daddy can catch up."

Joe looked at her, his mouth crooked. It was the exact look Elymas gave her when he doubted her.

"Remember, I said that if I get caught, you gotta run and don't worry about me? Get yourself to Canada?"

Joe nodded.

"Your daddy and I said the same thing about here. So I know he's gonna come find us."

Joe did not look convinced.

She grew thoughtful. "When it come to telling this lady about us, remember this: sometimes what you know is all you got. Can't nobody can take it from you. And you ain't gotta be giving it away. This white lady, she skittish. She ain't like some a them others we met. She could be nice and bring us food tonight and go to Hickox tomorrow just to get us outta her hair. We gonna be extra careful with her. But this secret we got? It be dangerous, so we gotta play it right. We *yes, yes, yes* her until we can't."

"Why didn't we just go to that store? Like the man said?"

"When'd you get so full a questions?" Imari replied bitterly. "Get that water like I told you."

Joe passed Helen in the yard. She gave him a jug.

"Now be quiet," she said. "You know how to be quiet?"

"Yes ma'am," he whispered. "Yes."

Helen reentered the shed with a full plate of food and a quilt under her arm. She set her handkerchief on the ground, as if they were out for a midnight picnic.

She handed Imari the quilt, thinking she might never see it again. It was a whole cloth quilt made from the same gray fabric as the girls' school uniforms, one that she and the other pupils had worked on after Augustin had come calling. Each section of the needlework was done by a different hand. Helen could still see the areas each girl had stitched. Even Miss Manahan had sewn a section. Augustin found it ugly.

"What a fine quilt," Imari said, examining the workmanship. "We gonna take good care of it."

The shed door opened. Helen scrambled to her feet as though fully expecting the slave catchers to come striding inside. Instead, Joe entered with the water jug filled, his front wet. He gave it to his mother, who lifted it to her mouth and drank deeply.

"You must have some of the food or your strength will not be restored," said Helen.

Joe reached in, but quick as lightning, Imari slapped his hand.

"When has you ever grabbed without thanking our Lord?" Imari whispered. Joe clucked his tongue. "You thank the lady and you thank God."

"Thank you, lady," he mumbled. "Thank you, God." This time as his hand shot toward the food, there was no slap.

"I thank you too, missus." Imari took a biscuit.

"So, you're from Frankfort?" asked Helen, watching Imari.

"Passed through there." The woman nibbled on the biscuit, then picked up a piece of fish, smelled it, and returned it to the plate.

"Where are you heading?" asked Helen, trying to sound light, but turning her focus to Joe. He ate with deep concentration, never meeting her eye.

"Albany, ma'am," said Imari.

"Really." Helen paused for effect. "Then why did you choose to walk west from Frankfort?"

"No, not Albany," said Imari quickly. "That other town?" She looked to Joe, who seemed to act like he hadn't heard her. "The one that sound like Albany, but ain't. Oh my. I got myself confused."

"You mean Auburn," said Helen, instantly regretting her propensity to help.

"That the one," said Imari. "My husband got himself some work there, Auburn."

"So your husband is letting you walk all the way when the baby is so close?"

Joe dropped the remains of his food onto the plate. "Why we still talking?" he asked, a little too loudly. "Ain't it time to rest up for to-morrow?" He threw himself to the dirt floor and lay on his side, his head on his hands and his knees bent. He tugged on the quilt and Imari leaned forward so he could pull part of it over himself. He pushed his eyes closed, but his lids fluttered like leaves in a stiff wind.

Imari patted the quilt. "He a brave little man, like his daddy. During the storm, we pray for sanctuary—you give us that. When we be hungry, we pray for food and you fed us. We don't want you to get in no trouble." She stopped talking and raised her gaze to meet Helen's. "So, you take your quilt." She pulled it back, uncovering Joe's curled body. He tugged his legs to his chest. "And we be gone tomorrow." She pushed the quilt toward Helen, her arms outstretched.

"No," cried Helen. "Leave him covered."

Imari did not move. "I promise you, missus. We getting outta here. But I don't know what this baby gonna do. God be watching. And He a harsh judge."

A groan escaped Helen's lips. Almost to herself, she pleaded, "I don't know what to do." She looked back and forth between the two, emotions playing across her face. Finally, she pushed the quilt back to Imari. "Keep it. I'll bring you breakfast," she said, rising. "But then you must find a way to move on."

"Thank you, ma'am. You doing the right thing." Imari eased herself to the dirt floor and lay next to Joe, spreading the quilt over her and her boy. She rubbed her stomach, murmuring the little lullaby. Joe joined her humming the melody, his eyes closed tight.

Helen sighed and left, closing the door. A sharp clear sky confronted her. She looked to heaven. *God,* she thought, *was that right? Am I doing as You wish?*

The Milky Way, usually such a dependable sight, as puffy as a strip of clouds across the top of the sky, was outshone by the glare of the moon. Everything was still. Only Helen and the eternal stars were really awake. The moon was almost too bright to stare at, but just as she turned to leave the yard, she remembered the comet. Augustin had said that it would be in Ursa Major.

She moved her eyes toward the west. There was the Big Dipper, the first section of a constellation that her father had identified for her. He was always teaching her something, about the stars, or how to make a fire hot enough to melt iron—or right from wrong.

She remembered how she had been sent to fetch him from the blacksmith shop one cold night in December. She took a seat on a tall section of tree trunk that had been bolted into the floor. Normally it served as a workplace, but she liked to pretend that the tree had grown there to provide her a spot to watch her father at his business. As he stoked the bellows, the fire in the brick hearth blazed. It warmed her face and set the snow dripping from her boots. Later, as she rode home on his wide shoulders, he had pointed to the sky and traced out the handle and cup of the Big Dipper. He drew the line from the cup's outer lip up to the North Star.

Now she stood in Augustin's yard and saw the comet, its tail shooting out of the top of the Dipper. And though it was silent and unmoving, the sight of it sped her heart. In all the wide sky, how could such a thing be exactly where Augustin had said it would be?

She thought again of her father. The morning after her mother and brother had been put into the ground, Helen found him hanging from a low beam in the kitchen of their cabin, his toes almost scraping the floorboards. She grabbed his legs and tried to lift him so she could relieve the horrible crease in his neck, but she was not strong enough. She ran and pulled her uncle from the shop. He had to cut her father down. Once he was on the floor, Helen grabbed his hand, but it was already cold. And now, here was the tail of the comet, shooting out of the Dipper like steam rising from a red-hot iron bar plunged into the water of a cooling barrel.

* * *

After Helen left the shed, Joe stopped humming. "We going, or ain't we?"

"You seen how I talked to her?" Imari asked.

"I seen you got caught in a lie."

"Not that," she said, annoyed. "She gotta be told what to do. But I can't do that direct. It gotta be her idea. So I push and plead. That's how you talk to white folks. Make them feel like they's in charge."

"So, we ain't going."

"I got what we needed, a place to sleep. You remember that." She patted his shoulder. "Sleep tonight as good as you can." As she rolled onto her side, her mind began to wander over the day. Hickox had already been on the property and here they were, two plums ripe for picking. Not only that, this childish white lady had caught them within a few minutes of their arrival. Guilt had worked to get food and a dirt floor for the night, but clearly the woman wasn't committed to helping runaways. Imari thought for the hundredth time that she had been foolish to not have gone to the place arranged for them. Walking away from that candle stub in the window might have been the mistake that finally ended this journey. And it would be all her fault. Too nervy. Too rash. Too confident. She always told herself that Elymas's natural caution was a drag on their progress. She wanted to get going. To get to freedom. But the slave catcher was a dreadful shadow. Hadn't he already had his hands on Elymas? The uncertainty of his fate played on her mind. She kept up what seemed like a crazy hope that her husband had wriggled free from Hickox and that somehow he would catch up. They had an agreement. If they got separated, go to Utica and find the Galway house. It was a last resort. Every moment of every day she questioned her decision to run when she saw Elymas struggling with Hickox. If it had been just her—if she hadn't had Joe with her and wasn't trying to protect the baby—she'd have fought the elder slave catcher. Ripped him to pieces—if she could. Elymas's last word to her was "Run." Anger flared in her belly. What right did he have to sacrifice himself? He should be here now. That had been the plan. Again, she pictured him with Hickox bearing down. She might never know his fate. Deliberately shoving aside the vision of him so helpless, she told herself that he could have gotten away. We waiting right here for him to catch up, she decided.

* * *

Back inside, Helen tiptoed past the library where Augustin slept. His accident would be keeping him away from her bedchamber. During their
honeymoon month in New York, his moods were so varied that she
had not been able to predict his intentions when the inevitable rapping
came at her door. Sometimes he arrived elated and in a ravenous mood.
Those nights she had to be ready to accommodate his lust. One evening,
he was melancholy and lay on his side upon the bedcovers with a pillow
hugged to his chest. He grabbed her hand and drew her arm around
his body, so that Helen had no choice but to press herself into his back
until sleep slackened his grip. Once, he paced the floor and described
a complicated stock gambit that had collapsed and apparently caused
him a considerable loss of capital. Helen was not even certain what his
business was. She had asked and he had answered, but she could not
work out the difference between bonds, coins, specie, notes, and stocks,
or how they impacted him, or her. Tonight, to have him confined downstairs promised the relief of uninterrupted sleep.

Just as she had her hand on the wooden banister to go upstairs, she
heard a moan from the library. A second cry of Augustin's pain reached
her ears. She knocked softly and entered. The smell of pipe tobacco and
liniment hung in the air. A lamp on the side table burned low.

"Maggie?" asked Augustin.

"It's your wife," answered Helen.

"Emma?"

She exhaled. "No. Helen." Now that they were no longer traveling,
she felt Mrs. Galway around every corner of his house. Where am I in
his heart? she wondered.

"Forgive me, my dear," said Augustin, coming around. "I was
dreaming."

"I'll let you sleep." She turned to go.

"No," he said sharply. Then a little softer, "Please, sit with me for
a while."

He looked pale and damp as he lay on the daybed. White sheets en-
veloped him. A tan wool blanket lay in a disordered heap on the floor.
Helen picked it up and spread it over him. When the cover pressed
against his broken leg, he winced.

"I'm so sorry. I didn't mean to hurt you," she said.

"It's no matter."

She put her palm on his forehead, as she had with the younger girls at school. He was warm, but not feverish. He clutched a lacy handkerchief and she plucked it out of his hand. The corner had the monogram *E. G.* embroidered on it. Annoyed, she dabbed at his forehead with it.

"That damnable doctor should be the one to do this," he said. "He is, no doubt, sleeping peacefully upstairs while my pain solution has worn off."

"Shall I fetch him?"

"No. Let him alone. He availed himself of my wine," said Augustin as he fussed with the blanket. "Too much of it, clearly." He was thoughtful for a moment, his attention finally settling on the tea table. "See that medicine vial over there?"

On the table sat some liquor bottles as well as the doctor's stethoscope, tinctures, and medical instruments. "You see the brown one that says *Opium?*"

"Maybe I should call the doctor."

"No need to rouse him. I know the dose," he said. "Put some brandy—the French label at the center of the tray—into a glass there and add twenty-five drops. See the pipette, use that."

Helen pursed her lips, but obeyed. Using the thin glass tube, she counted out the opium drops with care.

Augustin lifted his head and drank the brandy down in a gulp. He sighed, resting back on the pillow, and closed his eyes. Helen pulled the ottoman to the side of the daybed and sat. She took the glass from him and turned it in her hand, focusing on the remaining drops of brandy as they slid around the bottom.

Augustin appeared to sleep. The medication must have already relieved him. She stood and put the ottoman back near his smoking chair. A crumpled piece of paper on the table drew her attention. She brought it toward the lamp and ironed out the sheet with her palm. She read Hickox's notice several times, her heart sinking. So Imari, or really "Suzy," had lied. They *were* runaway slaves. It also said that she was dangerous. And of course her husband wasn't working in Auburn. He had run with her . . . and been captured. She clenched her jaw, furious at how she had been lied to, angry enough to confront the woman.

Her husband began to cough, his eyes flipping open like startled birds. She hid the slave notice behind her back and kneeled at his bedside.

"Can I help?" she asked.

His cough subsided. "Stay with me," he said, clearing his throat.

"I have something to tell you." Preparing to confess the presence of the slaves, Helen remembered how Imari had said that God was watching. She had to be sure of her husband's opinions before she revealed her secret—at least for tonight. "Rather, I want to ask you something."

"Anything you want, my dear," he slurred, smiling blearily.

"I understand that you're in an organization that discusses what to do with the Negroes and the slaves."

"We do a lot more than talk, a lot more."

"But you care about what happens to them?"

"We're building a place for them in Africa." He jabbed his finger in the air. "It's a place to send the free Negroes, much better than they will ever find here—much, much better. It will end slavery." His eyelids fluttered. "Like we did here in New York."

"And they'll all live in Africa? There are no masters?"

"They'll all be free men." He focused on her. "Why is this on your mind?"

He and his organization might be able to help the two, but she had to be sure. Augustin looked on the verge of sleep. "Those men who visited you today," she began, "the slave catchers, they don't bring people to Africa, do they?"

"You are confusing runaways with freed men. Hickox and Swift are chasing bad slaves, criminals, who've left their homes."

"Oh. So . . . who goes to Africa?"

"Are you wondering about that fishmonger, Horace? A man like Horace would do well in Liberia. He's smart. Ready. Once this leg is mended, I'll speak to him. You watch. But don't worry any more about it. You should be thinking about our children, a healthy boy or two whenever they may come . . ." He trailed off.

"Would you send Maggie to Africa?"

Augustin's eyes opened. "Never." He raised himself on his elbows, but fell back down again. "Maggie is too important to this house."

Without warning, sleep seemed to have gotten the better of him. Helen stewed. His organization would be of no help. "Imari" and "Joe" weren't criminals, at least she didn't think so. But they had lied. Well, what else could one expect from runaways? With the slave notice in her hand, she went out the side door into the backyard to confront them.

The shed door swung open, ushering in a blast of cool air. Imari and Joe froze in their places. Helen swept in.

"So, *Suzy* and *Joey*, I know who you really are now." Helen held up a lantern. She stood over the two prone figures gripping a crumpled piece of paper. "According to this, you are runaway slaves from Virginia. And you're dangerous." She shoved the paper toward the woman, who did not raise her hand to take it.

"I am . . . I can . . ." Imari began.

Joe, sitting up now, kept his eyes low.

"You cannot deny what is printed right here." Helen drew the paper back and read: "*Escaped from the Barnwell Plantation, Virginia . . . a Yellow Wench, 30 years old, bright, named Suzy. With her is a Negro Boy of 10 years named Joey. She is 8 months with child . . . Suzy is of light complexion, freckled, well-spoken . . . and DANGEROUS. The boy is of dark complexion, bushy red hair, skinny limbed.*" She paused, lowered the paper, and glared at them. "*Originally ran with a Mulatto Man called Elymas, aged 30, since recaptured.*" Staring down on Imari, she continued, "It says there's a $150 reward for you. What do you have to say for yourself?"

"That say Elymas been captured? Let me see."

Helen seemed taken aback and handed her the notice.

Imari studied the paper, trying to focus on it, wiping away some tears. There it was. Captured. She could no longer deny his fate.

"He ain't gonna catch up, is he?" asked Joe with bitterness.

"No," she said. Letting go of the idea was impossible. He had to catch up. Why live if he couldn't be with them? "He gone." No longer able to restrain herself, she sobbed.

Helen, her hand on her chest, kneeled down. "I'm sorry." Silence filled the shed. "If you go back with this Mr. Hickox, you'll be reunited with your husband, won't you?"

Imari began to tremble. "Missus, sorry, but you don't understand the way things is. We ain't never gonna see him again."

"Why is that? Won't he be returned to his master?"

Imari swallowed hard. "Sometimes if you run and get caught in the neighborhood, you might get a whipping and maybe Master, he keep you. Elymas is a blacksmith, so he important to the farm. But he got caught way up in New Jersey, I think. He got a taste a freedom, at least that's how Master will look at it."

"He's a blacksmith? So was my father. I didn't think you people—"

"That we smart enough?"

"That's not, um, no. That's not what I meant."

"I'm sorry, missus," Imari said. "There ain't no reason for you to know how it go where we come from."

"My teacher, Miss Manahan, said that the master is like a very stern father."

"Father," said Imari, shaking her head. "Let me tell you, Elymas be a real father. He cared so much for his boy here and this one in here," she rubbed her pregnant belly, "that he run right at Hickox so we could get away. And what he gonna get for that? He gonna get sold to the soul drivers."

"Soul drivers?"

"They buy the slaves nobody wants. Runaways, troublemakers, people Master can't afford to feed. They go from plantation to plantation riding tall on they horses. We seen them come down the road with fifty, maybe a hundred slaves, all chained together in one long row. Men, yes. And women and children too. Just like me and Joe here. Chained up and walking clear to the cotton and sugar fields down south. Master told me they walking all the way to New Orleans to be sold on the block."

"But that's just cruel," said Helen, color rising to her cheeks.

"Missus, that what we running from."

"That's not what I've been told."

"You gotta know the truth. I ain't never showed this to nobody." Imari pulled aside her shawl and rolled up the sleeve of her blouse. There on her arm, standing out so tall it cast its own shadow, was a long scar that slashed across her skin. "That be from a whip."

"I feel sick," said Helen. "Does it still hurt?" She leaned in to look again.

"It don't hurt here," said Imari, indicating the scar. "It hurt here." She pointed to her head. "And you never know when the whip gonna come your way. Bad things happen, missus. All the time. You think you ain't never gonna be surprised by it again, but then, *thwack*, and you feel the bite, or your child does, or your momma. Missus, if you tell Hickox that we here—all that, whipping and soul drivers, that gonna happen to us too." Drawing both arms around her stomach, she looked straight into Helen's face. "You the only friend this baby got in the world."

"Me? How can that be?"

"You stand between this baby and death."

Helen's mouth opened as if to protest.

"And if this baby lives, you the only one that can keep him from being sold on the block."

Helen rocked back, the animation draining from her body.

Imari continued, "This baby like a piece a meat to them slave-catching dogs. They mouths dripping wet thinking about them pieces a gold—just like Judas. Forget about me, missus, think a this here helpless baby."

Helen brought her hands to her face. "I can't . . ." she said through tears.

"There ain't no 'I can't,'" said Imari.

"How dare you speak to me like that?" Helen said, wiping her face. "I don't even know why I should be responsible."

Imari closed her eyes, lids stretching, inside corners trembling. Huge tears fell down her face and landed on her cheeks, dripping onto her shawl. "Oh Lord," she cried, looking to the ceiling, hands up in appeal. "This my punishment, Lord? I prayed. I done my best, but I lost my man and now we stuck here. And now you don't send me no help? Why hate me, Lord?" She sobbed, her thin shoulders heaving. She brought her palms together and again looked up toward the heavens. "Please, God, please. Have mercy. Hate me, okay. But don't hate my baby."

Helen shivered as if she were being dragged under the freezing waters of the Ballou.

Imari continued to weep and Helen embraced her.

"I'm so sorry," Helen moaned. "I'm a stupid girl. God doesn't hate you." She paused. "I don't hate you."

CHAPTER NINE

WHEN THE WHITE LADY LEFT THEM ALONE, Joe threw the quilt off and was on his feet, pacing among the clutter. "What we supposed to do now?" he asked in an angry whisper. "If Poppa said go, we oughta go."

Imari sighed deeply. "No. I can't move. Elymas might . . ."

"He ain't coming," Joe hissed. His mother held her head in her hands. He cleared his throat. "We oughta go right now to the man we was supposed to meet."

"I can't."

Joe kneeled beside her. "I'll help you."

"You gonna help? All right, go get me a real big carriage and make sure it got a fine Negro in livery hanging off the back."

Joe got to his feet and folded his arms across his chest.

"Listen, boy. I can't move. This baby need me to be still. So we gotta wait. Then we move. You got that?"

"Let me go now and look for him," the boy said eagerly.

"You ain't getting outta my sight. You all I got left. Besides, it be night and Hickox be out there waiting. Swoop down on you like a chicken hawk. Tomorrow be good enough."

Joe threw himself down, pulling the quilt over himself and his mother. In the dark, his mind went to his father. At first, after they got separated, he had expected him to appear. Upon waking he would sit up looking around, knowing that Poppa would be right there, close enough to touch. It was only after they moved across the water to New York City that he secretly lost hope. He must have been killed, Joe decided. Otherwise he would have found them. Joe didn't dare suggest that to his mother. Every day she said he would "catch up," even as they traveled farther and farther toward wherever it was they were going.

When he remembered that Poppa wasn't with them it felt like he had an animal inside chewing on his guts, sometimes his chest, sometimes his stomach, sometimes his very bowels.

He yawned and blinked and thought back to the plantation's blacksmith shop, where his father sweat from dawn till dusk supplying the plantation with nails and other forged iron, making and repairing farm and garden tools, patching cooking pots, and furnishing horses with shoes he crafted special for each animal. Whenever Joe had the opportunity, he watched his father, often receiving lectures on the art and craft of ironwork.

"Here come Mr. De Vries," Joe warned one morning when he spotted the overseer striding toward them. Elymas stopped hammering a barrel strap and pumped the bellows, which reddened the coal fire and sharply raised the temperature of the shop. Elymas winked at him and picked up a rag to wipe the sweat and soot off his neck.

De Vries stepped in. "Damn," he said, "how do you darkies take this kinda heat?"

"Don't know, Mr. De Vries," said Elymas.

"I reckon it's in your blood, ain't it?"

"If you says so, Mr. De Vries."

"I need me a collar all chained up and ready by tonight," said the overseer.

"That a mighty big job, Mr. De Vries," said Elymas, a look of alarm on his face.

"It ain't for you, if that's your concern." De Vries strolled casually over to some pieces of chain that hung on the shop's wall and brushed his hand across them. The jangle of the metal filled the room.

"No sir. Thanks," said Elymas. "But—"

De Vries swung a yard of chain, slamming it down on the worktable, scattering tools and nails. Elymas leaped back, almost stumbling into the fire. Joe screamed.

"You want a taste to get you moving?" De Vries said softly.

"No sir. Sorry, sir," said Elymas, his eyes flashing toward Joe. "I gonna get 'em to you when they done. I be real fast."

De Vries strode out. Elymas threw a rod of charcoal iron at the fire so hard that red fragments flew out of the hearth and scattered to the dirt floor.

"Pick them up," Elymas said, shoving a pair of tongs toward Joe. "Fast now or the shop gonna burn up."

In bare feet, Joe slowly moved about, grasping small bits of burning coal and depositing them back into the hearth. Elymas extracted the red-hot iron and began to hammer. Each deafening blow vibrated in Joe's head. As the iron collar began to take shape, Elymas's rage seemed to grow. He produced two half circles that could be joined by two locks, but he looked unsatisfied.

He filed and pounded the inner surface of the collar, checking it often with his gloved hand. Finally, he plunged the collar halves into the water barrel to cool them.

"Get over here, boy," he said. "Run your finger along the inside, there."

Joe passed his hand over the still-warm edge and inside face of the collar.

"You don't feel no bump?"

Joe shook his head.

"They ain't no tiny hook that gonna cut nobody, right?"

"They clean," said Joe.

Elymas handed him the collar halves and a length of chain. "Run them to Mr. De Vries. Don't say nothing but *yes sir* or *no sir*."

Joe nodded.

"Repeat it," said Elymas.

"*Yes sir* and *no sir*," said Joe.

"No sass now. No nothing."

"Yes sir."

"You meet me back at the cabin. We got work to do."

At the cabin, Joe found Elymas staring into a small outdoor cook fire.

"I ain't never making no more chains." He took a branch of pine that Joe had stacked that morning and brought it to the fire so he could set the end to blaze. The dry part of the bark quickly sparked into a white-hot flame. He held it over his head. "Show me where you find this here wood."

Joe led him to a wind-felled tree. There they selected a few long logs and carried them to the edge of the Potomac.

"We gotta store 'em up so they don't look like nothing but what the river wash down," Elymas told Joe. "Don't tie nothing together till we ready."

Joe asked, "Ready for what?" But Poppa would not say.

As he lay in the shed now, he closed his eyes remembering the river and how more than once Elymas had warned him to stay away from the water. Despite that, he knew the terrain and where the shore quickly became a sheer wall of rock near the great gorge. He knew the rapids where the current swept around an elbow of land.

That summer, during an almost unendurable hot spell, he had secretly eased his way into the river, inch by inch. At first he shivered in the cold, but he forged ahead one small step at a time. When he was up to his chest, his feet struggled to maintain contact with the rocky bottom. Finally, he held his breath, pinched his nose shut, and submerged himself completely. He opened his eyes and saw fish and eels and floating vegetation. His mind filled with questions, but there was no one he could ask.

The secluded power he felt in the water was intoxicating. He could barely even look at the river without stripping off his shirt and pants and diving in. He taught himself how to swim and grew stronger, challenging his new power in the current. In an effort to stay near the bottom, he held a heavy stone. With his free hand he scattered schools of fish and snatched up terrified crawdads, watching as their tiny claws pinched uselessly. He imagined himself a river-god, like the type that his elderly friend Quack described in his stories about Africa. Late at night as he lay on his pallet, he practiced holding his breath.

Along with other children, he was assigned to the garbage gang. But he tried to rise before the morning work horn just so he could spend time savoring the water's buoyant, cooling embrace before the stinking work began.

In the shed, he dreamed that he was sitting at the edge of the river in the darkness. Stars sparkled on the surface. Leaves shifted off to his right and he thought that his father had arrived. He tried to ask, *That you?* but his mouth seemed full of mud. He noticed the warmth of a nearby body and reached out, expecting to feel the coarse linen of his father's shirt, but instead grabbed a thick, fibrous pelt. Something stuck its muzzle into his ear. The click of a wet mouth thundered in his head and he felt hot breath across his neck. The animal rose up and squeezed him between massive forearms. It was the bear. Joe's legs would not move. His throat closed. His elbows shoved at the massive body as it pressed against him. There was no escape.

Suddenly awake, he frantically turned his head left and right before realizing he was in the shed. He tried to blink away the dream. Even here—so far from the plantation—he had escaped nothing.

Careful to be silent, he slipped out from under the quilt. His momma stirred, but did not wake. Streaks of bluish light came through the slats of the wall. He eased up the iron door latch and pushed out into the night. The cool breeze blowing off the creek embraced him. Body heat had mostly dried his clothing, with only a few folds still damp. Solid and bright, the moon hung over the western horizon. He looked up at the sky to orient himself by the Big Dipper and once again saw the long white mark in the Dipper's cup. Someone told his mother that it was something called a *comet*, but to him it looked like a tear in the heavens. He watched to see if the white streak would grow, allowing long-dead ghosts a chance to pour back into the realm of the living.

Before their journey, he had no idea how big the world was. He could not understand why his father and mother had ever started. They'd left warm hay mattresses and traded them for the cold dirt of shed floors and damp culverts. What sense did that make?

Another whisper of wind blew off the water. Joe shivered. He was pretty certain that they must have been moving farther and farther away from the sun. Perhaps that tear in the sky meant that Canada existed behind the curtain of stars and they were finally getting close. He shoved his hands into his armpits, warming the tips of his fingers. There could be no harm just looking around for the place where the Frankfort man said their contact was supposed to be. I'll get back before Momma wakes up, he thought. He stayed in the shadows and slipped out of the yard, walking to the corner of two wide streets. After checking to see that nobody was about, he crossed to the western side of the wide road so that the shadows of the trees hid his progress. The only way to return was to know your steps, so he studied the house he had just left. Secure that he would recognize it later, he kept the moon on his left and moved down the street.

He passed a building that smelled of yeasty spoiled beer. On Christmas day, Master Arnold had barrels of beer brought out to the slave cabins and Elymas and the other men had rushed over with bowls. His father smelled of beer when he hoisted Joe on his shoulders and danced around a blazing bonfire. They were told that every day until the New Year more barrels would appear. Almost everyone drank themselves silly and had stinging headaches the next morning. Quack, who was so old he seldom left the fire he tended, hissed that it was "Master's way a breaking us. We glad to work after eight mornings a beer sickness."

Thereafter, Elymas had only taken a cup or two. "Just enough to get me happy," he said. Joe had been happy too, because on his father's shoulders he towered over the other children.

The farther he got away from the shed, the less he stayed to the shadows. Most houses were dark, but one window glowed. He crouched low and watched a shadow darken the glass. He skittered across the yard on his hands and toes, keeping his head up and his ears open. Just below the window he kneeled. He held the wooden frame and pulled himself up slowly until he was able to see inside. A thin, sharp-eyed, gray-haired white man in a comfortably old brocade robe strode about the room. He paused in front of a cheerful fire. Joe took in the entire messy array of things. The room was so full that it seemed like nobody could actually live in it. Every bit of furniture was taller, larger, and had more fabric than any he'd seen before. Pictures hung on the walls. Dried flowers sat undisturbed under a bell-shaped piece of glass.

The old man grabbed his candle and crossed the room to a hanging cabinet with crammed shelves. He picked up a heavy bound book and seemed interested in it until he suddenly slammed it closed. He crossed to a black wooden desk whose upper doors were thrown open and bursting with rolled papers and disorderly stacks of books. He turned, his fingers to his lips, and met Joe's eyes through the window.

He straightened and rushed to the door. Joe ran. He heard the man open the front door and call to him, but the words "Boy, get back here!" faded as his feet carried him far from the shed and his mother.

Out of breath, he kneeled in the shadow of a large building. He heard the birds far to the east beginning to chirp. The noise of their morning song moved toward him, tree by tree. The first blush of rose appeared in the sky. He should be getting back, but he feared the old man might be watching for him and he still hadn't found their contact.

THE THIRD MRS. GALWAY

A series of whistles came from down the road and he emerged from his hiding place to take a look.

Ahead of him a wooden bridge arched over the canal. As he got closer, on the other side down near the water, he saw two mules. One was being ridden by a white boy, bigger than himself, holding a lantern that threw its light onto the towpath. A cable stretched behind them to the bow of a long, low freighter coming from the west. It was loaded with barrels. The mules went under the bridge and Joe ran to the eastern side and saw them emerge, still plodding along, in no particular hurry. The lad on the mule straightened on his perch. A second set of mules came from the east, they too pulling a vessel. By rights the ship traveling closest to the towpath had the right of way. The boat coming from the west was supposed to slow, allowing the other mule team to step over the towline and pull its boat over the sinking cord. But the boy driving the freighter showed no signs of slowing. Canal men on the second boat began whistling to alert him. Still he moved on, even goosing the mules to speed up. Shouts and curses flew from the second boat, urging him to stop and let them pass. He did not yield.

By this time, Joe was leaning over the short rail of the bridge and hanging above the canal. He laughed at the battle of nerves between the two drivers. The boy from the second boat leaped off his mount and ran toward the oncoming mules. He made a grab for the harness of the team, but the original boy slashed his whip at his opponent. Stung, the second boy had no choice but to run back and stop his mules and lift his towline, thereby allowing the interloper to pass under. The men aboard the first boat jeered as the two ships crossed.

Joe hooted and clapped with delight, when suddenly he was grabbed from behind.

"Got you!" shouted a man.

For a moment, Joe thought it was the bear from his dream, but he turned and saw the slave catcher Hickox who had been chasing them for all those miles.

"Swift, get over here!" yelled the slaver.

Joe squirmed in terror, kicking his legs wildly as Hickox dangled him in the air. Just as Swift arrived, Joe's left foot found its target. Hickox buckled in pain and released him. Without a second of thought, Joe hurtled himself over the bridge and into the chilly canal, hitting the surface flat and hard. The bow of the second boat struck him and dragged him below the water. The air was knocked out of him. The canal water, thick with end-of-season sludge, flowed past his head. His shoulder scraped against the rough concrete bottom. If he didn't work his way higher, he knew he would be crushed. His fingers found purchase between the boat's planks and he wrenched himself free. Gripping the tiny spaces between the wood, he held on for the few seconds it took for the ship to pass below the bridge. His lungs burned and his heart pounded in his chest. He propelled himself to the surface and floated, inhaling deeply.

Joe opened his eyes and saw the looming darkness of a second bridge. Right at its center, he let go of the boat and swam hard toward the far side of the canal. He paused, hand on the canal's wall, sucking in breath. Across the water, footfalls hurried along the towpath.

"Joey, come on out, boy! We won't hurt ya!"

Joe ducked beneath the surface, still hearing the slave catchers' muffled calls. A third boat passed between himself and the towpath. He pushed off from the wall and met it a few yards from the canal's side. Again, he allowed himself to be pulled along, this time back in the direction he'd come and far from the sharp eyes of Hickox. When he saw the original bridge he had been on, he kept himself low. Just then he noticed a new current entering the canal. It smelled a bit of stale beer. It had to be the same creek that ran behind the shed. Shoving off from the third boat, he swam upstream and found himself in the colder water of the creek. After fighting against the flow, he crawled on shore. Just before he collapsed, he noticed a tiny window with a candle that, though almost down to its nub, still burned.

A few minutes later, a man in a white apron picked up the exhausted, soaking-wet boy and brought him inside his shop, placing him on a cot near a great domed brick oven common to his trade.

CHAPTER TEN

IMARI TOO HAD BEEN DREAMING. She was back in Virginia, and Elymas was coming to her on a Saturday night. Her worry drained away as she looked into her husband's light-brown eyes, warm with anticipation. His soft lips pressed against hers. Her palm brushed the tightly curled hair that trailed down the back of his neck toward his muscled shoulders. His bulky body pressed against her. But she noticed a flicker of pain from her stomach. Elymas rose, sliding through her hands, slowly easing beyond the reach of her fingertips. He floated through the roof of the cabin and into the darkness of the night sky. Just as she was about to cry out, to try to follow him, the shed door swung open. From behind the screen of baskets, she saw the silhouette of a man, and for a moment she believed that Elymas had finally caught up. But as the stranger leaned into the building, she strangled the impulse to call his name.

"Anybody in here?" he asked.

Imari held her breath as a tear, heavy with disappointment, eased down her cheek. Whoever the man was, he might be able to feel the warmth of sleep lingering in the air. She held completely still—all the time wanting to reach over and touch Joe.

With a sharp shake of his head, the man withdrew and snapped the door closed. She let warm air rush out of her nostrils. The man's footsteps retreated. He hummed as he moved about in the next building. Joe's spot was empty and cold. A man prowling around and Joe gone? Stupid boy. If he couldn't understand the danger, a good switching would straighten him out.

She moved to rise. A pain stabbed her—back to groin. She needed Elymas. He could run after their son and bring him back, or better yet, have had the strength to keep him hidden. But, she thought, trying to push away panic, Joe could hide better than a beat dog. He would come back, he had better. But Elymas?

Time was, her husband hadn't had much desire to run. He said he was grateful that God had seen fit to keep the three of them together after Master James died. Blacksmithing suited him fine. Even when he was only making hooks for the slaves to hang their clothing on, he liked the satisfaction of having something to show for his sweat. And running was dangerous.

After Master James's death, the slaves had been divided between his three children. Still dressed in their mourning finery, they'd taken turns drawing each slave's name from a battered box. While Elymas, Imari, and Joe had all been chosen by Master Arnold, many families had been split apart. One couple, Sammy and Lizzie, about the same age as Imari and Elymas, had been separated when Master Paul, the youngest son, took all his slaves over thirty miles away to his wife's family plantation.

Sammy, a tall thin fellow whose work as a carpenter was rarely judged faulty, asked repeatedly for a weeklong pass to visit his wife. Master Arnold said, "Soon. Not while we're planting." Then, "Soon. Not while we're weeding." And once, "Wait until Christmas, then we shall see." Several months passed and Sammy told Elymas that he was missing his Lizzie and planned to take off one Saturday night to walk the thirty miles and be back before the Monday morning's work call.

Sunday's dawn came and the slave patrol arrived at the Barnwell Plantation with Sammy, his long skinny arms pinned by iron restraints, his ankles cuffed and chained, and a rope around his neck. Bloody bruises marbled his face and shoulders. A stony, straight-backed man high on a horse held the other end of the rope, his frosty blue eyes sharp. The slaves gathered around.

Master Arnold came out of the house seeming to be surprised that Sammy had left the farm. "Why did you do this to me?" said the master.

"My wife, she be sick when she got took away, Master," said Sammy.

"Why didn't you ask me to write to Master Paul and inquire?"

"You do that for me, Master?"

Master Arnold looked up at the patroller holding the rope. "Mr. Hickox?"

"Sir," said Hickox.

Nervousness grew as the Barnwell blacks, intent on reading what the master would do, began to fidget and sweat and wipe their mouths.

"You love your wife?" asked Master Arnold.

"Yes sir. More than anything," said Sammy.

"Take him to the market," Master Arnold said to Hickox.

A cry of shock went through the gathered slaves.

Sammy fell to his knees, chains clanking. "If you sells me, I'll never see her, Master. Please don't. I won't go again. I'll wait for Christmas to come, like you say, Master."

"Now, Mr. Hickox."

The slave catcher tugged on the rope.

Elymas turned his back to the scene, his body rigid. Sammy's appeals mixed with sobs from the other slaves who must have allowed themselves to remember their own splintered families. Imari, choked by dread, watched Hickox drag Sammy away. Master Arnold surveyed the assembled slaves. "All of you remember this!" he shouted. "I am not my daddy. There is no disobedience here now. No slacking off. You want to stay with your families? Well, act like it." He strode quickly back to the house as Sammy disappeared down the road.

One night at the beginning of July when Imari and Elymas lay in bed together, her on her side, him curling around her, one hand on her belly, she mentioned the dangerous business of running.

"But them harvest tools ain't fixed up yet," he said. "I can't leave all them folks to work with busted tools, can I?"

"Master Arnold, he say he gonna sell somebody. Might be you or me. Or Joe."

"Why he gonna sell me? I ain't run nowhere," Elymas snapped. "And who gonna do the fixing?" He softened. "And his momma, Missus Bea? That old woman need you, don't she? Plus, you gonna have that baby. He knows that. Master Arnold do what he got to. He ain't gonna sell Joe. He knows I be teaching him how to smith." Elymas pinched Imari's cheek. "Don't go thinking too much." He moved to kiss her neck.

"What we think don't matter for nothing," she responded, turning to face him. "He ain't no smart man."

"You miss his daddy or something?" said Elymas, up on one elbow. She could feel his annoyance in the dark.

"No," she said tartly. "He don't run things good, not like Master James."

"Master James," Elymas shot back, "I don't never wanna hear his name again."

"But Master Arnold, he said someone gotta get sold." She crossed her arms over her chest.

"You don't know everything," said Elymas, quietly. He pulled her into his arms. "Anyways, we can't run now." He kissed her cheek. "Not till that baby be born." He slipped his hand over her belly and between her thighs.

She let the matter drop, but a shroud of worry began to weigh down her days. She knew that God takes care of the birds of the air and, she'd been told, might be depended upon to take care of the humans on the ground, but so far as she could tell, He had a downright blindness when it came to watching out for the slave.

Daylight began to warm the gloomy shed. Imari sat up. She meant to count her blessings, but instead could only see her losses. Jimmy, she thought, tapping her heart three times, my firstborn—sold off. Momma, dead before her time. And Elymas captured, like he'd never even existed. He must still be alive. She directed her mind to what she knew about her husband, rebuilding him the way a person might reconstruct a cabin after a fire.

Thirty years ago, when Elymas had arrived from the slave market only a week old and with a fresh injury on his foot—one that earned the Barnwells a discount—he joined the other infants in the slave nursery. Since he didn't have a natural mother like the others, he was fed by Abby, who'd recently birthed a stillborn. Elymas and Imari and the other infant slaves had been swaddled and weaned together by pregnant slaves who were too close to their lying-in time for heavy work.

At eight years old, they both graduated to the garbage gang that moved around the plantation picking up refuse. The trash was separated. Food scraps and such went into a pile near the kitchen garden to rot and be used the following year to enrich the soil. Some items from the master's house, like pieces of material, old clothing, or chipped crockery, were taken by the slaves and reused. The rest was burned.

As they grew, Imari singled out Elymas for special attention. One sulky-hot afternoon when they were both about ten years old, he ran by her carrying a freshly filled water bucket that was intended to soothe the parched throats of the field hands. She poked out her thin ankle and sent him sprawling. The water arched in the air like a clear rainbow before splashing to the dirt, raising its own mini dust storm.

Elymas pulled himself off the ground, wheezing and angry. "Why you go and do that?"

"I didn't do nothing," she responded.

"You sure did," he said, outraged. Unsure of what to do, he raised his hand to slap her. Their eyes locked. He stopped midswing. He took a breath and made an attempt to reengage his hand, but the gesture had lost its force. "You just a girl," he said, then spat on the ground. "Ain't even worth hitting."

For a while, whenever he crossed her path, he squinted at her, lips pressed tightly together, his normally smooth brow a lumpy field. She knew he no longer considered her as unimportant as some sow bug. If it seemed like he had taken her for granted, her shin found a way to remind him. He never hit her, instead resorting to pinching her warm springy skin and, with a look of glee, twisting it until she yelped in pain and surprise. If there was a bruise on her, no matter what the source, he claimed to have caused it.

One Sunday, when they were thirteen and were excused from their morning duties, he from the blacksmith shop and she from attending to Missus Bea's demands, they strolled together down the steep, leafy path between the master's house and the river to hear one of the elder slaves, known to all as the Reverend, preach. They moved in and out of fleeting columns of smoky light as the sun shone through the early morning fog. As they neared the shore, the trees thinned and Imari was surrounded by brightness. Elymas noticed a long, dark, purple slash that wrapped halfway around her upper arm.

"I seen I got you real good," he said. He caught up with her and lightly rubbed his thumb over her welt.

"Ouch," she said, pulling away. She stopped in sight of the river and the circle of slaves who had come out to the service. "You must be one dumb nigger to want to own every lick I get," she whispered.

"You got switched?" he said, now seriously looking her over for other signs of a beating.

"Well, that ain't from no pinch a yours."

His spine shifted, each vertebra stacking itself into a perfect, board-straight line. "Who done it?"

"You can't do nothing about it, so I ain't even gonna say."

"Don't tell me what I can't do," he said.

"I ain't gonna be the one to get you killed," she hissed.

He rubbed his index finger along his upper lip, touching the few curled hairs that had recently sprouted. "That there don't look like a willow switch done it. And it ain't no cane mark, too thin." He poked his finger into the spot on her back where a longer weapon, like a bull-whip, would have caused further damage. She yelped and twisted away.

"Keep your hands off a me," she said. "I ain't yours to touch any-time you like."

"I know who done it," he whispered.

"It ain't none a your business," she said, looking over her shoulder toward the gathered slaves. Folks took their seats on tree trunks that had been arranged in rows. Her mother waved and nodded to an empty space.

"Why the overseer done it?" asked Elymas. "He know you Missus Bea's girl. He ain't got no business with nobody in the house."

Imari's face grew hard. She knotted her hands into fists and started toward her mother. Elymas stepped in her way.

"Why you running from me?" he asked.

"You mind what you gotta mind," she said through her teeth.

"He after you?"

Imari pivoted and stalked up the hill.

Elymas ran and caught her by the arm. She winced. "He after you?" he shouted.

Her eyes flicked to the service. The Reverend was telling everyone to quiet down. Children who had been dancing around the circle were captured and seated on laps.

Imari looked at Elymas. "Don't do nothing," she said. But down deep in her belly she felt a tingle of excitement.

A month later, Imari woke to the urgent clanging of a bell and the smell of smoke. She heard shouts and staggered out of her mother's cabin. Slaves were being roused from their beds by Master Paul's shouts of "Fire!" He held a flaming torch that lit the open yard between the slave cabins and threw wild shadows on the surrounding trees. "Grab your buckets! We need water!"

Imari unhooked her bucket from the outside wall of the cabin and rushed to the shore. The moon, low and fat in the eastern sky, cast a jittery reflection on the Potomac. She waded into the cold river. As she turned to bring the water toward the fire, she saw Elymas. He quickly averted his eyes.

When Imari reached the top of the hill, she saw that one of the small buildings, a little way from the main house, was ablaze. Bright flames, sparks, and smoke roared into the air. Slaves and the master's family worked together throwing water on the fire, but the heat that radiated from the building pushed them back. Master James ordered everyone away just before the front wall of the structure collapsed into a burning heap.

Elymas stood next to Imari. She knew that it was the overseer's house, burning as quickly as if the devil himself were pumping a set of bellows. But the overseer was nowhere in sight. He had not been near the slave cabins to sound the alarm. He was not now moving people into a line to make a bucket brigade, or instructing slaves to douse the nearby buildings and the flames that spread across the dry grass. Master James and his boys were doing all of that.

Imari slid her gaze away from the scene and looked at Elymas. His face was placid and the sweat on his chest reflected the orange dance of the fire. With deliberate slowness he turned toward her and stared into her eyes. Her throat tightened and her heart beat so hard that her fingers throbbed with its rhythm. She understood it all. The overseer was dead—lying, no doubt, among the flames and embers of his house. With that one look, she knew that Elymas was not afraid to risk everything for her. The line that had started with the overseer raising his hand to crack the whip that caused the welt now wound her and Elymas together as tightly as a wedding knot.

Later, Elymas pulled her into the woods and she let him touch her anywhere he liked. She let herself be his, never underestimating his anger again.

C HAPTER ELEVEN

HORACE WILBERFORCE KNEW THE BEST PLACES for digging worms. When your profession is fish, you'd best be a master at sniffing out the fattest, liveliest crawlers in town. He also knew just when each of the town's comely black cooks boiled morning coffee, rolled out biscuits, and whipped up eggs. Putting those two chunks of knowledge together was one of his talents. It did no good to hunt in the same place more than once a week. As a matter of fact, if he timed his worming and his flirting just right, he might get breakfast as well as a flaky biscuit and a bit of ham to wrap in his kerchief and save for later. Being about the business before dawn was crucial for catching the worms and demonstrating a level of motivation that the gals in charge of those generous kitchens liked to see in a man.

Once dressed, he put on his droopy hat and grabbed his pail and his broken-handled shovel. He made his way from his shack on Water Street, behind Bagg's Hotel, and up the hill toward the Galway house. The leaves had been dropping and there were moist spots behind the Galway barn where a few shovels of dirt could turn up a dozen industrious, fat worms. Maggie was never so easy to pry breakfast out of, but it had been a while since he'd gone there and he was feeling lucky.

He approached, careful to avoid disturbing the house. The only lamp burning was in the room next to the kitchen, Maggie's bedroom. He slipped off the street and headed to the yard. On the path he paused at the shed. Something seemed different, but what? He took another step, dismissing the feeling as the kind of nonsense that comes with the dawn, and continued to the barn. Galway's mare snuffled in her stall looking for feed. Horace tiptoed behind the building, intent on surprising his prey. Worms weren't stupid. They knew his tread and if he shook their territory, they would flee through the earth just as fast as a fish slips through impatient hands. After yesterday's rain, the worming was good. He got thirty or so tucked away in his bucket with a bit of dirt and a few leaves for cover.

He heard Maggie singing and smelled the smoke from her morning cook fire. When he came around the corner he thought that surely she was the very best person to see in the early morning light. She stood at the well, lowering the water pail into the cold pool at the bottom.

"Now you let me do that, Miss Maggie," he said.

Maggie continued working the rope. "Ain't seen you for a while. All them prettier cooks sick a you?"

Horace smiled and took charge of the well pulley's handle. His shoulders pulled a little as he lifted the heavy wooden bucket.

"You out collecting Mr. Augustin's worms?" asked Maggie.

"Last time I look, worms belong to the soil."

"And he owns the soil, don't he?"

"Why we talking about worms, when they's secondary?" He locked the pulley in place and grabbed the bucket. Maggie pointed to a water jug and the kettle. Horace poured in the fresh water. He straightened.

"Well, pick them up," she said, walking back toward the kitchen.

She put a hunk of fatback onto a hot griddle and poured out four circles of batter. They snapped and bubbled.

"Why you toting water? Your cistern still broke?" He put the jug in the dry sink and the kettle on the stove.

"Don't you never mind what's broke and what's fixed around here."

"Remember, I'm here . . . if *you* ever break," he said, cuffing her cheek. He looked over her shoulder at the pancakes, mouth moist.

"Who says I'm broke?" snapped Maggie. "Men, you think you know everything. And don't go pretending that I'm the reason you come. I ain't no fool."

"You got me there. I come to see if Mr. Galway agree to us getting hitched."

"You want an old woman like me, huh? You know I don't come with no food." She turned the cakes over on the black pan.

"It ain't about food now. I'm guessing you a little neglected. I could take care a you real good."

Maggie laughed. "You're just plain outta your mind if you think that I'm gonna live in your poor little shack, when I got all this right here. I don't need no husband telling me what to do." She flipped three steaming-hot pancakes onto a plate. "You want some?"

"You know I do."

She hid the plate of cakes behind her back. "I got just one request," she said, as Horace tried to reach around her. She stopped him with an irritated glance. "I told Mr. Augustin that I'd get a boy to help him. He done broke his leg and he needs some boy to do for him. You got a nephew or somebody?"

Horace's belly stirred like a tornado. "Broke it, huh? That's too bad." There was no nephew, but what did it matter? If a nephew was the only thing standing between himself and breakfast, he'd find one right quick. "You know I got whatever you need. Now, hand over them hotcakes."

While Horace sat and ate, Maggie took bites of her own breakfast. She bustled around putting the coffee to boil and cutting thick slices of smoked ham. A bell rang over the plaque that read, *Dining Room*. She looked up and went right back to her business. Horace studied her. The bell rang again with more force behind the pull and again she continued working.

After a few more moments, a blond gentleman with dark circles under his eyes burst through the dining room door. Horace whipped off his hat and stood over his mostly empty plate.

"There's two of you?" The doctor looked Horace over with startled indignation. "Oh, I see. You feed your suitors before your employer?"

"You suddenly in charge and I don't know about it?" said Maggie, a carving knife in one hand.

"I forgot you were the queen of Third Street," said the man, smoldering with rage. "When might I expect some food and coffee, Your Majesty?"

Horace had seen Maggie's temper rise before. He looked from one to the other thinking he had no idea what she might do.

"If you want a bite a breakfast outta this kitchen, you'll wait till seven when I serve it." She stabbed the knife into the carving block. The gentleman jumped back. "You come early, you get nothing. You come late, you get it cold. I got too much to do to be running every time you get it in your head to ring that bell."

"And feeding a shiftless beau is 'too much to do'? We shall see about that," the doctor said, looking flustered. He turned on Horace. "You come with me."

Horace grabbed the remaining pancake off his plate, winked at Maggie, and followed the man into the hallway. As he watched the doctor knock and open the library door, he remembered his daddy warning him about men like this. *They likely to toss you down like you ain't nothing and stand on your back, just to see the view.*

Inside the room, Augustin was covered in sweat, his eyes red. "I've been awake for hours," he said, his tone biting.

"How are you? Any pain?" McCooke went to the bedside and felt his patient's head.

"Of course I'm in pain. That medicine you gave me wore off." Augustin noticed Horace standing quietly in the open doorway. "What the devil are you doing here?"

"I caught your cook's paramour stealing food in the kitchen." McCooke went to the side table and poured some brandy into a glass and counted out the drops of opium. Augustin watched as he stirred. The doctor brought the mixture to him and he drank it in one swift draft. The effect seemed instantaneous. He sighed and closed his eyes for a moment of total relaxation. Finally, he shook himself, opened his eyes, and took in his audience.

"Did you say stealing? Where was Maggie?"

"Eating right next to him—as close as two conspirators."

Augustin laughed and then grabbed his leg and moaned. "Maggie is in charge of the kitchen, Doctor," he said, as he tried to breathe through the pain. "I suggest, for your health, you stay out of there." He turned slowly and tried to ease his broken leg out of the bed. "Horace, come here, boy, and get me out of this confounded bed. You take the other side, Doctor. You both need to earn your bread."

"Sorry your leg got broke," said Horace, as he joined the doctor at Augustin's side. Each lifted him under a shoulder and with care helped him to the chair, where he settled with some difficulty.

"I best be getting out to that river, Mr. Galway," said Horace. "Maggie told me you want a boy. I'll find you one and send him over."

"Wait a moment," said Augustin. "I've been meaning to ask you how that fish business is doing."

"They's biting good, Mr. Galway, and I know where to find 'em."

"Yes, yes. That's good, but Horace, you have to ask yourself, is that enough?"

"Well now, sir," Horace started, his throat thickening so suddenly that he had to clear it, "I been thinking that if I could get me a few dollars built up I could open myself up a shop. That way I could salt some a them fish. Maybe smoke a few and sell them. Make getting through winter a lot easier."

"Is that so?"

"And . . . I was thinking maybe you'd be . . . maybe you'd lend me some money, just to get started. I don't need much."

The doctor snorted. Augustin looked at him through narrowed eyes. McCooke busied himself pouring a shot of brandy. A slight tremor rattled his hand.

"I've been thinking about your situation too," said Augustin, focusing back on the fishmonger. "You see, I was at a meeting of the Colonization Society the other night. I have an idea that could make you into a big man."

"Me?" Horace replied. "Begging your pardon. I don't need to be no big man or nothing. I just need me a little bit a help."

"Oh, this is help. It's an opportunity. A man like you here in Utica? How high can you ever hope to get?"

"I don't follow, sir."

"You have an enterprising attitude. You could be the leader of men. That can't be said for everyone of your race. You know what's happening right now in Liberia?"

"Liberia?"

"Africa. The land of your ancestors. The new colony we're building. We don't take just everyone. We want only the most industrious and temperate. People like you. I would speak for you, put my reputation on the line. You'd be among peers there—not a Negro in the white man's land. A boy like you could rise to the very top."

"Africa? But sir, I don't know about no Africa. I know Utica. Born here. Lived here my whole life."

"You could be a leader there. And that will never happen here," continued Augustin. "Just think, right now we are setting aside five cleared acres, planting vegetables, and putting a comfortable cottage on it just for you. The Colonization Society is putting fifty dollars into each plot. A man could live well on five acres. Say a number of you boys get together and you want to grow sugar, cotton, or coffee—you get more land. Why, an enterprising man could get rich. You helped us build that canal, didn't you? You've got the expertise."

"You put me on the bend of any creek around Utica, I don't care if it be the blackest night, and you spin me around, I'm gonna find my way home."

"All I'm asking is that you think about it. Get in there before all the good spots are taken. We need to have some ambitious men as the foundation there. When those waves of uneducated slaves arrive they'll need a strong hand to guide them. Slavery won't last forever and there needs to be someplace for them to go. Look at what the white man has done with the wilderness here. You could go there and do the same thing."

"I'll get you that boy," said Horace, retreating.

"Think about it," said Augustin.

"Yes sir."

Horace appeared back in the kitchen. Maggie was filling a tray with coffee, pancakes, and ham. "What'd he say? He don't care about no breakfast, I'm sure."

"Mr. Galway say he thinking 'bout me. When a white man start thinking 'bout the black man—well. That ain't likely to be a good thing. He been talking to you about Africa?"

"Don't be no fool," said Maggie as she lifted the tray. "Africa? What I gotta do with Africa? Now don't forget to water and feed that horse before you go. Earn that sandwich I made for you there."

Horace put the sandwich into his kerchief and tucked it in his pocket. Once outside he lowered the bucket into the well. The eastern sky was just lightening. For years he had enjoyed his exchanges with Mr. Galway. The financier had always stood out as being fair to the black man and had an ease that other whites lacked. But this was different. Horace relied on his business and Maggie's kitchen. Would all of this be lost if he refused go to Africa? There had been some talk in the black neighborhood around Post Street that fever and death stalked the newcomers in Liberia. Just yesterday Schoolmaster Freeman, who ran Utica's School for Persons of Color, had given him a newspaper that said the colonists in Liberia had been attacked by nearby tribes.

Did Mr. Galway know this? If so, then maybe he really was like all the other whites. What was so wrong about just living here? Why should he get kicked out?

As Horace passed the shed, he again had a strange feeling. He noticed that the tall grass had been trampled in front. He listened at the entrance. Silence. He opened the door and stuck his head in.

"Anybody in here?" Absolute stillness pervaded the inside. Something felt strange. He closed the door and told himself that it was nothing, just his mind playing tricks. He made his way to the barn where he mucked out the stall and watered and fed the horse, thereby earning his sandwich.

Upstairs, Helen watched Horace out her window. She barely breathed as he approached the shed. When he appeared to see nothing amiss after going into the barn, she figured that Imari and Joe must have left during the night. It was for the best, what with the slave catchers dropping by the house. Now at least she could just do her sewing and start to settle into her new home. Maybe today she would look into the nursery. When had it been furnished? Mrs. Galway was almost forty when she died. The linens and baby clothing had to be at least a decade old. Today she would see to it. If only that doctor wasn't around. She must make some excuse and check the shed to see that no evidence of the runaways remained. Why, Imari and Joe might be halfway to . . . She realized that she had no idea where they were going. Imari had mentioned that some man was supposed to help them. They must have gone to him. She hoped they arrived safely and nobody besides her had read the notices and turned them in to Mr. Hickox. To think of what might befall a woman that far gone with child. No. She would drive the two slaves from her mind. They were on their way and she had done her Christian duty by risking herself and bringing them food and the quilt. Whether it was also her Christian duty to turn them over to the authorities no longer mattered. Perhaps she should drop by St. John's Church and go to confession. She had done right and wrong, both. It would be good to discuss this with Father Quarters.

She hesitated at the top of the stairs. If she went down the main staircase, Dr. McCooke was sure to be lurking nearby. It seemed clear that a few hours later in the day he would still be there. For all she knew he might still be living on the very same floor as she a year from now. Instead of stiffening herself and facing him, she slipped down the servants' stairs to the kitchen, drawn by the smell of the griddle cakes.

"Morning, missus. I was just gonna bring you some food." Maggie put a plateful of pancakes down on a tray. "You want it in the dining room?"

"No thank you." Helen brightened. "I'm so hungry, I'll eat it right here."

"I bet you're hungry," said Maggie. "I seen someone's been dipping into those biscuits and fish last night."

Helen froze. She thought, foolishly, that the missing food would not be noticed. "You saw that?" she said, deliberately easing herself onto a stool. Maggie smiled as she moved the plate of pancakes, butter, and syrup to the table.

"A course. And I know that doctor woulda licked the plate clean."

Helen nodded and started to eat. Again, she looked at the cook, fear troubling her stomach. Imari and Joe had to have moved on, she assured herself. Otherwise Horace would have found them this morning.

"And you got a little shine to you today," said Maggie.

"I do?" said Helen.

"You do. Maybe we're gonna have somebody new living here before too long."

"You mean the doctor?" said Helen, frowning.

"Not that darned loafer. He's a pain in my side." Maggie looked pointedly to Helen's stomach and then back to her face. "Maybe you don't even know." She leaned in and whispered, "You got your monthlies?"

"Oh my." Helen blushed and was about to change the subject when she stopped to think. "Well," she began, "I had them before the wedding. And . . . huh."

"We'll be looking out then," said Maggie, putting a plate of ham and a pot of tea on the table. "But while we wait, you'd best eat like they's one more sitting at the table."

Could it be? Was it possible she was with child already? Perhaps that was why she had been thinking about the nursery this morning. If she was to have a baby, especially a boy, Augustin would surely stop comparing her to Mrs. Galway. Let that lady finally lie at peace. With an heir in her belly, maybe she could let her husband know that Dr.

McCooke upset her nerves. That would certainly not be good for the babe . . . if there is a babe.

Helen ate her fill. There were many things to do this morning, she thought with a brightening sense of possibility. Looking to the nursery, going to confession, and, of course, checking on Augustin. He had seemed so distressed last night. Perhaps she might even brave another trip to Bagg's Square, this time not shopping for dinner, but to look for cloth to make new nursery curtains and to buy some sewing supplies. If she was to have a baby, there was much to prepare.

She stood, ready to begin, when the shed again caught her eye. They would not risk still being here, would they? She shivered. After I was so kind? No. The quilt? The food? They could not impose on me any further, could they?

"I gotta see to Mr. Augustin and get them breakfast dishes outta the library," said Maggie. "You got enough to eat, missus?"

Helen laughed nervously. "Yes. Thank you."

The instant Maggie went through the door to the front of the house, Helen ran out of the kitchen, down the back porch stairs, across the lawn, and burst into the shed.

There was no sign of anyone. Helen bit her lip. "Hello?" she whispered.

"That you, missus?" came Imari's voice.

Helen circled around the baskets and stood looking down on the woman. "You're still here," she said, not knowing if she was relieved or angry. "I imagined you'd be gone."

"Missus—"

"And where is Joe?"

"He be right back, missus. Don't worry about Joe none. I gotta tell you something."

"This is going to be another excuse, isn't it?" said Helen.

"Please sit down and hear what I gotta say."

Helen looked around the shed, growing exasperated. Finally, she pulled a bucket over and sat.

"This here baby. He, or she, they the one in charge now," said Imari. "Not me and not you. Maybe God, if He ain't too busy with somebody else. This here baby can't go nowhere. I ain't even stood up. Been trying for the longest, but it ain't working."

Helen kneeled, thinking that she might try to lift her. "We should get you a doctor then."

"I don't trust no doctor," said Imari.

Helen pictured McCooke smiling at himself in a mirror. "But you said that there was a man who was going to help you, didn't you?"

"Yes," said Imari. "But it ain't like he knows where I be."

"I can go find him." Helen made to rise.

Imari grabbed her arm and pulled her back down. "This ain't no easy business. You can't just burst in on the man and say you got a couple a people for him."

After Helen settled back down, Imari told her everything she knew.

CHAPTER TWELVE

MAGGIE HAD JUST CLEARED the breakfast dishes from the library and was complaining to Augustin about his lack of appetite, when a knock came at the front door. Sheriff Osborn appeared, smoothing down a few locks of his gray hair that normally saw little daylight from under his hat. Some tufts were in such a scramble that it was unclear if they ever behaved well without a heavy dose of Sunday hair oil. But the Lord's Day was now two days gone and no remnant of the treatment remained, nor would any new oil be applied before church attendance required it.

"Mr. Galway, sir," said Osborn, standing before him, fretting the edge of his tan hat, "I'd a never troubled you if I'd knowed that you was lame. But a young man I got in my lockup wrote you last night." He handed the folded letter to Augustin.

"Locked up?" Augustin grumbled. "Perhaps you are mistaking me for that rascal Alvan Stewart. Defending prisoners is more in his line."

The doctor, who had been sitting comfortably in a chair adjacent to the liquor supply, laughed merrily.

Osborn smoothed his wayward hair with a palm. "He expects an answer."

Augustin grunted and unfolded the paper. His body began rocking back and forth. "Ha," he laughed. "You've really plucked a fatted goose. What's the total amount that Mr. King, Judge Hayden, and *you* demand for Mr. Anwell's freedom?"

"Anwell?" said McCooke.

"Son of Llewelyn Anwell, Little Falls. A rich man, if there ever was one. Collaborated with him on a few contracts and now his son is begging for my help." Augustin smiled. He imagined the elder Anwell's innocent, indulgent face. Their mutual contract with the state to supply lumber to build the canal between Utica and Herkimer would have been disadvantageous if Anwell had negotiated the deal. A great engineer, but naive in the ways of the world.

Sheriff Osborn stated an amount, including an extra dollar above the cost of the food. Augustin withdrew a key ring from the breast pocket of his vest and gave it to McCooke. "Get the strongbox out of the bottom drawer of the desk."

A second key opened the box as it sat on Augustin's lap. He withdrew a few bills and gave them to the sheriff. "Doctor, write a note, will you? Tell young Mr. Anwell that he may come by once he is released."

McCooke complied, using one piece of paper for the letter to Mr. Anwell and a second to note the name *Llewelyn Anwell. Little Falls. Wealthy.*

"Speaking of Alvan Stewart," said Osborn, "you seen these handbills for this anti-slavery convention?" He offered a printed flyer to Augustin. "October 21. That ain't too far off. Plain folk are getting pretty riled up. Could get violent if the abolitionists go ahead and meet."

"Abolition?" said McCooke. "I thought you were shipping them all back to Africa."

Augustin flicked his hand toward the doctor and then was quiet for a moment. "The Democrats are using the convention to beat up the Whigs—as if they had any control of Stewart and his ilk. Breaking the convention up, as Beardsley and Hayden have called for, could spark a riot. And if the abolitionists are successful, it will encourage the Negroes of Post Street to believe all sorts of rubbish."

"How do we stop 'em?" asked Osborn.

Dr. McCooke rose and handed an envelope to Osborn. "I know. That morning we lock the doors of every church, schoolroom, and meetinghouse in town," he said, smiling conspiratorially. "Then the lovers of the Negroes will have to meet outside in Chancellor Square."

"Are you an imbecile or just trying to fatten your purse setting broken bones and removing shot from backsides?" said Augustin gruffly. "No. We must obey the rule of law or we are no better than the abolitionists." He thought a moment. "Will Alvan Stewart listen to reason?"

"So, we should *prevent* the convention?" said McCooke, amiably, looking from one man to the other.

"How? With force of arms?" replied Augustin, sneering. "Does freedom of speech and assembly mean nothing to you? My father fought
for those rights in the revolution." He banged his fist on the strongbox,
setting off waves of pain. He clamped his teeth and grunted, "Damn
you. Look what you did with your foolishness."

Osborn, money tucked into his pants pocket and with the reply to
Pryce Anwell in hand, edged out the door.

McCooke retreated to his medical bag and began rooting through
it. He pulled out several small vials and lined them up on the tea table.
Each had a little brown liquid at its base. "I'm afraid we have exhausted
the opium," started the doctor. "I could send your cook down to Williams & Hollister to get a fresh supply."

"Do it," said Augustin.

"But maybe it would be best, considering . . . well, the importance
of the medicine, that the task not be left to a member of the darker race.
Maybe I could go myself." The doctor paused, watching for Augustin's
reaction. He noted the almost imperceptible widening of the man's eyes
and the way the word *opium* triggered his patient's thumb to jump back
and forth across the tips of his fingers as if he were counting.

"You're the medical man," said Augustin.

"Yes," smiled McCooke. "It's just that I don't have the coin to re-
fill my stock. Perhaps you could . . ." The doctor nodded toward the
strongbox.

The muscles on the side of Augustin's jaw bulged as he produced
a sufficient amount of money for the doctor to accomplish his errand.
"Be quick about it," he said.

C HAPTER THIRTEEN

OWEN SYLVANUS SLID THE THICK wooden door out of its niche in the domed brick oven and set it on the floor. Hot air and the smell of fresh bread filled the back room of his shop. The wet boy he'd found on the creek bank sat up, looking panicked. He jumped off the hard cot that usually served as Sylvanus's resting spot during the quiet time between the cycles of rising dough that regulated his life. The baker's expertise in the ways of yeast had developed over thousands of loaves of bread. As he saw it, each springy ball of dough was a small version of life. You mix and you wait. You do your part and the catalyzer gets to its business. Everything else was up to the Creator.

"Be not afraid," said Sylvanus, holding his hands out. "I am a friend. It looked like thou needst one."

The boy moved toward the barred door at the back of the room. Suddenly, a furious pounding shook the wooden board that kept the door closed. He jumped back.

"Are they after thee?" whispered Sylvanus. Fear filled the child's eyes. The baker brought his finger to his lips and grabbed the boy's hand and pulled him to an area near the oven.

He called toward the door, "Just a moment. I shall be with thee." Quickly, he lifted a kneading table covered by a white cloth. Under the table there was an iron ring in the floor that opened a trapdoor leading to a tight crawl space. "Get inside."

The frightened boy obeyed. Sylvanus replaced the table and went to the back door. He moved the board aside. Hickox and Swift marched in scanning the room.

"Baker," said Hickox, "we are seeking a black boy with red hair who may have come this way. Have you seen him?"

"Thou hast come to the right place," said Sylvanus, "but too early. I see black boys all afternoon long. If thou needst hire one, just wait by the canal and thou shalt have thy pick. For the price of a few coins they will run hither and thither for thee just as they do for the canallers."

Hickox stepped back and studied the baker's flour-dusted black pants and simple white shirt. His eyes swung to a peg near the cot where a plain black coat and a wide-brimmed black hat hung.

"You're a Quaker," said Hickox. He nodded to Swift. "Look around."

"Thou art free to look. But I bake bread, not black boys." Sylvanus went to the opening of the oven and, with a long wooden peel, pulled fresh loaves out and stacked them on the kneading table. "Bread cannot be rushed," he said. "Nor ignored. Burning the Creator's gift is an act of alienation from the Light Within. Besides, hungry mouths on the packets await my labors."

"I don't doubt your word, for your people don't lie, do they?"

"Aye, a life led honestly is a simple life."

"But life's as complicated as a berry patch," said Hickox. "Particularly blackberries."

"He ain't here," said Swift.

"You checked behind those sacks of flour?"

"A course I did."

"If you are finished, I must meet my boats," said Sylvanus. He walked to the front of the shop, leaving Hickox and Swift staring hungrily at the bread. The baker returned to the room with a deep basket and began stacking the loaves into it. He looked over his shoulder and saw the two slave catchers lingering. He pulled a knife from his belt. Hickox stiffened. Sylvanus cut a large hunk off of a loaf and divided it in two. "You look hungry," he said, handing each a piece. He marched to the back door and replaced the board that held it tightly shut.

Swift took a healthy bite out of the bread. "Good," he said.

"I must make my boats." Sylvanus led them to the front door and out to the street. The small brass bell that hung from a bracket over the door tinkled. The Quaker turned the key in the lock.

From his hiding place, Joe heard the bell and the lock's snap. The crawl space under the floorboards was tight, but he lifted the trapdoor until a crack of light could be seen. The building's stillness convinced him that it was safe to work his legs through the hole and slide out. He surveyed the room. Almost at once he noticed half a loaf of bread on the kneading table. He tore off a hunk and stuffed it into his mouth. Before he unbarred the back door and slipped out to the area facing Ballou, he grabbed the rest of the loaf.

The sun had already risen above the horizon, casting long shadows of the leafless trees. Joe leaned against the back of the bakery and hoped that the brightness might warm him, but a cool morning breeze raised the gooseflesh instead. He could sneak his way back to his mother by sticking near the creek or by taking the street. A shiver went through him. He could not face the cold water again.

A single horse and carriage rattled by, heading east. Taking small steps and listening for any sound of a search, Joe moved to the corner of the building to get a peek at the cross street. The slave catchers were most likely hunting for him nearby, but he didn't see them. Few people were out, so he fixed his mind on the "walk" his father had trained him to do.

"Lots a people think black folks ain't worth a second look," Elymas had said as they neared a town early in the journey. "So that gonna work for us. You gotta walk like you going to the place you gone every day a your life. Don't look scared. Act like you so tired a walking this way that you don't hardly care about nothing." Elymas had assumed a slow, steady walk, arms relaxing at his sides, like the only thing important to him was to let the light shine down on him and mind his business.

Joe's chest grew tight as he thought about his daddy. Why had they kept on moving after Poppa was caught? They should have stayed close by if he was going to find them. His eyes suddenly went wet. But Poppa wasn't coming, and Momma knew it. That's why she kept on. Anger welled up in him. She lied all this way, he thought. Her and her secrets. It was unfair.

A sharp whistle from the canal brought him back. He didn't have time for feelings, so he bit the inside of his cheek and focused on getting himself back to the shed. He worked his way to the next corner, one that afforded him a view of the street he had originally come down under the cover of darkness.

Below him, an overloaded cart made a turn and headed in his direction. After a deep calming breath, he started ambling up the road with as carefree an attitude as he could manage, but with his whole consciousness focused on the progress of the cart as it neared. The driver was a slack sort of white fellow and the barrels that the cart carried were stacked two high. As the vehicle came parallel with Joe, he veered as if to cross the street, and within a few steps he grasped the wagon's tailboard, leaped on, and stowed away.

After a block, with the slave catchers probably somewhere behind him, he risked a peek out. He saw the house of the sleepless old man and knew he was close. Maybe, he thought, Momma will still be asleep and she won't even know I run off. He felt for the loaf of bread in his pocket. She still thinks I'm a baby, but when I bring her this food she'll know I'm old enough. Almost too late, he recognized the house he'd left that morning and vaulted out of the cart. He ran to the side of the building and toward the relative safety of the shed.

Just as he came around the house, he smacked into the solid bosom of a black woman wearing an apron.

"There you are," she said, grabbing his shoulder, her fingers digging into his flesh. "You're Horace's kin, right?"

Joe, so startled about being in her grasp, simply opened his mouth and emitted no sound.

The lady shook him. "Don't you tell me that your uncle sent me a fool. Are you a fool?"

"No, Mammy," he stammered.

"Mammy? Maybe you *are* a fool. I ain't nobody's mammy. You call me Miss Maggie. You call him Mr. Galway, or sir. You look smart and I'll give you meals. You understand? No talking back. No stealing. You be ready when he calls. And if that doctor tries to make you his slave, you say nice as you can, 'No, Doc, I gotta be ready for Mr. Galway.' You understand?"

"Yes, Ma . . . Miss Maggie," said Joe. He dared a look behind him at the shed. It was just across the grass.

"Now what do you tell that doctor when he starts bossing you around?"

"I ain't no slave."

"A course you ain't no slave. You're getting wages. Well, food, but that is wages enough for some fool boy. You say, 'I gotta be ready for Mr. Galway.' You got that?"

"Yes, Miss Maggie."

"What's your name?"

"Joe—b. Job."

"Well then, Job, come inside and I'll give you a hunk a bacon and some griddle cakes while I hunt up some a Mr. Galway's old clothes for you. It looks like you've been chewed on by a swarm of beetles."

C HAPTER FOURTEEN

ANTICIPATION WHIRLED IN Dr. McCooke's breast as he sauntered toward Bagg's Square, looking to all the world like a consummate medical man, complete with his case of instruments and tonics. In his pocket was enough cash for a few drinks, at least one round with a willing woman, and the opium that worked miracles—keeping his patient quiet and out of pain. Perhaps his "lean luck" had finally ended. Now he could finally build himself back up after his mother ran the plantation into the dirt. Really it was her "overseer" Billy who should be blamed. That African seduced her weak mind and pretended that he could run a complex operation as well as a white man. The blow had been staggering. It threw his whole life's plan into the refuse pile. No wonder I drink, he thought. Anyone in the same circumstances would. He just had to confine his fun to afternoons and evenings. It was the morning drinking that got me in trouble. Here in Utica I am beginning anew on a good footing. No need for a mistake or two to ruin my whole life. Even he had been heartbroken by the loss of pretty Miss Duphorne of Albany. When he thought about it, the fault had been entirely the servants' for not following his instructions to the letter.

His fortune in finding Galway injured and in need of his type of personal, on the mark, sunup-to-sunup services, put the doctor in an excellent position. Galway's house featured food (never mind the effrontery of the surly black cook) and that beautiful, too-young wife. All he had to do was sit in Galway's library and the whole of Utica's finest might parade by to pay their respects. He pictured the gouty feet of important well-fed gentlemen, the dyspeptic matrons upset by their rich suppers, and the lovely shy daughters overcome with ague, whose passions wanted cooling.

As he ascended the John Street Bridge, he heard his name being called. Hickox and Swift climbed up from the canal's towpath.

"Doctor, I trust that Mr. Galway fares well?" said Hickox.

"He is suffering," answered the doctor. "But I'm in almost constant attendance."

"It's comforting to have absolute confidence in his care," said Hickox, studying the doctor. "I wanted to let you know that I saw one of my two fugitives just this morning."

"You caught one, eh?" asked the doctor, intrigued.

"Caught, then lost." Hickox scowled. Swift looked to the sky. "It was the boy, but he may have drowned. If you hear of a corpse with his description, I'd be obliged to get a chance to inspect it."

"Drowned, eh? Terrible way to die."

"But perhaps the Lord spared him and he might yet be returned to his proper place."

"I don't know why I'd be informed, but if I am, I'll certainly reach you."

"I have tracked these two across hundreds of miles, Doctor." Hickox grinned, showing a set of yellow-brown tobacco-stained teeth. "They had many paths open to them and yet they came here. It may be chance, but it may be by design."

"And my part in this grand design?" asked McCooke. "I should let you know that as a rule, I'll have nothing to do with those people. No good ever comes of it."

"How very perceptive of you. But I have lived very close with them. Men in my line of work who underestimate the cunning of the Negro don't catch the Negro. Any intelligence you gather will be rewarded."

The doctor smiled, raising his eyebrow and wondering why the slaver believed him to be in a position to be helpful. Hickox nodded, and he and Swift crossed the street and jumped back down to the towpath.

McCooke continued toward Bagg's Square. He noticed one of Hickox's advertisements at the corner of a building and reread the description of the two fugitives. Shrugging, he saw that he was in front of Dupré's House of Sugar Confections. In the window, pastries and cakes and honeyed almonds drew his eye. His mouth dampened, thinking of all the sweets that could be had. Perhaps young Helen Galway might look on him favorably if he presented her a little gift, maybe a macaroon. Being in her good graces and having a little fun could make his stay easier and perhaps indefinite.

The doctor noticed a reflection in the shop window. A sizable man, broad across the shoulders and with an intelligent face, was in a tugging match for a sheaf of papers with a hulking, brutish man.

"You rogue be damned!" shouted the smarter-looking man.

McCooke turned. The big man had on a fine topcoat and tall hat. His menacing attacker and a thin, haggard accomplice appeared to be straight from a grog house, their homespun coats dirty and their pants worn thin at the knees.

"You ain't getting away with *treason*, Stewart," growled the brute. He wrenched the papers out of the well-dressed man's hands and tossed them in a heap. While the gentleman bent to retrieve them, the lanky man leaped forward and brought up his knee, flattening his opponent's nose and knocking off his top hat, sending it sailing through the air.

McCooke's eye followed the hat. He cringed when it hit the pavement, picking up a considerable amount of dirt. Before he had time to restrain himself, he swung his medical case and whacked the lanky man soundly on the back.

"Hey," he cried, turning toward McCooke, "you a low-dog traitor too?" He advanced a few steps toward the doctor.

McCooke backed away, looking for an escape route. "Touch me and I'll send for the sheriff."

"There he comes now," said the well-dressed man, who had dropped to one knee and was holding a handkerchief against his face. "His deputies too."

The two grogshop men looked hastily up the street and then retreated, shouting, "Go on with it, Stewart, and we'll be there to send you to hell!"

The doctor bent to recover the top hat. He brushed off the dirt and handed it to the man they called Stewart, who was swabbing his face with a handkerchief stained with bright-red blood. He smoothed down his ruffled brown hair and replaced his hat.

McCooke looked around and, seeing no lawman, drew his eyebrows together in confusion.

"Sometimes a clever scheme is as good as a sheriff."

"You might have a black eye there," said McCooke.

"I think I should thank you that I don't have a broken neck to go along with it. The name's Alvan Stewart, Esq." The man pulled off his glove and offered McCooke his powerful hand. "I didn't think they could best me. Going to have to get quicker."

The doctor noticed that under the expensive clothing, Stewart appeared to be as fit as a draft horse. A breeze caught the dropped papers and shuffled them, sending a few fluttering toward the gutter. McCooke stamped his foot on the stack and retrieved them. He straightened.

"Dr. Corliss McCooke, at your service." He handed the papers to Stewart, retaining one. It was the notice for the Anti-Slavery Society convention. "Were you taking these down?"

"No. Putting them up."

"Surely not," said McCooke. "You want the Negroes to stay?"

"Indeed. I'm the man who invited the Anti-Slavery Society to Utica," said Stewart, rubbing his nose with the bloody cloth and then stuffing it in his pocket.

The doctor hesitated. He appraised the lawyer's clothing—finely made suit, perhaps from Albany, or even a New York City tailor. The tall hat was new, with none of the beaver fur ticked or damaged from wear. The topcoat was of the kind of soft warm wool that took extra care to maintain. Stewart's long Roman nose and vivid gray eyes added to his look of nobility.

"I suppose," said the doctor thoughtfully, "that those two gentlemen were opposed to your plan?"

"These are grave times indeed. And we all must stand up for what we believe." Stewart fished in a pocket and produced a crisp white calling card. "I'm in your debt."

The doctor took the card. "Nonsense, but if you need me, I am currently at Augustin Galway's house attending to his injury."

"Galway? Sorry to hear that he's unwell."

"You may contact me there if you meet other rogues," said the doctor with a wink.

Stewart nodded and started up John Street, stopping now and again to pin handbills on buildings and rails.

Indeed, thought the doctor, my fortunes have not only reversed in a mere thirty-six hours, they have positively soared. Even if Stewart was on the wrong side of reality when it came to the blacks, he might be a useful friend. Perhaps there was no desire the doctor could not attain, if he kept his wits and capitalized on the Fates' gracious gifts.

C HAPTER FIFTEEN

HELEN STEPPED OUT OF THE SHED and stared at the wide basin of Ballou Creek. A chilly wind shook the branches in a nearby stand of trees. Clumps of brown cattails and reeds lined the bank. She imagined herself sinking quietly to the bottom of the basin, embraced by the cold water. What relief. No more runaways, no more husband, no more pressure to be perfect. And her own lack of sympathy. It embarrassed her. The pain of it was fresh and sharp. But did that justify her volunteering to find Imari's contact? It seemed like the only way to be rid of them. More than that, imagine being as helpless as those two runaways.

They had been placed in her path—by God or the devil, she did not know. Only one month ago she had promised to obey her husband, and now this woman had somehow drawn her into sin. Yet they required food, water, clothing, and help. *Her* help. The righteous, she remembered from her lessons, had no idea of the day or the hour when God might come. The alternative was to call in the slave catchers, and that she could not do.

She looked again at the trees. Did they not bend in a storm? Once they died and became brittle they broke apart in a strong wind. She decided to bend. Imari had told her all she knew about the man willing to help them. Helen must find that man.

In the empty kitchen, she wrapped up the remains of her breakfast and selected a few more biscuits from the pantry. Maggie's voice rang out from the front of the house, something about "Horace's nephew." Helen ran into the shed to drop off the food.

Maggie was in the kitchen when she returned.

"You were right about my being hungry," said Helen. "I ate a few more of your delicious biscuits." She passed Maggie on her way toward the front of the house.

"Why you out at that dirty shed, missus?" asked Maggie.

"Pardon?" said Helen, her hand frozen in the middle of pushing the door open.

"No other place on this property got so many spiders and creepers and Lord knows what all else." Maggie removed a leaf attached to a length of insect silk from her shoulder. "That ain't no place to spend time."

"I was thinking about a garden," said Helen. "Maybe in the spring."

"If you want a garden, we'll get someone to set it up. Don't go messing around out there. Now, I almost forgot. Horace sent over his nephew, Job, to help Mr. Augustin. You see him in the library, don't pay him no attention."

Helen frowned as she entered the library to ask permission to go to Bagg's Square. The boy would be yet another person from whom she had to keep secrets. The sooner she could go downtown and find Imari's contact, the better. In the hallway, she checked herself in the mirror. Hanging off her sleeve was a dust-darkened spiderweb. She brushed it away and noticed several more clinging to her maroon skirt. Once she had righted herself, she put on a smile and opened the library door.

Augustin sat in his chair, skin pale, with two red circles brightening his cheeks. She saw the backside of Horace's skinny nephew as he bent behind the tea table.

"Helen, my dear," said Augustin, his voice strained and tired, "you look distressed. Is anything wrong?"

"I'm just worried about you."

The boy straightened. Helen's eyes widened.

"What are you doing in here?" she said, shocked. Joe was in the house? With Augustin? Everything that she had planned now stood on its head.

"There is no need for alarm," said her husband. "Job is here to help me."

Joe stared at her.

Helen tasted bile in her mouth. Her hands shook. This is where he had gone? How had things gotten so out of hand so quickly? She suddenly remembered that the runaway-slave notice had mentioned Joe's unmistakable red hair. At any moment the slave catchers could barge in and see him. She must confess it all to Augustin. This was too much. He might not notice the boy's hair, but Dr. McCooke would connect the description of the boy with Job's sudden appearance. Anyone might. As she opened her mouth to tell the truth, she noticed Joe's fear.

"My dear," said Augustin, "what's the matter?"

Helen focused herself on the one thing she could change. "That hair," she cried. "He might be full of lice." She rushed to the corner and jerked the bell pull to summon Maggie.

"Lice? You're imagining things," said Augustin. "Maggie says he's a good boy."

Maggie appeared.

Helen turned on her. "Now you look here," she said, hysteria edging into her voice. "This boy may have brought vermin into this house and I won't have it. You must shave his head clean."

"Missus," said Maggie, "I checked him myself."

"You shave his head this instant or I shall." For a moment Helen and Joe made eye contact. He had his hand on his hair and looked startled. She had no choice but to continue.

Maggie stepped forward and put her hand on Joe's shoulders.

"It must happen instantly," said Helen.

"Mr. Augustin?" Maggie said.

He shrugged. "Do it."

Maggie moved Joe to the door. She turned back and peered at Helen through narrowed eyes, a frown dragging down the corners of her mouth. "I never heard a such a fuss about one skinny black boy," she said as she left.

"And take off those eyebrows too," Helen added before the door was firmly closed.

"That was in very bad form," said Augustin in a low firm voice. "You have made your life here more difficult. I don't have time to intervene between you two. She deserves respect."

Helen's arms shot above her head. "You don't even know what's happening!"

"What do you mean?" said Augustin.

"I mean that . . . you . . ." She scrambled to think of what to say. "I may be with child."

All the anger melted from Augustin's face. He opened his arms. "Oh, my dear, my dear. Come here."

Helen froze, spine stiff. Lord, what have I done? The idea had only been suggested by Maggie, but there was no going back. She moved to Augustin's side. He grabbed her hand and kissed it. Pulling urgently, he brought her to her knees. He kissed her forehead and drew her into his arms.

"Are you certain?" he whispered.

She nodded, aware of having a new lie to confess.

"You have made me live again," he said.

C HAPTER SIXTEEN

HORACE RELAXED BEHIND his fish stand as he waited for his regular customers. The Mohawk had been kind to him that morning, providing a variety of perch, trout, catfish, and bass. Perhaps later tonight he could take some of his earnings and see if there were any goings-on around Post Street that suited his fancy. As he fingered the handkerchief in his pocket, checking to make certain no river water had dampened Maggie's sandwich, he remembered that he still had not found a "nephew" to send to Mr. Galway. It would keep.

He retrieved that week's copy of the *Oneida Whig* from under the stand and set himself to reading the news of the nation, when something on page two caught his eye. A blistering waterfall of words condemned the upcoming statewide abolition convention. He could not think of a more unlikely place than Utica for such a thing. Just as he was settling in to read the column in full, he noticed the two slave catchers walking directly toward the stand. The older one's smile brought a shiver up his back. He stopped reading, shook the paper, and pretended to use it to shoo away flies before laying it, abolition story side down, over the fish.

"Something caught your eye, boy?" said Hickox as he approached.

"No sir. Just swatting them flies." Horace grabbed the newspaper off the fish. "Seen anything to suit you, sir? They's fresh. Swimming this morning, on your plate tonight."

Hickox nodded to Swift, who circled around the cart and grabbed the newspaper out of Horace's hand.

"Hey now," said Horace, alarmed. "You want a damp old newspaper, all right. But they got new clean copies right there in the hotel."

"The paper doesn't interest me," Hickox said, taking it from Swift. "I want to know why it interests *you*." He scanned the crumpled pages until he found the article on the abolition convention. He directed his chilly blue eyes at Horace. "If I peeled you like an apple, I'd find an abolitionist under that black skin, isn't that so? It's true of all your kind."

"Don't know nothing about all that big stuff, mister." Horace glanced around the square hoping for a friendly face. "I only know about fish."

"I have a little reading material of my own," said Hickox, producing a copy of his runaway-slave notice.

Horace glanced at it. A gnawing pain developed in his stomach. Someone was being hunted and now here was the wolf pack sniffing at him. A black man might be kidnapped by frustrated slave catchers and sold into a life of bondage without warning. It was not impossible. As a matter of fact, it had happened in the great city of New York. Such stories appeared in the abolitionist newspapers that were passed hand to hand on Post Street. Whenever a slave catcher arrived in Utica, news traveled rapidly. He himself had discussed the arrival of these two with Schoolmaster Freeman.

"I ain't seen 'em," Horace said, trying to hand the notice back.

"Now look, boy," said Hickox, smiling and pointing at the top of the notice. "You see right there? It says $150 reward. That's more money than you see all year. Maybe in ten years. Money like that could make you an important man." Hickox extended himself over the cart and leaned toward Horace. "From this spot you can see the whole city stroll by. Just open your eyes and see what you see. No one has to know where I got my information. You understand?"

"Yes sir. I got it, but I still ain't seen them two."

"Good. Good. But you're going to keep alert," said Hickox. "You know what happens when someone keeps the whereabouts of stolen property a secret?"

"Stolen?" said Horace.

"They stole themselves. Same as if your fish here got up and swam off. Their rightful and forgiving owner is waiting at home with open arms." Hickox ran an appraising eye over Horace. "You're a businessman. Minding your business, I understand. Here is your problem: anybody who obstructs, hinders, harbors, or conceals an escaped slave pays five hundred dollars or goes to jail. That's the law and it's a lot of big words, but I'll gamble you know what they mean."

"I ain't seen 'em. I ain't seen nobody."

"And I believe you, boy," said Hickox. "But if you get some word about them, you have to speak the truth." He produced a leather pouch, and after some fiddling, he pulled out two large golden coins and rubbed them together between his thumb and index finger. "You ever seen a Spanish doubloon, Fishmonger?"

Horace watched the coins circle each other. "No sir."

"Isn't having $150 weighing down your purse better than owing five hundred and being thrown in jail—for a couple of *strangers*?"

Horace's throat tightened. Just for a moment, he allowed himself to think of what $150 would buy, like a sparkling window for his shack that would allow in the sun and replace the drafty plug he had now. He'd buy a new overcoat before the winter freeze and a pair of boots that didn't leak. But mostly he thought about the glorious sign he would hang over his new shop: *Horace's Fresh Fish*.

"I have such confidence in you," said Hickox, "that I'm giving you this now." He flipped the coins one by one toward Horace. "An advance of eight dollars on that $150."

The doubloons glowed in Horace's palm.

"Don't stand in my way, Fishmonger," said Hickox. "Others who traveled that path have found nothing but woe."

C HAPTER SEVENTEEN

PRYCE ANWELL BURST OUT of the watchhouse and into the sun a free man. He smoothed the nap of his long-tailed jacket. Since its dunking in the canal, the garment had shrunk and wrinkled. Amazingly enough, his tall beaver-skin hat appeared to be undamaged by its time in the water, but the leather sweatband had tightened enough to leave a red mark across his forehead. His shirt collar was still damp, but at least it was passably clean, thanks to Mrs. Osborn's insistence that she "give it a good scrubbing." Sheriff Osborn said that Pryce "better obey" the summons to Mr. Galway's house if he did not want to anger his new benefactor—a man, the sheriff assured him, "terribly ticklish about insults."

Following the sheriff's directions, Pryce proceeded across Bleecker and began to take in the newness and apparent prosperity of the neighborhood. Perhaps someday, he thought, he might settle in just such a place. Really, anywhere in Utica would work, as long as it was nowhere near the canal. He made himself happy thinking of coming home in the evening to one of the fine houses along the street. What kind of work would he be doing? he wondered. The earnest face of his father burst into his thoughts, dissipating the vison. Settling here was crazy. He'd had nothing but trouble since his less-than-glorious arrival. All he could do now was fulfill his promise to thank Mr. Galway, beg him for a few more dollars (to be paid back at some future date), and resume his tiresome journey out to Buffalo and back to Little Falls. He prayed that his father never got word of the ordeal.

As he proceeded, he brightened. Perhaps his luggage might still be on board the boat or waiting to be retrieved at Utica's canal house. Wait, he thought suddenly, they wouldn't have written to his father, would they? A wave of anxiety crushed his mood. A picture flashed through his mind: a letter—detailing his idiotic belly flop—arriving in Little Falls that very morning. Shaking his head as if to dislodge the idea, he remembered that the boat hadn't even slowed down for him. He couldn't imagine the captain putting quill to paper, much less paying for the postage.

How disappointed the old man would be if he heard about the fiasco. Pryce turned his mind to solving his immediate problems. First: borrow more money. Second: catch up with the packet and find out if a letter had been sent. If so, write and deny everything. If not, write and say that things were going along as planned.

He approached the Galway residence. It was very fine with white clapboard siding, five windows across the second story, four chimneys, an elliptical window in its triangular pediment, and tall pilasters with arches attached to the front wall. The decorative fanlight over the solid oak door matched the pane design of the sidelight windows. The man must be quite prosperous indeed.

Pryce decided that if his father's assessment was correct, Mr. Galway would be happy to help. But Father was too trusting sometimes.

Because the elder Anwell was so nice, people often underestimated him. But he seemed to recognize successful projects, ones that brought profit, as if they sparkled, while the failures rarely caught his fancy. His father floated along, lighting on one idea after another. A steep drop in the riverbed, ignored by most, produced the vision of a water-powered sawmill that his father designed and had built. The tall pines nearby could be rolled to the very edge of the construction area. There they were fed into one end of the building and sliced their length by giant whirring blades. The wood emerging ready to use from the other, thereby eliminating the cost of transporting the lumber to the canal's work site.

When Anwell senior had studied the turgid waters of the Mohawk, he imagined a new mountain of stone arranged into an arched bridge that held the canal in a straight line, an aqueduct that would carry people and freight in total calm and comfort thirty feet above the anarchy of the raging spring melt that could wash away another engineer's set of locks. The structure became a part of the landscape as if it had always been there, just waiting for someone to place the stone blocks in the right order. The money poured in as his father flitted on to another idea, another problem whose solution would come to life, as if it had sprung from the head of Zeus.

Pryce felt that if he had inherited the old man's vision he would see his future with that same luminosity and know which way to go. But to him rocks were rocks and trees stood until someone else cut them down. And planks were produced with noise and sweat and violence.

He lifted the heavy brass knocker on Galway's front door, banging it against the strike plate. A face peeped at him from the sidelight window. With a start, he recognized Miss O'Connell. He blinked as if he might clear this improbability. She stared at him with a look of alarm.

He suddenly realized the frightening impression he must be making—a strange man who had followed her and was filthy enough to have spent the night in jail.

Regaining his composure, he tried to pull his hat off his head, but the shrunken band gripped his forehead until he applied such force that, for a moment, it felt as if the leather had ripped away some of his skin. He touched his brow to check for blood, remembered where he stood, and bowed abruptly.

"I found you," he called through the glass.

Her brow crinkled. She opened the door and pushed her head out, glancing nervously behind her as if her employer might be angry to have her lollygagging around the entranceway. A sharp red blush climbed up her cheeks. "What are you doing *here*?" she said.

Pryce bowed again, slowly and with a smile of satisfaction at her blush. "I'm here to thank Mr. Galway."

"You know Mr. Galway?"

"No, he . . . helped me out with a difficulty."

"So, this," she said, her finger wagging back and forth between them, "is just some coincidence?"

"Helen, who the devil is it?" called a voice from inside. "It had better be Dr. McCooke."

Helen stepped aside, allowing Pryce into the foyer. A pleading look came into her eyes. "Don't mention the canal," she whispered. "I'll ask Mr. Galway if he can see you now," she said louder and with a formal tone.

The moment she disappeared, Pryce revised his mission. First: forget engineering. Second: ask for an additional loan and suggest that he work off his debt as Mr. Galway's clerk. That would give him plenty of time to smite the girl's first and second impressions and properly present himself as a suitor. If Mr. Galway didn't hire him, surely such a successful man could suggest another place.

Pryce shook himself. This notion was ridiculous. The logical thing would be to get back on the packet boat. Later, if he was still interested in pursuing Miss O'Connell, he could write to her and press his suit on paper.

Helen returned to the hallway and indicated that he should enter the room. He straightened his back and nipped quickly in. Their eyes met as he passed. Forget about Father, he mused. She was worth any risk. He would stay and woo her, even if it meant working somewhere as horrid as King's Victualing House.

Helen followed Pryce into the library.

"Well," said Augustin, gripping the arms of his chair and looking pleased. "So you're Llewelyn Anwell's son."

"At your service," said Pryce.

"It seems to me that I've been at *your* service," said Augustin. No one moved until he broke the awkward silence: "I'm jesting. Sit down, sit down."

"I will leave you to your business," Helen said, swiftly gathering up some needlework from the sofa.

"No, Helen, stay," Augustin said.

She nodded to him, shut the door, and went to an overstuffed chair by the window. In her lap, she knit her fingers, rubbing knuckle by knuckle.

As Pryce took a seat on the couch, he thought it curious that the maid, or housekeeper, or governess, or whoever she was, be asked to stay.

Augustin shifted. A groan sounded deep in his throat. He gripped his thigh, massaging it with the heel of his palm. "As you can see, I'm indisposed."

"I'm sorry that you're not well," said Pryce, noticing that his own hands were subtly smoothing the short fur of his hat. He put the hat aside and tried to fold his fingers together, but even that felt awkward. "I won't prevail upon you for long. First, I'm grateful for your kind help during my recent *crisis*."

Pryce glanced at Helen. Confusion darkened her face.

"Your predicament wasn't all that grave," said Augustin. "But why was it *I* who had to save you? Did someone finally swindle your father into bankruptcy?"

"Both his finances and physical health are excellent. He mentioned you before I left. He prayed for your continued good health."

"A lot of good that did me," said Augustin with a tight smile. Helen scowled.

"Yes, I suppose it didn't—or I mean did—I mean," said Pryce. "I'm sure he will be unhappy when he hears that you're unwell."

"And I'm sure he'll get over the upset in a matter of moments." Augustin studied the young man.

Pryce felt his face brighten in embarrassment. "I must ask you the favor of not letting my father know," he said, looking at his nervous fingers. He glanced at Helen.

"Know about what?" said Augustin

Pryce's head swung back to Galway. "About the unjustified situation with Mr. King. It would be . . . inconvenient."

"A secret, eh?" said Augustin, a playful gleam in his eye. "I bet you've more secrets than a son of Llewelyn Anwell ought. Well, he is a kind man. When it comes to fathers, *you're* one of the lucky ones."

The front door banged open and Dr. McCooke hustled into the room as if to announce that Napoleon had risen from his grave. He stopped and stared at Pryce.

Augustin focused all his energy on the doctor. "What the devil took you so long?"

McCooke lifted his chin and smiled broadly. "Success on a mission of medical necessity sometimes takes longer than anticipated." He crossed to the liquor table and opened his medical bag. "But," he said, focusing on Augustin, "success I did have."

"Helen," said Augustin, "take Mr. Anwell into the parlor and entertain him for a moment."

As she closed the library door, she noticed the doctor slap his hands together and rub them up and down before withdrawing a vial of opium from his medicine bag. Something about the gesture troubled her, but she shut her husband and the doctor in and crossed the foyer to a double set of French doors and opened them wide.

The room had not been used since the first Mrs. Galway had been consigned to the earth. Though a fire had been laid in the fieldstone fireplace, it had not been lit. Helen pulled open the brocade drapes and sunlight streamed through the windows, revealing the swirl of dust stirred up by her presence.

"I tried to find you," said Pryce in a low murmur, moving toward her. "You just disappeared."

"Then how did you follow me here?" she asked, glancing toward the hall.

"Miss O'Connell . . ."

Helen stiffened. "It's Mrs. Galway."

Pryce froze, his face slack. "Mrs. Galway? What? . . . You said . . ."

"I know what I said," she snapped. Sighing, she straightened her left hand. The gold of her wedding band glinted in the sun. Why had she brought this humiliation upon herself? She was Mrs. Galway until death. The weight of it sank into her. "I misspoke—that is, I'm still getting used to it. I'm sorry to have confused you."

He stood straight-backed, hands at his sides. "I want to apologize. My behavior's been abominable. Had I known you were married . . ." He trailed off. "But I *didn't* follow you."

"I'm sorry I misled you."

"I *tried* to follow you," he said, shrugging. "You were too quick, or I too slow." He smiled at her warmly.

Her eyes went damp. "I'm sorry, Mr. Anwell. Truly." She egded toward the foyer. "But I must go. Mr. Galway will have the doctor call you." She stepped to the threshold of the room.

"It's just that you were so adorably serious with your sketchbook," he said.

She stopped, suspended for a moment. "Please, don't continue. I'll be in trouble if anyone hears this kind of talk," she said, turning, a softness on her face.

Pryce focused on the floor. "I should be the one to go." He glanced up, resolute. "Give your husband my thanks. I'll repay his kindness as soon as I'm able."

The door to the library swung open and Dr. McCooke's head appeared. "Mr. Galway says he needs to see you both."

Helen and Pryce stole a fleeting glance at one another.

"Mr. Anwell, Helen," called Augustin from his seat, "the doctor has told me the most interesting thing." He put his hands on the arms of his chair and began to lift himself.

"No, no," said McCooke as he rushed to Augustin's side, "you mustn't stand."

Helen moved quickly to him and kneeled by his chair. "Please, don't injure yourself further."

Augustin turned to her with bright eyes, "The doctor tells me that tonight a telescope is being brought from Hamilton College and set up in Chancellor Square. We'll all be able to see Halley's comet, as if it has been brought down from the heavens to blaze before our eyes." Again, he tried to lift himself.

The doctor laid his hand on Augustin's shoulder. "Stay seated, sir."

Helen looked at McCooke. "What does he mean? Surely he can't go anywhere."

"Your leg will be further damaged." McCooke's voice was steady and low. "Try to get some sleep."

"Sleep?" said Augustin, agitated. "While the heavens are opening their mysteries and revealing themselves?" He made another attempt to stand before collapsing into the chair.

"Let yourself heal," said McCooke. "I'm here to see to you."

The doctor's calming words had taken some effect and Augustin's head relaxed against the chair's tall back, cradled by the curve of its wing. "Forgive me. I am rather tired." He placed his hand over Helen's. "God is inviting us to marvel at His work. My dear, you can't miss the summons."

"I'm not missing anything," she murmured.

"The doctor says I can't go," he whispered. "But *you* must."

"I will stay by your side," Helen insisted.

"I'd be happy—" started the doctor.

"Tell her," called Augustin to Pryce as he lingered in the doorway, "this happens only once in a lifetime."

"Mr. Galway is correct," said Pryce, quietly. "Halley's comet hasn't been seen since 1759 and won't return for another seventy-five years."

"You must take her, Mr. Anwell," Augustin pressed, a patina of sweat polishing his brow. "Mrs. Galway cannot be alone on the street after dark."

Helen leaned back on her heels.

The doctor looked at Galway, frustration evident on his face.

Pryce stepped forward, animated. "I'd be honored to take Mrs. Galway anywhere you please," he said. "But I have no place to stay. It pains me to remind you that all my money was lost in the canal."

"Of course," said Augustin. He inhaled as if starting a new thought, but his eyes closed. A few silent seconds passed and everyone in the room bent toward him. His head drooped. He caught himself and resumed as if he had not paused: "Go to the National Hotel, it's just below the canal on Genesee Street. Speak to Richard Sanger, he's the proprietor. Tell him to charge your food and lodgings to my account."

"Sir, I thank you for your kindness, but I'm already in your debt."

"Yes, you certainly are. But you see, I insist . . ." Augustin trailed off, his eyes fluttering until the lids quieted and he seemed to fall asleep.

McCooke led them out of the library. "As you can see, Mr. . . . ?"

"Pryce Anwell."

"Oh, the convict?" said McCooke with a chuckle. Helen's head spun in Pryce's direction. He looked aggrieved. "You can see that Mr. Galway is having some difficulties," continued the doctor, his focus shifting to Helen. "Mrs. Galway, it's not prudent to go out to view the comet."

She broke away. "My husband made himself quite clear. Once in a lifetime, he said." She turned to Pryce. "Mr. Anwell, I'll expect you at sunset. Perhaps Mr. Galway will be able to sustain himself for a longer visit after a nap."

"I'll be here promptly," said Pryce. He nodded to McCooke. Helen and the doctor watched as he let himself out.

"Sounds like fun," smiled the doctor. "We three shall attend together."

CHAPTER EIGHTEEN

THE SHED WAS A DISMAL PLACE. Over their months of travel, Imari had slept in swamps, in hidey-holes, on the bare ground, in attics, under chicken coops, on cots, in the holds of ships, in dusty cellars, and once, on a feather mattress. But the thought of spending another night on the dirt floor filled her with despair.

She felt the baby shift. He or she would not rest. God, she prayed, I have nothing left. Let me have this one. No husband. No friends. Not even the strength to get onto my legs. Where is Joe? He might be in the hands a the demon Hickox.

She pictured the boy in chains, his thin limbs dragged down by their weight. Or worse, they might be whipping him into betraying her.

Joe had been a miracle. There had been two others who never even had a chance at life. And her firstborn, poor Jimmy. Sold off for looking too much like a yellow Master James for his wife to live with. Imari tapped on her heart as she always did when Jimmy came to mind. It crippled her to even think where her poor light-skinned boy might be. The child was only four when Master James sold him. The man never said where he sold Jimmy or to whom. It was like he couldn't get rid of the evidence of his sin quick enough. The world opened its jaws and swallowed Jimmy whole.

When she was carrying Joe, her fourth, Master James had brought in a doctor, a filthy old man with long white hairs sprouting from his eyebrows, nose, ears, and one small crop coming out of a brown witch's teat on his cheek. He had laid her out on her mother's own pallet and put his nasty hands all over her without even saying "Good morning," like she was a thing.

Once the exam was over, he and Master James stepped outside. She crept to the entrance. They talked about her "slippery womb." Slippery? As if Jimmy had just slid out of her.

The doctor had said, "Sell the wench. She's no breeder. Ain't worth the feed."

Master James laughed. "She has her uses."

Despite the doctor's opinion, Joe held on.

She shifted her back, trying to find a comfortable position. This new baby seemed strong enough. It had survived all these miles.

They had decided to set out on a moonless Saturday night in late July. She was about six months with child. The sun had been relentless during the day and most of the slaves moved their bedding outside hoping for cool air off the Potomac.

Imari knew that there was never a time when everyone could be expected to be asleep. She made Elymas leave the cabin first and head to the shack where the slaves did their private business. He was to work his way through the trees over to the shore where he and Joe had constructed a raft. She and Joe joined him about an hour later and hoped that no one would put the two departures together.

They intended to float across the Potomac to Maryland. She had never been on the water and when Elymas proposed their means of escape, she begged him to find another way. He guessed that they might be carried downriver a mile or two, thereby getting a good head start. She finally conceded.

When they pushed off from the shore, frigid water came up between the logs. A swift current grabbed the raft. Their roughly made oars would not get them to the other side. It was impossible to see anything ahead as they were buffeted by the moving water. The raft's wood pieces moved like an accordion. After being bucked an inch or two into the air, Imari and Joe gave up trying to row and hung on to the leather straps that Elymas had added—just in case. Water surged over the wood and soaked them as they rode the swells. The ropes that held the contraption together loosened. Elymas tried to keep the raft in one piece with his whole body. Once the knots gave way, sections tore loose. As it broke apart, Elymas grabbed Joe and hauled him close. Imari clutched a single log that whipped like the tail of a snake as the river rushed her away. In the darkness she lost sight of them. Through the roar of the rapids, she heard Elymas franticly calling for her.

A rock outcropping as large as a horse suddenly appeared. The log slapped against it. She spun, ending up facing backward. Smaller stones scraped against her, but she could not get a grip on anything solid.

Suddenly, she was tangled in the limbs of a downed tree. The remains of the raft ripped out of her hands. The force of the water pushed her down. Waves covered her head. She held her breath and grasped large branches, pulling herself to the surface. She coughed and sputtered but, hand over hand, dragged herself toward the thicker arms of the tree. The crush of the water and the weight of her saturated dress sapped her strength, yet she continued, knowing that to weaken meant death. Soon her knees rubbed the riverbed. She crawled to the beach and collapsed. Where were Joe and Elymas?

She yelled for them. Only the Potomac answered. She cried bitterly. With no strength left, she rested her head on her weary arms and moved no farther.

It was not until after the sun rose and woke her from exhausted sleep that she saw that she had landed on a sandy finger at the end of a wooded island. She was close enough to the Maryland shore to see people moving about. On that side of the island, the river was calm with no white water to mock her.

She dared not draw attention, but pulled her heavy wet skirts out of the sand and moved to the safety of the trees. She shucked off petticoats and squeezed water out of her dress. Her shoes, shawl, and head rag were gone. She rested against a tree and tried to concentrate on the babe in her stomach. Had it survived?

As she rubbed her belly, trying to coax the life inside her to stir, she realized how crazy they had been. They had known nothing about nothing. Only now did she see the jeopardy that she had brought upon the unborn child—upon them all. Eyes closed, she prayed to God to let this mistake come out right. Let them all survive. The river had scrubbed her of her pride.

Splashing sounds reached her ears and she moved through the trees until she saw Elymas and Joe walking in ankle-deep water. Quick as lightning, Elymas plunged his hand into the river and came back out with a floppy black eel. Her stomach rumbled and the baby, as if it too were watching, gave her notice that it was alive and ready to eat.

"I knew you was strong," she said, and ran to her family, throwing her arms around them.

Now, in the quiet of the shed, Imari laughed ruefully to herself. She wondered: if they had turned around at the island, found some way to get back to the plantation before dawn on Monday, might they not still be together?

"We ain't crossing that river again," Elymas had said. "We just gonna get kilt if we try. I don't wanna die like no drowned dog." So they did not turn back.

Other than her first hours on the island, she had rarely been alone. After keeping her boy close for so long, how could she have lost him now? At the plantation, she thought, I didn't protect him from Master Arnold. But why had Joe suddenly run off? Anger stirred her. Now he gonna get sold down south. He ain't never gonna get no freedom. If he was in Hickox's clutches it was his own fault. Thinking he knew better than she. Everything could be lost in a second. She closed her eyes. He deserved better—such a useful boy, so smart. Now it had to all be for the baby.

She sighed. If only being separated for a few hours by the river had been their biggest trouble on this long journey. Elymas, Elymas, she thought desperately, are you really not coming? Can I give you up and move to the next place? She should have lashed herself to Joe last night. That would have stopped the boy from wandering. Well, there was no changing the past. God seemed to care so little for the present, He could not be expected to go setting right the yesterdays of a slave.

She caught herself. No. Never again a slave.

After leaving the doctor in the hallway, Helen went upstairs to her room to prepare to look for the man Imari had said would help. The thought of the smitten Mr. Anwell brought a girlish smile to her lips. Under Miss Manahan's care she'd seldom encountered handsome, brash young gentlemen. The boys and the dreadful leering men she'd met on her walks to the canal had been horrible, ill-mannered ruffians. But Mr. Anwell was so dashing, and the daring way he had flirted with her from the top of the packet boat—he seemed reckless to woo her. Would she be able to keep him at bay in the dark square, with the night sky above them? Why, he might be so bold as to try to steal a kiss. In the mirror, she noted how happy she looked. It was wrong to even entertain such ideas. But before she was able to push the thought of his kiss out of her head, she imagined him coming to her bed. Once again her face burned. Augustin seemed blinded by opium, or surely he would have noticed the young man's attentions. The doctor certainly noticed. She left her room resolved to not think about him or anything else except finding Imari's contact.

She opened the hall linen closet and pulled a knitted woolen blanket from the shelf. A chamber pot sat on the floor. How would she get them to Imari? Certainly, she should be able to go wherever she liked, no matter what Maggie thought. She felt a stab of guilt about Maggie. The cook had been very kind to her. If there had been another way to handle the situation with Joe, she didn't know what it could be. She didn't want to think that she might have ruined her relationship with . . . well, the only kind person in the house. Life was capricious. She believed that leaving school and marrying would bring her freedom, but that was the assumption of a girl, not the reality of a wife. Even if this was now her house, she couldn't just march out to the shed.

And now there was Joe. She could think of no way to get him out without raising more questions. She had covered it over with Augustin. Now she had to try to mend the breach with Maggie. And Imari must be told that Joe was a part of the household.

She came to the first floor and stopped outside the kitchen door. Maggie seemed to be talking to Joe and saying something that sounded like "crazy come from crazy," which she assumed to be about her own father's manner of death. She wanted to burst in and stop Maggie's wagging tongue. Poppa was not crazy. He was heartbroken. The cook lived in the comfort of this house. How could she know what he had felt? How could she know anything?

Behind the door Maggie grew quiet. Helen backed away. She lit a taper from one of the sconces in the hallway and stepped down into the basement's dark dampness. After some searching, she found an empty flour sack. She lifted it from a low table. Several potato bugs dropped to the dirt floor and scuttled away. Startled, she dropped the sack and then, mad that she had been scared, flicked the bag a few times to clear it. She put in the blanket and chamber pot and went back upstairs.

At the kitchen, she paused once again and heard Maggie whisper,

"You ain't gotta do nothing that lady says." Everything had gotten so complicated so quickly. Perhaps she should stop right where she was, before there was real trouble, and confess to Augustin. Maybe he would forgive her if she explained that there was a man who was supposed to help the runaways. Maybe he would let them proceed on their way. But, she remembered, the slave catchers had come to the house. Did they have that privilege with everyone in town?

She had already wronged Joe; she would not wrong him again. If only she could find the man who was to help. She would risk it. Confess later, if need be.

She entered the kitchen. The back of Joe's newly shaved head greeted her, now dotted with cuts and abrasions. The skin where his hair had been was much lighter than his neck. Africans browned in the sun? There was so much that she didn't know.

Both he and Maggie turned and looked at her. Without his eyebrows, Joe looked like a weird elfish spirit with a glowing dome.

"Maggie," said Helen, "I must apologize. I treated you badly."

"You ain't gotta say nothing to me, ma'am," replied Maggie, as she turned away and swept Joe's hair into a dustpan. "I'm just a cook. Lady of the house don't gotta say she's sorry to no cook."

"But I should have trusted your judgment," said Helen. She looked at the boy. "Job, is it? I'm sorry to have scared you."

"You ain't gotta be sorry to no black boy," Maggie said, emptying the dustpan into a pail of food shavings. "Anyway, we going to town to tell Horace what's what so Job's people don't think we went crazy on the boy."

Joe's eyes pleaded with Helen to save him.

"Wait," said Helen. "I need his help in the shed. I mean, Mr. Galway may be waking soon and doesn't Job need to be here? Besides, I have an errand in Bagg's Square and I will explain to Horace what happened."

Maggie looked at her finally, her face cross. "Yes ma'am. If you say so, ma'am." She picked up the razor and the slop pan. "We're here to do what you say, ma'am. No reason you gotta be nice." She stalked to the porch and threw the dirty water onto the lawn. Puffs of white shaving soap dappled the grass like early snow.

Helen tasted bitterness on her tongue. She supposed that she deserved the comment. "Come with me, Job," she said as she passed Maggie on the porch.

"You just told me he's gotta be ready for Mr. Augustin."

"He will be," said Helen. Carrying her loaded flour sack, she stepped down the stairs and across the yard.

"I just dressed him up nice," called Maggie. "He ain't gonna be fit for the house after that shed."

Helen pressed on.

Imari gasped when she saw Joe's shaved head. Helen explained the haircut and how the ruse had to be maintained, at least for the day. The boy gave his mother half a loaf of bread as well as bacon from Maggie's breakfast. Their reunion was short and tear filled. Joe said nothing about almost being captured.

"I'm going to find your contact, the Quaker," said Helen. "Joe, you must leave here now so that Maggie doesn't come looking."

"I ain't going back," Joe declared.

"Get yourself back," Imari snapped, "and you play at being happy to serve that man. You play like this is the happiest you ever been and raise no fuss. You obey that cook too. She sound like trouble."

"She nice," said Joe.

"You too young to know," said Imari with finality.

Once again Helen stood over the canal, this time on the Third Street Bridge. The memory of Mr. Anwell burned her cheeks. Was she really so captivating that he'd become mesmerized by her and fell into the canal? And to have agreed to see the comet with him was a willful folly. But it would be fun to once again have someone with whom to discuss the stars. That couldn't be bad, could it?

It was time to find Imari's contact. She had few clues. He was a Quaker with a shop. What kind of shop, Imari could not say. He could be found by a candle burning in a tiny window at night. According to Imari, the shop was on the south side of the canal, near Ballou Creek.

The whole area held many of Helen's most happy memories. Just ahead was the building that had been her father's blacksmith shop. Now the place was run by Mr. Rees. Her mouth felt dry even seeing it again. That happy past, did it really exist? Every assumption she'd had was false—ripped away by reality. Even yesterday's assumptions no longer stood. Five years ago this area had been almost empty. Now the intersection of Ballou Creek and the canal was a bustling area of businesses. To add to her frustration, every fourth man looked like he could be a Quaker. Was she to stop strangers and quiz them about whether they helped slaves escape?

Just east of Third Street the businesses thinned out as the developed part of the city gave way to streams, trees, and ungraded dirt roads. Across the creek was the soap and candle factory; black smoke from rendering animal fat made the air feel greasy. It seemed too big to be harboring runaway slaves. Such illegal business had to be furtive. The more people who knew a secret like that, the less likely it would be kept. No, she was looking for a smaller establishment. One run by a husband and wife, maybe, or a single proprietor. Eliminating Mr. Rees was easy—he was a Welsh Presbyterian. Next to the soap factory was the Crinan Brewery. Did Quakers drink? She thought that they must be temperate, but she didn't know for sure. And if you were yourself not a drinker, did that prohibit you from brewing beer?

I'm getting nowhere, she decided. I haven't even been inside one business or asked one question. Perhaps it would help to begin with a sort of a survey. I'll walk past each place and see what I can eliminate. When I have a few prospects, I'll come back and enter them one by one. She started back up Third Street, passing a shoemaker—possible, but it wouldn't be open late at night. There was the American Hotel, which seemed unlikely, not isolated enough. And one could absolutely rule out Deputy Mitchell's house. On the corner of the block stood a small two-story building. The sign said, *Owen Sylvanus: Baker*.

Nothing looked obvious. This search was ridiculous. And she could feel herself dismissing places like the shoemaker's simply because they were unknown to her.

She began to walk toward home, but stopped. How could she tell Imari that she had failed? The woman had escaped from a cruel master and come hundreds of miles. Yet, was Helen herself too cowardly to go into a few shops and look around for a Quaker? She had not been nearly so timid before her wedding. What was it about the state of marriage that had pushed her into this crystalline fragility? It could not be borne. She had to succeed—if not for them, then for her own self-respect. And it was the only way to be rid of them.

Just then she spied a roundish man carrying a large basket into the bakery. It backed up onto the creek, as Imari had said it would. In his black coat, white shirt, and wide-brimmed black hat, he certainly looked like a Quaker. Didn't Joe have some bread in his pocket? She glanced around furtively. There was nothing wrong with entering a shop, yet her pulse was up and her face was hot. A bell jingled when she opened the door. Inside, the comforting smell of yeast and freshly baked bread got her mouth watering.

"A moment, please," came a voice from the back of the shop.

Helen noticed that there was a lock on the door leading to the rear of the store. Curious, she thought.

"How may I help thee?" said the baker, closing the door firmly.

At least he seemed to be a Quaker, but she had no idea what to say. A direct question would not be trusted. Too much innuendo might also draw suspicion.

"I had a taste of some delicious bread this morning," she started, "and I wanted to see if it came from here."

"Didst thou come from a packet boat?" he said, grinning.

"No."

He paused. "Bagg's Hotel, perhaps?"

"No."

"Thou must tell me more. Most of my humble products are purchased by the canalboats or the hotels. Few buy from the shop."

"This was not a whole loaf. But the heel resembled these," she said, indicating the loaves on the counter.

"I fear that my bread is not so unique," he said. He began to brush flour from his pants.

"The way I came to have the bread was unique. It was brought my way by a rusty-headed black boy."

He stopped brushing, looked at her, and picked up a rag to wipe the counter. "Rusty-headed, thou sayest?"

"The bread was very fresh."

"When didst thou eat this bread?"

"This very morning. The boy and his mother are friends of mine."

"I see. How fare thy friends?"

"They are not hungry, yet still they yearn."

"Bread sates the body, but not the hunger."

"These two were told that there was help for their yearning to be found in a shop in Utica," she said. "Have I found the right place?"

Sylvanus looked to the door and then studied Helen. "Thou hast."

CHAPTER NINETEEN

WHEN MAGGIE ESCORTED the abolitionist Alvan Stewart into the library, Augustin was sitting up with clear-eyed attention, showing neither weakness nor pain. Stewart, whose wide chest might have served him better on a loading dock than in a court of law, moved with grace. He clutched Augustin's hand in both of his and took care not to jostle the injured leg.

"You be needing anything?" asked Maggie.

"Bring a new bottle of brandy," said Augustin.

"Tea for me, if you please," said Stewart.

"It'd please me if everybody just drunk tea," said Maggie, eyeing McCooke on her way out.

"Mr. Galway, sir," said Stewart, "your physician told me that you'd been injured."

Augustin turned to McCooke. "Is this true, Doctor? Are you talking about town?"

"I was explaining why I'm not living at my usual lodgings—Clarke's," said McCooke.

"Usual lodging? You were probably driven out," said Augustin. "Perhaps Stewart here will take up your case. You like unwinnable causes, do you not, Mr. Stewart?"

"Nothing is unwinnable, but some victories take more time," replied Stewart, smiling.

"Getting the doctor back inside a temperance house may take you a lifetime."

"Clarke did not know who he was evicting," said McCooke heatedly, a glass of sherry in his hand. "I have a letter of recommendation from Mrs. Elizabeth Preston McDowell Benton, Senator Benton's wife—he's the one who shot . . ."

Augustin glared at the doctor as if he had just interrupted some important business. McCooke stopped talking, his mouth hanging open. Galway gestured for Stewart to take a seat on the sofa. The lawyer folded his frame onto it.

"You're optimistic," said Augustin to Stewart. "I wish I could be too. I'm afraid I fall in with those who try to see the world for what it is."

"Optimism and realism are not antagonists," said Stewart.

Maggie reentered with the china service. At the tea table next to Augustin, she clucked her cheek and sighed. The surface was littered with empty bottles. Turning, she laid the tray with a clatter on the table in front of Stewart. After shaking her head, she collected the spent brandy and wine bottles, tucking three under her left arm and one under her right.

"They's plenty a *tea* right there, Mr. Augustin. Maybe you want me to pour you some?" she suggested.

"Your hands seem to be full," said Stewart. "I'll pour." He leaned over the table and began to manage the cups and saucers.

"He likes it sweet," said Maggie. "Just a dash a the cream."

"You know his tastes," said Stewart.

"I'd be some special kinda fool if I don't know what he wants after more than forty years."

Stewart looked to Augustin. "Forty, is that right?"

"You may go, Maggie," said Augustin.

"A little more sugar," she said as she passed Stewart. He obliged and handed Augustin the cup. Satisfied, Maggie withdrew.

"To answer your unasked question," said Augustin, stirring his tea, "yes, she was, at one time, owned by my family. But now, of course, she gets a wage, board, and Sundays off."

"And now she thinks she owns *you*," muttered McCooke.

"I'll not hear you disdain her," growled Augustin.

"My apologies," said the doctor, withdrawing slightly. He picked a book off the shelf nearby and sat as if to read.

"I didn't know your family had owned slaves," said Stewart. "Impressive that she still serves here. It would seem that you're uniquely qualified to talk sense into your Colonization Society colleagues."

"How's that?"

"Some of your number are using our forthcoming anti-slavery convention to create an atmosphere of fear and intimidation."

"I'll vouch for that," said the doctor. "But, Mr. Stewart, those ruffians couldn't be Colonization Society members. That's how I met him. You see—"

"I understand," interrupted Augustin, "that there is indeed some . . . passion about the issues. But I know these men. It's all just talk."

"According to some," said Stewart, "I am either trying to resurrect Nat Turner so that he can slit every white throat—or I am an idiot."

"Nobody argues both?" said Augustin, his eyebrows raised in mock innocence. "Your abolition convention is deliberately provocative. Of that, I'm sure you're aware. Even as a reasonable man, I worry that there'll be violence because you'll fill the streets with radicals."

"The violence," said Stewart, "if it comes, will not be from the abolition society."

"No. It will come from the uneducated mob whose minds shouldn't be inflamed with dangerous talk of freeing millions of Negroes," said Augustin.

"Is it not hypocritical to moan about violence," said Stewart, leaning in, "when your society's own Congressman Beardsley speaks of destroying the city to prevent the convention from occurring?"

The blood rose in Augustin's face. "It's you who are the hypocrite." He pointed to the center of Stewart's chest. "If the men of the street promise violence, how in good conscience can you continue to organize?"

Stewart rose, placed his hands behind his back, and began to pace the room. "I'm tempted to make a speech, but if you will allow . . . Your family were, I am sure, loving and benevolent slaveholders, correct?"

Augustin set his jaw. His teacup and saucer rattled as he put them on the table. "As you can see, Maggie has chosen to remain right here."

"That's what I'm saying. They were good. But even if others were half as good, it's not enough in the eyes of God. The apostle Paul places 'man stealers' on par with 'murderers of mothers' and 'whoremongers.' Not the best company with which to be associated, correct?"

"Our country inherited slavery," said Augustin through clenched teeth. "As did I." He noticed that Stewart looked delighted. He pursed his lips and took a moment to master his feelings, pasting on a grin that showed no warmth. "For now, slavery is the law among our Southern neighbors. Each generation works at improving the laws. We are but masons chipping away at a crude and unpolished block of marble to reveal the perfect form at the core of the stone."

Stewart moved in, towering over him. "That's a lovely sentiment, but we both know that the men who make laws are carnal beings. There are many reasons why one provision or another might be written. Laws are riddled with compromises—to suit the strongest. Agreed?"

"Yes."

"Then is not God's law higher than mortal law?" asked Stewart, smiling once again.

"Are you, as an officer of the court, advocating that each individual should decide which law to obey and which to ignore?"

"These issues must be considered by our lawmaking masons. If our task is to chip away at the marble, then should there not be free discussion?"

"I have made that point exactly, have I not, Doctor?" asked Augustin.

"I seem to remember something like that," answered the doctor, gulping down his sherry.

"It follows," said Stewart, "that if I cancel the convention, society's masonry tools will lie fallow and nothing will change." He straightened himself to his full height. "Therefore, I do not concern myself with the threats of violence."

CHAPTER TWENTY

BY THE TIME HELEN ARRIVED home, the sun had passed over the hills of New Hartford and hung in the western sky, waiting for its chance to dip below the horizon. She had secured a promise from Mr. Sylvanus to come to the shed at midnight. And, just so that no one got suspicious about her trip downtown, she had bought several skeins of soft yarn and a few yards of raw muslin. She needed to seem like she was making ready for the child. Once the runaways had moved on and she determined if she really carried a babe, she could get started on other preparations.

From the kitchen window, she saw that Maggie was directing Joe to split up wood for the fire. He wielded the ax with uncertainty.

"Where you been that you ain't learned to use a hatchet?" Helen heard Maggie ask. Joe struggled to free the blade from the log in which it was partly buried. There was no way she could get to Imari just yet to explain tonight's plan.

She looked in on Augustin and found her husband sleeping in his chair, his hair out of place, an open book on his lap, and glasses on his nose. The doctor snoozed on the couch, his handsome face smooth and untroubled, a red and white knitted blanket draped over his body. Before him stood a brandy bottle and a snifter half-filled with dark liquor.

Maybe, Helen hoped, the doctor will sleep until after Mr. Anwell calls. There was little time to get ready for his arrival and she wanted to make certain that the woman he would escort tonight was the same one who had so mesmerized him on the bridge.

Joe came into the library, his arms filled with split wood. Helen put her index finger to her lips. At the woodbin, Joe struggled to place the logs, but lost control of the pile. They crashed to the ground in a thud.

McCooke sat up. "What?" He looked at Joe with an unfocused gaze. "Who are you?"

"Nobody," Joe said.

"What happened to your head?" asked the doctor in a slur of words.

"Nothing," replied Joe.

The doctor nodded and seemed to accept the answer. He relaxed, plumped his pillow, drew up the knitted blanket, and fell back to sleep.

Helen motioned Joe out of the room and quietly closed the library door. "The man you are supposed to see will be at the shed at midnight. Make sure to let your mother know."

Joe nodded.

"Now back to work with you."

The boy went to the kitchen.

Helen grabbed her skirts and ran up the stairs with heat rising in her breast. It would not be proper to think of this as a social engagement. Mr. Anwell was Augustin's guest. One of the tasks of the lady of the house was to make guests as comfortable as possible. Really, she was merely performing a wife's duty by allowing herself to be taken to the comet viewing. Apparently, the entire town would be out in Chancellor Square. Appearing with him might cause talk, but since it was evident that only a few people knew that she was now Mrs. Galway, she dismissed the thought. The world would be too busy looking at the comet to be wondering about her.

The outfit she selected—a deep-blue and green dress with puffed sleeves that gathered at the elbows, flared out over the forearms, and finished with a trim of scalloped white lace—gave, she felt, the impression of a lady of great fashion.

She heard the heavy knock on the front door and her heart surged. Mr. Anwell had already arrived and she had not yet even selected a hat. As she pulled on her gloves, she heard the doctor answer the door. Something was motivating him—certainly not a sense of decency.

The hat she chose had a stiff brim that stood straight up from her head, so that she could see the sky. It framed her face nicely, and the sapphire bow at the front complemented the dress and set off her cool white skin. On her way out, she grabbed a striking lace cape to cover her neck and shoulders from the October chill.

Downstairs, Mr. Anwell was in conversation with Augustin. The doctor was merrily filling three glasses.

"I believe that it was Herschel's *sister* who discovered the comets," said Pryce. "Well, some of them."

"That's right," said Augustin. "The sister."

"Did *a woman* discover Halley's comet?" asked Helen. All eyes turned to her.

The doctor smiled brightly, raising his glass as if to salute her. Mr. Anwell stood, appearing to be favorably impressed by her outfit. Her husband, dark circles under his eyes, regarded her crossly.

"No," said McCooke. "Halley did."

"If you'll permit a second correction, sir," said Pryce. He looked at Helen with cautious, neutral eyes. "Technically the comet had been known since antiquity. Halley identified several historical sightings as a reappearance of the same comet and accurately predicted its return. Herschel's sister Caroline discovered many comets, but not Halley's."

The doctor looked pointedly at Pryce.

"We've found the right person to expand your knowledge, my dear," said Augustin.

She went to her husband's side. "I should stay here with you."

"Nonsense," he said. "Not when you've finally gone to the trouble of putting aside that school dress and put on a proper frock."

Stung, Helen straightened. "I can change, if you desire."

"More nonsense," he said. "Doctor, weren't you about to pass out some brandy?"

The doctor quickly drained his glass, poured a bit more, and came from behind the liquor table with glasses for Augustin and Pryce.

"Careful, Doctor. We need you sober," said Augustin.

"My hand is steady and I am ready," responded McCooke.

"Your hand is steadily filling your glass," Augustin noted.

"For that, I blame you," said McCooke, laughing. "Quality demands quantity." He distributed the liquor, showing exaggerated care and surety in his motions.

"It is very fine stuff," said Pryce.

"Finer than your father's reserve?" asked Augustin.

"Father's a temperance man, spirits are forbidden. He's very well acquainted with ale."

"Temperance men?" said Augustin. "My father always said they were a dull breed. Not Llewelyn, of course."

Pryce seemed on the verge of commenting when Helen stepped forward.

"Should we not be going? As you can see my husband is tired."

"Go ahead," said Augustin. "I'm fatigued and feel some pain coming on. Doctor? I need you." He nodded to the medical bag and the doctor's shoulders sank. McCooke eyed Pryce for a moment with a look that Helen took to be strong dislike. He reluctantly began fishing in his medical bag.

"Helen," Augustin continued, "see if Maggie will join you. It would be a good idea. You understand, don't you, my dear?"

"As you wish," said Helen. She squeezed his shoulder again and went to the door. Pryce bowed to Augustin and followed her out.

"Maggie?" Pryce asked when they were in the passageway.

"The cook," she said, smiling. "She is annoyed with me, rightly, I think."

In the kitchen, Maggie sat in a rocking chair, smoking a pipe and looking out the open back door at the darkening yard. She remained seated when Helen and Pryce entered. "Mr. Augustin told me he ain't hungry and not to cook no food, if that's why you're here."

Helen bit her lip. "Mr. Galway thought you might like to come and view the comet."

"The comet? What kinda fool goes out at night asking for trouble? That there comet's got Mr. Augustin so dizzy he broke his leg. Besides, if you ask me, it don't look like much."

"So, you've seen it?" asked Pryce.

"I ain't trying to see no comet. Besides, I got things to do. I can't be wasting my time on what's in the sky when I got a bunch a cares right down here on earth."

"I can assure you that the comet is perfectly safe," said Pryce.

Maggie pulled a long puff out of the pipe. "You think I'm a fool."

"No, I, uh, only meant . . ."

"Do you know what's creeping around them streets at night? You got your head up in them stars so much you don't see what's right in front a you. You go ahead and be some hungry bear's supper."

"Very well, Maggie," said Helen. She indicated to Pryce to step out of the room. When he was gone she asked, "Where's Job?"

"Home, I suspect."

"Good," she said, peering out at the backyard before leaving the kitchen.

Maggie heard the front door close. Without hurry, she set down her pipe. As she rose, she steadied herself with one hand. The other reached around to her lower back to ease the ache from the day's work. She lit the wick on a whale oil lantern, brightening the room. From behind the back door, she retrieved a musket that she kept ready to kill raccoons and other varmints in the yard. She stepped onto the porch and held the light high, illuminating a circle around her and causing her shadow to shift on the doorframe. She stamped her foot on the cover of the empty cistern to warn, with a resounding *boom-boom*, whatever creatures were lurking nearby. If they wanted to keep their heads and not end up in a stew, she was to be avoided. After hearing padded feet scuttling through dry leaves, she stepped off the porch.

Something was going on in that shed and she meant to find out what.

CHAPTER TWENTY-ONE

AS HELEN AND PRYCE WORKED their way across Bleecker Street toward Chancellor Square the silence between them accumulated, one moment atop the next, making it difficult to begin a conversation, either intelligent or casual. Thoughts darted around Helen's head like a swarm of fireflies, but no idea settled long enough to be articulated. She sneaked a peek at Pryce. In the soft rose of dusk, he seemed to be looking at everything, from the tops of trees, to the flickering flames of the streetlamps, to the polished paving stones, rather than at her. Several times he gathered his breath as if he were about to comment, but he never did.

She resolved to remark upon the cloudlessness of the sky when suddenly, as if a stage curtain had been pulled back, the broad square came into view. Stately elm trees lined the perimeter, their limbs still decorated with a few bright-yellow leaves, stretching toward the indigo sky. People arrived from every direction carrying oil lamps. Bull's-eye lanterns bobbed and sparkled throughout the expanse. Children, thrilled to be out of doors instead of tucked away under wool blankets, tumbled and laughed, eluding parental entreaties to behave.

"It's just like a pixie's garden," said Helen, her eyes wide with excitement. Without a thought, she broke away from Pryce, rushed across one of the gravel paths that bisected the area like a great pie, and stood on the tips of her shoes in the grass. She closed her eyes.

Pryce bounded after her. The breeze of his arrival stirred the soft hairs on her cheek and cooled her eyelids. She felt as if she had stolen away from home and could pass the evening any way she pleased.

A few measures of Irish dance music drifted into her ear. People gathered around a man playing a small triangular harp. After a quick look back at Pryce, she ran over and joined the crowd. The instrument rested in the lap of a middle-aged gentleman in worn knee britches, thin stockings, and a formerly grand overcoat, now threadbare at the hem and elbows. A case sat open at his feet with a few coins bright against the dark velvet lining. His arms encircled the blond wood harp, pulling it toward his shoulder like a loyal friend. His long fingers furiously danced back and forth, adroitly plucking the metal strings, bringing forth vibrations both sharp and resonant. Several men hopped and kicked in time. When the music ended with a flourish, Helen joined the clapping. The musician started a new song, slow and sad, playing with his eyes shut, head swaying with the rise and fall of the tune's strains. Helen's throat tightened. The music, one of Piper Jackson's ballads, stirred a forgotten memory of sitting on her father's lap, her arms around his neck, tears wetting her cheeks over the loss of a small metal figure of a horse he had forged for her. He'd softly sung a Gaelic lullaby, easing her pain until all she felt was the serenity and safety she found in his arms.

"Look over there," said Pryce.

Helen dabbed her handkerchief under her eyes and looked toward the middle of the park. Driving around the central reflecting pool was a peculiar-looking wagon, outfitted with great springs carrying a sturdy wooden box painted with the word *Rittenhouse* in gold leaf. Three men jumped off the driver's bench and removed the container's top, which had been padded with cotton-stuffed muslin. They extracted a tall brass tripod and carefully set it upright on a large piece of flat slate.

"That must be the telescope from Hamilton College," said Pryce.

They hurried to where the men were attaching a long brass tube to the tripod stand. A second smaller box, perhaps a foot in length, was pulled from the original crate. The encircling crowd hushed.

"That's the eyepiece," whispered Pryce. "All of this equipment is extremely delicate."

"Have you ever looked through a telescope?" asked Helen.

"Only once. It was miraculous," said Pryce. "It shows how mystifyingly complicated the universe is. And it lets you gaze into the past."

"The past?"

Pryce straightened and turned his face to the sky. His profile was silhouetted against the last glow of twilight. "We think we see a star, but what we really see is the light from that star. It could take two million years for that light to travel to earth. But by the time the light reaches us, the star may already be dead."

Helen looked up. The Big Dipper glittered and she again saw the white smudge that was Halley's comet. "Many things that are dead still shine," she said. "My father has been gone for five years. He knew so much about the constellations. Sometimes when I look up I feel like he's still carrying me on his shoulders and pointing out each grouping. I've forgotten much of what he taught me."

"It's all right to not know something. Remaining ignorant is the sin."

"Perhaps tonight I'll repent some of my sins," she said.

He glanced at her with a surprised smile, cleared his throat, and looked away. She immediately regretted being so forward and felt the pinpricks of a blush.

"Look," said Pryce, a little too loudly. A washed-out young man, with pimply white skin and lank yellow hair, fitted the eyepiece into the telescope. He swiveled the contraption around so that it pointed north, toward Deerfield and the hills beyond. He raised the great brass tube toward the sky.

"He's sighting for the comet," said Pryce.

Helen raised her hand to her mouth in alarm. "Won't his eye be burned if he sees it?"

Pryce laughed. "No one ever died looking through a telescope."

The young man said, "There it is," and the gathered crowd moved closer. Helen leaned forward in spite of her fear, almost waiting for the poor man to scream in agony from looking at a blazing ball of fire.

He took his eye away from the lens and peered at her. "Would you like to see, miss?"

Helen looked at Pryce. "Me? Are you sure it's safe?"

He nodded and she approached. She held her breath and looked through the eyepiece. Everyone on earth dropped away as she examined the white blur of the comet. She had fully expected to see a scorching bright orb, something that was worthy of the poem she had read describing planets shrinking before a "fearsome flaming comet." Though it was trailed by a large tail, it sat murky as a hailstone shadowed by a ghostly white shroud. Her eye followed it as it drifted across the circle of the telescope's sight. "I lost it," she said.

"That's just the rotation of the earth," said Pryce. "May I?"

She stepped aside and allowed him to look through the eyepiece and reposition the device.

"Amazing," he said to the blond man.

"Give somebody else a chance," said an intelligent-looking older man with long stringy hair and an old-fashioned tricorn hat.

Helen quickly bent in for one more look. "I don't see any fire. Now it looks like a gob of cream floating in a cup of tea."

"It's not fair," grumbled the older man.

They moved away as the onlookers pushed toward the telescope.

"You found it amazing?" she said, her voice a little shaky. They cleared the knot of people. "I feel rather dull."

"The sensational reputation that comets have," he said, "does make reality a little disappointing. But studying them increases human knowledge, which brings us closer to understanding a small sliver of God's plan."

They moved a few steps.

"We don't need to see through the device to enjoy an evening of contemplating the firmaments," continued Pryce. "That is, if the *bears* refrain from eating us."

They both laughed.

A silhouette in black crepe appeared at Helen's side.

"I did not expect to find you here, Mrs. Galway," said Miss Manahan.

The smile fell from Helen's face. Coughing, she extracted a handkerchief from her sleeve. "How nice to see you."

"I have been awaiting a call from you," said the older lady.

"Forgive me." Helen noticed that she was waving the cloth like a person about to surrender arms and stuffed it back into her sleeve. "You and the girls have been much on my mind."

Miss Manahan cast her eye in Pryce's direction. "Helen?"

"Oh," said Helen, again flustered. She awkwardly gestured to Pryce. "This is Mr. Anwell of Little Falls. He's visiting Utica as Mr. Galway's guest."

Pryce, who seemed to sense how nervous Helen had become, bowed low—restraining his hat with his hand.

"This is my schoolteacher, the mistress of Miss Manahan's Female Institute."

The lady did not offer her hand, instead slightly inclining her head in his direction. "The girls will be expecting you," she said to Helen. She brought her candle lantern up and studied Pryce's face. "It is a singular occurrence when one of our poor number gets to travel as far as you have, young lady, and they are expecting a full report." She squinted at Pryce once more before departing.

As she marched away, Helen's shoulders sagged.

Pryce leaned in, whispering, "I believe that we have survived the bear."

Helen's hand quickly covered her mouth, but her eyes narrowed and she rocked with stifled laughter.

A light streaked across the sky. Several people declared that they had seen a shooting star.

"We're here to look at the heavens," Helen said, with an attitude of business. "According to my husband, you can teach me something. So, what do you think when you look up?"

Pryce breathed deeply and took in the wide expanse of sky. "I think about a magnificent being who can see the whole universe, past, present, and future, like we see the forest from the top of a mountain. What an exquisite creation He's made for us—an act of love, really."

Helen found herself not looking to the sky, but instead noticing the contours and smoothness of his face and the intensity of his concentration.

"He wants us to gaze as deep and as far as possible," Pryce continued. "The study of astronomy is a form of pure reverence."

"It sounds like a prayer when you say it."

"To ignore the beauty God made for us," said Pryce, clearing his throat, "is to insult His work."

Helen deliberately looked away and bent her head back and searched the sky. "There's Cassiopeia and her babe, Little Cassiopeia," she said, her arm outstretched, finger pointing. "And the next is . . . what's the name?"

"Cygnus? There? The great swan. Follow the long chain of stars that make up its neck, to the bright star of the bird's eye. That is the Albireo, which is so splendidly bright because it's a double star. One is blue, the other yellow. They revolve around one another. Pulled together by gravity. As they draw closer, the speed of their orbits increases, as if in anticipation. As they move away, they slow as if in mourning."

Helen let herself look at him in the warm light of the lanterns. Her emotions welled up in her throat and, afraid he might notice, she directed her gaze back to the night sky.

The bluish tint of Cygnus's eye sparkled. She imagined soaring past the trees and out of the square, above it all. Her life in Utica faded into nothingness. She flew past the moon and the rings of Saturn before turning out into open space. Oh, to possess a real companion throughout time. A yellow to complement one's blue.

"And what are *you* thinking of now?" asked Pryce.

"That it must be quiet up there. It's so loud and rude and complicated on earth. I'd like to be floating around in the sky, to grow wings and glide on the currents of ether and have no one making demands of me, no one to take care of." Their eyes met. "It seems like paradise."

"Yes," he sighed. "No canal locks to study."

"What?"

"Nothing. It's just that the infinite is exquisite and *almost* everything else is mundane. But it's also cold . . ." His gloved index finger stretched toward her left hand and touched it. She did not move away, but instead turned to focus intently at the stars. "And lonely . . ." His finger's pad traced the rib of her glove from her wrist to the tip of her pinkie. "And mostly empty . . ." Her breath caught and her little finger rose, allowing Pryce to continue his voyage around and then down into the space between her pinkie and ring finger. "And I couldn't follow you there . . ." She gave his finger a gentle squeeze, like an involuntary contraction, and he went on tracing the silhouette of her hand. "And I so want to follow you."

She spread her knuckles and allowed him to explore the next valley. Every scintilla of focus was on his finger's journey. As she watched the sky, her body pulsed with life. She pictured them floating on a current of air and coupling. A tingle of pleasure lit up her skin. It was all she could do to resist the ache to turn and pull him into an embrace.

"Ah, there you are," came an out-of-breath voice from behind them. The two broke apart and turned to see Dr. McCooke. A moment of confusion crossed his face as he cast his eye from one to the other. He seemed to decide something and smiled mildly. "Having fun without me?" he asked.

Helen stood solidly, determined not to betray any emotion. "How is Mr. Galway?" she asked.

"It's simple," said the doctor, an element of professional pride in his tone. "If he doesn't rest, he won't heal."

She noticed a slight tremor in his hand. "And what sort of medicine is this opium?"

"One that's come down through the ages as a soother of pain and a bringer of sleep. It's perfectly safe."

Helen turned away and looked up at the comet.

Pryce began to fill the silence: "Comets are actually rather hazy. The tail looks solid, but is really just a trail."

Helen turned back to the doctor, a look of determination on her face. "If rest is all he requires, why are you in residence?"

"That's his preference. The best families often require my live-in services. My old patroness, Mrs. Elizabeth Preston McDowell Benton, wife of Senator—"

"Then why is he in so much pain?" interrupted Helen. "I've seen other broken limbs. Two splints and a few tight wrappings do the work. The patient does not require medicine."

"I didn't realize that you had such a deep store of medical knowledge," said McCooke with a chuckle, winking at Pryce. "I had to attend college and learn my way about the body by dissecting Negro corpses." He gamely poked Pryce with his elbow. "Imagine a lady studying a well-formed naked buck, eh?"

Helen set her mouth and said nothing. Inside she smoldered with indignation.

"It's too cold for you to be out," said McCooke. "Really, Mr. Anwell, you should have known that." He turned conspiratorially to Pryce. "Women are so delicate and they get overexcited. No doubt it's the stimulation of the comet. It's time to get her back home." The doctor tried to take her by the arm. She pulled away. He turned toward Pryce. "Good evening, Mr. Anwell." McCooke stepped between the pair. "Mrs. Galway, I will accompany you home, now." He wound his arm around hers.

"I will call on Mr. Galway tomorrow," said Pryce. His eyes met Helen's and they watched each other even as the doctor steered her away.

McCooke murmured close to her ear, "Acting the coquette, eh? So soon after the nuptials?"

"You insult me."

"I'd like to play too."

She stopped and pulled her arm away. "Mr. Galway is the one who insisted that Mr. Anwell escort me tonight."

"We all like a little harmless fun. No one needs to be the wiser."

Helen fell silent. He patted her hand as they moved across Bleecker Street toward the Galway home. Dr. McCooke once again considered his improving fortune. He'd been around women like this before, demure and innocent, but if you got them behind a curtain they turned into tigers. That was certainly the case of pretty little Miss Duphorne of Albany. Such a shame that the servants let her die. Helen Galway was young too, but she was a woman of experience and they almost always found a way to slip from their great height. It might take multiple tries with her, but the reward would be worth the effort.

"Now," he said as he glanced around the street. About a block behind, he saw a gloomy figure heading in their direction. He opened his light and blew out the flame. "How about you favor me with a bit of what you just gave that boy?"

"What do you mean?" Before Helen could move away, he pulled her to him and maneuvered her to a darkened area between two houses, just off the walk.

"You are so beautiful," he whispered. "I've quite fallen for you."

"Doctor, I'm leaving." She tried to move, but he held her tight.

"Quiet or someone will catch us," he said playfully, pressing her against the wall. His lips met hers. Her resistance was strong, so he released her and stepped back into the shadow of the building, a finger to his lips. He smiled. Now they shared a secret.

She hurried back into the street, where she caught up to a lady in black crepe.

"Miss Manahan," she said, slipping her arm through the woman's bent elbow, "we're going the same way, I think."

"I'm sure we are, Mrs. Galway." The schoolkeeper looked back toward the doctor, but he remained in a deep shadow. Helen urged her away.

The doctor smiled. He would let that kiss marinate. Women loved to be pursued. They resisted and resisted until the moment of surrender. It was part of the game and he excelled at playing it.

CHAPTER TWENTY-TWO

AFTER JOE HAD SPLIT the wood and loaded it into the bins through-out the house, drawn water and filled all the jugs in the upstairs rooms, helped Maggie wash down the kitchen, and fed and mucked out the horse, he had been given a fat sandwich, surprised with a warm hug from Maggie, and dismissed for the day. He wrapped the food in his new kerchief so that he might share it with his mother and fled to the street so that it would seem like he was heading downtown. He looked like a dapper boy, clad in Augustin's old wool trousers, jacket, and topped off with a matching wool cap. One block away, near the home of the sleepless old man, he turned east and swung around so he could follow the banks of the Ballou to the back of the Galway property. He peeked out from behind the horse barn and through the open kitchen door saw Maggie in the dimly lit room in a rocking chair, her attention directed to the backyard. He crouched low and, careful to make little noise, worked his way to a brambly area between the horse barn and the shed. His jacket caught on thorns as he crept to the corner where his mother lay just on the other side of the wall.

He tapped and when he heard her soft reply, he stifled the urge to cry.

"I can't come to you," he whispered, his voice breaking. "That cook be watching."

"Don't you worry. She gonna sleep soon enough. Take cover and keep your eyes on *her*."

"We gonna leave at midnight, at least that's what the white lady say."

"Pray that God puts some strength into my legs. You go now, like I told you."

"But—"

"Go on. Keep a watch out."

Joe crossed his arms and didn't move. She was always telling him do this, do that, don't touch, be quiet, stand up, sit down, and don't ask—like he was a baby. Today was bad enough. Miss Maggie had not given him a moment of rest.

"You still there?" whispered Imari. "I ain't hear you moving."

"But I be tired," he said.

"Don't pick now to get fresh," she said, her voice sharp even through the shed's wall. "You gonna get to sleeping soon. Go on now."

Joe stamped his foot, but slowly crawled behind a scrubby berry bush by the barn. He plucked off a few of the raspberries that still hung on the canes and ate them while thinking about his sandwich. It looked very fine, thick with ham on two stout pieces of bread that Maggie had lined with butter. His mouth watered just thinking about it. But his daddy had told him that the baby inside his momma needed food too. Getting born, it seemed, was hungry business.

He ran his hand over the scratchy surface of his head, picking at small scabs and rubbing the spots where a few hairs had been missed by the straight razor. His encounter with Hickox had terrified him. It was plain luck that he got away, but somehow keeping it from his mother felt good. She had her secrets and now he had them too. As he went over what happened, he realized it would be important for her to know. Hickox had proof that they were there. But explaining it meant telling the truth about swimming in the Potomac by himself, and that information was his own, too good to share.

Joe watched Maggie reach over her shoulder and pull a burning stick from the cookstove. Her face brightened as she put a pipe between her lips and sucked fire into the bowl. He liked her, despite Imari's warning. Miss Maggie ran him from one task to another, and seemed to be mad at him when he was confused, but when she shaved his head, she was more tender than anyone had ever been—except his own mother.

All around him the sounds of evening settled on the neighborhood. The Galways' horse munched the oats and fresh hay that Joe had set out. Off to his right, the hiss and *cha-chunga* of a steam engine slowed, and after several minutes he heard men come out from a building. They called "Night" to each other before going their separate ways. Animals moved about in the grass. Deer came out of their daytime hiding places in the woods for a drink from the creek. Mrs. Galway and the visitor entered the kitchen and then left. He heard the front door open and close.

Miss Maggie blew a smoke ring, which made Joe smile. He had not seen a woman smoking since he was with his Grandma Abby, the woman who had raised Elymas as her own. A tall, thin woman who could see over the heads of many of the men, Grandma Abby could blow a smoke ring and then quick as that, shoot out a second that passed right through the middle of the first. Because of her height, she became the only woman on the plantation to learn the art of growing and processing tobacco. During the day, she toiled in the blazing-hot fields. She wielded a hoe with precision, chopping up weeds and keeping the rows clear. Her nimble fingers pruned suckers, nipped flower buds, and crushed hungry green worms. At night, she brought out her small pouch of tobacco, loaded a handmade pipe, and smoked as she "let the work outta my bones." During the harvest season, he watched her set up the drying fires in the tall barn, where the sheaves of leaves hung from every rack and rafter. The fires had to be carefully monitored so as not to burn too hot and ruin the tobacco, turning it black and sour, but not too low as to prolong the drying process. During curing, she hardly slept. But when she did rest, and allowed him to cuddle up in her lap, she smelled of woodsmoke and the rich caramel scent of tobacco. He had come to love the way the blue smoke that rose from the bowl of her pipe tickled his nose. Occasionally, he begged for a few puffs. One day, after watching her blow a series of rings that floated on the air, thinning out and then disappearing in a light breeze coming off the river, he tried to make his lips form the perfect O to shoot out a ring for himself. She laughed and claimed that he looked like "a runt of a god putting on a high and mighty fuss about nothing."

His mother didn't like the old lady sharing the tobacco with him, so he kept his requests to a minimum when she was around. But he looked forward to those stolen moments and the feel of the warm smoke in his mouth and the dizziness and exhilaration he felt after he got his chance. There had been no tobacco since they left the plantation, which had bothered him at first. Miss Maggie might share a plug with him, if he asked her right. In fact, he had not smoked since the day Master Arnold had offered him a fat pouch of tobacco "for nothing."

Joe broke away from his thoughts about the plantation. Maggie stood, lit a lantern, and came out to the porch; he saw the musket she carried.

A cold sweat sprang from his skin as she came down the stairs and crept toward the shed. She set down the lantern, cocked the gun, brought it into firing position, and looked around as if, in the growing darkness, there were a pack of slavers ready to pounce. With careful, silent steps, she moved to the shed's door.

"Wait!" Joe called, springing to his feet.

She turned, gun pointed in his direction. "Who's that?"

"Me—Job," he said, stepping forward.

"Job?" She lowered the gun. "I just about *shot* you—like a damn dog. Why you still here, boy?" She picked up the lantern and shone it toward him. "You done scared me half to death. Go home."

"I ain't got no home."

"Go to your Uncle Horace's then," she said.

Joe approached. "But, but, he told me to stay here."

"Oh my blistered backside. Ain't you got no sense? You shoulda told me. You gonna sleep in that shed? Does Mrs. Galway know that? Is that what you two was fixing up out here?" Maggie grabbed him by the arm. "Don't you never hide on me. Go to the porch and sit. Go on."

He backed away, keeping his eye on her. She drew up the musket and went for the door, opening it quickly. He surged forward, arms flailing, scrambling for the gun. A blast of shot and sparks flew into the shed. Flickers of light went everywhere. Thick smoke filled the air. The bang was so loud that it took him a few moments to realize that he could hear a new sound—his mother's choking wail.

Imari had heard her son shout. The words she understood of the cook's reply were "shot you." She tried to leap to her feet, but her legs failed her. He was in danger and she could do nothing. Her hands shook in fear and frustration. She listened. The tone of his voice sounded mature as he tried to get the cook and the gun away from the shed. He was giving her time, perhaps only a moment, to make herself as small as possible. She leaned against the cabinet and pulled her legs as close as they could go to her rounded belly. She hugged the unborn child as if to shield it from harm. The wall of junk would not hide her from someone who knew the correct spot of every item on the property. And then there was the smell. She had been in the shed for more than a day without a way to dispose of waste.

The door thumped open and a gust of cold air rushed in, bringing the hairs on her arms upright. She heard a struggle and then the room was full of light and noise. She felt the stings of a dozen hornets on her left side, down her arms, back, and legs. She cried out, but thick smoke caught in her throat and the smell of bad eggs filled her nose.

Joe shoved the baskets aside and fell to his knees beside her.

"Momma," he wept. "Sorry, sorry."

Imari gasped for air. He wrapped his arms around her as she slumped into his body. Just before she blacked out, she heard a woman's voice shouting, "Get outta my way!"

Maggie and Joe carried Imari into the house and pulled her into the cook's room off the kitchen, carefully placing her on the bed.

"Oh Lord, oh Lord," Maggie said as she tried to staunch the blood with her apron. "Job, take that sheet and hold in that blood."

She ran into the kitchen and added some wood to the cookstove's firebox and moved the kettle onto the plate burner.

Augustin called to her from the library.

"Oh please, not now," Maggie said.

He called again, panic edging into his voice. She ducked into her room, told Joe to keep pressing off the blood, and ran to the library.

"What was that?" Augustin called from the daybed.

"That's just me. Shooting one of them old nasty raccoons."

"I thought I heard a woman scream. Was that you?"

"Me? No," said Maggie as she fussed with Augustin's blanket. "That was the raccoon. Terribly peculiar, wasn't it? Must be some lady didn't do no good in her human life, so she came back as an animal."

"What's all that on your apron?"

Maggie looked down and noticed Imari's blood. "Oh, that's nothing. Don't you worry none. I got water on. I'll bring you some tea."

"Where is the doctor? I need my medicine," Augustin complained, crossing his arms.

"Who knows where that dirty old doctor keep hisself. I'll get you what you need, just like always." She went to the liquor table and lifted the opium bottle. "This the one, right? For pain?"

"Yes, thirty drops," said Augustin.

Maggie measured out the drops and added a splash of brandy to the glass, looked at him, and added a second splash. As she turned, she dropped the opium bottle into her pocket.

"Now you drink that down. You don't need that doctor. Don't I always take care a you?"

"You always do."

Maggie hurried to the door. "Get some sleep. I'll check on you in a bit."

She was almost out the door when Augustin asked, "Did she die?"

"What?" she said, frozen.

"The raccoon, did she die?"

"A course. Her spirit be on to some other critter by now, poor lady."

In the kitchen, she poured steaming water into a bowl and grabbed clean rags from her supply. She lit an oil lantern and hurried back into her room. Imari blinked rapidly. Joe sat next to her, his hands dark with blood. Maggie gave him a clean rag and took his place.

"She gonna die?" asked Joe.

"Now don't you worry. That's just a little bird shot. Ain't gonna be too deep." She looked over Imari's body. "Boy, you clean up and close them curtains. In the kitchen too. Then go get my lantern from the yard and bring that musket back. Don't wanna leave that around."

Joe looked at his mother. She focused on him, squinting.

"You heard the lady," she said weakly. After Joe cleared the room she grabbed Maggie's arm. "Did the baby get shot?"

"Now you're in the house and gotta be quiet," whispered Maggie as she lifted the bloody sheet. "I know you're hurting, but don't raise no noise." Maggie seized a pair of scissors out of her sewing basket. "Gotta cut that blouse and skirt off to see what I done."

"I don't care about no clothes," whispered Imari. "My baby. That's all that matters. It ain't moving."

Maggie swallowed hard and worked the scissors through the waistband of the skirt, pushing back the material. She brought the lamp closer. Imari's stomach was dark with blood. Maggie wet a rag and began to clean. Imari flinched. Maggie stopped.

"I'm sorry. But . . ."

"Keep going," said Imari.

Maggie brought the lamp up close and inspected each wound. Several deep slashes marked her belly.

"What you seeing?" asked Imari, lifting her head.

"It looks like . . ." Maggie shook her head in relief. "Thank you, Lord," she cried. "None a the shot went in. Thank you, thank you, Lord." She looked at Imari. "You got some scratches where the shot cut you as it went on by. But none a them pellets got into your belly. I didn't hurt the baby."

Imari squeezed Maggie's hand. Her head fell back on the pillow, eyelids fluttering.

Joe stood in the doorway. "She gonna live?"

"A course," said Maggie. "But we gotta dig out every piece a that shot. And she can't make no noise. You gotta help me, Job. You gotta be a man and help your momma."

"Joe. My name ain't Job."

"And what's your momma's name?"

"Imari."

"Imari. Pretty name for a pretty gal. You two on the run?"

Joe's eyes flashed to his mother. "Yes," he said.

Maggie pulled out the vial of opium. "Okay, okay then, this is what I need you to do . . ."

CHAPTER TWENTY-THREE

PRYCE FELT HELPLESS as he watched Dr. McCooke lead Helen out of the square. His stomach soured. Should he follow them? That might have been the very same impulse that had caused his improper advances. In the parlor, she had begged him to do nothing to harm her reputation and now this had happened. Beastly bodily impulses. He was no better than a rutting cur.

Curse this city. He'd hardly had one good moment in it since he'd crossed its borders. He would call on Mr. Galway in the morning and try for a loan to get himself back home. But it didn't matter. If necessary, he would walk the thirty miles to Little Falls. Of course, when Father finds out I've cut the trip short and wasted his money—and know less than nothing about engineering—he will give me that sad look that says, *I still love you*. It's like I'm still a boy. But I'm a man and must face the brutal truth. Miss O'Connell is *Mrs. Galway* and there isn't a thing I can or *should* do about it. Yet, there can't be affection between those two. And she is so . . . alive.

At the National Hotel, the sounds of the taproom filtered out through the entranceway to the wide street-level veranda. Light poured through the tall windows and inside many men opted to refresh themselves with food and drink, completely ignoring the comet.

All the seats on the wooden benches that stretched the full width of the hotel porch were filled save one, next to a large gentleman who was reading a copy of the *Oneida Whig*. Pryce dropped down and stared at the carts passing through the pools of light cast by the streetlamps along Genesee. Galway had paid his way out of jail, paid all his lodging expenses, and even trusted him with his wife, and all the man had received in return was betrayal. A blast of laughter exploded from the bar. Why resist leaving? At this point there was no other honorable choice.

The fellow next to him shook his newspaper. "Damn liars," he murmured, crumpling up the periodocal and throwing it to the ground.

Pryce flinched.

"Pardon me," said the big man, noticing him for the first time. "Reading the paper's an obligation, but I am compelled to spend my precious time fighting the most outrageous falsehoods."

"You in the newspaper business, sir?" inquired Pryce.

"At this moment, I seem to be engaged in the business of *making* the news. Alvan Stewart, Esq., at your service."

Pryce perked up. "Pryce Anwell, lately of Little Falls. Forever of Little Falls, I suppose. How are you making news?"

"Shall I tell you and risk creating another enemy?"

"Me? Don't have me arrested and we'll be fine."

"Though I'm a lawyer, I don't usually have strangers arrested to build my practice." Stewart appeared to be measuring Pryce. "Are you a colonizationist or an abolitionist?"

"Excuse me?"

"Slavery, my friend. Should it be ended by colonizing the slaves in Africa, or setting them free now?"

"I haven't given it any thought," said the young man. "I feel sorry about what those slaves must endure."

"What will we become if we don't think much about our fellow human beings?" mused Stewart.

"I've never enslaved anybody," said Pryce amiably. "And I don't plan to."

"True, we seem far from it here," said Stewart, leaning back casually. "I wonder. That shirt—is it made of cotton?"

Pryce nodded.

"Of course it is. Ever indulged in tobacco?" The young man began to answer when Stewart held up his finger. "No? I can see you maybe enjoy a good smoke occasionally, not enough to call it an indulgence. Add sugar to your tea? Eat your mother's plum pudding at holiday time? We all have. We all benefit from slavery, don't you see?"

"How can I help doing what everyone else does?" asked Pryce.

"That's an important question." Stewart dug into his pocket. He handed a folded notice to Pryce. "Perhaps my upcoming abolition convention will help you figure that out."

"Convention?"

"In just a few weeks hundreds of dedicated men will come to Utica to create the New York Anti-Slavery Society." Stewart retrieved the newspaper and flattened its pages. "We are coming together to demand immediate emancipation of the slaves. What do you think about that?"

"It sounds rather dangerous. There's a lot of them, isn't there?"

"We think about two and a half million."

"Let loose two and a half million? It sounds crazy. Won't there be violence?"

"From the slave owners? They will resent it," said Stewart, studying the young man.

"No, from the slaves."

"They yearn to be free. Would you fight the man who opened your cage?"

Pryce thought back to what he was doing to Mr. Galway and shivered. "Your convention sounds quite interesting, and I'd like to be there, but I'll be gone. My father expects me home."

"Too bad. We need young men like you." Stewart's attention shifted to the right, toward the sound of clinking irons. Two men on horseback appeared out of the shadows and approached the hotel. Shackles dangled from their saddles. "Slave catchers. Hickox, and the big one is Swift. They have been ripping down my convention signs and putting up their foul notice about two runaways. I have been returning the favor. We are at silent war for the eyes of Utica."

"Runaway slaves? Through here?"

"Yes. And their numbers increase each year. Soon the dribble will be an unstoppable flood to rival Noah's. Those wretched unfortunates will wipe out slavery with their own legs."

A hotel groom approached the slave catchers. Before handing the reins of their horses to him, Swift and Hickox gathered their weapons.

"Leave them saddled," Hickox instructed. "Fodder and water only. We've more calls to make."

The groom started away. Hickox called him back and whispered something in his ear. The groom nodded in Stewart's direction.

"My little handbill war has just escalated," said Stewart, standing. "It's best I leave."

Pryce stood also. "Is it safe for you?" He looked at the two slave catchers. Now that they were approaching the porch, the younger one looked grossly strong and the older dangerously stony. "I think I shall go for a walk as well."

"Come along then," said Stewart as he stepped to the street. Pryce turned rigidly and followed. Stewart headed up Genesee, but when he came to the canal bridge, he hopped over the railing and down to the dark towpath. Pryce followed and as soon as he hit the gravel, he was pulled under the bridge.

"Quiet," whispered Stewart. "They may not have noticed." He pushed Pryce under the center of the bridge. Above them footsteps echoed on the paving stones.

"This is the way he went, ain't it?" said one voice, as its owner stepped onto the bridge's timbers.

"Shut up and listen," said the other.

Pryce heard the wood of the bridge creak. A sprinkle of dirt fell on his shoulder. Afraid to move, he let it lie.

"Look under the bridge," said the second man.

Pryce held his breath as Stewart pressed them back against the musty wall.

Above them, Swift went to the east side of the bridge, kneeled, and bent his thick torso. Pryce saw his head silhouetted in the approaching light of a canal boy's lantern.

"See anybody?" asked Hickox from above.

"Maybe," said Swift. The light crept toward Stewart and Pryce's position. But without warning, one of the tow mules neighed and reared up, spooked by Swift's head. The boy struck Swift with his staff.

"Hey!" shouted the slaver, holding his ear.

"You want your head ripped off?" yelled the boy. "Keep it right there, brother."

"Ya think you can just whip me?" roared Swift.

Stewart pulled Pryce away from the argument. They trotted quickly along the towpath until they came to the next bridge and climbed back to the street. The abolitionist cast his eye about.

"I thought I was watching those two," he whispered. "Now they're watching *me*."

"What will they do if they catch you?" asked Pryce, looking over his shoulder.

"Plenty of men in this city would rejoice if I became incapacitated by some *accident* and unable to carry on with the convention."

Pryce started to laugh and then clapped his hand over his mouth.

Stewart raised his eyebrow. "Levity at my demise? You are a callow youth."

"You must admit—that was rather thrilling."

"Since I announced the convention, every day has brought new *thrills*, as you call them," said Stewart. "When do you leave for Little Falls?"

"My situation is complicated. I lost all my money and have a debt to pay."

"And I've dragged you into my business as the most hated man in Utica. My apologies."

Pryce laughed again. "At least yours is a noble reason to be hated." His hand twitched as he remembered its trip around Helen's fingers.

Stewart stood squarely before Pryce, his face serious. "Now, have you the stomach to follow our slave catchers and see where they're sniffing?"

"You mean there's more that might happen?"

"Those two are in Utica for some reason. I need to know if it has anything to do with my convention."

"More thrills?" asked Pryce.

"It may be foolhardy. Are you feeling bold or cautious?"

"I feel like I *want* to be bold," said Pryce, "Sir, you have me for the next few hours—before I leave for home."

"Good lad," said the abolitionist. "Let's hope we don't regret this."

Horace considered his profitable day. After the slave catchers had left him with the two Spanish doubloons, he'd sold off most of his stock. As the dark of night came upon the city, he found himself trying to decide what to do with the gold pieces. His shack held all his possessions: fishing equipment and clothing, some dishes and fry pans, cooking utensils, a few pieces of furniture rescued from the oblivion of the streets and lovingly oiled clean, bedding with a mattress stuffed each summer with new hay, a stack of recent newspapers collected from the refuse piles of the steam-powered printshops, a potbellied stove that had been in his daddy's shack, his supply of salted fish put by for winter, and a box that held his papers proving that he had been born a free man of free parents.

Before today, he *never* worried about the security of his belongings. Thieves knew that breaking into the cabin of a black man—a fishmonger's at that—would net them very little. But now the two doubloons weighed on his mind. They jangled differently than the other coins, their tone a constant reminder of their evil source. He should never have accepted them and he felt certain that the slave catchers would not let him give them back. They were his responsibility.

If he spoke to a friend about what to do, there would be awkward questions. Some might even suspect that he had turned to crime. No matter what story he gave, he knew that certain people would see the coins in the same light as Judas's thirty pieces of silver. Normally he could tell his problem to Mr. Galway, who seemed to have everything figured out when it came to money. But after the morning's discussion, the man's agenda seemed to include making him cross the wild ocean and die in Africa from either fever or an attack by tribes hostile to the colonizers.

Perhaps Schoolmaster Freeman might have an idea of how to safely store the doubloons. Being an educated man, he generally avoided irrational theories and speculations. Maybe it would be best not to admit to Freeman that it was he who had the coin problem. He headed up to the schoolmaster's home on Post Street, all the while hearing the unnerving clang of Spanish gold.

With its boardinghouses and taverns, Post Street's reputation was decidedly bawdy, but most of the people who lived on the single-block street were focused on securing an income and keeping their children's bellies full. Apart from the friendly, food-providing cooks Horace cultivated, almost all the people of color lived in the two-story, whitewashed, wooden buildings with pitched roofs and small stoops that lined the street. He rounded the corner of Burnet and saw people still out and about, enjoying the autumn night, their lanterns shedding pools of light at their feet as they talked to neighbors. In the shadows, a few young men coaxed kisses from their sweethearts.

For the most part, the white citizens of Utica stayed away from Post Street. A few whites lived there and those who inhabited the adjacent streets had a nodding relationship with their black fellows and kept to their own. The whites who came at night brought with them the behaviors and demands that led to the street's spicy character. There would always be men ready to profit from unsavory doings.

Horace glanced behind him and was surprised to see Dr. McCooke approaching from Bleecker, making his way into the neighborhood. Horace stepped up onto a narrow porch that was shaded by a second-story balcony, lowered his hat, and leaned one shoulder against the wall, pretending to be drunk. McCooke paid no attention and proceeded down the street toward one of the houses in which favors of an intimate type could be purchased.

Suddenly, couples began to part, boys going one way and girls another. Neighbors tipped their hats and retreated to their homes as if in a hurry. Horace snuck to the edge of the stoop and tried to figure out what was happening. He instantly recognized the outline of the two slave catchers as they slowly rode their horses up the street. Behind him, he heard the sound of people traveling through the backyards of the block. Some of them may have had prices on their heads and would be of interest to Hickox and Swift.

McCooke headed straight for them. Hickox leaned down to shake the doctor's hand.

Horace ducked between two houses and, instead of departing as the other men had, sneaked up closer. He got to the back of Schoolmaster Freeman's house and judged that he must be pretty near the three whites. He slipped up the rear staircase and when he knocked on the Freemans' door, he was quickly admitted. The schoolmaster's son put his finger to his lips and led Horace to the front parlor. The entire family, Freeman, his wife, and two girls, were sitting by the open window, listening to the white men's conversation. Horace kneeled close to the frame, his ear hot with the desire to find out what it was all about.

"Just appeared in the house."

"Red hair?"

"Bald as a melon. But a very fresh shave. Still a few bloody scrapes from the blade."

"Is he still there?"

"I have no idea."

"Thank you, Doctor."

"So is that worth anything? I'm happy to cut the house's Negro population in half."

"We shall see."

The sound of the horses moving away broke up the Freeman family.

"Are those the two gentlemen we saw yesterday, Mr. Wilberforce?" asked Freeman.

"They's the ones," answered Horace. "Come sniffing around the stand this morning. Tried to get me to help round up them runaways. Even gave me this here paper." As he slipped the slave notice out of his pocket, he heard the gold coins clap against each other. They sounded as loud as church bells on a Sunday morning. "That doctor was at the Galway place this morning," he added.

"There any young boys there?" asked Freeman. "They were discussing a boy with a freshly shaved head." Freeman quickly read the notice.

"Maggie be looking for a boy. Ask me to find her one."

"It sounds like she found one herself. And the slave catcher made a point to ask about red hair. They might go there looking for this 'Joey' mentioned in the notice."

"I gotta warn Maggie," said Horace, moving quickly for the door.

CHAPTER TWENTY-FOUR

THE LIBRARY WAS DARK when Helen returned to the house. There had to be a way to tell Augustin about the doctor's behavior and at least bring up her doubts about the opium. His snore, the same noise that kept her awake and staring into the darkness whenever he accidentally fell asleep in her bed, could be heard before she even opened the door. She almost stalked up the stairs, disgusted with him, but remembered his injury and went in. Embers still glowed in the large fireplace. She turned up an oil lamp. The light shone on the creamy face of a pendulum clock. It was past eleven, not yet time for the baker, Mr. Sylvanus, to arrive and help get Imari and Joe away.

There was something about Augustin's sleeping face that caught her. With one more glance at the clock, she decided that there was plenty of time before she had to go back to that shed. Reaching out, she put the back of her hand on Augustin's forehead. It was clammy, but not feverish. She plucked a few stray hairs off his face. Even in the peace of sleep, the skin around his eyes crinkled. Deep lines fell from the outside of his wide nostrils to the corners of his mouth. He was a handsome man, but thin blue veins snaked at his temples and the skin under his chin hung loosely about his face. His head and rusty beard were frosted with gray.

Mr. Anwell had whiskers too. Except, of course, *he* had no gray, no wrinkles, no slackening skin, nothing but striking green eyes that danced at the thought of seeing the comet.

How he had dazzled her with his knowledge of the night sky. She imagined spending hours looking through a telescope with him to guide her eye. Unconsciously, she traced the path that his finger had made around her hand's contours. Shivers of joy spread around her belly, tightening her bosom and raising heat below her waist.

Augustin sighed, his shoulders twitched, and the tip of his tongue darted out of his mouth to wet his lips. But this was the man to whom she was bound. She brought the lamp to his injured leg. It was dry and warm beneath her fingers. Perhaps a bit swollen, but that was to be expected. His leg would heal and he would be visiting her bedroom again. If she was not already with child, she would be soon enough. That was her lot. Mr. Anwell had to be avoided. Imari and Joe must be turned over to Mr. Sylvanus. And Dr. McCooke had to be expelled.

She thought that she had better say her goodbyes to the fugitives and make certain they were fully prepared. Having them in the shed had been very trying. But the story that Imari told her about the way she had been treated at the plantation—well, she would not soon forget that. She knew nothing about slavery, nothing. Clearly Miss Manahan was wrong when she had taught that slaves were part of the family. Perhaps, she thought, I can ask Imari why she stayed as long as she did—and why she left.

Helen slipped out of the library. The doctor had not yet returned. She would never allow him to take the liberties he assumed were his due as a man, but solving that problem had to wait.

Light came from under the kitchen door, so she went out the side of the house. When she got to the back corner of the building, she saw the full moon shining over the treetops. With much deliberateness, she crept toward the quiet yard. Light glowed from the kitchen window, and as she came forward, she noticed that the curtains had been drawn. Maggie's bedroom window was ablaze behind muslin fabric.

The shed door was wide open. Helen hurried across the lawn. The smell of burnt black powder lingered inside. Her hands began to shake.

"Imari?" she whispered. "Joe?"

The wall of baskets was in disarray. She rushed to the farthest recess and found the quilt and blanket, but no Imari. A shiver went through her. Could Mr. Sylvanus have already been here and taken them away? Had they been captured? If so, Augustin would have been awakened. Everyone would know that she had been guilty of hiding them. The evidence must be gotten rid of. She swept the bedding into her arms and grabbed the chamber pot. Behind the shed, she heaved the pot's contents into the night. She went back to the house and brought everything to the basement. There she wrapped the pot in the blankets and shoved the package deep into the dusty shelves.

Maggie *had* to know what was going on. There was nothing to do but face her.

In the empty kitchen, a lamp burned on the table. Muffled sounds and the ping of metal hitting metal came from the cook's bedroom. Helen tapped on the door. The sounds stopped.

"Maggie, it's Helen."

A chair scraped on the floor. Maggie opened the door a crack. "You alone?"

"Yes," whispered Helen.

The door swung open. Inside Imari lay on her side with her eyes pressed shut. Several candles and lanterns surrounded her. Joe held her hand and talked softly in her ear. Bloody pieces of cotton dotted her arm and back. Her left leg was speckled with dark holes that leaked onto the bed.

Maggie pulled Helen into the room and shut the door. "She got shot. Bird shot. I done it." Maggie looked back at the prone figure. "By mistake."

"Imari," said Helen, going to her knees by the bed, "are you all right?"

The woman opened her eyes, but then her irises rolled up and her lids fluttered.

"I gave her some a Mr. Augustin's medicine," said the cook.

"I know you?" asked Imari, now focused on Helen's face.

"We gotta get the pellets outta her," said Maggie. "I'm mostly done, praise heaven."

The clock in the hallway began to strike midnight.

"Joe," said Helen, "you remember that bread maker you met this morning?"

"Yes ma'am," Joe nodded.

"He might be out at the shed this moment—come to take you both away. Go outside and quietly bring him in."

"She can't go nowhere," said Maggie.

"Of course," said Helen. "But Joe, bring him in. He may be of some help."

Joe left.

Maggie sat at Imari's side. "I'm gonna start digging again, Imari. You gotta hold quiet." She picked up the knife and focused on an open wound. "Missus, bring that light a little closer."

Helen moved the lamp and could see a wet round ball just under the surface of the skin.

"This one's not too bad," said Maggie. "Now sister, you hold still and be quiet." Maggie's eyes flashed to Helen, who began speaking softly in Imari's ear.

"Quiet . . . shush . . . I know it hurts, but be calm and quiet. You're going to be all right. Elymas would want you to be brave."

"Elymas," said Imari in full voice.

Maggie dropped the knife.

"Shush," said Helen to Imari.

"What'd she say?" asked Maggie.

"Elymas coming?" asked Imari, sitting up.

"Yes," said Helen. "He wants you to be quiet."

Maggie stared at Imari. "Who's Elymas?"

"Her husband."

Maggie went to the head of the bed. "Where you from?"

"They're from Virginia," whispered Helen. "At least that's what the slave notice said."

A tremor rattled Maggie's hand.

"Elymas was recaptured," Helen continued.

Maggie's breathing became strained. "Elymas was my granddaddy's name . . . and . . ." She tried to pick the knife up off the floor. Both her hands quaked. "I can't do no more. You gotta take over." She pointed to her vacated seat.

Helen's brows rose. "I can't," she said, hiding her face in her hands.

"You know her?" said Maggie, wiping her wrist across her eyes. "'Cause she's gonna die and take the baby to the grave if we don't get that shot out."

Helen looked at the poor soul on the bed. "Yes, I want to help."

"Good then. Pick up that knife."

Helen obeyed.

"You gotta lay the knife flat against her skin at the edge a the hole. Firm now, but don't cover it up. You're gonna press with your thumb and see if the shot pops out. If it don't, you gotta dig." Maggie turned to

Imari. "You're gonna bite your voice now. Quiet. Here it comes."

Maggie nodded and Helen began to squeeze. Imari whimpered deep in her throat. Helen pressed again. The shot pushed above the surface.

"That's it," said Maggie.

Helen grabbed the ball and dropped it into the tin pan. It made a satisfying ping.

Outside, Joe went to the shed. Over the miles, he had honed an ability to hear men who were trying to be quiet. He could not describe exactly what it was that alerted him to another person's presence, sometimes breathing, or slight movements to stretch a limb, or the clicking of bones. But there was often more of an absence of sound, as if bugs and mice were holding still too. That is what he felt in the shed.

"Baker?" he whispered to the room.

"Aye," replied Sylvanus.

"They want you inside," said Joe.

"Who be *they*?"

"The cook and the missus."

"Is thy momma in there too?"

"She got shot," said Joe.

"Does she . . . still walk among us?" asked Sylvanus, as delicately as he could.

"She ain't walking nowhere," said Joe. "We had to carry her to the house."

"Does she still have the breath of life?"

"Oh, yeah," said Joe. "She got that."

Joe and Sylvanus stepped out of the shed. Without warning, Joe was taken up and lifted off the ground. He came nose to nose with Horace, whose face twisted in anger.

"Why you pretending to be my kin?" Horace snarled.

Joe struggled wildly, arms pushing, legs thrashing. His foot found Horace's knee and brought them both to the ground. Horace rolled on top of him and pinned him against the grass.

"You that boy they's looking for, ain't that right?"

"Leave the boy," whispered Sylvanus.

Horace kept his knees on Joe's arms while looking up, surprised to see the baker. "What this got to do with you, Mr. Sylvanus?"

"Thou must be quiet," said Sylvanus. "Let the boy go."

Horace stood and dragged Joe to his feet.

"Now, Brother Wilberforce, what has drawn thee to this place?"

"Them slavers be looking for a black boy just like this one here. I gotta warn Miss Maggie that they's heading this way." He looked at Joe, "If you is who I think you is."

"Headed here now?" asked Sylvanus.

"I ran ahead a them. They was on Post Street."

"Quickly now, we must get thee out of here." Sylvanus bent to take Joe's hand.

"I ain't leaving without Momma," said Joe, breaking free and running to the house.

The two followed him into the kitchen, where Sylvanus extinguished the lantern on the chopping block. Joe rushed into Maggie's bedroom followed by Horace and the baker.

"Kill them lights," Horace hissed. Maggie blew out the candle flames as Helen shut down the lamp's wick. "Them slavers heading this way for this here boy. That his momma there?"

"What will we do?" said Helen, standing and rushing toward the door.

Sylvanus blocked her way. "Stay quiet." He pulled the door closed.

Two burning torches could be seen through the curtains; they were crossing the yard. They paused outside the shed. Sounds of a violent search came through the window. Horace parted the muslin curtain and risked a look.

"It's them," he said. The torches disappeared into the horse barn.

"Missus," Maggie said to Helen, "you gotta go out there and throw them off. Say they woke you. Make them tell you what they're doing. Go out the front door and keep them away from here."

"But . . ." started Helen, "wouldn't you be better at this?"

"Them types ain't never gonna give no black cook no attention. It's gotta be you."

Helen nodded and hurried out.

Helen ran through the house and out the front door. As she rounded the building, Hickox came out of the barn with the torch. At the back corner of the house she paused. The older slaver stopped between the barn and the shed.

"Smell that?" he said to Swift. He brought the fire low and looked carefully at the ground. "It's wet over here."

Helen cursed herself about the chamber pot. She was about to call out to them when she felt dampness on her fingers. Imari's blood—it could be nothing else. Trembling, she reached up her sleeve, pulled out a handkerchief, and wiped her hands clean.

"Excuse me?" she said, too softly. In the dark, the men did not notice her. She didn't believe that she could stop the slavers. But just on the other side of the wall, Imari and Joe and the others were depending on her. Her insides felt as shaky as a pudding. She had no idea what she would say, but one hand gripped the corner of the house and the other clenched into a fist. "What are you doing back here?" she demanded.

The men looked up. Hickox raised the torch. "Who's that?"

"It is Mrs. Galway," she said from the darkness, "and I ask again: what are you doing on my property?"

"We're authorized to search for runaway slaves," said Hickox, his voice gruff and unyielding.

She held her ground: "Slaves here? Have you Mr. Galway's permission?"

"That's not necessary," the man barked.

"How dare you, sir."

Hickox's shoulders drooped. He stalked toward Helen with Swift following. "Mrs. Galway, we have every right—"

"Every right to break into our buildings and throw our belongings around? Shall I find you searching under our very beds?" Helen felt her anger rising. "You will explain yourselves to Mr. Galway."

The slavers did not move.

Helen drew herself up. "Right now." And she marched toward the front of the house with her back straight and her head held high. Out of the corner of her eye, she saw them follow.

As soon as the slave catchers cleared the back, Horace and Joe sneaked out to the porch. Horace crept to the corner of the house and saw the two following Helen around to the front. He signaled to Joe, who ran to the shed. Horace rushed over to the barn. Joe returned to the porch with a coil of hemp rope. Horace came back with a tall foot-wide plank, which Joe took inside.

Working silently, Maggie and Sylvanus wrapped Imari in sheets and blankets, careful of her wounds. They took the plank from Joe, laid it flat on the bed, and pulled Imari onto it. Joe began to wind the rope around both his mother and the board, entwining the two the way a caterpillar secures itself to a tree branch. Imari had been given a second dose of the opium and moaned softly as the ropes tightened around her body.

"It's life or death now," whispered Maggie at Imari's ear. "Not just for you, for all of us. Be quiet. Think about the baby and bite down that pain."

Imari's eyes flicked open. She nodded.

Horace came in and together the four lifted her and brought her out to the kitchen.

"Watch out," whispered Horace. "That cistern trapdoor, it's wide open."

They moved toward the porch. Indeed, there was a square opening in the floor of the porch. Nearby lay the cover, which usually sat tightly in the slot. Belowground, the cement walls of the cistern were smooth and dark.

"Augustin," said Helen, standing over the daybed, shaking him awake. "Tell them that they cannot search our property."

"What?" Augustin looked about uncertainly and brought both hands to his eyes. "What's going on?" He stared at the two men. "Who are you? Where's Maggie?"

"These two have wrecked the shed and torn apart the barn," said Helen.

"Mr. Galway. It is your *old friend* Abel Hickox, sir."

Augustin roused himself. "I don't understand. How dare you come into my home at night. Tearing down my barn?" He tried to straighten himself. "Helen, help me, for God's sake. Get another pillow."

She obeyed, bringing him a fringed pillow and helping him to sit upright.

"Sir," said Hickox, "we had intelligence that suggested those runaways—you remember the runaways to which I am referring, yes? One of them was working right in the house."

"What an outrageous accusation," said Augustin.

"But," said Dr. McCooke, suddenly appearing in the library doorway, "the problem is that it is true. You have been duped by your own cook. That little bastard tried to disguise himself by shaving his head."

"He is Mr. Horace's nephew," said Helen. "And I was the one who demanded he be shaved. He had lice and I didn't want him to bring any vermin into the house."

As Hickox examined her, a sudden coating of sweat broke beneath her clothing.

"Mr. Galway, we have found evidence in and around your outbuilding to confirm our suspicions," said Hickox. "We need to search the house."

"Now?"

"Tomorrow will be too late. If they have found a confederate, you and your household are in danger. Mr. Colby was murdered trying to capture them. These slaves have evaded me for hundreds of miles. Perhaps your cook knows something about it?"

Augustin darkened and turned to Helen. "Ask Maggie to come in."

"She's probably asleep."

"Just bring her." He turned to McCooke. "You, Doctor, are going to regret bringing these two scoundrels into my home. Now get me to that chair."

Helen went out the door.

Hickox narrowed his eyes. "We'll accompany Mrs. Galway."

"Maggie will not fight me," said Helen, loudly.

"These people are desperate," said Hickox, nodding to Swift. "She should not go alone."

They followed her.

During the discussion in the library, Horace and Sylvanus struggled with the rope as they tried to lower Imari, secure in her cocoon, through the trapdoor into the dry cistern. Their muscles strained and the rope burned their hands. She had been mostly quiet, but at any moment they might slip and drop her. The pain from such a fall would be too much for her.

Joe kept watch at the side of the house, and Maggie listened at the swinging kitchen door. She could hear no distinct words, but it was clear that the slave catchers refused to leave. She stripped off her bloody apron and ran to her dresser. Quickly, she stepped out of her clothing and dragged on a clean white nightgown. On the way back through the kitchen, she rinsed her hands. Horace and Sylvanus fought with the rope. The sound of Helen's voice saying her name came from the hallway. She knew they were approaching.

Maggie rushed to the swinging kitchen door and burst through it into the front hallway, pausing only to let the door hit her in the back so that she could be certain it was closed.

"Who's that waking up Mr. Augustin?" she bellowed. Muscling past the slavers, she rushed into the library and planted herself by Augustin. "You trying to kill him?"

Augustin called, "Hickox. You wanted to see her, well here she is."

Hickox and Swift reentered the room while Helen lingered in the hallway. She quickly went to the kitchen door, opening it a crack. The two men, a rope in their hands, struggled over the cistern's trapdoor.

Sylvanus looked like he was braced against the lip of the porch. Horace hung over the trapdoor, one foot on each side. His arm quivered with effort when, out of the darkness, a new man appeared and took hold of the rope between Horace and Sylvanus. And Pryce was suddenly on the porch. He glanced at her and took his place behind the baker, wrapping the rope around his forearm in an effort to stabilize Imari's descent into the cistern. Helen's heart rose. Pryce looked up toward the kitchen and nodded. Helen almost sobbed in relief, but quickly shut the kitchen door and rushed into the library.

The doctor pointed at Maggie. "Don't listen to that shrew. She's hiding something."

"Treat her with respect," snapped Augustin.

Hickox grabbed a candle and brought it close to Maggie's nightdress. She stepped back. "Stop looking me up and down. I ain't for sale." She turned to Augustin, her hands on her hips. "Am I?" Her face was gray with rage.

"Don't be absurd," said Augustin, coloring.

"You were harboring a boy," said Hickox. "Where is he?"

"Home explaining to his momma why he got shaved like a moldy ham." Maggie looked around and found Helen at the threshold of the room. "Mrs. Galway didn't like his look, ain't that right?"

"It is as I said." Everyone turned toward Helen. Her stomach tightened, but she tried to look fierce. "He might have had lice. In close quarters it only takes one child to infect the entire household."

"You've been duped by that cook. *They* all stick together. Isn't that right, Mr. Hickox?" said the doctor.

"Quiet. You've caused enough trouble," said Augustin. "Let us get this business over with. Maggie, is Job a runaway slave?"

"No, he ain't," said Maggie. "He's Horace's nephew."

"Mr. Galway," said Hickox soothingly, "we would like to be at our beds as much as you. We tried to avoid waking you, but Mrs. Galway insisted. Again, I am sorry."

"Thank you," said Augustin.

"However, these slaves are dangerous. I fear that they have been secreted on your property. Maybe no one knew." Hickox looked at Maggie, squinting.

"Don't go give me no evil eye!" yelled Maggie.

"Sir, for your own protection and for the safety of the ladies," said Hickox, "we must search the property."

Augustin glanced from the slaver to Maggie, to Helen, to McCooke. "Do it," he said. "But be quick about it."

Helen stepped forward. "Really, Augustin? They have your permission?"

"Wait," said the doctor. "Shouldn't you be frightened?"

"Just what do you mean, Dr. McCooke?"

"I . . . I mean, we are all here to protect you. That cook might be involved with dangerous slaves."

"Protect me?" said Helen, looking like she wanted to slap the doctor.

"They ain't no slaves in here," said Maggie, "dangerous or otherwise."

"But there's you," said the doctor. "You're one troublesome nigger."

"Doctor!" shouted Augustin. "You will stop this right now!"

Maggie turned her eyes to McCooke. "He brought them slavers to the house. And he says *I'm* lying."

"Mr. Galway, we must get about our business," said Hickox.

Simultaneously, on the back porch, Horace, Stewart, Pryce, and Sylvanus lowered Imari, inch by inch, until the board touched bottom. She cried softly, her voice echoing around the smooth cement walls of the cistern.

"Boy," said Horace, "get on over here." Joe obeyed. "You men hold her there." Stewart, Sylvanus, and Pryce set their feet and nodded. Horace released the rope and turned to Joe. "I'm gonna drop you in there so you can guide her down easy. No bumping. No noise."

Joe sat on the edge of the hole. Horace kneeled over the opening. He rubbed his burned hands and then grabbed Joe around the wrists and pulled him over the edge, lowering him into the dark hole. Horace's head and shoulders went in as the boy's feet kicked, trying to feel the bottom.

"Quick, Mr. Sylvanus," whispered Stewart, "grab his legs."

The baker crawled over and secured Horace.

Maggie's voice pierced the night.

Inside the house, Hickox strode out of the library. Helen, Maggie, and Swift followed close behind.

"Doctor, stay here," commanded Augustin, stopping him.

"Mr. Swift," said Hickox, already in the hallway, "search the shed." Swift left by the front door. "Now, to the kitchen. That way, I think." He pointed to the door.

"Yes, that's the kitchen," said Helen loudly.

Maggie rushed around from behind them and stood in front of the swinging door. "If you tear my kitchen up," she yelled, "or break even one a Mr. Augustin's teacups, I'll give you a lickin'!" She stared at Hickox. "See if I don't."

"You heard your master. Move aside," said Hickox, grabbing her upper arm and shoving her aside. She lost her balance and crashed to the floor with a thud. Helen rushed to her.

"You nothing but a devil!" shouted Maggie. "Throw an old woman to the floor!"

"What's happening?" yelled Augustin from the library.

The slave catcher drew his sidearm and pointed it at Maggie.

"Now you gonna shoot me?"

Helen placed herself between them. "Don't you dare hurt her."

"He's gonna shoot an old woman in her nightclothes."

"Doctor, I demand to know what is happening," said Augustin. Mc-Cooke ran to the hall.

"She's hiding something," insisted the doctor. "I know these people."

"You are a nincompoop," said Augustin. "Get me up. I need to go out there."

"Shut up, you blubbering bitch!" shouted Hickox.

He shouldered the door open and found the kitchen dark and empty. A sound, like metal scraping against metal, came from Maggie's bedroom. Pointing his gun in the direction of the noise, he moved cautiously through the room to the back door and opened it. "Mr. Swift," he roared, "get in here!"

Maggie and Helen entered at the same time. The doctor, with Augustin leaning on his shoulder, came up behind. McCooke maneuvered Augustin onto Maggie's stool. Swift thundered over the porch, into the kitchen.

"You must see her treachery for your own good," said McCooke to Augustin.

"Shut up," said Augustin.

"Behind that door," Hickox indicated. Swift drew a short-barreled musket.

"You stay outta my bedroom," said Maggie, running toward them.

Hickox pointed his weapon at her. Helen grabbed her hand and pulled her back. They watched Swift in horror. He moved to the bedroom. With one kick, the door swung open.

"Don't shoot," came a man's terrified voice.

"Got you," said Swift. He dragged the man into the kitchen, threw him to the ground, and aimed the musket at his head.

Hickox raised a lantern. Horace Wilberforce lay naked on the floor of the kitchen. A blanket had been dragged along with him. He reached out to pull it around him, but the slaver stamped his foot onto it.

Maggie shook herself and dropped to her knees, draping herself around Horace and spreading her nightclothes across his lap.

"Now you happy?" Maggie hissed. "You done discovered my big secret. Horace here is my man."

As he looked at Horace, Augustin's face grew dark. A shiver racked his frame. He focused on Hickox. "Take your brute and never enter my property again."

Hickox, his body rigid and sidearm still in his hand, met Augustin's outraged gaze and then cast a murderous eye on Dr. McCooke.

"That boy may be hidden," argued the doctor. "Question *her*, not me."

"To all of us comes our moment of reckoning," said Hickox. He turned to Galway. "The wolf may already be at your door."

"Go!" yelled Augustin. The slave catchers withdrew.

Maggie nodded to Horace, who wrapped the blanket close and disappeared into her room.

Another shiver racked Augustin.

"Too much excitement for you," said McCooke lightly, as if nothing extraordinary had happened. "We must get you back to bed." He took his patient's arm.

Helen stepped forward. "Is that it? Dr. McCooke brings those villains into our house and nothing happens?"

"Your husband is an ill man," said the doctor, smartly. "He needs my services and can't be disturbed any further."

"Both of you, be quiet," said Augustin, teeth chattering. He turned to his wife. "Just get me back to the library."

Helen's mouth opened to oppose her husband, but she saw fear and pain in his eyes. She took one arm. McCooke took the other. Together the two bore the weight of the man and moved slowly toward the front of the house.

"Maggie," Augustin called, "get Horace out of here."

"Yes sir, Mr. Augustin," she said.

Within a few steps, Helen felt a discomfort in her abdomen. It must be from the day's exertions, she thought. With difficulty, she continued to the library and helped settle her husband in bed, carefully lifting his injured leg and setting it on soft feather pillows.

"Get me that opium," said Augustin, breathing hard and gritting his rattling teeth. His hands quivered as he raised the sheet, making it seem as if a wintry breeze had blown through the room.

"Mrs. Elizabeth Preston McDowell Benton also grew very fatigued," said the doctor as he rummaged through his medicine bag. "But all she needed was steady doses," he pulled out a vial of brown liquid and counted drops into a tumbler, "until she completely recovered herself."

"Shut up and give me the opium," said Augustin.

Helen put her hand on her husband's shoulder, head close to his ear. "This man is not your friend," she said in a low tone. "He has . . . other designs." She felt fever radiating from his core.

He started to cough and suddenly turned his head and vomited into a towel.

"Doctor," Helen cried.

McCooke sauntered over, the dose of opium-laced brandy in his hand. "We must let the spasm pass," he said. As Augustin retched, McCooke leaned toward her and spoke quietly: "Older people are so difficult. I wonder how you . . . Well, we endure what we must. You're so beautiful. The respectful thing would be for you to be surrounded by the proper servants. And I don't mean ignorant Negroes."

Helen turned away from him and put her hand on Augustin's shoulder as he heaved and coughed.

McCooke again bent to her ear. "You must understand the danger that cook represents. My mother made the mistake of trusting an African. Father died and she put the black boy in charge as overseer of the plantation. I was away, of course. Medical school. Nothing *I* could have done. When I got back that presumptuous nigger had lost everything. We were worse than poor because *we* knew what we lost. I sold that boy so fast." He smirked. "He found himself chained up and walking to New Orleans to the slave market there. He had the vanity to think he was as good as my father. I kicked his black ass all the way to hell."

"Doctor," Helen snapped. "Your patient."

He stepped to Augustin's side. "You don't know how the blacks are. Smile in your face and stab you in the back," he whispered. "I have my eye on that cook. She'll soon be on the street. I promise you. I'll get you a proper lady's maid. Won't that be nice? A nice white girl to style your hair? Someone to talk to?"

She stared at McCooke, her hand unconsciously brushing back some stray curls.

He cocked his eyebrow and smiled. "You really are lovely. You deserve what's due a lady. Let me assist you."

"Anything," she begged. "Just help him."

"Of course. That's why I'm here. Don't worry. I'll get him right." The coughing stopped and McCooke handed the glass to Galway. "Here you go. Drink that down. That's right."

Helen backed away. He had somehow defeated her. As she left, the stitch in the bottom of her stomach sharpened. In the hallway, a frustrated sob escaped her. Just then, around the kitchen door, she saw a crack of light. Maggie waved her over and pulled her into the room.

"We're getting her outta that cistern and into the bedroom," she whispered, nodding toward Sylvanus, Stewart, and Horace, as they pulled Imari up through the trapdoor. "Mr. Augustin's mad?"

"Aren't you afraid that Hickox will return?"

"That white boy gone and followed them to be sure a where they're going."

Despite herself, Helen felt a twinge of disappointment. "Augustin had some kind of attack," she murmured, "and the doctor is tending to him. You must be careful. Dr. McCooke said he's watching you."

"He gets too close to the stove, he might just find himself burnt up."

"I'm sorry," said Helen. "I tried to warn Augustin about the doctor." Several tears fell down her cheek.

"You done good tonight," said Maggie, patting Helen's shoulder. She dabbed at the tears with the cuff of her nightgown. "We won 'cause a you. Nobody hurt or killed or captured. We got a ways to go, but tonight, we won." Maggie held her candle high and studied Helen's face. "You look tired. Go to bed. I'll finish with Imari and take care a things back here."

Pryce hustled to keep close to the two slavers as they rode toward the National Hotel.

"Whatta we do now?" asked Swift.

"You shut up," said the older man. "Unless you've suddenly grown a brain."

The younger slaver seemed to be trying to master a potent rage. They passed Chancellor Square, now empty of the comet-sighting crowd. Pryce thought back to his time with Helen. Had he just seen her helping with an escaped slave? It was impossible, but there she'd been. Who was she, really? Then he remembered: she was a married woman. He huffed in frustration.

Swift turned. Pryce's heart suddenly accelerated, making itself felt in a most urgent way. He veered into the park.

"Now what are *you* looking at?" demanded Hickox.

Pryce thought he heard the muscular man say, "Nothing. Must have been a cat."

Back on Bleecker Street, Stewart's large form moved in Pryce's direction.

"That them?" whispered Stewart as he approached.

"They seem to be heading to their hotel. Did you get that poor woman out of the cistern?"

"With some difficulty, yes." Stewart shook his head. "To have illegal doings happen so close to the convention is unfortunate."

"Does . . . does this sort of thing happen often?"

"No." Stewart considered for a moment. "At least, not here. It's better if I don't know all that goes on, frankly. I have a job to do. A populace to enlighten. So charging around at midnight and narrowly avoiding men like those? It doesn't help the two and a half million in chains." He leaned over Pryce. "Must you go back home? Didn't you say you have a debt to pay?" He thumped the young man on the shoulder. "Why not stay for a few weeks and help me? I'll give you a fair wage and throw in boarding at my home."

Pryce straightened. Could he? He had never imagined helping someone hide from the authorities. His heart was still pumping wildly in his chest. Such exhilaration. And Helen. He could see her again. And he'd be able to pay back Mr. Galway . . . Helen's husband. His shoulders drooped. "I've strewn my path with follies that would have been completely avoided by a man following an honorable course."

"Good works outweigh the bad," said Stewart. "After the convention, you can pay your debt. Just think—you will be able to tell your friends that you were there at the founding of the New York State Anti-Slavery Society."

Pryce's father believed the round-trip journey should take two weeks, but he had allowed that his son might need to occasionally get off the boat so as not to go mad. This meant he might have as long as three weeks before he was expected to return to Little Falls. He would stay and help *do* something. As for his father, he didn't need to know anything about the delay, not right away, at least. He would enlighten him—soon.

"I'll do it," Pryce said in a jolly tone. "Maybe Utica isn't all bad." He pumped Stewart's hand.

"The jury has yet to decide that," said Stewart.

* * *

Hickox threw his stony body against the door of his room at the National Hotel. The wood absorbed the blow and bumped him back into the hallway. The night had been a disaster. They had been ordered off the property and now the damnable key would not turn in the lock. It was all because of that murderess. He and Swift would not be allowed back in the house without solid proof and the sheriff. She might just slip through his grasp again. After Mr. Colby's shocking death, he had pursued her using every resource he possessed and she was still nothing but smoke.

At best, chasing slaves was a thankless job, but one in which he took much pride. He was a bulwark against disorder and the return of the reign of Chaos. On the nighttime roads and trails of Virginia, he chased those who refused to accept the place the good Lord made for them. Occasionally the task took him farther. In his experience, only the most determined, the craftiest, the most ruthless runaways made it this far, and never without help. Were it not for men like himself the world would disintegrate and the final bloody battle—an insurrection led by a new Nat Turner and carried out by pitiless murderers—would surely begin.

"Let me try," said Swift. He shouldered past Hickox, grabbed the key from his hand, and jiggled it in the heavy metal lock. "Sometimes it ain't about power, but having the touch."

"Judging from your ugly face, you got touched a little too often," said Hickox.

Swift dragged his finger down the broken ridge of his nose then shook his hand. "You gotta relax sometimes. Learned that in the ring. Too rigid and you break your own bones."

He turned his attention to the lock and tried the key. The mechanism clicked and the door sprang open. He stepped aside as Hickox stalked into the room, stopping at the window over the canal to peer out. Swift fell on his bed, the springs squeaking under his bulk.

Hickox noticed a sealed letter on the floor. He picked it up, recognized the handwriting, and ripped into it like a man might tear open a lacy privacy curtain in a whore's bedroom. He threw the letter to the ground.

"Barnwell's not a quarter of his father!" he shouted. "That imbecile."

Swift rubbed his face in exhausted confusion. "What'd it say?"

"That nigger? The one Mr. Colby gave his very life to catch? He's escaped again."

"But you got your money, right?"

"You simpleton. He's coming here. I know it." Hickox stooped to grab the letter. "This is dated October 1. Why am I just receiving it?"

"We was in New York then."

"We must prepare. That bitch might be having her baby right now. If she does, she and the boy will move on, or at least change locations."

"How do you know they's still even here? It looked quiet to me."

"Because even a snail leaves a trail and that trail stopped at Galway's."

PART TWO

CHAPTER TWENTY-FIVE

IN THE DAYS AFTER the slave catchers had searched the property, it was as if three different fortresses had been erected in the house. Only necessary words were spoken across their borders.

Maggie ruled in the kitchen and her bedroom. From all appearances, she went about her normal duties. But most of her focus was on the two people in her room behind the locked door. She slept on the floor while Imari and Joe shared her bed. For their sakes, she partially ceded the care of Augustin to the doctor. All the curtains at the back of the house were drawn day and night. People with nothing to hide did not keep their windows obscured. That in itself was an admission of guilt, but it could not be helped. In her opinion, the woman was much too close to giving birth to be moved.

Imari had submitted to Maggie's ministering and gained strength, but was still in much discomfort. Twenty-three lead balls had been removed from her body. After having poultices of comfrey leaves applied to each and every wound, and cleanings with the cook's own witch hazel solution, her injuries had scabbed over, but remained very tender. The unborn child clung to life, giving Imari a daily reminder of its commitment to be born with hiccups and kicks that stretched the long bird shot wounds across her stomach. She and Maggie talked for hours. In the quiet times, when Maggie was at her work, Imari obsessed about her missing husband, imagining him hurt, or sold, or dead. Occasionally she had feverish visions of him coming toward her, finally catching up.

Joe paced the small bedroom feeling like a cat stuck in a tree whose lone view was of a pack of barking dogs. His only relief from his confinement was sleep. But if Maggie and his mother were talking, he closed his eyes, slowed his breathing, and listened to everything they said—learning much with every conversation.

Augustin stayed in the library, floating between the intensity of his pain and the depth of his opium-induced oblivion. Maggie told him that "Job" refused to come back to work. No new boy would be hired, she said. "I'll take care a everything. Like always."

"That is what I prefer," he replied.

Dr. McCooke kept Augustin supplied with medicine, and himself with alcohol. During the days, he sipped from crystal glassware or, while about town, took small nips from his brand-new silver flask. Evenings he drank his fill promising that come morning, he would abstain. But at sunrise his shaking hands would betray him and he'd keep at the spirits despite his best intentions. He often escaped the house and went downtown to restock, with Galway's money in his pocket. A sliver of his mind wondered if having this much access to liquor was ruining him. The ghost of poor Miss Duphorne of Albany fluttered at the edge of his consciousness, but he turned his thoughts away before she fully materialized. At the house, he seemed to keep his distance from Maggie and Helen. If he dared to step into the kitchen, the cook picked up the closest knife and started hacking away at whatever food was in front of her. She took to carrying an impressively large specimen of cutlery, tucked into the strings of her apron, even while she served. He often lingered in the hallway outside Helen's bedroom, but never attempted any communication.

Helen sequestered herself in her chambers. Using the fabric that she had bought in town, she sewed tiny nightgowns and infant's dresses, decorating the garments with intricate needlework at the necks and hems. Mostly she imagined Imari's baby wearing them, occasionally dreaming about how her own child would fill out the clothing. She took her meals alone. Maggie brought in food and gave her reports about Imari's condition. Both women agreed that the doctor was actively watching them and so they did nothing to bring attention to the fugitives. Helen only joined her husband when summoned.

Pryce Anwell was much on her mind. She relived the time they'd spent together in Chancellor Square, conversing like equals. He had been part of Imari and Joe's rescue, and in that he knew her greatest secret. And he had taken the risk of trailing the slave catchers so that the others would be safe. But would she see him again? The problem wasn't just the watchful eyes of the doctor. It was the sin of it. Numerous times she resolved to not think of Pryce, but her mind was stuck deep in the mud of desire. With each rendition, the memories of him warped themselves into even more seductive fantasies. Every time she pushed out the lurid thoughts and worked to cleanse her mind of temptation, she found herself in another version, committing the same base actions. According to all she had learned in the church, she was now marked by the scarlet stain of intent.

Nothing she tried, not reading, not embroidery, not even prayer, washed her clean. One morning, she sat looking at the evergreen outside her window. The low autumn sun broke through the clouds, throwing streaks of light into the room. She became aware of the girls next door as they recited poetry. Their voices chimed in unison, the sound rising and falling with the breeze off Ballou basin.

"Nature imparts her gifts to all;
And every creature, large or small,
That frolics in the sea or strand,
Receives some favors at her hand."

Helen recognized the verse of the Greek poet Anacreon of Ionia. She got up and opened the window, allowing invigorating air into the stale room and sending the dust swirling away. Her voice rose to join the others:

"To man, more bountifully kind,
She gave the nobler powers of mind;
And woman, too, was not forgot;
Both grace and beauty are her lot,
Whose potent influence will prevail
When wisdom, wit, and weapons fail."

It was the *fundamentum* for Miss Manahan's lecture on female influence. The lady had incorporated Reverend Austin's notes for his book *A Voice to Youth*, which had been given to many of the city's headmasters and mistresses in anticipation of its publication. The book, the reverend hoped, would become "mandatory material for each child to purchase and consult with frequency."

Helen had never truly considered the meaning of the poem, but repeating it as an adult in her own home, she heard the words anew. Was it true that all she had was grace and beauty? Did women possess no wisdom or wit? It was absurd. She had been surrounded by girls with both those attributes, and more. Miss Manahan would never have been able to run a school without learning and cleverness. Maggie was more like a ship's captain than a mere deckhand. Why, even a female runaway slave proved to have been a formidable adversary to Hickox.

A knock rattled the door. Helen turned away from the window. A weakness came over her and she paused by the bed, one hand on the carved maple post, her fingers gripping the contours of the turned wooden spiral. She noticed a wisp of pain in her abdomen and wondered if her breakfast of eggs and toast had not settled properly.

"Missus?" said Maggie, through the door. "Mr. Augustin wants to see you."

Helen opened the door and met Maggie's eyes. They both looked as if they wanted to speak, but the cook raised her index finger to her lips. "I gotta get us some supper," she said in a normal voice. "Maybe go pick up a big fat trout from Horace and make Mr. Augustin his favorite."

"Do you know why he summoned me?" whispered Helen.

"I don't know what's what with that man no more." Maggie lowered her voice. "That darn doctor proof a that."

Helen smiled. If Maggie could still joke, then she herself would stand straight and face whatever trouble awaited her. She took the cook's hand and together they walked down the stairs. At the library, Maggie gave a nod and left by the side door. Helen felt very heavy, but squared herself and entered the library.

The doctor lounged on the sofa, a pipe in his hand. Smoke hung in the air. Didn't decent men restrict this sort of activity to right after a good dinner, and only when there was company?

Her husband sat in the winged armchair, his leg elevated on the stool. His eyes were unfocused and sweat beaded on his temples. It had been more than ten days since the slave catchers had searched the house and Augustin seemed worse, not better.

"Are you ill?" said Helen, alarmed. She approached the sofa. "What is the meaning of this, Doctor?" She withdrew her handkerchief and dabbed at the perspiration.

"I'm fine," Augustin said, waving her away.

"It'll pass," said McCooke lazily. He leaned forward and retrieved a half-full glass from the table. "Perhaps he's just in need of a little more feminine kindness."

"I can speak for myself," snarled Augustin. He turned to her, softening and taking her hand. "Helen, the doctor tells me that you've been locked in your room for days. Are you all right, my dear?"

Helen's free hand traveled to her lower belly and surreptitiously she pressed at the stitch of discomfort that had lingered there. "I wish that you wouldn't discuss me with him."

Augustin narrowed his eyes. "We are—that is, I am—concerned about your welfare. It's not right that a lady be confined in her room—unless she is ill."

The corner of her lip rose in a smirk. What did Augustin know about what a lady needed? He appeared to her to be among the people who believed that ladies possessed only grace and beauty. She thought that once she finished with her duties, she should be free to choose what to do with her time. "I am not ailing. There's no need for the doctor to be involved in my affairs."

"I don't appreciate your sudden willfulness, my dear. It is unbecoming. Since you say that you are not convalescing, you should take the air. It would be better for the baby."

Helen stepped back, about to reply, when her knees weakened. A dark spot clouded her vision. Stabbing pains erupted in her lower abdomen and she found herself on the floor.

She tried to sit up, but groaned as another sharp pain pushed her back on one elbow. Her skirts were in disarray. She reached to cover herself and saw a bright-red stain of fresh blood. The doctor was quickly upon her.

"Don't you touch me." She tried to push him away.

"You're bleeding. You must let me see," McCooke demanded as he tried to lift her skirt.

She kneed him in the jaw.

"Stop fighting," he said, rubbing his chin. "Allow me to just see what the devil is—"

The cramp worsened. She curled herself into a tight ball.

"Helen," said Augustin, "let the doctor help."

"No!" she screamed, hoping that Maggie was still close.

"This is clearly a womb problem," McCooke said, again pulling at her skirts.

She slapped his face.

"She's hysterical," the doctor said, holding his cheek, his voice high and furious. He struck her face with his open hand.

"For God's sake!" cried Augustin.

Helen's head swung away from McCooke. Just as a curtain of black descended over her eyes, she heard him say, "Sir, she must be fully examined."

CHAPTER TWENTY-SIX

HORACE SAW THE TWO slavers marching toward him. Hickox bringing his partner along meant more trouble. Since the night at the Galway house, he had been getting almost daily visits from the elder slave catcher. Everyone knew it. No black person had bought a fish from him in days, lest they too come to Hickox's notice. This reduction in business was testing him. Somehow, he lost the two doubloons on the night they hid the runaways. His dream of setting up a shop crumbled to dust. He dare not go to the Galway house, for he did not want to know where the runaways were now hidden. Truth be told, he was angry at Maggie. She should never have involved herself in this business and, by extension, implicated him.

"Boy," said Hickox as he approached the cart, "you're holding a secret. And I suspect it's burning your fishy fingers by now."

"Mr. Hickox, sir, I swear I got no idea what you on about."

"You know something, I've been the very soul of patience. Have I harmed you?"

"No sir."

"No sir, I have not." Hickox eyed him. "I like you. You're a man of business. It's rare to see one of your kind putting in the effort. Building something."

"Thank you, sir," said Horace, his eye warily traveling from one man to the other.

"But you see, I have to put all of that aside." Hickox paused, his finger tapping on his temple, as if thinking of the best course of action. He stepped closer to the fishmonger. "Now, I could order Mr. Swift to flay you right here. In times of extreme need, he has done it. And enjoyed it."

Swift moved his hand to his whip and nodded to Horace, who took a few steps back. Several passersby lingered, waiting to see what might happen.

"You're lucky, because we both know that this is not Mr. Swift's natural homeland. Ah, the sweet South, where the African knows his place. No one would blink at the sight of a white man making sure that it stays that way. Why, they would slap him on the back in the most honest fraternity."

Horace felt sweat on his upper lip and ran his coat sleeve across his mouth. "Now, Mr. Hickox, sir," he said, his hands up, palms facing the slave catcher, "I'm doing my best. I ain't lying to you."

"As I see it, you owe me two doubloons."

"Pardon me, sir. Somebody got them coins that night. My pants was off when he," pointing to Swift, "was in the room and—"

"You calling me a thief?"

"No sir, I ain't. Just supposing you mighta seen is all."

"Perhaps it was that cook you're so fond of." Hickox looked to the sky. "While you were in a passionate embrace, if relations between two of your kind could be called anything but animal lust. Perhaps the lady took what she believed was her due for fornicating with a beast like you."

Horace's ears turned red as he swallowed back a flame of rage.

"So as I see it, we shall be taking all your fish. Mr. Swift?" One by one, Swift dropped each flopping fish to the walkway and dug his boot into their soft flesh while they tried to swim away. The pressure of his heel split their bellies, spilling their viscera onto the chilly ground. "This is only a small part of what you owe. Trust me when I tell you that we shall get the rest."

"I wish," Swift said as he crushed a beautiful rainbow trout under his foot, "that this was you." It took several minutes to kill the entire stock. The walkway was slippery with skin, flesh, bone, and blood.

Horace dropped to his haunches amid the ruin, his arms covering his face. The slavers departed, cutting through the few onlookers.

Finally, Horace began scraping up the mess, knowing full well that nobody would buy fish from a cart that was surrounded by putrefaction. A few people tried to speak to him, but he heard nothing. He scooped some remains into his bucket and plodded one block to the edge of the Mohawk River and consigned the flesh back to its source.

He sloshed the bucket in the current until it was clean and filled it with water. When he returned, he washed the smaller bits of fish into the street.

As he came back from his second trip, he found Maggie, fists at her hips, shopping basket on a clean spot of ground, staring at the mess. One eyebrow shot up as she focused on him.

"You gone crazy?" she asked.

He squinted at her and said nothing. They both watched as he splashed water on the sidewalk, sending a swirl of muck sloshing into the street.

"Who done this?" demanded Maggie, her voice rising in anger.

"You know who." He kneeled and took a battered catfish in his hands. Its whiskers stood out, still whole, while its body hung in tatters. "Just swimming this morning. You didn't even get to feed nobody."

"Why'd he done it to you?"

"Next time it's me they grind into the dirt." Horace dumped the fish into the bucket. "You watch and see."

"But he ain't cornered me," she said.

"You's Mr. Galway's girl," he spat.

She kept her lips tightly pursed as she studied him. He would not meet her eye, but instead kept filling the bucket and shaking his head. She sighed. "You want help?"

"You can't do nothing," he said, and resumed loading the bucket.

"Here." She removed a sandwich wrapped in a white kerchief from her pocket. "You ain't been by, so I brung you this." She held it toward him.

He looked up, eyes red. "Thank you." He rose and moved away from her, shoving the sandwich into his jacket pocket. Maggie lingered a few moments, watching him. Finally, she shook her head, picked up her groceries, and proceeded east along Main Street toward her last stop of the morning, the Sylvanus Bakery.

Alvan Stewart sat at his desk. Morning light streamed through his window, brightening the room. Though his office was neat, with well-ordered law books on level shelves and a stack of to-be-submitted briefs in a handsome wooden box, a litter of papers surrounded his feet. Each sheet had ink on it: writing, strike-outs, scribbles of half-arranged thoughts, and unpromising beginnings. He dropped a new leaf to add to its fellows. If the Colonization Society already hated him, how could he win over any wavering members when he spoke at their meeting tonight?

His attention was drawn to the partially charred scarecrow with a tall top hat and roughed-up tailcoat that hung high in the corner of his office. A sign was attached to the noose around the form's neck. It read, *Alvan Stewart, Traitor.* He kept the effigy in order to remember that mistaken men, once passionately emboldened, were hard to stop and impossible to control.

His own safety didn't trouble him. Instead he worried about his new assistant, Pryce. After yesterday's hours of organizing for the upcoming convention, he had suggested that the young man sit in the lobby of the National Hotel and monitor the comings and goings of Hickox and Swift. The two slave catchers had lingered in the city and now the convention was fast apporaching. Knowing what they were doing seemed important, but Pryce had not returned to Stewart's home and was uncharacteristically late. He prayed that the lad had not drawn attention and been attacked. He stood, deciding to make a circuit of the town and look for him, when the street door opened.

Pryce came slowly up the stairs and met him on the landing.

"Where the devil have you been?" asked Stewart.

"Watching the slavers."

"All night?"

Pryce drifted into the office and removed his coat, brushing off a few pine needles and bits of dry leaves before hanging it on a crowded rack.

"Mr. Swift didn't stay in the hotel. Around midnight, he went out alone. I followed him."

"I told you, just sit in the lobby," said the lawyer.

Pryce shrugged. "He secreted himself outside Galway's home. At sunrise, he retreated back to the hotel."

"Our ruse was not believed," said Stewart, crossing his arms. "Never follow him again."

Pryce had not only been watching Swift. He'd been sitting under the evergreen below the window he believed to be Helen's. It was the first time he'd been near the house since he and Stewart had helped hide the runaways. It didn't matter if she had no idea of his presence, because he filled the time with dreams about saving her from Swift, or some other danger. Whatever the imagined scenario, he vanquished the foe and she ran to him filled with gratitude and surrender. Now he looked at Stewart. "Do you think I ought to tell Mr. Galway about Swift?"

"I've another idea." Stewart brought out a stack of letters from his desk drawer. "We have to figure out where all these out-of-town gentlemen will be staying once they arrive for the convention." He slapped the correspondence down on a spare writing table. "Note each person's itinerary. Make reservations. And prepare a list so that we can dispatch each to their rooms."

"All of them?"

Stewart nodded and sat back at his desk.

Pryce slumped in the chair and thumbed through the stack. He picked up a letter and began to read. After a moment, he dropped it back on the table. "I really think Mr. Galway ought to know that his house is being watched."

"The question is," said Stewart, "does that expose his cook to any danger? If the runaways are still there, will this information spur Galway to some detrimental action?"

"I hadn't thought of that," said Pryce.

"No, clearly you had not."

The young man lifted a different piece of mail and stared at it, but the words wouldn't come together into sentences. "Maybe he already knows about the slaves."

"He's unlikely to be part of the conspiracy," said the lawyer. "Colonization men don't do that sort of thing."

Disappointed, Pryce turned his chair to get more of the sunlight onto the letter, ruffling it and trying to focus his mind. "Maybe I should go over there and offer my help to that cook."

"Do you want to put them all in danger?" asked Stewart gruffly. "Besides, the Negroes have been helping each other escape from slavery since the barbaric practice began. I doubt she needs your help." He picked up his quill and dipped it into the inkstand. His hand hovered over a clean sheet and there it froze. After a few moments, he slid the feather back into the ink in frustration. "I wonder if Galway is privy to any plan to disrupt the convention. He's an important member of the Colonization Society. Maybe he's well enough to go to tonight's meeting." Stewart looked at Pryce, whose eyes were sparkling and at full attention. "Perhaps we should pay him a visit—to check on his health."

Pryce was on his feet and already at the coatrack.

Sylvanus knew about patience. It took time to nurture the gooey, yeasty starters that worked their will on the flour, sugar, salt, and water he fed them. Quiet time was not wasted time. Often, he found himself rewarded for simply sitting with his chin in his hand waiting for the next step to introduce itself. On this day, he let his thoughts drift to the question that often captivated him—the difference between the mortal being and the soul. During everyday work, while measuring and mixing the ingredients of his dough, or cutting wood to heat the great domed oven, his soul flew above while his back and arms carried on. But during his deliveries of the finished loaves, the soul inhabited his body once again as he bargained and laughed and occasionally argued with his customers. During the night, when the body was at rest, his soul might play the most amusing tricks on him, making him believe some outrageous circumstance had befallen him. And his legs sometimes kicked off the blankets, leaving him shivering on the cot. But it was still difficult to imagine how the two might be separated. Having no immediate answer to these heavy questions never troubled him. Instead, he simply waited for the Creator to toss in a pinch of understanding to salt his thoughts.

With his morning deliveries complete, this was his position, chin in hand, when Maggie came through the front door, setting off the tinkle of the bell. Sylvanus smiled, eyes bright.

"Hast thou the need for my sort of bread? Thou seemest like a person who only serves her own."

Maggie looked around the shop, eyes lingering over the loaves stacked on the counter. "Well, that's mighty fine-looking bread there," she said. "Maybe I should just give up on my own." After surveying the store, she pointed to the back.

Sylvanus stood. "Thou and I are the only ones about."

Maggie put her basket down. "She's getting close with the baby. I suspect it'll be any day now. And I got that nosy doctor trying to find out whatever he can. A crying baby's gonna be hard to hide."

"Yes."

"And I ain't gonna let nobody else near her till the baby come."

"Thou art wise. If thou wilt shelter her for another week or two, 'twill be much better for her and the babe."

"Week or two? If that baby got the colic . . . I don't know."

"I know a man outside Oriskany. A good Quaker with his good wife. They live alone. Thou mayest trust him with thy charges. I shall write about our need."

The door swung open, causing the bell to tinkle. Both Maggie and Sylvanus stiffened.

"Morning, Sister Myrick," said the baker. "How be the good reverend?"

Maggie turned for the door, eyes down, giving Mrs. Myrick plenty of room to pass. As the cook retrieved her basket, Sylvanus called to her: "Don't forget thy loaf."

Maggie turned back and grabbed the bread. "I thank you. What's Mr. Galway gonna say if I come back with no bread? He's gonna say I'm getting on, that's what he's gonna say."

CHAPTER TWENTY-SEVEN

McCOOKE KNEELED BY Helen's unconscious form. He wrapped one arm around her trunk, the other went to the back of her knees.

Augustin called to him, "She is with child. Save them, I beg you."

"I'll determine if she's in that condition," said the doctor, lifting her from the floor and thinking that his moment had come. He'd be her savior. She'd be grateful and his stay could turn out to be very pleasant— and longer. He approached the library door. "Females exaggerate. Only a medical exam can say for certain."

"Be careful with her, Doctor."

As McCooke pushed into the hallway, he heard Augustin declare, "God, I know I am a sinner, but I beg you to please protect the baby and my wife."

He can pray, thought McCooke, but I'll be the one doing the saving.

Helen's head was thrown back over the doctor's arm, her milky throat, long and luxurious, exposed. He felt her warmth through her clothing. Shaking himself to clear his head, he pushed his mind to the problem at hand. She might be having a miscarriage or just an incident of suppression of the menses. The doctor had his doubts that a man over forty could produce seed strong enough to impregnate such a young wife. Not that it was impossible, but old sperm might instead produce a horror.

As he reached the top of the stairs, he caught a glimpse of something floating near the ceiling. He staggered. Miss Duphorne's ghost loomed over him. A waterfall of blood washed down her body, staining the front of her nightdress. His temples started to pound and his legs weakened. Fearing that he might drop Mrs. Galway, he rushed into his own room and put her on the bed. He grabbed his head. The apparition couldn't be real. Glancing into the hallway, he calmed. She was gone, but he turned to the bed and saw Helen and his poor dead Little Darling in the exact same position. They appeared to merge. The violent pounding in his temples returned.

Suddenly and with great clarity, he remembered that it was his attempted abortion that had started Miss Duphorne's bleeding. When he'd determined that she carried a child, she became terrified of her parents' reaction to her ruination. Of course, the baby can never be born, he had said, convincing her that he would carry off the procedure without any harm. Their tryst would remain secret. McCooke believed that if Miss Duphorne's father knew that he had spoiled "Little Jenny," the last thing he would ever see was a lead ball emerging out of the sparks and fire of a flintlock.

She could only have been a few months pregnant. If they waited, the quickening would come, and the punishment, if caught, would be hanging rather than some other less permanent sentence.

At his direction, she had taken extremely hot baths while drinking purgatives and laxatives, but still the proof of their sin remained. They met in the barn so that she might leap from the loft, hoping to stir the womb to spit out the fetus. Nothing happened but a twisted ankle. He knew that some men employed violence trying to kill an unborn unwanted baby, but he didn't have the heart to injure such a female. Finally, he decided to try a direct injection of olive oil and near-to-scalding water into the womb. It might have worked, but the syringe meant to deliver the concoction must have accidentally perforated her womb.

He closed his eyes and opened them again. Mrs. Galway lay prone on the bed. There had to be a different outcome for her, or all was lost. He noticed that his hands shook like an old man's. The only way to calm himself and stop the trembling that had infected his entire body was to take another drink. Clearly, the few sips earlier this morning would not be enough at a time like this. Dropping to his knees, he fumbled under the bed for a bottle of brandy he had secreted there.

After several steadying gulps, it occurred to him that they might be disturbed by the cook, who had an absolute mania against him. He decided to employ the lock on his door, lest he be stopped from rendering treatment. For all he knew, the Negro might call in some kind of Native medicine man to perform magic over the poor lady. One never knew with the colored races. No, he must be the one to bring her back to life. He turned the key and heard the lock engage with a solid click.

Now that he thought about it—she had fought him so hard that, for her own good, she needed to be restrained. If in the middle of determining the state of her womb she began to thrash, she might tear herself apart. It only made sense to bind her hands. He removed a pillow cover and carefully knotted it around her wrists before tying the other end to the bedpost. Everything depended on this exam going perfectly.

On her way up Third Street, Maggie saw Alvan Stewart and Pryce Anwell crossing Bleecker and heading for the porch of the Galway house. She slowed her pace. It might be dangerous for her to be seen with them. Let the doctor open the door, she thought.

She watched them knock. They went unanswered. Damn that doctor, he might be nosing around in her kitchen, trying to get into her bedroom. The two visitors looked through the sidelight windows that framed the entranceway and appeared to be disturbed. They pounded on the door and pulled on the handle with no apparent luck. Maggie quickened her pace.

She came to the porch, breathing hard. "Why you trying to break—"

"Mr. Galway is in distress," said Stewart, stopping her.

Augustin lay on the floor in the foyer. Dropping the basket, she fumbled trying to extract a substantial key ring from her dress pocket. As soon as she got the door unlocked, she rushed to him. Stewart and Pryce followed her. All three tried to lift Galway.

He grasped Maggie's arm. "No. Leave me. It's Helen. Upstairs. The doctor is examining her. The baby."

"Alone with her?" Maggie rose with some difficulty. "I'll see to that doctor," she said, rushing to the staircase. "Help him." She climbed quickly to the second floor.

"Assist her if you can," said Stewart to Pryce. "I'll take care of Mr. Galway."

Pryce charged up the stairs two at a time.

Maggie entered Helen's chambers and found them empty. She ran back out and saw the doctor's door closed tight. Pryce came up the stairs just as she discovered that the door was locked. He moved her aside and threw himself against the solid wood. She shouldered him out of the way and again used her keys. When she opened the door, Helen lay on the bed and the doctor was drying his bloody hands on a white towel.

"If you've come to save her from the white man's medicine, you are too late."

"Too late?" shouted Pryce. "Is she dead?"

"Of course not," said the doctor, indignant.

"Outta my way," said Maggie.

The doctor stepped between her and the bed. Maggie used her forearm to deliver a powerful chop against McCooke's throat, sending him coughing and stumbling away.

"She is my patient," the doctor croaked. "Do not meddle with her."

"Get him outta here," ordered Maggie.

Pryce stood between McCooke and the bed. The doctor tried to go around him, but the younger man shoved him back "Step away," he said, speaking in a slow deliberate voice. When the doctor didn't move he pushed him until he was in the hallway. "Don't make me knock you down the stairs."

Inside, Maggie quickly pulled a ladder-back chair from its place and wedged it under the door handle. Helen was unconscious. The cook smoothed down the girl's dress and gently shook her shoulders. Her eyes blinked open and she smiled faintly.

"I was calling for you," she said in a faraway voice. Her brow knotted. "Is he still here?"

"You're safe now," said Maggie.

Tears fell down Helen's face. "He was . . . touching me."

Maggie's jaw clenched. "He's locked out. I seen to it."

Helen tried to sit up. Her hands pulled against the binding at her wrists.

"Stop now," Maggie soothed. "You're pulling them knots tighter. Cutting off the blood." She inspected the bindings.

"In my sitting room," said Helen in the childlike voice. "Scissors."

By the time Maggie finished, she had helped Helen to her room, washed and dressed her, and put the girl down to sleep. She carried a bundle of sheets and garments to the kitchen to soak in cold salt water. Now that she had the ammunition, it was time to realize her most fervent wish.

At the library door, she heard Augustin's anguished cry and went in. Stewart and Pryce were stationed at either side of the bed, holding him down. The doctor stood at the end, Augustin's injured leg in his hands. He was pressing around the flesh with his thumbs and forefingers. Augustin whimpered in pain.

"What you doing to him?" demanded Maggie.

"Quiet," said McCooke.

Stewart replied, "It seems that his leg has sustained further damage."

Just then the doctor grabbed Augustin's foot and pulled sharply. Galway screamed in agony.

"Stop!" Maggie shouted, hurrying to the bed.

Once again, McCooke ran his fingers over the leg, probing. Finally, he stood upright. "Sir, I've reset the bone. You have thrown your recovery back weeks. I would not be surprised if you have a permanent limp." He grabbed two pieces of wood and the rolled-up bandage and began splinting the break.

Augustin's cries filled the room.

"Take your dirty hands off a him, Doctor," said Maggie. She slapped his arm away.

"I will not be disrespected by *her*." He threw the roll of bandages to the floor.

"Maggie?" said Augustin with much difficulty. "How is Helen?"

"I gotta talk to Mr. Augustin—alone." Maggie picked up his hand and brought it to the side of her face. Immediately his breathing eased.

"Perhaps we should be leaving," said Stewart, looking at the two. He cleared his throat. "But someone must attend to that leg." He directed his gaze at the doctor. "He seems to have an infection."

"And what," asked the doctor, "would you know about that?"

"You keep your mouth shut," ordered Maggie. She addressed Stewart and Pryce: "It would be a particular favor to me if you'd wait in the hall." She glared at the doctor. "Get out."

The doctor tugged down his vest. "Sir, I will not be ordered about by a nigger." His eye traveled to Augustin's hand entwined with Maggie's. "*Any* nigger."

Augustin, his voice phlegmy and full of pain, said, "I will hear her, gentlemen. Alone."

Twenty minutes later, Stewart and Pryce had their hands filled with the doctor's clothing, personal belongings, and his empty valise. They carried them to the street and placed everything on top of the medical bag that sat, as did the doctor, on the curbside.

Maggie listened to Augustin's uneven breathing. The opium she administered after the doctor had reset his leg put him in a stupor. Splints and wrappings had to be put on, but she let him rest before beginning the painful process. If he stirred and disturbed the break again, things would go worse for the man and she didn't want that.

She had been his most steady companion in life. They had lived with each other for his entire existence—with only a five-year lapse when he took rooms in New York City so that he could learn the business of finance. She had stood at his side when his parents were buried and was there when his first wife followed them into the hereafter. And now the hope that he had planted within Miss Helen was gone as well. How life whittled you down, she thought, lopping off piece after piece, until you were nothing but bone.

Her own expectations had been similarly shaved. She was just fourteen years old on July 4, 1799, the day New York's Gradual Emancipation Act went into effect. She had such faith back then. That summer morning, when she awakened and began helping her momma with the chores, they both talked about what life would be like after they were freed. Maggie knew that even though *she* had to continue to serve until 1827, any child she had would be born free, not a slave who could be sold. That expectation seemed stupid now, looking back, understanding how so many things had been beyond her control.

The long wait proved too much for her mother. She died of fever in 1804—twenty-three years short of freedom. Young Augustin had demanded that his father give her a proper burial with a preacher. He even took Maggie's hand at the graveside.

Her throat tightened. The tears might gather if she kept on thinking of all that had passed. She set her jaw and decided that it was time to work—the only salve she allowed herself, besides the occasional bowl of tobacco.

Pulling back the blanket and sheet, she saw that his leg was blotchy and pink with messy bandages covering a nasty gash where the bone had come through. She laid the back of her hand on his calf and it felt warm. Could it be that Mr. Stewart was right about an infection? Some cabbage leaves might draw out any poisons. Some honey around the broken skin would help. She would see to it, make sure he got better, now that the doctor could no longer cause trouble.

Augustin stirred. Immediately his face curdled in pain.

"I know you're hurting," said Maggie, "but I gotta splint up that leg."

"Brandy," said Augustin.

Maggie squeezed his hand. "You think you at a party?"

A faint smile crossed his lips. "Even a priest drinks in church. Just to get him through."

"You gonna act like a priest now?"

"Oh, never that bad."

They both laughed. Maggie got the brandy and propped him up. After several good-sized swallows, he nodded. She took three thick books off the shelves and put them next to his leg, one above the break near his knee, and two by his ankle.

"I'm gonna need your help. I can pick up the leg, but you gotta slide them books under so that I can wrap it up."

"One more brandy," he said, handing her the glass.

As she refilled it, she said, "You about ready for religious orders."

He screwed up his mouth, looking grim, then downed the alcohol. He gasped and panted as she lifted his knee and foot, carefully maintaining the angle so she didn't undo the doctor's work. His hands quaked as he slipped each book into place, falling back against the pillows, still breathing hard when it was finished. She gave him another measure of brandy, which he had to hold in both shaking hands as she went about lining up the splints and carefully binding them to his leg.

"You gonna be laid up for a while," she said, minding his pain out of the corner of her eye. He grunted. "Maybe that society a yours gonna fall apart without you."

"The Colonization Society?"

"Maybe if you ain't there, they's gonna just give up," she said, wrapping his leg.

"Nonsense," he said. And after a pause, "Why bring them up?" He sipped his brandy, wincing as she tried to adjust him.

"Oh, I don't care. But I ain't picking up and going to no Africa."

"You certainly are not," he said.

"But that's what your society wants, ain't it? All a us go? Take us-selves outta their sight?"

"That's what some of them want."

"What do *you* want?"

He watched her as she kept focused on her task. "I want your people to have a chance to run your own lives. I don't think you will ever get that here. There's too much prejudice."

"Don't I run my own life?"

"Are you looking to go off and live with *Horace*?" he said with a snide tone.

Maggie met his eye. "And if I was?"

"Are you?"

"I ain't," she said, moving back to the bandages.

"Then why are you . . . don't I treat you well?"

"I just want to know how much freedom I got."

"You made your choice—to stay with me."

"I sure did," Maggie said, standing up straight. She leaned in, took Augustin's glass, and went to the bar. "But I'm still the servant and you're still the master."

"Damn it. Tell me what you're on about," he said, twisting to get a look at her. "If you want to move in with *him*, I can't stop you."

"I don't think no priest swears like that," she said, and pointed up. "Careful, He'll hear you." She picked up the opium bottle, added a few drops to the brandy, and handed him the mixture. "You and me, we both lived all our lives right here. Both our mommas died in this house."

"What's your point?"

"What goes on in my room is my business, right?"

"So, this *is* about Horace."

"No. It's about if my room is mine. Because if it's mine, then every-thing in it's mine."

"Legally, the furniture . . ." he began, then looked at her standing over him. "Well, all right, I agree, it's all yours."

"Good. Then if them lousy stinking slavers ever come back, you to tell them to keep outta my room."

Galway stared at her, but didn't object.

CHAPTER TWENTY-EIGHT

THOUGHTS SWIRLED IN Stewart's mind as he and Pryce advanced along Bleecker Street. Galway was an opponent—even if the man refrained from joining the chorus howling for his blood. Still, seeing him so broken had shaken the lawyer. On a human level, it was a lesson about the impermanence of life. You could be working hard, doing what you thought was God's will, only to be struck down before the task was half-finished. And what do I leave behind, he thought, a pile of legal briefs? An attempted convention that might crumble in my hands? If a startled horse runs me down, who would carry on the work?

"That doctor is a scoundrel," said Pryce.

Stewart's eyes cut to his young assistant. "One scoundrel hardly changes the equation."

"Oh," said Pryce, seeming chastened.

A few yellow elm leaves tumbled across the street. "But," said Stewart, "one good man working for a righteous cause, why, that's worth a hundred crooked politicians, good-hearted fools, or lying doctors." He went quiet for a moment. "The wind blows freely, until it comes against a brick wall. Right now, the Colonization Society blows hot with federal money to send free Negroes to Africa. Almost all the most important citizens of Utica, like Mr. Galway, call themselves members of the society. Everything seems to be moving toward colonization. But if all the free men and women are transported out of America, slavery won't die, it will entrench and expand into the territories. Do you see what I mean?"

"I guess so," said Pryce. "I've been trying to sell that abolition newspaper, the *Standard and Democrat*, but people won't buy it."

"I'm glad you've tried. The very best thing you've done is read it."

"The paper really does rile one up," said Pryce.

They arrived back at Stewart's law office and climbed upstairs. Pryce went to the stack of unsold newspapers. Stewart focused intently on the young man. "I think you've made yourself ready to be part of that brick wall," he said. "You'll speak at the meeting of the Colonization Society tonight."

"Me?" Pryce sat down with a thud, feeling a little sick. Working in the office and answering letters was one thing, but speaking? It would mean that he really believed that the slaves should be freed immediately. He supposed that if he had been held in jail for longer than a few hours, he would have been mad for freedom. Maybe this was the right thing. He felt a twinkle of delight that Stewart was rewarding all his work nailing up convention notices and, in the process, destroying the runaway-slave advertisements. "You should be the one to speak at any debate."

"They haven't invited me," said Stewart. "We'll go to their meeting and when they open the floor for discussion, you stand up and speak in favor of our plans."

The delight wilted in Pryce's breast. "Will they allow it?" He glanced up at the half-burned effigy above Stewart's desk.

"Allow?" The lawyer banged his fist on the desk. Pryce flinched. "They claim to believe in democracy, let them prove it. The meeting won't just be the Colonization Society. The public will be there, men of work and business." He rose and strode to the window. "We can't cede their hearts to our opponents." He turned, his face animated. "They've hardened against me. You'll open a new front on the battlefield."

"What will I say?"

Stewart clasped his enormous hands behind his back. "For some, Negroes are no better than beasts of burden, put on the planet to be used as slaves. Those men pucker their lips and slobber for slaveholders as 'our poor Southern brethren.' To them, Negroes are savages. Opinions like that won't be changed."

"Surely a moral argument about the evils of slavery will show them their mistake."

Stewart grimaced and shook his head. "They already know the arguments. What we must do is shake the insides of the men who have come there with open minds. Speak to those who have bone and sinew and who know what it means to toil. We are told that *benevolent* slave owners instruct their charges in religion. They are painted as fatherly, bringing the childlike Negroes into a state of grace. Refer to the slaves as Christians. Use your Bible. If we are all Christians, then we have no right to enslave another believer."

"Aren't most slaves rather ignorant?"

"An educated slave is a dangerous slave. Have you never met an educated black man?" asked Stewart, amiably.

Pryce shook his head.

"You will at the convention, trust me." He put his hand on the young man's shoulder and gave it a squeeze. Pryce felt the strength of the older man's grip and found himself leaning into it. He straightened, afraid that Stewart had noticed his weakness.

"Come, let's work on a few points so that you're prepared." The lawyer took his seat, passing quill and paper across the desk.

Pryce scratched notes, all the while hoping that his father would never find out about him speaking on behalf of the slaves. The old man should have received the letter he sent home by now. It had already been over a week since he sat himself down at the small writing desk, knowing that if he neglected to send the promised dispatches along the way to Buffalo, his mother and father would be worried. He had to appear to be moving along on the appointed trip and learning as he went. He thought he might wax on about the genius of the canal system, or try to explain the workings of the locks to his mother. Or throw in a detail or two about the scenery. Father probably never traveled far beyond Little Falls, he thought. He felt guilty about trying to fool them. Maybe he could simply admit that he had taken a position at a lawyer's office and intended to organize an abolition convention—and he didn't care who knew. He grabbed the quill and dipped it into the ink. The image of the old man, mourning the loss of his only son to maintain the family business, bloomed in his mind. Best to keep it short, he thought.

Dear Mother and Father,

I am well. I trust you are both in good health. I'm studying the canal very closely. I'm now well past Utica. I'll write again soon.

Your devoted son

Well past Utica? It was idiotic. Scratching it out, he knew that the sentence gave away the entire game. He turned the period after *write again soon* into a comma and added *from Lockport*. Satisfied, he believed that would hold them off.

That night, the room at Miller's Hall looked packed with colonization men. Pryce stood on Whitesboro Street peering through the entryway doors. Most chairs were either occupied or reserved by the presence of a topcoat and hat. Tobacco smoke hovered in billowing clouds. He stepped inside just as a burst of laughter came from a knot of men at the back of the hall. A tall fellow at the center held forth on some issue that appeared to be of the deepest interest. From under his furrowed brow, the man's sharp gaze focused on one person, then the next. He seemed to be making certain they would all be ready to act together if the necessity arose.

Stewart stood behind Pryce and murmured in his ear, "That's Congressman Samuel Beardsley. Never at a loss for words. He'll be speaking. He always speaks."

Pryce was about to turn. Stewart stopped him.

"Pretend you don't know me. Move in a little and I will point out a few of the others."

The young man found a place at the back wall.

"See the smart-looking man there," said Stewart, "just inside Beardsley's circle?"

Pryce noticed the judge who had sentenced him to spend the night in jail. "I know him—too well."

Judge Chester Hayden leaned against a back-row chair, his hands folded across his stomach, silent and alert.

"He's lapping up every morsel of information for later use," said the lawyer. "He can be dangerous."

Pryce swallowed, his throat suddenly dry. What would he say to these men to change their hearts? A shiver went through him. "I can't do this."

"Nonsense," said Stewart. "There are others here. You're not alone." He patted Pryce on the shoulder and pressed him to move forward and take a seat.

Pryce plodded ahead, wishing that the floor would open and swallow him down whole. He found a place and felt his own insides quivering. He touched his pockets and felt the notes. All he had to do was read them. The thought did nothing to calm him. Stewart sat behind him.

The meeting was finally called to order.

"Representative Beardsley," called the chairman, "we would like you to open up."

"Thank you, sir. Most kind," started Beardsley, coming forward to the dais. The audience settled as he looked around the room, appearing to take each man's measure. Finally, at a moment of perfect silence, he began: "Lest we forget, it has been just four years since the devil Nat Turner and his confederates slaughtered sixty-five souls—from innocent babes to mothers and grandmothers, to men defending their families—all savagely murdered in their homes, on their lands, and in our country. Yes. I said *our* country," said Beardsley, his deep voice vibrating in Pryce's chest. "It is precisely because of those deaths that we know how dangerous the situation in the South is. That is why we must stop this abolition convention. Don't let these agitators sully Utica's reputation with the stench of bloody treason."

Shouts of "Hear! Hear!" and "Huzzah!" temporarily silenced Beardsley. Pryce looked around. Most of the men were cheering, but among them were some who looked thoughtful, not yet convinced. Beardsley put up his hands and the crowd grew silent.

"No one can sleep easy in their beds as long as abolitionists and their allies try to pollute the minds of the slaves and tear this country asunder. We won't let this convention and the return of the comet combine in the minds of rebel slaves as a pretext to begin another bloody insurrection. Rather than allowing Utica to be turned into the headquarters of abolitionism in New York State, I would almost prefer to see the city swept from the face of the earth, like Sodom and Gomorrah.

"And let's talk about slavery. It is allowed in our Constitution. We in New York have gradually done away with it. How can we ask anything different of our Southern brothers? Abolitionism is nothing but a fetid form of federalism. So, what is our plan? How do we intend to deal with the growing tide of free Negroes? The colony of Liberia has been established on Africa's coast to welcome them back to their fatherland. If they are able, let them build there as we have built here."

Roars of approval filled the meetinghouse and echoed off the plaster ceiling.

Pryce looked around, confused. In all the papers there were regular reports from Liberia stating that the death rate of black colonists was staggeringly high. These men must be told the truth, he thought. If they were to make decisions, someone should tell them the facts. He found himself on his feet.

"Africa?" he yelled. All eyes swung in his direction. His hand shook at his sides as he turned to the congressman. "Liberia's in trouble. The colony is failing. Just last week there were reports of attacks from hostile tribes. Fever kills even more. At least half of the colonists who go there die."

"Silence!" roared the chairman, a stick-thin man with a protruding Adam's apple.

Congressman Beardsley focused his razor-like eyes on Pryce. "Who are you, sir? You're not from Utica."

"I am Pryce Anwell, a visitor to your fair city."

"By way of Sheriff Osborn's jail—if I recall," said Judge Hayden, rising, his snide tone drawing attention. "We don't need your liberation fancies here, Mr. Anwell. You and Stewart are clearly resolved to press forward with this convention and thus endanger our brothers in the South." The judge now turned to Beardsley and the chair. "Is there a man here who believes that if the people of the North tried to abolish the system of slavery, that the South would not forthwith disband themselves from the Union? The abolitionists say it is their right to meet here in Utica. Therefore a man may also contend that he has a right to smoke a cigar in my gunpowder house. Abolition is disunion."

"You can't fix Liberia by attacking me," cried Pryce. "The people you wish to remove were born here. They have as much right to call themselves citizens as you do."

Outrage buzzed around him, as if he had hit a wasp's nest with a stone. He turned to Stewart. Black spots swarmed his vision. The lawyer steadied him. Pryce sank into his chair.

"I ask you, Representative Beardsley," boomed Stewart, standing, "if you found yourself in chains, denied your freedom, whipped, prevented from entering into the sacrament of marriage, unable to stop your own children from being ripped from their mother's arms and sold to the highest bidder, would you not find that cruel AND unusual punishment? And if it be cruel and unusual for you, why is it different for the Negro? Where in the Constitution does it say that protections against such punishments are only for white men?"

"The Constitution of the United States," intoned Judge Hayden, "protects the rights of free men, including slave owners. You know that, Mr. Stewart, better than anyone. We cannot allow the Negroes' impressionable minds to be warped. If the country goes Stewart's way, it's a guarantee that the throats of slaveholders will be slashed. Cost what it may—no regard for what's right." He opened his arms wide as if embracing the audience. "We admit that originally it was wrong to reduce men to slavery, but when we have them in our midst, incompetent to the rights of citizens, should we discharge them from our care and let them perish through their inability to provide for themselves? If we must provide for them, is it not better for them, and us, that they should be provided for in the relations in which they now stand? If you immediately set free two and a half million uneducated slaves, our economy will be in ruins. The Union will be broken into pieces. Let the slaveholding states decide their own fate. As long as the law says that slavery exists, we must uphold it to preserve the Union."

Words drifted over Pryce's head. The burning shame of failure consumed him. This night was testing him and he had crumbled. If only there was a way to crawl out the door and leave Utica. But where to go? Buffalo? Back to Little Falls? He imagined the pain on the old man's face. Not smart enough. To return a failure? He couldn't do it.

"What Union?" yelled Stewart. "These lovers of the Union refuse to hear the bitter grief which rises from the mouth of every slave straight to God's ear."

Two rows in front of Pryce, a well-dressed man with a brocade waistcoat wobbled to his feet. "You, Stewart," he said, pointing with vague aim at the lawyer, "offend God's ear right now." Those around him laughed. He brought a heavy mug of beer to his lips. "I'll do our Lord a service," he said, and threw the glass, which showered Pryce with ale and bounced off Stewart's cheek, cutting him.

"If we here in Utica," responded Stewart, ignoring the injury and raising himself to his full height, "encounter so much noisy violence as we try to plead the cause of abolition, imagine the poor slave. Can he object to his own cruel and adulterous master?" Stewart fixed his gaze on the man in the waistcoat. "Does the *drunkard* listen to the voice of the slave?"

With sudden energy, the gentleman lunged toward the big lawyer, his arms flailing and hands grasping. He fell onto Pryce, who shoved him backward. A group of spectators cushioned the man's descent. Several surged toward Pryce and Stewart, but the lawyer shouldered them away.

"If it's right to liberate slaves in fifty years, then it's right now!" Stewart shouted.

The rhythmic banging of the chairman's gavel filled Pryce's ears. The room felt hot, as if the breath of a thousand bellows poured out of the angry men. The smell of cigars grew thick and the oil lamps seemed to be flashing in unison.

"Come on, my boy," said Stewart, grabbing his sleeve and moving them toward the door. "A good man knows when to retreat." At the entranceway, Stewart turned back to the assembly and called out, "We leave you to your castles in the air!"

They stepped away and a chilly October breeze filled Pryce's lungs. His vision cleared and he saw Oriskany Street and the distant lights of Genesee.

Stewart started laughing. "You wanted thrills, well now we've got them." He punched the young man's shoulder. "You were bold, my boy. Got up on your legs. And at your first meeting. That's more than most men do in their entire lives."

Pryce stopped and found Stewart smiling at him, nodding, merry despite the cut.

"You're a true abolitionist now," said the lawyer. "You've survived your first mobbing." He slapped Pryce's back. "Good job."

At once, Pryce's throat tightened and he felt the sting of tears.

Stewart nodded and threw his arm around the younger man's shoulders.

Pryce gulped down the emotion. He thrust his head back and hollered, "Woo-hoo!" Maybe he would never tell his father where he was. He grinned as the two hurried up the street.

CHAPTER TWENTY-NINE

A NEW BREEZE STIRRED the night air. The sky—cloudless, moonless, and no longer featuring the comet—sparkled. Jupiter flickered behind a few remaining oak leaves on its rise through the eastern sky.

Off the kitchen, inside Maggie's small room, Imari sat bolstered by pillows as she sipped beef tea and listened to the cook tell the story of the day. Joe lay motionless on the far side of the bed, his back to the women.

"Miss Helen gonna be all right?" Imari asked.

"I pray the Lord keeps her safe after the day she got," said Maggie.

"Well, I know He ain't wasting no time on me," said Imari, smiling. "So best He be looking after her, poor child." She paused. "Did she lose it?"

"If she had one, yes. But I don't know. And that dirty doctor ain't no better at guessing."

"Turns out she a brave girl," said Imari. "I can't believe all you said she done to help me."

"Believe it," said Maggie.

Imari rubbed the heel of her hand along the right side of her belly. "I got me some gas." She pressed her side a little harder. "Oh my."

After days of conversation, while Imari recovered from the bird shot, the cook's attachment to her and the boy had grown in a way that she had not allowed with anyone else.

"You got pain?"

"Naw," said Imari. "It gonna pass right on."

"I wanna ask you something. You know I ain't gonna tell nobody nothing."

Imari nodded. "You better to us than anybody. Go ahead. Ask."

Maggie hesitated, suddenly filled with a nervous pulse. She frowned at her apron and began picking at specks of dried food. She brushed the crumbs into her hand and felt the graininess between her fingers. "I know you coulda stayed in New York City," she said, looking up at Imari. "So why'd you come all this way up to Utica?"

"True, Utica a long way, but we can't wait in New York. We stay with one fine black man, Mr. David Ruggles, he picks us up the first day, right when we get to the harbor. He be educated. Got his own books even. He tells us that Hickox sniffing around in town. That paddyroller, he like a lynx—good nose, patient, smart. And I still be broke up 'cause we lost Elymas."

Maggie uncovered the chamber pot, tossing the crumbs into it before replacing the lid. "How old's Elymas?" she asked as she slid the pot under the bed with her foot.

"I don't rightly know," said Imari, slowly. "I seen something about him once. But it don't say nothing except how much Master James paid for him and such."

"He weren't born there?"

"No ma'am."

"Him and you about the same age?"

"He been around my whole life. Really, I ain't never been without him. Him and me, we come up together." Imari's eyes shone as if she were lost in a memory of him.

"How old are *you*?"

"My momma don't read or nothing, so I don't know exact. But the moon was high and she counted from that. Near as I can figure, about thirty years old. I feel like a hundred." Maggie only nodded. Imari's nose crinkled. "Oh," she said, "this here tea ain't sitting right."

Maggie took the cup. "So, this Ruggles, he told you about Hickox?"

"He figure that if we stay, there gonna be big trouble, for us and him too. He scrapes together his own money 'cause he don't think he got time to wait until he can ask his friends or nothing. He puts us on a steamer up the Hudson River. So off we go. I got a veil on. Joe, he dressed like a little girl." She smiled, her eyes happy with the memory. "He hate that," she whispered. "Now don't you go telling that I told you."

Maggie smiled too. "I bet he ain't good as no girl."

"Well, we here." They both snickered.

"You ain't answered me," said Maggie, getting serious again. "Why Utica?"

"That just how it go," replied Imari, shrugging. "We ain't in charge."

"Now," said Maggie, leaning slightly forward, her eyes sharp, watching Imari closely, "I'm asking for God's honest."

"Mr. Ruggles sent me here. That's the truth."

"Now ain't that something," said Maggie, leaning back and crossing her arms. "I ask you direct. You gotta know that the truth is more than not lying."

"What do you want?" said Imari, holding her gaze.

"It's a big world. There's a lot between Virginia and Utica. But here you is. So why? The whole story."

Moments passed with Imari quiet. She met the cook's gaze. "You can't say nothing to Miss Helen."

"I ain't got no reason to tell nobody."

"Well, Missus Bea? One day she don't feel too good, so she sends me to the kitchen to get her a little something to settle her. Master James seen me leaving her room and he got that look—you know how they get." She glanced at Joe to make sure he was still asleep.

Maggie nodded.

"Like they suddenly struck with the best idea they ever had, and ain't nothing gonna put them off. So Master James, he grabs my hand and pulls me into his room. He got one right next to Missus Bea. I guess he like to think that maybe she gonna catch him at it or something 'cause that ain't the only time he done it to me there. Only that day we go into his office. He got a big desk and he spends a lot a time there scratching in his books.

"Well, he gets up on me and gets to it just like he wanted, but he sweating like a slave out in the tobacco field. I catch him in the light from the window and he don't look so good. Next thing I know, he twists up his face and moans real strange and crash down—dead."

Maggie gasped and crossed herself. "I ain't gonna say he didn't have it coming, but you musta been scared."

Imari looked at the ground, shaking her head. "At first I don't understand. But he don't move. Finally, I gotta push him into his chair to get out from under." She put her hands together and raised them. "How can *dying* be so quiet?" She relaxed and again rubbed her belly. "He the biggest thing in my life, never let me alone. There ain't almost nothing that I done, no move that I make, no decision, no pain, nothing happy that he don't know about. Master James be that big for me. And he just leaves life? His soul there inside him and then gone? He don't even cry out? Just like that, he ain't nothing but empty skin?"

"What'd you do?" asked Maggie.

Imari shivered. "First off, I didn't know what to do and I just sorta stood there looking at him, like someone was gonna come help me. I know I got to shake that off, so I go to the door between his room and Missus Bea. She snoring like some kinda bear. Her husband dead and she lost in a dream. Best to leave her be, poor woman.

"I know if he gets found like he was . . . you know . . . they gonna look at me and accuse me a something. So I get him dressed proper and lean him over his desk, real peaceful like. I check and there ain't nobody coming to look for him, so I think maybe I can find something, a little money or something. I go back and get to looking on his desk and that big book he got. This the thing he spend his life scratching in and look-ing at. So I open it up and there be Elymas's name."

"You can read?" Maggie straightened. Imari nodded. Her voice quivering, Maggie asked, "What'd it say?"

"It say: *July 13, 1805. Bought. Male. Infant. Elymas. $75 from Thomas Galway of Utica, New York. Via Abel Hickox.*"

Maggie appeared to be sitting quietly, but a whirl of memories bat-tered her heart. Her stomach twisted like a wrung-out towel. Over the years, there had been no real reason to suppose she would ever see her little lost baby again. Anytime hope warmed her breast she denied it, turning her mind to the present and all the tasks that awaited her. After she was officially emancipated in 1827, along with all the remaining slaves in New York State, she thought about moving out of the Galway house. But the irrational idea that little Elymas might be somewhere nearby crying out for her . . . looking . . . yearning . . . stopped her before she even packed a dish. If she felt the notion resurfacing, she ruthlessly shoved it down, knowing that for her life to move forward she had to give up on the baby. But had life moved on after Elymas had been stolen? She had no husband, no other children, no real intimacy. Overwhelming grief had seized her thirty years ago and everything after that stood still—except time.

She remembered the day that frost had painted the grass sparkling white and there was still plenty of autumn left before the ground froze hard and life shrank down to fit inside four walls. Augustin had entered the kitchen from the back just as she opened the bread oven. He was a handsome young man, powerful and easy in his movements, filled with assurance that his path forward would be smooth. Cold air came in with him, rushing along the floor, moving her skirts and circling her ankles. She noticed his smile and then quickly looked away and pushed some tree bark onto the stone surface of the bread oven.

"What're you doing?" he had asked, grabbing a piece of kindling and holding it over the flame of the cooking fire.

"It's Monday," she said, appearing disinterested. "Every Monday since you been born the bread gets baked."

"I know." He looked down as if wounded somehow, then he handed her the burning stick and she brought it to the pile of bark.

"You got no work to do?" she asked, shifting to the wood stack. She selected a sturdy log. Once in the fire, wisps of yellow-orange flames licked around the limb, dancing in each cleft, turning it black. A snapping spark flew out of the oven, bouncing off her mouth.

"Are you burned?" Augustin asked, cupping her chin in his hand. His fingers brushed her lips. The softness of his touch erased the sting of the ember. Before she knew what was coming, he kissed her. Stunned and excited, her tongue mingled with his. The kiss seemed a natural answer to all the teasing they had engaged in over the years. He leaned on her and pinned her against the fireplace, whispering, "I love you," again and again, as his hips pushed against her. Just as she was about to shove him away, he maneuvered her to the floor and lifted her skirts. She tried to keep them in order, but he pressed himself into her. Through her shock, she understood that trouble had come her way.

Eight months later, Augustin's father, Thomas, called her into the library and accused her of being with child, though he had used a much harsher term. He demanded to know who the father was, color rising on his neck until it was almost purple. When she refused to tell him, he struck her across the face. Frightened and in tears, she admitted that the perpetrator had been Augustin. He was summoned to the room.

"What is the meaning of this?" Thomas barked at the young man. "Did you fuck this nigger of ours?" He slammed his fist on the tea table. "Because she's carrying someone's bastard and she says it's yours."

"I . . . I," started Augustin. Maggie watched him, her eyes pleading. He squared his shoulders. "I will do what's right."

"Do what's right?" the old man bellowed. "It is far too late for that." He strode to his son and slapped him too.

Augustin staggered, unbelieving.

"You disgust me," said his father. The old man paced the room. "Leave. I don't want to see you again today."

Augustin slinked out.

The elder Galway summoned the stable boy and ordered that his closed carriage be readied for a long journey. He hired two men to switch off driving them day and night, changing horses often. Maggie was imprisoned inside the darkened coach for what felt like days. She barely saw the light until they arrived at a slave market in Richmond, Virginia.

Weak with fatigue, she was placed in a pen with other women. When her labor pains started—hurried along by the journey, she figured—she was moved to a dingy room with a single bed. A slight woman named Peg attended her, bringing water and some bread. Peg never looked into Maggie's eyes. Over the pain-filled hours, she almost forgot where she was and that she was to be sold. Peg helped her through, staying until she placed the wet crying baby on Maggie's stomach. The boy found her breast and began to suckle on her yellowy milk. Maggie closed her eyes and imagined that she was at home and that everything was safe. As the child took nourishment, something inside her soul had aligned.

She woke to Peg bringing her food.

"He got a name?" asked Peg.

"He's Elymas," said Maggie. "Just like my granddaddy." She stroked the infant's head. "What's gonna happen to us?"

"Far as I know, Mr. Hickox, a dealer for a plantation up the Potomac, talking to your master."

"He gonna buy us both?"

"Maybe," said Peg, patting her hand. "I ain't heard." She looked away. "Just keep praying."

Hours passed with little Elymas suckling and sleeping and looking up at Maggie's face so seriously that her heart soared, even in the shabby room. After three days she overheard voices outside. She sat up fearing that she was the topic.

The conviction that she and the baby would be parted seized her. Panic set in and she began to frantically search the room for something, anything to help her. One look at an old blackened woodstove and she knew what she had to do. She pulled a small fingernail knife from the pocket of her clothing where she had secreted it during the journey south. She carefully unwrapped the tiny baby and laid him on the bed. He looked up at her, seeming amused by this new situation. His little feet waved in the air. She seized one of them and kissed it. "I'm sorry," she said, and then as fast as she could, she carved a few lines across his sole. He screamed. Before anyone could unlock the door, she ran to the stove and swiped her finger along the soot that had built up above the opening. She managed to get back to Elymas and rub the black soot into the wounds she'd made.

The man she would come to know as Hickox burst in.

"She's killing it," he barked, pushing her aside and sweeping the baby into his arms. "Take it, Abby," he called to a tall dark woman, who relieved the slaver of his burden.

"Don't take him," Maggie begged Abby. For a moment, the two women's eyes met. Maggie detected a pitiful look of loss. That's me now, she thought, as the tall woman hurried from the room.

Energized, Maggie lurched toward the door.

Hickox stepped in and swatted her with the back of his hand. She crumpled to the floor.

"What are you doing with my baby?" screamed Maggie, holding her face. "Who are you?" She forced herself to her feet and stumbled toward him.

Hickox grabbed her by the throat and threw her to the bed.

Maggie rose, still reaching for the lost babe. Hickox shut the solid wood door with a bang and turned the lock. She tried to wrench it open, her anguished cries reverberating off the walls. After pounding until her hands were bloody and bruised, she finally moved back to the bed and curled up with her emptiness. Hours passed. She slept fitfully, awakening with a terrible certainty that something was missing. The single image of Elymas's little face as he looked up at her filled her mind. She sobbed until she again fell into unconsciousness.

Time passed, and during her waking hours she knew that somewhere in the great big world on the other side of the wall was her
baby with that man and woman. How could they know what an infant
needs? She touched her aching chest. Wetness. Yellow stains marked her
night shift. Her breasts swelled with milk, but she had no tiny babe to
suckle. Please, God, she prayed, bring him back.

The door opened. Filled with hope, she struggled to her feet and
saw Augustin. He must have the baby with him, she thought, rushing
toward him.

"Give him to me," she said. "I need to feed him."

"The infant is gone," he said, his voice harsh, but his eyes appealing
to her as if he were still a boy seeking her approval.

"Dead?" she wept. That devil must have murdered the poor little
child.

"Forget him if you can," said Augustin, straining to keep his voice
from cracking. "It will be easier if you forget."

"How?" she screamed. "You think you can just forget? He's *your*
son too!"

Augustin looked stricken.

She shoved past him. "Elymas! I'm coming."

Augustin followed her down the hallway, finally grabbing her
around the waist. She fought, arms swinging wildly. They fell to the
floor. A wave of frustration pressed her down. Her strength melted
away.

"He's gone," said Augustin, desperately. "But you've been saved.
Father agreed to let you come home."

"*You* did that?" sobbed Maggie, pushing herself up to her elbows.
He nodded. "You stupid, stupid man. It's all ruined. If you let me go,
let me be with my baby, maybe I coulda thought kindly about you . . .
But now?"

"Hit me," he said.

Maggie didn't move.

"I'm sorry," he murmured. "There was no other way for you to
come home."

She looked at him with hard eyes. "You do that for me, or for you?"

On the road out of Virginia, Thomas Galway did all the driving. Maggie sat alone on one bench of the carriage, Augustin across from her. She kept waiting for a chance to run and find Elymas, but her weakened body betrayed her. Sick of looking at Augustin's contrite face, she curled up under a blanket, her head covered. He tried to talk with her, occasionally pulling down the blanket, but she only looked away, too dead inside to even fight.

Thomas, apparently disgusted by his son's simpering attitude, detoured to New York City. There, Augustin was instructed to "learn the banking trade," and was left to make his way in the world.

When she was back in Utica, she tried to forget the boy, telling herself he was dead, pushing any thought of him out of her mind. At first, she forced herself to forget the image of the tiny baby at her breast, a thousand times a day. Then, for a time, she focused on punishing Augustin's father. As long as she felt constant pain, he would too. Sometimes she planted a thorn in his shoe or a burr in his clothing. When he complained, she rejoiced. She spent time carefully choosing river pebbles to secrete under his sheets in the exact spots where his bad hip rested. Once, when he was recovering from a nasty gash on his hand, she boiled his bandages in peppercorns, inflaming the wound. Each time she saw his reaction, her strength grew.

Five years later, Thomas Galway finally died, not of anything she did, she was almost certain. She let herself celebrate. Anytime she felt melancholy, she summoned the vision of his gray and lifeless corpse. Augustin, now a wealthy man, returned to Utica to bury his father. With him was his beautiful new bride, Emma.

After the pair moved into the house, it was awkward for both Maggie and Augustin. But they seemed to grow accustomed to seeing each other again. The little lost boy was never mentioned. Emma made a special effort to be a benevolent slaveholder and though she never knew about the child, her bright presence did much to mend the rift between Maggie and Augustin.

Some time after that, Maggie went a full day without remembering Elymas. When had that happened, exactly? She never forgot the baby who had looked at her with such seriousness, but she rarely allowed herself to revisit that pain.

Now back in her own bedroom, she looked at Joe—her grandson— and the woman who was carrying her second grandchild. Some part of

Elymas had been returned to her. The miracle she had hardly allowed herself to pray for had come to pass. Everything had now changed. She decided to wait just a little while before she told anyone, giving the information time to settle.

CHAPTER THIRTY

THE UNEXPECTED PASSENGER in the coach that the wealthy New York silk merchant and ardent abolitionist Lewis Tappan had hired to drive his party from Albany to Utica, was a short, powerfully built, bright man with a wide-open face and a deep indent between his brows, as if his mother had laid her thumb against him while he grew. He wore a suit, borrowed from Mr. Ruggles, who sat next to him. Though the outfit was of a handsome cut, it pulled at his shoulders and sagged at the knees. His head had been freshly shaved, his rusty hair left behind in New York City. A passerby would see a prosperous Negro with a limp and an unsightly scar at the corner of his mouth. The passenger felt a lightness of heart that had been absent from his last months. He was alive, no longer in chains, riding in a fine coach, among powerful friends, and heading for the city where, according to Mr. Ruggles, his wife and son said they would be waiting for him—if the Great Lord had allowed them to get that far.

Elymas had last glimpsed his family from the chilly ground in the woods outside Hightstown, New Jersey. He thought back to that terrible moment. The previous few days of travel had gone well, until they arrived in Allentown, where they couldn't find their contact. The ladies in Bordentown had said that there was supposed to be a barn with an oil lamp in the window. They passed by a number of barns in the small hamlet, but they were all dark and shut up tight. Finally, with the birds beginning their morning chatter and the sky starting to lighten, they decided to rest behind a huge gristmill. The water from the millstream flooded over the stones in the creek bed. The back of the building looked quiet enough.

"You sit a bit," Elymas said to Imari.

"We gotta stick together," she said.

Elymas tried to calm himself. Sometimes it felt like she wouldn't let him protect her. Besides, she'd been moving very slowly the last few hours.

"Look," he said, trying to keep his voice even, "there gotta be someplace right around here where we can bed down for a few hours. Me and Joe will find it out. We gonna be all right."

He grabbed her hand and helped her sink to the ground. He could see the irritation on her face.

"You watch yourselves," she said.

He nodded, realizing she might be mad at herself for being at the end of her strength. Who wouldn't be tired? he thought.

He and the boy moved away, their feet stirring fallen leaves. "Gonna have to be outside today," said Elymas.

"Again?" moaned Joe.

Elymas felt himself getting angry. Wasn't all this running and hiding for Joe's own future? He's most a why we left. He oughta know at least that much. Imari ain't the only one who's tired, he thought. My own cot in the back of the blacksmith shop would feel pretty good about now. But here we are, seeking safety in the land a tricks. That Joe had let himself be trapped by Master Arnold—he shoulda been smarter than that, shoulda listened to me more, obeyed, not let himself be fooled. Running was the only way out. Master Arnold made sure a that. Elymas clamped his jaw shut, teeth pressed together. So what did the boy have to complain about? The rhythm of Joe's steps, about one and a half strides for each of his own, reminded him that his son was just too young to understand. Living on a plantation was normal for the boy. But he should know that they were running *to* a free life. A place where a man might feel like a man and where a woman was your own, not subject to a master's desires. Besides, all the boy's training in the blacksmith shop was going to be put to use soon. When we settle in Canada, I'll find a job and start saving and open up my own place. Me and Joe will work side by side and we'll be getting more than the leavings off Master's table. It'll be for us.

He was just about to reach out and cuff Joe's shoulder for complaining when, arms flailing, he tumbled into a divot in the land. Unhurt, he realized that the depression was just deep enough to shield them from view.

"You all right, Poppa?" asked Joe, alarmed.

"Yeah. Kick a bunch a them leaves in here while I get your momma. We gonna make us a nice bed and get some sleep."

Elymas soon returned with Imari. After a few disappointed glances, she allowed herself to be helped to the ground. Elymas covered her and Joe with leaves. Satisfied, he sat, pulling the leaves over himself until he could stretch out.

The sun rose and warmed them under their leafy blanket. Elymas drifted off to sleep, only to be woken when someone kicked his leg. He bolted upright and got on his feet fast. Looking at him was an angular black boy dressed in layers of torn clothing.

"My daddy watching for you," said the boy. "So's you best come with me."

"You?" Elymas said.

"Who told you to look for us?" asked Imari, sitting up.

"My daddy."

"Who told him?" she said.

Elymas pulled Imari to her feet. "You think this all right?"

"Why he out looking?" she whispered.

"My daddy say you was suppose to get here last night. Had a lantern in the barn over yonder and everything. So, just come on."

Joe was now up, looking tired and rubbing his eyes.

Imari's wariness infected Elymas with a tightness in his stomach. They'd been lost before, or had taken extra time to get to their next contact, but nobody ever came out searching. He leaned close to his wife's ear. "What choice we got?"

"Daddy say you gotta get hid away. He ain't gonna be there all day."

Imari looked at him. "I don't know."

"Let's go," said Elymas, deciding.

"I guess so," said Imari, and they followed as the child led them to a falling-down barn that they had not noticed before. The back quarter of the building was scorched from a fire and the wall had collapsed onto itself. The smell of burned wood filled the air. Inside they saw a good-sized wagon hooked up to a mule whose flanks were striped by its protruding ribs. Two block-and-tackle systems hung from the ceiling with barrels dangling from them. Elymas figured that the father, an older man with white hair, a long face, and long fingers, must do some sort of work out of the place.

"I got me a hidey-hole in this here wagon," the man bragged. "I'm gonna ride you to Hightstown."

"Where you want us to sleep?" asked Imari, looking around.

"You ain't sleeping, we going now," the man said.

"In the daylight?" asked Elymas.

"They's never looking on a bright day," said the man with pride. "You goes creeping around at night? Well, then the questions come. But daylight? Smooth as horsehide."

"But your boy here said we gotta get hid," said Elymas. "And them church ladies in Bordentown told us go right on past Hightstown, they say it ain't too safe around those parts on account a that big farm working a lot a hands, free and slave. They say to see the lady who runs the Cranbury Inn, next town over."

"Them old ladies don't know how things is over this way," said the man. "Look, we gonna hide you right here." He pointed to the wagon.

Again, Imari and Elymas pulled together to talk.

"I'm so tired, I can't think. Feeling every step today," she said, easing herself down on the back of the wagon and leaning into his chest.

He plucked a piece of dry oak leaf out of her hair and looked at its shiny brown side. He thought about the plantation and all the thousands of tobacco leaves that Momma Abby had tended and nurtured and dried with care, losing days of sleep at curing time. Had the Barnwells ever thanked her for that? No use getting mad now. Leave all them folks to the devil.

The long-faced man hopped into the wagon and raised a panel over the hidey-hole. "Alls you gots to do is lay back and I put this plank over you. Nice as nice. I covers you over with that there hay," he said, pointing to a pile near the door. "Maybe you even gets some sleep. Leave it to me." He smiled, but his face seemed unaccustomed to the gesture, barely allowing warmth into it. "Outside ain't safe," he said sternly. "Go this way or go that way." He indicated the door. "I ain't got time for no argument."

Elymas looked at Imari and thought of all the miles they'd come. He decided and brought his face down to Imari's belly. "We riding," he said to the baby.

Imari giggled, "Yeah, riding."

They lay down in the bed of the wagon, Joe between them. Just as the man was about to put the board down, Imari yelled for him to stop.

"Keep your woman quiet," said the man, the long indent between his nose and his lip deepening as he lowered the hidey-hole door.

Elymas heard the squeak of the pulleys, and through a crack he saw a barrel flying down, settling on top of them. He pounded on the wood yelling, "That ain't no hay!" He pushed the cover. It wouldn't budge. The second barrel also dropped on top. "Let us out!"

"Shut up," hissed the man. "You want us all to get caught?"

Elymas got quiet. He draped his arm over Joe, the odd angle twisting his elbow, and found Imari's hand.

The wagon started to move, bouncing up and down as it cleared the barn's threshold. There was no way to tell exactly where they were heading. Inside the hidey-hole, it got hot and Elymas felt himself falling asleep. He woke to a mournful bellow, like an unmilked cow stuck out in the field. Off to the left, there came another long tone. It was a horn, sharper than the first. They were joined by a third that brought to mind Gabriel's horn marking Judgment Day.

Elymas heard the man's son ask, "What that?"

"Trouble," the old man said. He must have slapped the reins on the mule because the cart sped up.

Elymas squeezed Imari's hand. "We best be ready to run," he said, as the road got rougher and they bounced in their hidey-hole.

The wagon turned hard to the left and Joe was thrown to his side. One of the barrels tipped and rolled off the wagon, thudding when it hit the ground. Elymas helped Joe flip onto his stomach and told him to push the panel up with his back. Even with his father's help it would not budge. The wagon tilted in what must have been a rut and all three tried to throw off the cover. The remaining barrel swayed. Another bump sent it rolling off the wagon. Elymas tossed off the hidey-hole door.

The boy yelled, "Poppa, they's getting out!"

The man pulled out his musket, but before he could fire, Elymas sprang forward, grabbed the gun, and threw him off the wagon. The boy jumped and Elymas and Joe took over the driver's seat while Imari clung to the side.

Ahead, Hickox and Colby stood with their long guns ready. Elymas pulled the mule half off the road. This gave them cover as they ran back and helped Imari off the wagon.

"Joe, grab that musket," said Elymas. "Follow me." The three started to run as the balls of shot whistled over their heads. Just then the horns started up again. All three came from close by. Elymas bent and picked up Imari and ran toward the sound. Joe followed.

The slave catchers took off after them. Before they could get too close, several black men appeared with pistols and muskets. They waved the fugitives past before crouching behind some trees, weapons drawn. A volley of shot was followed by shouts. The family ran until they spotted a gray house in a clearing. At an upper window, Elymas saw a bone-thin woman beckoning them. Shots boomed again and they rushed into the house. Once inside, they saw weapons secreted near each window. The occupants were ready for a siege.

A sweet-faced girl, with cheeks dotted by dark freckles, asked if they had been with the long-faced man. "We suspect him of betraying runaways, but we ain't been sure till now," she said.

Three of the armed men ran into the house and barred the door with a rough-split log. "We didn't hit nobody," said one. "But that shooting gonna draw more white folks—and they guns."

Elymas believed Hickox couldn't want them dead. What good would that do him? No money unless he had some flesh to sell. He chanced a look outside and saw the slaver, a dozen yards off, gathering with several white men.

The bone-thin gal called down the stairs, "Send up Sandy."

From the corner, a wrinkled woman rose from a chair. She bore the marks of extreme age: thin hair, raisiny skin, and a jaw no longer holding teeth. Her back curled like a shepherd's hook. She climbed the stairs with determined and deliberate steps. Elymas heard her voice crack as she called to the whites gathered at the fringes of the clearing.

"Who's out there?" she demanded. "Why you sneaking around my house?" She kept talking and talking, never giving them a chance to answer. "If you come near, I'm gonna shoot you." She sent one musket blast into the air to show that she was serious.

"Come on, Sandy!" yelled one of the whites. "We don't want trouble, but you got some bad folks in there!"

A man whispered to Elymas that the whites all knew her because she'd been mammy to many of them, so they might not shoot her.

Out the window, the old woman denied that anyone was in the house, but declared that they must stay out too.

Elymas, Imari, and Joe joined the others to make plans for escape. The group had been preparing and had dug a tunnel leading from the basement to the woods. Some of their friends who were still outside waited for a signal to start making noise and draw the whites away. Anybody who was a slave on the run would get out and move in the opposite direction. In total, five people waited in the cellar for the signal. A bell clanged and the group was told go, so they went. The tunnel, rough and uneven, wasn't tall enough to stand upright. You had to crawl if you were tall, but Imari and Joe, still carrying the musket, moved through it bent over. Elymas scampered on all fours like a spider, following the sounds of the two men ahead of him. When they reached the far end, the three men pushed open the trapdoor and emerged just beyond the edge of the woods. Once outside, Elymas turned and saw smoke coming from the road. He guessed that their defenders must have set the long-faced man's wagon on fire.

The white locals dashed toward the smoke. But Hickox and Colby spotted the ruse and instead ran toward Elymas and his family.

The other fugitives took off fast. Elymas grabbed Imari's hand and started to run, but he could see that she wouldn't be able to keep up. To carry her meant that they both might get caught. With only a quick look at his wife's worried face, he dropped her hand and reversed course, and ran in Hickox's direction. Imari screamed at him to stop. Hickox charged toward Elymas, who changed his path again. He thought that he was outrunning the slaver, when something grabbed his legs, pitching him to the ground and knocking the air straight out of his body. Around his ankles was a set of weighted ropes. As he clawed at them, the slave catcher pounced, crushing him into the dirt.

When he strained and looked over his back, he saw Imari struggling with Colby, the long-faced man's musket between them. Joe slammed the white man from behind. Imari had the gun and swung it by the barrel. The solid hardwood handle proved as good a weapon as gunpowder. Colby went down. That his wife and son hesitated and had not run immediately brought panic to Elymas's breast. He was still shouting

"Run!" when Hickox kicked him hard in the side. A dark cloud of pain blinded him.

That afternoon, after Elymas had been secured in leg chains, the slaver padlocked him to a buckboard next to the shrouded body of Colby. The wrappings on the corpse were stained brown at the head. On the road, he watched Colby bounce with each jolt. More than once he had to push the dead man away with his feet. Late that night, they arrived in Philadelphia by the post road. The slaver told him that a letter had been dispatched summoning Master Arnold to Baltimore.

The next day, Elymas and his captor got to Maryland. He spent two nights in the dingy cellar of the Admiral Fell Inn, shackled to the wall. A terrified white maid brought his meals, placing the plate on the dirt floor and pushing it within his reach with a long stick kept near the stairs for that purpose. At night, the rats came foraging and he feared he might become their meal. His entreaties to the girl for even a bit of kindling to fight them off went unheeded. He was alone in the gloom with time to contemplate all that had gone wrong. Hickox must have been on their heels and anticipated their route. Money most likely bought the betrayal by the long-faced man and his skinny son. He and Imari had put aside their misgivings, but even if they had rejected the man's help, the outcome might have been the same. At least neither his wife nor son were here in the dampness with him. They still got a chance, he thought. He turned his mind to survival and to him that meant running again.

Before the third night, Master Arnold had arrived and was brought by the slave catcher to the basement to inspect the captive.

Barnwell looked at him like he had never seen him before. "How could you?" he asked Elymas. "My father was good to you. Gave you the best job on the plantation. Wasn't that enough for you?"

At first Elymas tried to tamp down the fury that burned up his throat. He knew he should agree and hope that the man might be less guarded, but some hint of fear quavered in his master's eye. Without warning, he imagined this man taking everything—wife, son, the life he wanted to build—and destroying it. This little man had power, and had used it. The thought disgusted him. Master Arnold wasn't smart or strong. More like a turd to be scraped off the bottom of your shoe.

"You laid with my wife," said Elymas, the rage suddenly uncontrollable. "I still be a man."

Barnwell flinched. Hickox jammed the butt of his gun against the edge of Elymas's mouth, tearing open his lip.

"Now we need not bother with any more of his complaints," said Hickox, as the captive writhed in pain. "I know you want him to go back to work, but he didn't simply run off one night. A good deal of planning was involved."

"I have lost too much time and money hiring out his work," said Barnwell. "We need him at least through the harvest."

"I recommend that he be sold right here in Baltimore. I know a man, Woolfolk. He'll get you the highest price. Buy yourself a new man. One who is grateful for the trust placed in him." He put his hand on Barnwell's shoulder. "Now, about the female and boy."

"What about them?"

"So far, great expense has been incurred recovering them. Mr. Colby, of course, paid the ultimate price. As I indicated in my letter, it was the bitch who delivered the fatal strike. Cut your losses. Sell her and the boy to me and be done with it."

Elymas, mute after the blow, shot to his feet and strained against the limit of his chains. Hickox pulled Barnwell away and came at Elymas from the side, whipping him with his riding crop, delivering five stinging blows. Elymas dropped to one knee. He breathed hard, distracting himself from the explosive pain by vowing to remember this moment and find some way to pay the slaver back.

Hickox turned on Barnwell. "She is a murderer now. She isn't fit for anything but hanging. Keep the reward money, sign them over to me, and they shall never trouble you again."

The deal was struck. Barnwell paid Hickox's expenses, including the price for Colby's body to be returned to his mother.

Throughout the journey back to the plantation, Elymas kept his mind on one thing—that if Hickox made Barnwell an offer, Imari and Joe were still alive and running. That fact filled his heart with a fluttery lightness, until a vision of Imari in Hickox's clutches invaded his mind. The slaver seemed angry enough to hang her himself. Elymas began to finalize his plan.

Inside the blacksmith shop, he resumed the work he did before the

escape, except now both his ankles were shackled by long chains. One
of the armed local night patrollers watched him. At once, he set to repairing tools and getting the chores finished. All the while, he stoked the
furnace and kept a crucible of molten iron red-hot and ready to pour.

The patroller observed this activity with much diligence and without comment. However, after several hours, and having been out the
previous night at his normal work, the heat in the building began to
erode his alertness. Elymas noticed and stopped pounding iron, instead
rubbing the file up and down along the edges of tools, placing each one
silently on the tall table nearest the forge. He pumped the bellows and
carried his chains, lest their clinking disturb the man's light slumber.

After a while, snores emanated from the guard. Elymas drew close
to the fire, placing his chains neatly on the floor, links near his ankles
lined up in parallel. He grabbed the crucible with long-handled tongs
and poured the molten metal onto the chains. Heat transferred from
one to the other and up the links to the cuff around his ankle, burning
him. He held his breath and gritted his teeth. The chain directly under
the stream of red-hot iron weakened until he was able to simply yank
the bonds apart. The remaining chain was hot, but he could not risk
cooling it and raising a spurt of steam. In his gloved hands, he grabbed
the hot chains and ran for the river, careful to avoid the tobacco fields
and the overseer who watched the slaves in the darkening day. At the
river, he found one of the leftover logs from the original raft. He pushed
himself out into the current, the cold water soothing the blisters on his
ankles and the whip marks on his ribs.

In that way, he rode down the river, through the patch of rapids
that had previously torn their raft apart, and began again his journey
toward Utica.

A guffaw of laughter brought Elymas back into the present. Ruggles,
Tappan, and a black grocer named James W. Higgins were talking an-
imatedly about the upcoming abolition convention, but Elymas just
looked out the window, occasionally touching the scar on the corner
of his mouth, and nursing the belief that he was heading toward his
family.

CHAPTER THIRTY-ONE

IT WAS LATE IN THE DAY and the sky outside Maggie's window melted from deep purple to black. Joe slumbered on the floor in the corner, his feet resting on a three-legged wooden milking stool. Imari lay surrounded by pillows, in the same place on Maggie's bed that she had occupied for days. Imari was certain that the baby's time was approaching, but had deliberately hid that fact because she knew that the cook watched her for any signs of illness or want. Besides, the pains were neither regular nor intense.

"You got a name for the baby?" asked Maggie.

"It ain't decided," said Imari. She shifted her position on the bed to relieve the strain on her lower back. She let her mind stray to Elymas. They should be naming the baby together. That would never happen now. But the idea that he would catch up had been etched on her heart. It was hard to give up. She never should have run off after killing Colby. I shoulda beat in Hickox's head—or shot him.

"You best decide soon," said Maggie.

"It sorta depend on what the baby look like."

"What do you mean?"

"Will it look like Elymas? Or," she whispered, "like Master Arnold?" She met Maggie's surprised expression. "I don't know."

Maggie clucked her tongue and shook her head. "The new master too?"

"Like he can't stop himself, trying to be the master with his daddy's ghost flying over his head." She shuddered and then took a deep breath. "Missus Bea, she named Joe. I want to call him Elymas. But she say no. I brung him to her and she looks into his eyes and claims they's like saint's eyes. He a quiet baby, so she gets to thinking about which saint has the most patience. Well, that gotta be Joseph. Here, his wife giving birth to a boy who ain't his own and he don't care about it, but he gonna love baby Jesus anyway. That sound like a saint to me. She says that they ain't no other name for him but Joey."

"I hope he don't turn out to be no saint," said Maggie. "Saints, they gotta be good all the time, and who wants that?"

"You got a little bit a that devil in you," said Imari, smiling. But then the merriment dropped from her face. She lowered her voice. "Master Arnold, he got something bad in him. He like a cat that don't know if he want in or out, but he pretty sure about me being his territory. After I know the baby coming, I tried to stop him when he come knocking on Missus Bea's door with some excuse. She knew what he want too, told me to quote the seventh commandment, *Thou shalt not commit adultery*. That don't work with no man. I can't have him on me 'cause a being slippery. I told him he gonna hurt the baby. Well, now he gotta have me more. He don't care who know it. More than anything, it be like he mad at me."

"All that musta burned up Elymas's heart," said Maggie.

"Elymas be mad. He take some of it out on the iron. But Elymas burns. At the end, if we don't go, his temper might get him killed, is what."

"What set you all off?"

Imari thought for a moment, gauging Maggie. She lowered her voice, unsure if Joe was actually asleep. "We been talking about running and making some plans, but it wasn't like it had to be now. We be looking for a chance, but this here baby mean we gotta wait. I be working in Missus Bea's room, cleaning her little thingums while she nap. I hear Master Arnold in his daddy's office, talking with Hickox about how he gotta sell some of us right after the tobacco comes in. But that makes Elymas go? No. He don't believe it gonna touch him. We safe, he says. But how safe can we be if Master Arnold's daddy sold my Jimmy, his own son?" She tapped her heart softly.

Maggie shifted as if suddenly uncomfortable.

"You all right?" asked Imari.

"Now you're gonna take care a me too?" said Maggie. "Go on about Master Arnold."

"Nothing matters to them white men when they got they needs.

Don't care who gets they heart ripped out. At the very end of July, Master Arnold, he corner me outside Missus Bea's and pull me into his daddy's room. He pushing and pulling me to the office and he shove me on the rug. I turn over and I yell no at him. He goes stiff. Ain't never heard that word from a slave. On my knees, I beg and pretend like I know it's his own boy I carry. He ain't got no boys, so I figure that maybe he gonna want this one." Imari started to cry. "He don't say nothing. He turns to stone. Instead a yelling, he swings his leg back like he gonna kick the baby, but I scream like I never done and roll away. Suddenly, Missus Bea, she hears me, I guess. She busts in and whacks him right across the head and it looks like he gonna hit his own mother right back. Instead, he walks out. I think Missus Bea save me. Everything over."

Maggie reached out and grabbed Imari's hand. "What'd he go do?"

Imari pulled her close. "He take it out on poor Joe," she whispered. She waved Maggie closer and spoke into her ear: "He done to him what he wanted to do to me."

Joe's feet twitched, as if they knew what was being discussed. But the sleep that embraced him was as deep and muddy as the Potomac after a heavy rain. More than once he had blinked open his eyes only to have the tentacles of his dream push his lids down again.

He sat cross-legged on the bottom of the river with a large stone resting in his lap to keep him from floating away. The water cleared and he noticed the sun's shimmering light. All manner of fish and plants drifted past. Beside him, two dark tree trunks stood upright, and when he looked up, he saw that their leaves vibrated in the current. He realized that he no longer needed to hold his breath and began taking in water. He wanted to swim, but the stone trapped him. Again, he looked up. The tree branches swayed wildly. The trunks themselves began to bend and combine, driven lower by the violent storm. He fought with the rock. It became huge and he was soon dwarfed by it. The trees shook and swayed, churning up the water. At their base, he noticed the roots had transformed into paws. It was the bear, its pelt so black that it absorbed the sunlight. It opened its tan muzzle, revealing the sharp peaks of its white teeth and a cavernous pink mouth. It bent down, sharp claws tearing through the thick water, reaching for him. He screamed as its front paws tightened around his body and its bulk pushed him down into the muck at the bottom of the river.

When he sat up, suddenly awake, he was confronted by the startled faces of his mother and Maggie.

CHAPTER THIRTY-TWO

IN THE YELLOW CANDLELIGHT, clothed in her dressing gown, Helen stopped at her washstand, poured cold water into the basin, and brought some of it to her face in cupped hands. She tried to piece together the past hours . . . or days? She wasn't certain, but clearly remembered Maggie helping her get out of the bed and . . . had she somehow been in Dr. McCooke's bedroom? She pictured him looming above her, but her dreams had been so wild and peculiar that she wondered what was real.

A twinge of pain troubled her abdomen. Without warning, the memories filled her: the collapse in the library, McCooke's hands on her as she fought, and the draft of brandy and opium he had forced her to drink.

Each snippet came together until she imagined a tiny infant slipping through her fingers. Sadness bore down on her. The poor little babe never took a breath of air or felt sunlight on its face, she thought. There would be no warm cooing baby to hold and protect—only terrible emptiness. She sobbed. Was she to have nothing to love in this world? Surely the Lord was harsh.

In the mirror, her irises stood out against the redness of her eyes, still sharp in their brown-black luster. Her face was pale and drawn— somehow changed, more mature, she thought as she looked at herself from different angles. What did others see? A girl? A wife? A mother-to-be? Nothing seemed to fit anymore. Sighing, she patted herself dry with a cotton cloth and pressed back a few strands of hair. Without thinking, she brought her index fingers to her widow's peak and ran them along the hairline, circling her face. The gesture was a favorite of her mother's as she sang, *"My heart, my heart, my heart belongs to Hel-en."* To whom would *she* sing silly songs? A tear broke away from the corner of her eye and streaked across her skin to her lips. Salt. Her mother called the eyes God's ocean. *"Blue, green, gray, or dark brown, like you and your father, it does not matter. The salt is the proof."*

If only she could still run to her and hold her and ask her to please make sense of this life. A parade of sudden change had destroyed every illusion she'd held.

Outside, in the dark beyond her window, a branch snapped. Searing anger flared. It must be those awful slave catchers sneaking around and looking for Imari and Joe. The nearest object to her hand was a sizable bottle of eau de toilette that Augustin had purchased in New York over her objections. She rushed to the window, shoved back the curtain, pushed up the sash, and threw the bottle at a form below.

"Ow!" someone cried, and the overpowering odor of lilac, lavender, and geranium wafted up from the ground.

"You've been told—stay away," Helen hissed at the intruder.

"I'll withdraw, of course," came the distressed whisper of a male voice.

"Wait," Helen said as she fetched the candle and leaned out the window. "Who's that?" The light flickered down on Pryce.

"Your humble and obedient servant."

"Please forgive me," she whispered, a smile breaking on her lips. "I took you for one of those awful slave catchers. But why are you here?" She placed the candle on a table near the window and rested her hip on the sill. A long silence came from below. Pryce's shadow moved and leaves stirred. "You still there?" she whispered into the darkness.

Evergreen fronds brushed the side of the house and she understood that he was moving up the trunk of the pine tree, branch by branch.

Her heart pounded and she closed her eyes, remembering that when she had been no more than seven years old, she had climbed high up in a similar tree in the yard of her father's blacksmith shop. A gust of air had gently set the tree to swaying. Fear turned her body cold. But as she held on, she found that she liked the back-and-forth motion. Close by, she saw the blue-black strip of the Mohawk River as it meandered through the green valley. Buildings clustered around the canal. Beyond, the hills looked like sleeping cats, the humps of their backs resting easily against the sharp blue sky. She vowed to go up each day so that she might learn what people were doing. When she came down, her father said nothing about it and sent her home. The next day all the low branches of the evergreen had been sawed off. The trunk was bare far above her reach.

She opened her eyes. Pryce was near to her now. Her skin warmed. This was no girlish blush.

"You must go," she whispered.

"But I don't want to," he said. "You intrigue me."

"I?" she said, a hint of breathless eagerness in her voice. "I'm as plain as paper." In the murky light, Pryce inched toward her, steadying himself with nearby branches. The limb began to bend. "Careful," she whispered, her heartbeat quickening.

"Today I discovered that I'm bold."

"Don't come near," she said, bending toward him.

"You're a universe," he said as he extended his hand. "Please."

She stood on the tips of her toes, leaning on the window frame, one hand holding on, the other reaching, their fingers inches apart. He angled forward and for the very first time his skin touched hers. He slipped something flat and hard between her index and middle fingers. A breath caught in her throat.

She heard a crack. He dropped.

"Mr. Anwell!" she gasped, lunging toward him as if she might catch him, almost losing her balance.

He dangled from the limb by one arm, his feet pedaling the air. Helen dropped his token on the floor and covered her mouth, stifling a scream. He brought his free hand up and grasped the branch, beginning, hand over hand, to move closer to the house. Swinging his legs, he managed to rest his feet on the top of the first-floor window frame. Helen reached out and together they strained until he scrambled into her room and stood before her.

Each gripped the forearms of the other and in the flickering light of the candle, their eyes locked. Like a sigh of surrender, they came together, lips meeting. Helen, suddenly aflame, leaned into his body. Tears spilled down her face. To feel the sweet arms of affection around her. She clung to his thin strong frame. This is what love should be—two alike people, she thought. He kissed her moist cheeks.

"I love you," he said.

"I . . . I . . ." The words would not come. A vision of Augustin stifled her. The intensity of her desire for Pryce was nothing like what she'd experienced in all her nights with her husband. "This is wrong," she moaned, still holding him, her head bent back. "I am a sinner."

"I wanted to return after we hid the slaves," whispered Pryce. "But Stewart said I'd expose everyone to danger." He held her face and covered it with small kisses. "This can't be wrong."

"God watches us," she said, and pushed him away. But the moment his arms slackened, disappointment pulled down his features, and she rushed forward, embracing him again. His kisses ran up her neck to her ear. She explored his hair and the contours of his face. Through her thin robe, the coarse wool of his overcoat brushed against her uncorseted body. His hands squeezed her, fingers pressing into the softness around her waist. She thought again about stopping him, but decided—not yet. It was as if his touch warmed her whole being. In his arms, the pain in her loins transformed into an erotic ache. As her heat grew, the idea of not feeling this, of not following her desire, seemed impossible. Even though she knew that she should resist, she would not stop. Powerful need strummed her body.

Scared that she might cry out, she pulled back, trying to breathe. Their eyes met and she burst into sobs. The thought of lying with Augustin again sickened her. To have one's longing for love—fulfilled, yet a *mortal sin*. Did these kisses mean she was forever damned? There could be no confession to Father Quarters. Might he not tell Augustin that his wife was an adulteress? She would be cast out of the house, and deservedly so. Miss Manahan would not take her back—not after this.

"Don't cry," said Pryce, pressing her hand to his lips. "I'm sorry. I was a beast."

"Leave," she said, her voice thick with tears.

"Of course." He went to the window. As he sat on the sill, he looked back at her. "I love you—I want to be with you no matter what happens."

She ran to him and they kissed once again. "Go. Don't come back." Turning away, she wept into her hands.

He touched her arm. "I can't promise." Grabbing an evergreen branch, he swung to the ground, taking several limbs with him.

She watched him from the window, saw him rise unharmed. The memory of his touch made her whole body tingle. A little sparkle on the floor caught her eye. It was his gift, a small, thin river stone—smooth, dark gray, and flecked with bright bits of mica. Though it had once been circular, a divot had been chipped out of the edge so that it resembled a small heart.

How sentimental, she thought. She drew the present to her breast. A silly, boyish gift. Her chest swelled, brimming with feeling, breaking and mending, because she knew that before her marriage, love with him could have been possible. But now . . . she could not afford an illusion such as that.

In bed as she tried to sleep, the memory of Pryce drifted round and round. Augustin might have been within his rights to kill him like a raccoon in a tree, she thought, smiling. Miss Manahan would call him a demon leading her to hell. Climbing the evergreen had been the brashest, most daring thing any man had ever done for her. But it was she who had pulled him into her room, she who had almost lost herself. The demon resided in her own breast. Her place in hell might already be set. Disgrace would descend upon the house. It might be better to throw herself off the roof than to be found out. Augustin would believe it was because of the baby. At least she would leave this troubled world.

She rolled over and saw one of the little nightgowns lying flat on her table. Poor Imari and her unborn babe. She owed them something, Joe too. Killing herself instead of giving them help? It would be piling one unpardonable sin upon the last. Even if her immorality meant that she was forever tainted, at least she would be true to them. Finally resolved to check on them, she threw off her bedsheets and dressed in her old school frock.

No sound could be heard in the house, so she pushed her door open just enough to look across the hallway. The doctor's chamber stood empty. She peeked into the room. He was gone.

How had Augustin allowed that cancer under his roof? Wasn't part of the wedding contract that the husband had to provide a safe place for his family? He had time enough for drinking. Though it might sound cruel, perhaps she was better off without a baby. She had to think about what to do.

A new idea began to take shape. If a slave could leave her master, might not a wife do the same? What if this was not the place where she would be spending the rest of her life? Couldn't she just follow Pryce, and then run? The weight of this new awareness made her light-headed and she sat at the top of the elegant staircase, realizing that her life did not have to be this way.

If she too ran, any disgrace might be left behind in Utica. Why, there was a whole frontier to occupy. Her uncle had simply left on a packet boat. She was married because she had agreed to it and sworn in front of Father Quarters. That, and a wedding certificate, combined with the belief that she had no other choice, seemed like the only thing binding her to this place. And Pryce appeared ready to hazard any risk. But if she ran away with him, there was her soul to be considered. Surely the sin of desertion of her husband for another man would be met with God's vengeance.

She thought once again of Augustin. If she stayed and remained a good wife—if she never saw Pryce again—might she not atone? She did not want to hurt her husband. If he were left alone, he might crumble. In the weeks before their engagement and wedding he had seemed so melancholy. And though he was often short with her, it made him happy to instruct her. During the honeymoon, he clearly wanted to make her into a fine lady of whom he could be proud. He was not an affectionate man, but from all he had said about the departed Mrs. Galway, it was clear that there had been true tenderness. What did she owe him?

Miss Manahan had spoken about love growing over time, emphasizing the joys of children fusing the bonds between husband and wife. But the baby was gone and she knew now what real love felt like. Could it be that God had put a choice before her? It felt much like the serpent's temptation.

But oh, the thrill of the idea. The adventure of leaving and leaping into a life of love and purpose. It was what she had imagined when she pined away her days at school. There would not be dogs on her heels or slave catchers chasing her with chains. Imari had braved it all for her baby and her freedom. What would Helen do for hers?

A sound disturbed her contemplation. Straightening, she tried to determine from which direction it came. The noise started again. Someone was creeping slowly up the servants' staircase. Helen's heart began to beat furiously. In the pale light of the passageway she saw a crouching form at the threshold.

"Missus?" said Joe. "Miss Maggie sent me up. She say it time."

"I'll come," said Helen, giddy with relief. If a boy coming up the back stairs of her own house could produce such fright—could she be brave enough to embark on an entirely new life?

She passed the kitchen stove and felt heat radiating from the iron box. A cauldron of water simmered on the top. The bedroom door was open.

Imari rocked on the bed, a rolled white cloth pinched between her teeth. She bit down on it, pulling her eyes shut and crinkling her nose, as an intense labor pain shook her frame. Her muffled voice rose above the night's stillness. Maggie held her hand. The time had come. Visions of her mother's failed delivery filled Helen's head. She felt as if the air had gotten thin and couldn't spend another minute in that room. As she turned, about to run back to her chamber, Maggie called to her.

"We need more linens. Go upstairs and get some fresh sheets and bathing cloths."

Grateful for the task, Helen ran back up to the hallway closet and pulled a pile of sheets from the shelf. She dragged several towels from an upper ledge, sending a few tumbling to the floor. She took a moment to steady herself. This delivery might not be the same as the one that took her mother's life. Everything might happen normally. Oh, any price would be worth their safety. She kneeled, hands clasped. *God, extend your protection and be there to catch both the mother and child. Please don't punish them for my sins. If they live . . . I'll be a good wife. I'll forget Mr. Anwell.*

Wiping her eyes, she rose and returned to the kitchen, handing off the linens to Joe. A clanging sound came from the front. "That's Mr. Augustin," called Maggie.

"I'll see to him," said Helen. The cook nodded and went back to her patient.

At the door of the library, she could still hear the bell, though it was softer and less urgent. Would Augustin notice the sin written across her face? She took three shaky breaths, trying to compose herself.

Her husband lay on the daybed in the dark. She lit a lamp and brought it close. He appeared gray and sweat covered his brow. He did not seem to be conscious of her presence, though his eyes were open. The bell still moved in his hand, but the clapper merely slid across the brass. Helen lifted it from his fingers and noticed that his skin was clammy. A shiver went through him that did not abate.

"You're freezing," she said, and brought over a blanket. He pulled it up to his neck. She gently moved his chin toward the lamp and looked at his eyes. The pupils were constricted and his teeth chattered. "What's wrong?"

"I need the medicine," he said, his voice small.

"How I hate that medicine." Helen noticed that his leg had been wrapped anew. "Are you in pain?"

"Yes, it's terrible. I hurt all over. Do you see any medicine?"

"It is not good for you."

"How dare you withhold it?" he said angrily. Then pleading, "I'm in terrible pain."

She bit her lip. If Imari's baby was coming, it might be best if he were in a deep sleep. She looked around the bed and the liquor table until she found a bottle marked *Opium*. "One moment," she said, pouring forty drops into a snifter and adding a few inches of sherry. Augustin's hands trembled as he took the glass and drank it down. The effect was almost instantaneous. He relaxed, his breathing slowed, as if he had been rescued from danger. Eyes closed, he leaned his head back.

Helen took the snifter and pulled the ottoman close. She covered his hand with hers and studied the sharp changes in his face. His cheeks were drawn and the skin under his eyes hung off his bones. The lips parted as his breath flowed. Something about him seemed shrunken, as if a portion of his life had been siphoned off since the accident.

It was odd to be given the chance to study him. Up until that moment, he had loomed larger than life. Since their wedding every choice, every outfit, and every penny in her purse had been under his control. His decisions and wants could not be questioned, no matter how wrong they might be.

The horrible doctor was gone. But what would be Augustin's next dangerous decision?

His eyes opened. He focused on the hand that still held his. "Thank you," he said.

"For what?"

"Helping me."

Helen withdrew her arm. "I feel that giving you that medicine was not right."

"I need it," he said.

"The doctor is an evil man. I will not have him in the house again."

He bristled, raising his chest and throwing back his shoulders. "That's for me to decide."

"You're not thinking clearly. You allowed me to be unsafe in my own home."

A shutter went through him. "I . . . I . . . What you and Maggie manipulated—I acted because I had no choice." His eyes sharpened. "Was there ever a child? Or was that a phantom cooked up by you?"

"I manipulated nothing." Helen stood.

Augustin withdrew into himself, chin pulled into his chest. He looked up at her, eyes shining. "My mind is a muddle," he said in a quiet voice. "What I have done? I don't know. I'm coming apart. I've been feeling lost . . . for so long. When I married Mrs. Galway, she put me back together. I'm afraid I'm coming apart again." He brought his hands to his face and muffled a broken sob. "Can I ever be forgiven?"

"By me?" asked Helen.

"No. No." He looked at her as if surprised by her nearness. "My dear, you've married a very old sin. One for which I have never redeemed myself."

"We are all sinners."

"That cannot comfort me."

"You can tell me what it is," she said, bending close. "Confess it to me as you would a priest." His eyes fluttered closed and his hands froze in the air, like a man in a trance. She studied him until he relaxed and folded his arms across his breast and took deep regular breaths.

Just then, she heard Imari's cry coming from the back. She took one more look at Augustin. What "old sin"? she wondered.

CHAPTER THIRTY-THREE

STEWART PACED IN HIS OFFICE, the sooty effigy floating on the wall. Would tomorrow's conference be a repeat of the night when this scarecrow had earned its burn marks? It had happened months before, in January 1834. The First Presbyterian Church on Liberty and Washington Streets had been filled with spectators on the first of four nights of debates between the American Colonization Society and the Anti-Slavery Society. The Colonization Society's main traveling agent, Reverend Joshua Danforth, a sweet-tongued man with a handsome appearance and an attitude of angelic benevolence, took the audience through dozens of reasons for sending the free blacks away from their homes in the United States to the shores of Africa. Many nodded their approval when Danforth hit his main point, that building up Liberia would ease the way for the Southern masters to release their slaves. In Africa, he said, the Negroes would thrive and stop the "idleness, insubordination, and insurrection" that bedeviled the poor free wretches.

A larger audience gathered on the second night to hear Danforth's main opponent, Reverend Beriah Green, president of the Oneida Institute, a wiry rail-thin man filled with the zeal of God's abhorrence of slavery. After hearing both speakers quote scripture, there was much confusion over God's intentions when it came to the slaves. But despite initial resistance, many murmured their approval, as if Green had won them to his main point—that if a man saw a great wrong, it was his duty to oppose it. Stewart himself had spoken on the third night, when hundreds of people crushed onto the long benches straining to hear a series of locals speak, most on the side of colonization. Much affected by the reverend's ardent speech the night before, he thought he comported himself well, though not as eloquently as Green. On the fourth and final night, the crowd filled the aisles and a vote was taken, whether to support the Colonization Society's resolution, or reject it as the abolitionists had urged. As soon as the measure passed supporting the Liberian scheme, a throng had rushed to the streets where a gallows had already been constructed. From it hung two scarecrows—effigies of Green and Stewart. They were lit ablaze and rolled up and down Genesee Street, passing Stewart's own home. In the morning, on his porch, he found the burned likeness, the sign *Alvan Stewart, Traitor* still affixed to its neck. Those same passions might very well be ignited again tomorrow, Stewart thought.

The day had slipped away and grown dark as he tried to figure out how to bring into existence the statewide New York Anti-Slavery Society in the face of such opposition. Once again, tension in the city had reached a fevered pitch. But he knew that he must find a way to get the hard business of forging the organization completed before his enemies disrupted the entire enterprise. There could be no more delays in the long fight for freedom.

He believed that Pryce might still be at the courthouse attending a meeting crowded with "respectable mechanics"—the men who earned their bread by working in the industries of Utica and were duly proud of their calluses. There, it was anticipated, they would call on the town leaders to allow the next day's gathering at the Bleecker Street Presbyterian Church to go on unmolested. But it was far from clear if Utica's gentlemen of property and standing, after having spent weeks vilifying the convention as treasonous, would quietly retire and allow it to occur.

Downstairs, the street door opened and the scent of lilacs irritated Stewart's nose. Footsteps thundered up the stairs.

Pryce bustled in, his face agleam with energy.

Almost immediately Stewart's eyes began to sting. "What the devil is that smell?" he demanded.

"Is it that strong?" asked Pryce, removing his broad coat and pressing it to his nose. A wistful look clouded his eyes.

"For pity's sake, open the window."

Pryce complied and a chilly breeze cleared the room of the false scent of spring.

"I dropped by the mechanics' meeting. It's still going on," said Pryce, as he threw the offensive coat on a chair.

"Dropped by?" asked Stewart. "You didn't attend?"

"I . . . hum . . . had to—" Pryce stopped. His mind flew back to Helen, the feel of her in his arms, the look of passion in her eyes. And, of course, there was her anguish. His love for her had blotted out all sense of decorum. They had almost been incapable of controlling themselves. But her weeping—it crushed something within him. His actions had consequences and he wouldn't shrink from whatever they might be.

He saw Stewart studying him, so he composed himself before going on. "The mechanics have bogged down with procedures and haven't yet come up with any written proposals about our convention."

"*Our* convention?" said Stewart, amused. "So this is no longer just a job?"

Pryce blushed. "I think I've earned the right to call it that."

"Of course," said Stewart. "Did you meet the packet boats and coaches? Are people arriving?"

"Our delegates have been met and have been dispatched to the hotels and boardinghouses," said Pryce. "But, there was a group of about ten very rough-looking men who arrived on a boat from the east. They were unsightly, missing teeth and such—too poor for berths on a packet boat."

"Well, what of them?"

"They were met by an expensively dressed man and each was given a purse that I believe held money. One of them, a fellow with tangled black hair, said," Pryce cleared his throat, "'Utica ain't no bedder dan da Sixt Woid,' whatever that meant."

Stewart took the information with a knowing nod.

"They looked like trouble," said Pryce. He stopped and sniffed the air. "What's that smell?" He flew to the window and stuck his head out.

"I can smell nothing but that ridiculous perfume," coughed Stewart.

Pryce turned back, his eyes wide. "Fire. There's smoke coming from Bagg's Hotel!"

Horace raised a bit of tattered carpet and slapped it on the flames that licked his shack's outside wall. Smoke had driven him from his home. By the time he discovered the cause, the backside of the rickety structure was completely ablaze. The cinders, disturbed by his efforts, showered him in fiery sparks. His shirt smoldered. He felt a bite of pain and saw a glowing red ring spreading on his shoulder. He smothered it. Some of the servants from Bagg's Hotel burst from the stately building, shouting in alarm and, he assumed, checking to see if the fire was burning down their workplace. He ran around the shack and hurried through the door. Inside, flames leaped to the ceiling. He lunged to the broken-down dresser and grabbed a metal box. The heat blistered his hands. Springing back toward the entrance, he stumbled over his chair. The box flew from his fingers. He scrambled along the ground trying to find it. His lungs filled with smoke and he lost his bearings. The air burned his throat. He gasped and fought to clear his chest. Suddenly, a set of hands dragged him outside and, without warning, dunked him into the river. He screamed in shock, but Alvan Stewart held him steady, head above the surface.

"Cold water stops the burning," said Stewart.

"My box," groaned Horace, coughing violently. "What about my box? I had it . . . I had it in my hands."

"What's in it?" asked Stewart.

"My papers . . . Daddy's free papers . . . A lock a Momma's hair . . . Everything."

"Mr. Anwell," shouted Stewart, "look for a box! He was carrying one!"

Pryce ran toward the shack. The roof was fully aflame. The wind shifted and the fire roared toward him. He staggered back.

Men who appeared to be coming from the mechanics' meeting yelled for water and organized themselves into a bucket brigade. They worked hard, trying to douse the fire, but Horace saw that his home was completely destroyed.

Stewart dragged him out of the river. "I'm sorry," he said.

"It's all gone," said Horace, sinking to his knees. "Everything."

Stewart put his hand on the man's shoulder. "Look, if you need a place for the night," he pulled out his purse, "I can pay for it. At least you can be warm."

"Keep your money. I'm sleeping right here."

Just then Sylvanus appeared. He kneeled beside Horace. "Canst thou walk?"

"Leave me be." He pushed the baker away. Tears ran down his face. "Leave me be."

Sylvanus and Stewart reluctantly withdrew.

"Can you stay?" asked Stewart. He placed a few coins in the baker's hand. "For him. Tell me if you need more."

"That's kind of thee," said Sylvanus. "I shall stay."

The big lawyer disappeared into the knot of onlookers.

Pryce wandered through the crowd. He recognized the New York abolitionist Lewis Tappan, whom he had settled at Clarke's Temperance House that afternoon. Mr. Tappan, a rich and generously proportioned man who, Stewart had told Pryce, was the subject of death threats in "honorable Southern newspapers," and whose own town house had been sacked by an anti-abolition riot the year before, watched the blaze and the bystanders with sharp eyes.

"Do you think this is about tomorrow?" asked Pryce.

"Could be," said Tappan. "Your convention has been national news. There are many who would see us all hang for it."

"I'll try to determine the cause," said Pryce, moving away.

Tappan grabbed his arm. "Use caution," he said. He bent his head toward the group of rough out-of-town men. "I recognize some fellows from the Sixth Ward. They have been imported from the New York City riots."

Again, the wind shifted and the blistering heat changed direction. The mass of people parted for a moment. Standing back from the blaze was Hickox, his face calm. Swift stood with him, the red of the fire in his eyes.

A shudder of fear raged through Pryce. Until that point, the danger had been more theoretical, like a frontier story in the newspapers. He now understood that the stakes of tomorrow's convention had just been raised.

CHAPTER THIRTY-FOUR

As they stood in the hallway of Clarke's Temperance House, Elymas looked at the Utica directory over the shoulder of Mr. Ruggles.

"What do it say?" he asked.

"There's no Thomas Galway listed," said Ruggles.

"Gotta be something there," said Elymas, frustration tightening his voice. Ruggles and Higgins and Mr. Tappan had helped him get this far, but they cared more about tomorrow's big meeting than finding his family. Imari and Joe had to be somewhere. Since Ruggles had sent her this way, Elymas could not believe that he didn't know exactly where she'd be. He knew these folks had their secrets, but not when it was so important. And not after he had fought so hard to get here. The man had to know something. "Look again," he said, tapping the page impatiently.

"There's an Augustin Galway listed," said Ruggles.

"That gotta be it," said Elymas.

"Not necessarily," said Ruggles, looking at him. "It could be nothing."

"It be something and I need something. Show me how to get there."

As they studied the city map, several men ran by.

"What's happening?" asked Ruggles.

"Fire at Bagg's Hotel!" shouted one man as he passed.

"That's it," said Elymas. "I'm going."

"It's better if we're not involved," said Ruggles.

"I ain't going nowhere near no fire," said Elymas angrily. "I gotta find my family and folks ain't gonna be looking my way when there's burning to put down."

"Very well," said Ruggles. "Remember the whole town is in an uproar. A well-dressed Negro will draw unwanted attention. Things can get dangerous very quickly."

Elymas nodded, calming himself. "I thank you for your help. But this here be as close to finding out something about my people as a hammer be to a piece a hot iron. Just a few more swings and I got my answers."

Ruggles took his hand. "Good luck to you. Please remember me to your wife and boy," he said, looking into Elymas's eyes, his face pinched with concern. "If you find them. Don't take chances. If you are in need, come find me."

At the door Elymas turned back. "We gonna send you words once we get to Canada. After I get some work, I be sending you back this here suit."

"No need," said Ruggles. "Keep it and be warm." He looked over the top of his spectacles at Elymas. "You'll soon find out what winter really means." The two men laughed.

In front of Clarke's, Elymas saw men hurrying toward the fire. He took in a fortifying chestful of air, tasted the smoke, shook it off, and proceeded calmly up Genesee Street and crossed the canal. After all the miles and hardships and setbacks, he absolutely would not be denied any chance to find the mysterious man who had sold him as an infant. Imari and Joe might be harder to locate, but since he and Imari had planned to go to this house on their way to Canada, it was the only place he knew to look.

At Genesee Street, he turned left to walk across Bleecker toward Third. Almost immediately, he noticed a handsome white church whose tall windows stretched up to the second story, their pointed tops like a reverent acknowledgment of heaven above. The steeple pierced the night sky. For miles around, all would be able to find the church in times of trouble and celebration. He noticed a few black men minding their business. Maybe he and Joe could set up their blacksmith shop right here and get customers of all races.

Imari and Joe had to still be in Utica. The paddyroller Hickox had thrown their every plan into the dirt. But Mr. Ruggles himself had mentioned Imari's unwavering determination to get to this city. And if Elymas truly knew his wife, she would sit in one place, like a mule, waiting for him. That was, if she had made it this far. Before Ruggles put her on a steamship up the Hudson River, he wrote to his contact in Albany about her need to go her own way. Smiling, Elymas pictured the intensity of her request, unwavering enough to cause the abolitionist to write such a letter.

At the corner of Third and Bleecker, he stood in the street before the Galway house. When he had understood that tall Abby was not his natural mother and that he had not been born on the plantation, he thought of himself as a bit better than the other slaves. He loved Abby, but as a boy he had fancied that maybe he was more a captive African prince than a slave born of a slave. And he had finally proven that he was different. After all, he was no longer sweating in the plantation's blacksmith shop making slave collars. No. He was a free man in a free state.

Imari had brought it out in him. It was as if her soul lived at the top of a tree and could watch their lives unfold from a distance. She constantly thought far into their future. Because she worked in the house, some of the women who toiled in the fields didn't take to her. He was hated by some of the men because of his job. It meant that he and she had fit together. They had a reunion every Saturday and a parting every Monday. That pattern seemed to give her a demanding sense of time passing. She lived with urgency. And though it was often inconvenient and occasionally made him angry, he tried to as well.

A sudden shiver of fear rattled him. What if she wasn't there? What if she and Joe, knowing that he'd been captured, had moved on? It wasn't impossible. They would have been crazy to believe that he would come. All the time that he was alone, he had pictured them here at a fine house, somehow keeping hidden. But what if they weren't? For a moment he almost didn't want to know. If they left or had been captured, what would he do?

During the minutes that Elymas stood in the street in front of the Galway house collecting his courage, not one living soul passed. He couldn't just stand, he had to find out one way or another, so he leaned forward and approached a window. He peered into a lit room where a man lay in a small bed and a young woman removed a bell from his hand before mixing him a drink.

They seemed to be having some kind of intense discussion. Elymas found himself caught up in the drama. Was this the man who had sold him into slavery? He looked old and weak, nothing like the person who had haunted him since Imari had found the name Thomas Galway.

Suddenly, a pained cry pierced the air. He shivered. It was Imari. As he ran toward the sound, he could feel his heart pounding in his ears. The voice rang out again and he followed it around to the back. On the ground floor, lamps were lit behind curtains. He heard one woman, not his wife, talking in a calm and even way. After a few moments, the voice he had been waiting for came again. It was her. He was ready to wager his life on it.

He steeled himself and approached the porch. The second woman said, "Joe, bring me that hot water."

"Joe," he whispered, tapping on the door. "Joe, boy, open up." The footsteps in the room stopped. The curtain parted. Light from inside bathed his face. His own boy looked out at him, shaved bald as an apple—just like his daddy.

The door swung wide. Joe opened his mouth, but nothing came out. Elymas pulled him into an embrace. A hand from the house grabbed his arm. "Quickly, now, get inside." It was the young white woman from the other room.

Elymas picked up his boy and carried him into the kitchen.

"Poppa," said Joe, looking up, his voice breaking. He hugged Elymas tightly, head pressed against his stomach. "You was dead."

"You believe that?" asked Elymas. Joe nodded gravely. He pulled his son closer. "You stayed in my head. I came back to life for you."

"Who's there?" demanded a voice from the inner room.

Joe wriggled out of Elymas's embrace and ran to the door. "My poppa."

"Elymas?" called Imari.

He went to the doorway. She hung off the edge of the bed, feet on the floor, legs bent, elbows supporting her. Her bedclothes were pushed up above her knees and stained with sweat. Small welts peppered her left side. The skin of her neck and face shone bright red with strain. Their eyes met. She tried to catch her breath, but instead she erupted in sobs. A wave of pain and urgency seemed to swim over her body. She started to crumple. Elymas staggered back against one of the windows and then found his feet and rushed to her as her body tensed. Memories of her crowded his head. She was young and giving birth to her first, poor Jimmy. He'd had to swallow some pride to love another man's boy—only to lose him to the slave market. Then there were the babies that came too soon. They had mourned over them, but nothing felt right until Joe was born, his own boy. Now the time had come again. Though they never talked about it, he understood that this new child might not be his blood. No matter who was the father, he would die before allowing another baby to be sold as a slave as he had been.

Kneeling in front of his wife was an older black woman. She looked at him with tight-lipped curiosity. An uneasiness tightened his chest. Imari groaned again.

"Push," said the older woman, turning back to her.

He grabbed his wife's hand, kissed it, and then stood up uncertainly.

"Stay right here and help," said the older woman.

Imari nodded, so Elymas climbed on the bed behind her, lifting her and supporting her. He wrapped his knees and arms around her. She leaned into him. He felt her body mold to his. Her arms reached up and circled his neck. To be holding her again, to feel her alive and hot in his arms—the joy almost choked him. He felt a new labor pain build, radiating from her core and consuming her.

"I love you," he said into her ear, and covered her neck with kisses as she rocked and writhed and sweat in his embrace. "Let that baby go. I got you. Don't hold back no more. Be slippery, like they say."

She moaned again, a cry of effort that filled his soul with hope.

As the next pain approached she pushed with her whole being, straining to her limit.

"It's coming," said the older woman. "I see it."

"You there, Miss Slippery," said Elymas, "you let go a that baby."

Imari screamed and again put her whole self into the push.

"I got the head," the older woman said, a hand supporting the baby. "You're mostly there. One more push."

Imari braced herself against Elymas. He absorbed her power, leaning into her, eyes glued to the emerging baby, a reddish brown, like rich cherrywood, and covered with blood and birth fluid. The infant slid into the woman's hands. He and Imari fell back in a shudder of relief. He pushed her up and they leaned forward to look at it. The baby girl flinched in the cool air and began to cry. The two new parents embraced. The white woman stood transfixed in the doorway, tears streaming down her face. Joe, who Elymas knew had seen animals give birth, slid down the wall until he rested on the ground, stunned.

"She's a beauty. Brown as her daddy," said the woman, smiling as she wrapped the baby in a cloth. "Elymas, ain't it?" She placed the baby on her mother's belly. "I can't barely believe it." She turned. "Now Joe, get up, boy. Didn't I tell you I need water?"

Dr. McCooke had followed the well-dressed Negro to the back, around the Galway house. The man apparently had been admitted. If that was not an outrageous violation, a reason to get to the truth, he didn't know what was. Not only that, perhaps there was a bounty on this fellow's head too.

The doctor grabbed a large stone from the garden and intended to heave it through the cook's window. That would flush them all out. At the very least it would scare the cow who had gotten him ejected from the house without even a coin in his pocket. She had laid a tissue of lies before Galway. As far as he was concerned, there was nothing unusual about most of the examination he'd performed on Mrs. Galway. Yes, he conceded, his measures to restrain her may have been misinterpreted. If anything, they were too cautious. And it was unfortunate that he had performed the assessment of her condition in his own bedroom, but time mattered in a case such as hers and Galway had demanded she be saved. He pulled a small silver flask out of his breast pocket and took a drink, tipping the container almost vertical to shake out the last drop.

He heard a woman's groan. Someone fell against the window. The curtain opened just a bit. The doctor bent low and scooted over, listening to the unmistakable sounds of labor. Slowly, he brought his blue eye up to the parting of the muslin. There, in all her glory, was the female fugitive. She was a thin specimen, long of leg, strong-armed, and in the last moments of life's most difficult battle. The cook acted as midwife and seemed to have the situation under control. When the baby appeared, the doctor took in a sharp breath. He always marveled at the act of giving birth. It was almost a shame to turn this family over to Mr. Hickox. But how was any of this his fault? He didn't tell the slaves to run. He didn't tell the cook to hide them. He would only be following the law, and for that he knew he could expect a generous reward.

Still, he couldn't deny that even Negroes seemed to appreciate the wondrousness of birth. If that bitch cook had only kept quiet. She reminded him of Billy, that bastard overseer who must have tricked Mother into handing the responsibility for the plantation into his grimy black hands. Every time I wrote to her for money she had some excuse, always on the word of Billy. *Billy said the tobacco prices dropped. Billy said the harvest had not come in. Billy said that there was no money.* When it came time to pay for his final school year, there wasn't even money for that without selling the land, equipment, and slaves—including dear old Billy. Niggers were supposed to make one rich. They were responsible for his difficult pecuniary position from beginning to end. Really, the truth was that he had been on the verge of getting full access to Galway's accounts before that miserable cook stepped in.

Given his circumstances, it was impossible to pass up this gift from Providence. He might have been generous with that family and their newborn, oh yes, he might have let them continue on their way. But there was no way now. He'd been wronged and intended to set things right.

He lowered the rock, leaving it by the side of the house. What he had to do was locate the slave catchers. The capture—no, the reclamation—would be best if it happened fast, before the parents developed too strong an attachment to the babe. As of morning, they would be headed to their rightful place, their lawful place. His hands were tied. After all, if he did not get the reward money, someone else would.

CHAPTER THIRTY-FIVE

SYLVANUS THREW ONE of the final buckets of water on the fire that had eaten through Horace's home. The little shack was now no more than a pile of blackened cinders and wet ash. The blaze had been beaten and no other building had been damaged. He looked around and saw Horace trudging down the street like a man in a dream.

"I'm sorry, Brother Horace." Sylvanus caught up to him a little out of breath. "Didst thou save anything?"

"Everything I got you see right here," said Horace, raising his empty hands.

"How about thy fish cart? Did it survive?"

"They's just gonna burn that up too," said Horace.

Sylvanus put his arm across the man's shoulders. "Dost thou know who committed the act?"

"I say it's that slaver."

"Thou art in danger of further violence." Sylvanus thought for a moment. "Brother Stewart left these coins." He put them into Horace's palm. "Thou art burned. Come and stay with me. I will butter thy injuries."

"I'm staying right here," said Horace, turning back.

"Stay with me, at least until the convention is concluded."

Horace looked at him, surprised. He tried to speak, but his voice cracked and he began to cough.

Sylvanus patted his back. "Come, come. At least let me feed thee breakfast. I'm told my bread has restorative properties." He led Horace to the bakery.

After Sylvanus wrapped Horace's hands in bandages and fed him, he left to make his early morning deliveries. Horace stretched out on the cot near the still-warm oven, but found it hard to sleep. Whereas his shack had been filled with odds and ends, this place had only a few necessities—the domed oven, a nearby stack of wood, worktables, a set of drawers, a few pots and dishes, and the pegs for the baker's clothing. There was almost nothing at which to look.

All his thoughts were on the ashes of his home and his dashed dreams of securing a lift in life. The cart remained, but for how long? Even if he had known Hickox's plans, how could he defend his property? The slavers had guns. All he had were fishing poles—at least he used to have fishing poles. A man couldn't even keep himself alive without poles, and salt to preserve what he caught. Everybody needed a place to be warm and to secure food from thieves and dogs. That damn slaver still believed Horace knew something and could get around Maggie. Certainly she would rather die than let them capture someone under her protection. But sometimes she shut the door—even to him. And having runaways in the house? Well, she'd be extra cautious. And that yellow-haired doctor, hadn't he really brought the trouble to Maggie's kitchen? He treated her no better than a slave. Why should *he* benefit from the $150? The doctor's obvious disgust for Maggie made him want to see the man in the gutter, or his grave.

Horace never asked to be involved with all this. Now his lungs felt shallow and tight and his hands throbbed. Life would have been better if he'd never got himself into it. What did he owe Maggie, really? She gave him breakfast once in a while, when he could flatter her into it. If he helped her, he got a sandwich. The other cooks smiled when he came knocking. They were more pleasant and freer with their food. What had Maggie ever done for him?

It was going to take a while to heal, he couldn't just live off the baker. What he needed was money, much more than a few coins. Mr. Galway wouldn't give him anything unless he went to Africa. And Mr. Stewart had millions of slaves to save. How could Horace's own troubles ever be as important?

He had never before been involved with helping escaped slaves. He kept his nose out of such things. Knowing who was and who was not free baited no hooks. Risking jail for a stranger did not keep out the freezing wind. Spring storms would be no drier if he got involved with hiding slaves. The doctor and the runaways were Maggie's problem and somehow it had all spilled over onto him.

No one had given him anything. He dug the worms. He caught the fish. He built his cart with his own hands. He had his customers, of course, but that was commerce, not charity. He didn't bother with church. Sundays were for resting, so he rested. He didn't need a preacher to tell him that. He didn't need anyone. The reward money? Winter was on its way. One hundred and fifty dollars was an unimaginable sum.

But helping the men who had burned down his house? The thought sickened him. Was there some way to get their money and also cheat them out of their catch? Hickox looked like he knew every trick. But maybe there was a way.

He paused for a moment and looked around at the baker's home. The man's needs were simple. A roof, a few articles of clothing, food, and work. Horace was so tired of it all, the fishing, the gutting, the smell of rot. Maybe he'd never go back to it. But that took money. Of course, his daddy wouldn't rest in his grave if he knew that Horace had turned Judas. There had to be a way to fool the slaver. The thought made him roll over and stare at the white wall.

Another image popped into his head: a boy to dig up worms. He imagined himself, perfectly clean and well dressed, pointing out where to hunt. More than that, he saw himself doubling the catch if he could train a couple of boys up right. And what would hiring a storefront cost? About the same in Syracuse as in Utica. Did the Mohawk go through there? The canal did. That meant plenty of customers needing food. His mind drifted to the sign that he would put above the door to his store, *Horace's Fresh Fish*, with a rainbow trout on it, just to catch the eye. All it took was starter money. The kind of money that Mr. Galway got born with. The kind of money that a lawyer like Stewart might make in a few days. For them it was easy. If he had that kind of money he'd owe nobody. Instead, that damn Hickox was after him because of what Maggie and those slaves were doing. Really, Maggie and her friends *owed him*. They might all be sitting in jail if he hadn't been there to help. Should he let his life get ruined? No. He did not deserve to suffer for them. He needed to start anew somewhere, somehow.

One hundred and fifty dollars—he could almost feel it in his pocket.

CHAPTER THIRTY-SIX

THE SUN, STILL BELOW the horizon, began transforming the black sky to magenta, then to a vibrant peach. Birds chirped, declaring their territory. Deer grazed on the banks of the Ballou. People stirred on the Erie Canal. Several freight barges sat docked and ready to be restocked with food for their journey to Albany. Captains' wives gave Mr. Sylvanus a few coins for his fresh loaves, still warm from his oven, and brought them down to the galley to slice.

The gentlemen and ladies of Post Street, an industrious lot, were up early for their labors, be they in the livery stables, shops, hotels, lumberyards, mills, or sculleries.

In the finer houses around town, men of business—bankers, merchants, tradesmen, local and state politicians—stirred in their beds knowing that their day's schedule would be crowded. After they shaved their faces and dressed in their white shirts and dark pants, waistcoats and jackets, and after they had partaken of their breakfasts, they were to meet at the courthouse. It was known that among them a committee would be appointed, the Committee of 25. The men so chosen were to march the two and a half blocks to the Bleecker Street Presbyterian Church, where they would confront the abolitionists and stop them from convening their meeting to establish the statewide New York Anti-Slavery Society. Along the way, they expected that the less prosperous men of Utica, those who had been their audience during the last seven weeks of rancorous public meetings, fiery rhetoric, and scathing newspaper articles, would be swelling their ranks.

The proprietors of several grogshops, including Mr. King of King's Victualing House, had stayed awake all night and were just then readying their establishments to provide free spirits to all comers, paid for in secret by a few of the upstanding citizens expected to be among the chosen twenty-five.

Spread around in hotels, temperance houses, and private rooms, men who had made the arduous journey to Utica for the conference were trying to temper their anxiety and allow themselves a few more minutes of rest, for sleep had evaded many.

Pryce stopped in front of the Presbyterian church and looked at the orange and pink sky. The clouds' edges were etched in gold as the sun peeked over the earth. He had exhausted himself by pacing his room all night, his encounter with Helen filling his mind. Now he imagined her sweetly asleep, the light not yet having reached her bedroom window. Bounding up the stairs, he joined Stewart on the raised stone entranceway to the church, where the big man pushed on the heavy carved oak doors.

A familiar form slinked down Bleecker Street toward them. It was Dr. McCooke and he appeared to be coming from the direction of the Galway house. As the doctor drew closer, Pryce saw him attempt to drink from a small flask and, when he found it was empty, turn his eyes toward the church. At the moment of recognition, McCooke quickly crossed away from him and Stewart and passed, chin up, eyes forward. That doctor's just itching to be followed, thought Pryce. He started to run off the stone portico, an idea of beating the doctor senseless boiling in his mind, when Stewart pulled him up short.

"He's just another scoundrel," said the older man, his strong hand holding Pryce's shoulder.

The doctor hustled to the corner and turned down Genesee toward the National Hotel, where Hickox and Swift were still in residence.

"Today is about freeing the slaves," said Stewart, patting Pryce's arm. "Don't ever lose sight of that."

Pryce saw the lawyer's worried look and nodded solemnly. He promised himself that the doctor wouldn't escape him twice.

At the National Hotel, Dr. McCooke sent word to Hickox's room that he wished to talk. The answer arrived in the form of Swift.

"What do you want?"

"You, eh? I asked to speak to Mr. Hickox."

"He ain't interested in jawing with you."

"I've new information," said McCooke. "Only to be delivered to his own ear."

Swift did not waver.

"Two nuggets. He will not get them elsewhere."

Swift shook his head slowly.

"Very well," said the doctor. "You leave me no choice. I'll go to Sheriff Osborn. He'll be interested in bringing the fugitives to Judge Hayden at ten dollars a head."

Swift's pupils widened.

"Well," said the doctor, "I'm sure you two'll be heading out of town—empty-handed—once the sheriff has the group in custody. Good day to you, sir." He turned on his heel and started away.

Swift reached out and grabbed him.

The sun warmed Horace's neck as he tapped on the Galways' back door. The horse whinnied in the barn. Since Maggie did not seem to be in the kitchen, he decided to feed and water the poor animal. That would put the cook in a good mood and it was important he be allowed in this morning.

In the barn, Horace hummed nervously as he lifted dry hay from the bin and changed out the soiled bedding. Poor old horse. He had not been off the property in a while. Horace poured out some oats and winced as he grabbed the bucket to fetch fresh water.

Maggie's arms crossed over her chest as she looked down at Augustin. "Missus Helen don't like that opium so I say no."

"You push me beyond my limit."

"We ain't nowhere close to your limit," she said as she stretched a blanket over him. "You ain't ready to meet your maker." She shook her head. "I'm just about through with you. You remember that I'm a free woman?"

"Maggie," he said, his bottom lip quivering, "don't leave me." He brought her hand to his cheek. She felt tears wetting her fingertips. "I need you."

She tilted his face up and looked him in the eye. "All right then, you gotta do what I say. It ain't gonna be easy. But right now, you need to rest up and be ready."

"Whatever you say."

Maggie poured him a large glass of brandy. After a moment of thought, she added several drops of opium from the vial in her pocket. He took the drink between his shaking hands and brought it to his lips.

"Swallow that and we're gonna get you through." She tightened the curtains, further darkening the room. At the door, she looked back. He greedily sipped the drink. She pressed her lips together and nodded to him before leaving.

In the hallway, Maggie lingered at the bottom of the staircase. Imari, Elymas, the baby, and Joe were asleep in the guest room—at least she hoped they had finally been able to settle down. Everyone had been so exhausted after the birth that she decided to wait to let them know the truth. What difference would a few hours make? She'd tell them over breakfast and explain to Miss Helen how it had all happened, as best she could.

She would manage Augustin and keep him quiet. Lord knew he needed to rest. In a day or so, maybe a week, she would confess everything. After that, she'd go to Mr. Sylvanus and ask him what could be done to make the family safe. It can wait, she thought. She needed sleep herself, but she put it off until later, after her morning chores. Her heart still felt a little soft at seeing the child born. She shook her head and went through the door to the kitchen.

She opened the curtains for the first time in days. Her eye lit on Horace as he filled the horse's water bucket. She thought work was a good thing for him—move on from the killing of his fish. That's how she handled setbacks. Keep pushing each task forward. This one a little. That one a little. At some point, you could look back and see that you were in a new place—your sorrows and troubles behind you.

She opened the door. "Morning. Fine day for fishing, ain't it?"

He looked up. "I'm taking a day off. I only came by to see if you in need of any work around the house."

"You working or taking off? Make up your mind." She smiled at him.

"Now, why you so happy today? Don't hold back nothing. Share it with poor old Horace."

"I can't exactly say," she responded, and waved him closer. As he put the full bucket on the ground and came to her, she noticed the bandages on his hands. "What happened?"

"Oh, me not thinking, is all." He folded his arms behind his back. "You're happy, but can't say nothing? Ain't no secrets 'tween us, is there?"

She smiled, wide and open. "When you're done with the horse, come on in. I'll set the coffee on and fix you up enough food to keep you going. I got a lot to tell you. Can't even start, I got so much."

Imari shook herself awake. Elymas slept next to her, snoring loudly and still in his rumpled suit. Joe had collapsed on a carved walnut divan with a tufted cushion seat, his right leg and arm dangling off the edge. Imari watched as Helen rocked the baby and gently straightened her clothing. The room was as nice as Missus Bea's, and for the moment it was hers. The baby was alive and safe. Joe was still by her side. And Elymas had somehow found his way back to them. All of the planning and figuring, the years of yearning, a lifetime of slavery, all of it pushed to the side for this moment.

She wanted to savor it, but whenever she closed her eyes, she remembered how it felt to swing the musket and hit the slaver's head. And how he had dropped like a bird shot out of the sky. The action and its consequences were part of her now. That he was an evil man, she did not doubt, but the desperation that had driven her to the fatal moment, and the impact of the gun and the wet thud stayed with her like an anvil around her neck. The instant she saw that Colby was dead, relief and satisfaction had filled her heart. The victory faded as Hickox shoved her husband into the dirt. She brought up the musket, aimed, and pulled the trigger. Nothing happened. By that time the slaver had Elymas pinned and was going for his gun. Joe pulled her arm. Elymas yelled "Run!" over and over. The word stuck in her head and she followed the boy, run, run, run, run, repeating in her mind. Run, run, run, run, matched each thump of her feet.

Colby's death must have outraged the already stonehearted Hickox. It put them all in danger. If she had been strong enough to slip away last night and spare them all, she would have. Her gaze lingered on each member of her family as she memorized the details of the moment. Despite the warm fire and the calm in the room, she shivered as she looked at the infant. It was as if the promised noose already hovered above her own head.

The baby fussed and mewed.

"Let me," said Imari, glad for the distraction. "She hungry. I know the sound." Helen handed her over. Imari settled the infant to her breast and marveled at how much her trust in the young mistress of the house had grown. Here they lay, dependent on the woman who, a short time ago, wanted them off the property. After the betrayal by the long-faced black man, feverish need had propelled her actions. The innkeeper's wife who'd hidden them in the Cranbury Inn after Elymas's capture was a gruff, tough-minded lady. That type could often be called upon once they decided to act. Helen had been soft and subject to emotion. At first, influencing her had been crucial to their survival. But Imari knew that weak people could sway back in the opposite direction. Yet this young woman had not allowed herself to be bullied by Hickox or her husband. Imari smiled and nodded to Helen, who watched her quietly.

"You want to know what I done decided?" said Imari, after checking to see that the baby was suckling properly.

"Of course," said Helen.

"I know what her name gonna be." She looked at her little girl and ran a finger gently down the infant's long, perfectly smooth arm.

"Had you one all picked out?"

"Not till this minute," said Imari, her eyes flashing. "She gonna be Margaret Helen Galway."

Helen laughed and wiped away a tear.

Owen Sylvanus became known to many of the masters who piloted the 363 miles of Erie Canal as the chubby man who sold bread. Secretly, the masters' wives who loved to gossip referred to the man who delivered the bread as the Quaker Baker. Much more mystery swirled around him than his outward appearance might suggest. No one argued that his superb bread was overpriced, but for many his wide-brimmed black hat and outdated language remained a curiosity. Additionally, his habit of referring to their husbands as Brother So-and-so instead of Master Thus-and-such signaled a sure sign of disrespect. None, however, broached the issue to his face.

As his bread basket lightened and the coins in his pocket grew heavier, his mind stayed on the image of Horace, burned and broken over the loss of a box and the rubble of what had been his home. Sylvanus exited through the canalboat terminal, past the office of the toll collector. He paused for a minute to hear a rancorous argument between the collector and one of the masters. It seemed that the master's vessel had traversed the "long level," a section of the canal west of Utica with no locks, skipping the stations where he should have gotten his clearance papers endorsed. The implication was that he had been racing above the four-miles-per-hour limit. The normal penalty of twenty-five dollars was not imposed, but a lesser sum may have changed hands in the few moments of tense silence.

He chuckled, knowing that simple honesty and an adherence to the regulations kept him out of most conflicts. Of course, his rejection of the morally abhorrent law of slavery had given his life—he had to admit—more purpose. Particularly as of late. Perhaps after searching for Horace's box, he might visit the post office to see if he had received a reply from Oriskany with regard to a place for the mother, child, and expected infant. Sister Maggie had been properly concerned about moving the woman before her lying-in time. Yes, he decided, this work was far more important than all the bread his two hands could produce. And doing it gave the greatest satisfaction to his spirit, as well as some heart-enlivening moments.

He made his way through the bustle to Genesee before he saw the slave catchers hurrying out of the National Hotel, followed by Dr. Mc-Cooke. He quickly moved sideways to hide under the striped awning of a dry goods store. The younger slaver had a rifle, a whip, and a brace of chains. The elder carried pistols on his hips and a coil of rope swinging from his belt. They turned up the street and were quickly at the apex of the canal bridge.

A flood of perspiration covered Sylvanus's body as he began following them. I am just a simple baker, he thought. What will I do if I catch them? He quickened his pace and saw the slavers ahead, still on Genesee. I will just look at the direction of their travels. If they take the left turn toward the Galway house I shall sound the alarm.

Ahead, a knot of loud men had gathered in the busy crossing of Bleecker and Genesee. The trio he was following stopped and seemed to be confounded by the disturbance. Sylvanus grew closer. When the doctor peered behind him, the baker stiffened. He knows me not, remembered Sylvanus. He closed the distance between them and joined other bystanders at the corner.

A group of rough-looking, oddly dressed characters trotted past. Several carried stout canes. "Come on, laddies," shouted one of them, "dis way!"

Sheriff Osborn dashed in front of an arriving coach stacked high with luggage, and tried to swing around the group.

The older slave catcher waded into the mess and retrieved the sheriff. Once he had him safely out of harm's way, the lawman took a moment to remove his hat and tamp down his unruly and unoiled hair.

"The fugitives are secreted at Galway's," said the slave catcher. "We have a witness."

"Again?" said Osborn. "Ain't you already been through there once?"

"I've seen them," said the doctor. "There's a new one. They'll leave any second now."

Osborn nudged his hat higher on his forehead. "Don't you know that my hands is full?"

Sylvanus, galvanized by a shudder of pure fear, pushed forward shouting, "Let me pass!" He rounded the corner and trotted down Bleecker Street.

He looked neither left nor right as he hurried along, the remaining bread bouncing in his basket. They weigh me down, he thought, dumping the loaves in the gutter. A pain grew in his side as he hustled past John Street. He pressed the ache and noticed that his lungs felt as if they were filled with fire. What a sight I must be, a fat old man running down the road on a Fourth day morning. Stopping, he gasped for air and clutched a light pole to steady himself. Behind him the trio advanced. Curse it. I have been too content in life. If I could gain headway, I might be able to warn Sister Maggie. With renewed purpose, he forced himself forward, panting with the effort. His face felt hot. He passed Chancellor Square Park. There were still blocks to go. But he had to find a way to alert the poor runaways.

A gripping tightness poked his right calf. He stumbled and fell, scraping his hands and knees, sending his hat to the ground where it rolled lazily on its brim. Several passersby came to his aid. As he massaged his leg, he panted like a dog left in the sun.

"He is ill," cried a lady in an ocher dress. "We need a doctor."

A finely turned-out gentleman called, "You there. Dr. McCooke. This man needs help."

Sylvanus saw the doctor pull up short and the slave catchers stop.

"He's fine," said the older slaver. "Doctor, your other patient awaits you."

"Look to him," demanded the lady. "It is a problem of the heart."

"Yes," gasped Sylvanus, hoping to at least slow down the progress of the trio.

Dr. McCooke kneeled, his stethoscope ready.

"Doctor, you were the one who said our mission was urgent," said Hickox.

"A minute," said McCooke. He placed the wide end of the listening device against Sylvanus's chest. "Silence!" he shouted, seeming delighted to have onlookers crowd around him. After a few moments of pressing his ear to the instrument, the doctor looked up. "It is not his heart," he announced with the air of authority.

Sylvanus grasped the doctor's sleeve. "Thou must take some time about it, Brother, just to be certain."

"Doctor, your appointment with the lady," said the slave catcher.

"Yes, yes," said the doctor, a nervous cough passing his lips. He turned to the baker. "You are just shaken, old man. Go home and rest. That will be three dollars."

"Take thee to the devil!" shouted Sylvanus.

Hickox hauled McCooke to his feet. "You heard the man. On to the devil." And the two slavers, one on each side of the doctor, stalked away from Sylvanus toward the Galway house.

With the help of the lady and the gentleman, Sylvanus rose, wiping away frustrated tears.

He had failed them all.

CHAPTER THIRTY-SEVEN

OCTOBER 21 WAS THE DAY that had been planned for months. At precisely ten o'clock in the morning, Alvan Stewart took to the pulpit of the Bleecker Street Presbyterian Church. Behind him a banner, which had been stitched together by some of the ladies who felt the issue of abolition most keenly, hung across the chancel wall proclaiming *The New York Anti-Slavery Society* in broad yellow letters on a blue background. It was as if the organization already existed. Stewart knew better. He had an agenda that had to be approved by the body so that the business would be a fait accompli. He looked over the sea of faces squeezed into the rows of wooden pews. As he drew in a breath, his eyes came upon the men whom, when the Utica Anti-Slavery Society had first put out the call for the convention, he had only dared to hope might attend. Lewis Tappan, one of the principal financers of abolitionist publications, had come because a Virginia newspaper had put a $20,000 bounty on his brother Arthur, promising the money to anyone who delivered him "south of the Potomac—to be dealt with according to his merits." With him was the brilliant young Negro abolitionist David Ruggles, who ran a bookstore on Broadway and Lispenard in New York City. And there were the young faces, both light and dark, of students from the Oneida Institute of Science and Technology, who had been brought by his good friend Reverend Beriah Green. Stewart wondered if new effigies of himself and the reverend were right now being stuffed with hay. Near Green, he noticed Gerrit Smith, a very rich gentleman and a leading light of the Colonization Society. Smith had never promised to make an appearance, but Stewart knew that Green had been shaking the man's opinions. Perhaps the convention would push him in abolition's direction. The room was filled with steadfast men who might just be able to bring about freedom for the slaves. He settled his papers on the smooth wood surface of the lectern. The meeting was happening—no matter what. That was already a victory.

Stewart raised his hands. Conversations ended and all faces turned forward. He picked Pryce out of the snarl of delegates standing in the back of the sanctuary. The two men nodded to each other.

"Is it true," Stewart asked, his powerful deep voice bouncing off the whitewashed walls, "that the philanthropy which warms our hearts to organize for the release of the suffering slave stops our patriotism? Is it true that because we feel for bleeding humanity, that we wish to cut the throats of our white Southern countrymen?"

As the responses of "No!" and "False!" filled the church, Pryce studied the assembly. He felt certain that anyone who was working to disrupt them would make themselves known during Stewart's address. He scanned the many familiar faces, men he had greeted the previous day. They had traveled from across the state singly or in small groups. This morning, everyone looked engaged and hopeful.

"We have been proclaimed traitors to our dear native land, because we love its inhabitants, no matter their color," Stewart said. "Are those who accuse us the patriots? The so-called friends of the Union? *They* are willing to see eternal and unmitigated slavery for every colored man, woman, and child."

"*We're* the patriots," called a thin fellow with a wispy brown beard, known to Pryce as James DeLong, a member of the Common Council.

Stewart pointed to DeLong. "That's right, my friends. We are the patriots because we will not permit the great cancer of slavery to continue to grow on the neck of the Union."

The massive audience, upwards of four hundred men, rose in applause.

"Those Unionists," Stewart went on, "are willing to destroy you and me because we are not terrified at the roaring of the slaveholders, and because we feel for two and a half million men, women, and children who are now being offered at the shrine of cruelty, lust, and avarice."

As Stewart continued to hammer on the idea of slavery, Pryce noticed that the delegates seemed joined by the righteousness of their cause, each person gaining strength from having come together. It was as if they were no longer alone, even though they might be the only abolitionist in their village. Now, because they saw so many in this place, they too might believe that the fight for the immediate end of slavery was something that could be won.

Pryce found himself thinking about the pregnant woman at the Galway house. What would have happened to her if he and Stewart hadn't been there to help? He didn't know her condition now, but since the slave catchers still lingered in town, and the fishmonger's shack had been destroyed, clearly she and her boy were still under great threat. And Pryce knew, as he watched the assembly hoot and clap, that just two and a half blocks away, the Colonization Society was at that very moment choosing a committee of twenty-five prominent members to lead a march to their convention.

A shiver of fear troubled the budding abolitionist. How would he handle violence if it came? Stewart had said that he shouldn't use physical measures to counter any dissent. But if Dr. McCooke appeared, he would drag the man into the street and deal with him—he was a special case. His father would never even consider using violence or any weapon to defend the conference. Pryce burned to take his anger at McCooke out on someone, but would that help the cause? The Founding Fathers had picked up weapons, as had the men who fought in 1812. However, here in this church, among so many peaceable men, he decided armaments would be sacrilege. It was his job to protect the delegates—if he could—but without resorting to the methods the doctor or the slave catchers might use. Squaring his shoulders, he resolved to be vigilant and ready to isolate anyone who tried to disrupt the convention.

"You," Stewart said, pointing at his audience, "are the representatives of American liberty. If today you are driven from this sacred temple, dedicated to God, by an infuriated mob, then, my brethren, wherever you go, liberty will go. Where you abide, liberty will abide."

Just then, the doors of the church banged open. Pryce recognized Representative Samuel Beardsley, tall and well dressed with an upright thatch of brown hair, surging up the aisle.

"Damn the fanatics!" Beardsley yelled, his crystal clear voice shattering the mood of the assembled. Pryce knew he had to do something, but could one manhandle a congressman? As he moved toward the older man to slow him down, Beardsley cut left with astonishing agility and continued forward. The other ushers stood still with shocked faces,

their only defense a waving of hands, a flattening of palms, and an out-
stretching of fingers. Once at the front of the room, Beardsley turned
and Pryce followed his eyes. The back of the sanctuary filled with the
Committee of 25, each a well-dressed gentleman.

"Sit down, Beardsley!" bellowed Stewart.

The congressman dashed to a position in front of the podium. "We,
the *true* leaders of Utica," he began, "some of our number *duly* elected,
do hereby declare this dangerous convention an *amalgamation*. You
traitors would celebrate if our guiding document, the Constitution,
went into the flames of another bloody slave uprising. We officially
declare this convention a *danger* and demand that it be disbanded." His
steely gaze swept across the attendees. "This is your chance. Leave now
or face the consequences."

Stewart, red-faced and puffing out his chest, marched toward the
representative. "How *dare* you threaten violence. You claim to love the
Constitution. We're a peaceful assembly. The Declaration of Indepen-
dence states that all men are created equal. Are not the Negroes men of
flesh and blood?" He turned to the audience. "I ask you all, when will
this nation live up to our founders' intent?"

Beardsley pushed in front of him. "Get up here, Judge," he called,
and waved to Chester Hayden, who marched forward, dressed in his
impressive black robes. The congressman grasped Hayden's hand and
pulled him up the steps.

Pryce seized the other arm and tugged him backward. The judge
turned on him, face burning with outrage. "You just bought a few more
nights in jail."

Pryce slackened his grip and Beardsley jerked the judge forward.

"We, the patriotic Committee of 25," Beardsley said in a command-
ing voice, "represent true Uticans. Now, hustle the traitors out."

As Pryce yelled to the ushers to close the doors, two of the imported
ruffians from the Sixth Ward stepped to either side of him, picked him
off the floor, and hurled him into the audience, where he knocked down
several men. He staggered to his feet, only to see a portly hunter in
tweed trousers releasing a pack of dogs. Each hound ran in a different
direction and soon the hall was filled with the sounds of barks and
howls. Pryce pushed into the aisle and tried to grab one of the beasts,
but the sleek short-haired pointer snapped at his wrist. He let it run.

Angry men, far more than the twenty-five, continued to charge into the sanctuary. Stewart attempted to regain order, but he was shouted down. A chant of "Give us Stewart!" swept through the intruders.

A few agitators closed in on the big lawyer, trying to grab him. Pryce surged forward and began tearing men away from his friend. The ruffians from New York wrestled him to the back of the room and delivered several thumps to his chest. As he gasped for breath, he saw the elderly secretary, Reverend Oliver Wetmore, struggling with a man over the minutes of the convention. The reverend twisted away from his attacker, laying in a sharp elbow to the lout's jaw. As Wetmore's assailant stumbled back, the papers scattered into the air and fell to the floor where they were soiled and torn underfoot.

Hymnals flew. Some of the interlopers noticed Negroes among the assembled. Epithets of the most brutal nature were hurled at them. Black and white abolitionists locked arms. A cry of "Amalgamators!" came from one of the better-dressed rioters.

A pug-nosed, powerfully built canal runner threw his arms around Stewart and tried to drag him off the riser. Pryce spotted the attack. He leaped onto a pew and used the backs of the seats like stepping-stones to dash across the sanctuary. Just before he reached the pulpit, Stewart planted his feet, thrust out his arms, and threw off his attacker. The canal runner staggered toward the seats, meeting Pryce, who leaped for the man and grabbed his coat. The garment, newly purchased that week, was torn in half.

Gerrit Smith looked shocked at the mayhem caused by his confederates in the Colonization Society. He climbed onto the seat of his pew. "These men have the right to assemble!" he yelled. "You are trying to silence debate and that I cannot allow." He opened his arms wide. "Delegates, your discussions will be heard. Come to Peterboro and tomorrow I will guarantee you my protection."

Lewis Tappan shouted to Stewart, "Motion for adjournment!"

Mr. Ruggles, whose arms were locked with his friend Higgins and a white abolitionist, cried, "Second!"

Stewart hobbled back to the lectern, shouted, "Adjourned!" and slammed the gavel to the podium with an earsplitting crack.

Abolitionists fled the church in ones, twos, and threes. Those with linked arms pulled themselves through the aisles and were met on the street by the growing mob. The fleeing conventioneers were pelted with mud, stones, and eggs. Many were jeered and chased through the streets. Some retreated to their hotel rooms, others to their homes.

Pryce joined Stewart on the altar. "We must get you to safety."

"I have to go home and be ready if they come to burn it down," said Stewart, his face flushed with excitement. "Go find Josiah Tripp. Tell him to bring his carpentry tools to my house. Hurry, man, we must build barricades before they get organized."

CHAPTER THIRTY-EIGHT

FINISHED WITH HIS CHORES, Horace came from the barn and looked through the open kitchen door, surprised to see Maggie asleep in her chair, arms across her stomach. He hesitated, foot already poised to tap on the doorjamb. A shiver of regret tightened his chest. Hers was a good soul, gruff but straight. But it was her fault that his belongings had been destroyed. That was the truth of it. He no longer even had a rickety roof over his head.

A cold wind blew off the Ballou. It smelled like the soil and fore-told of an autumn storm. Behind it he knew the wind of winter rushed toward Utica and there was not a thing he could do to stop it. Survival —his own—was in jeopardy. Somehow it had come to this. His face was wet and he swiped at it with his sleeve. Shaking himself, he locked his jaw and rapped on the wood with his boot. Maggie lifted her head, a smile bursting across her face.

"I guess I fell asleep," she said as she rose. "Come on in." She pulled a steaming pot of coffee off the stove and added a few pieces of split wood to the firebox.

"Now what got you so tired?" asked Horace. He smiled, but again felt the sting of shame biting at his gut. He'd been in this kitchen a thousand times, but never as a spy.

Gripping his wrists, she flipped his hands over and saw the stained bandages. "Burns?" she said.

He nodded.

"I'll fix you up once I'm done with a few chores. Don't go nowhere."

"You too nice," he said, choking a little.

"Don't tell nobody." She smiled and poured him a bowl of coffee. As she worked, producing two plates of scrambled eggs, each with a thick slice of ham, she told him about the birth of the baby girl.

Horace winced at the mention of the infant. Filled with the information Hickox sought, he felt as if searing-hot stones were pressing against his back. He suddenly understood that his plan was all wrong. He couldn't go through with it. Maggie joined him at the table.

"That sounds mighty exciting," he said, smiling, relieved of the guilt. He took her hand and was on the verge of telling her about the fire when a shadow darkened the kitchen door and the two old friends turned to see a silhouette surrounded by a halo of bright morning light.

Abel Hickox passed through in the doorway, pistols drawn. Horace's hands shot up in surrender, but Maggie leaped to her feet and reached behind the open door for her musket. Hickox fired at her and the ball, propelled by the exploding black powder, cut through the air and sliced off the tip of the pinkie on her outstretched left hand. It ricocheted off the stove with a loud *pong*, and flew out the window, shattering one of the panes. A man's yelp came from outside.

Both the shot and Maggie's scream reverberated through the house. Hickox grabbed her by the collar and shoved her toward the table. He seized the musket from its place. Horace, arms still raised, saw the slaver's second loaded pistol move back in his direction. Maggie clutched her bleeding hand. A bell rang furiously from the front of the house.

"McCooke!" roared Hickox.

The doctor, hands trembling, came to the door. "That almost killed me," he said, setting down his medical bag.

"You have a patient," said Hickox.

Blood oozed down Maggie's sleeve as she tried to stanch the wound. The doctor went to her. She kicked him hard.

"Damn you," said McCooke, grabbing his calf, "I'm trying to help."

Maggie spat with amazing accuracy and potency, hitting him square in the face.

Hickox tossed Maggie's musket to McCooke. "Watch her," he said. He grabbed Horace by the shirt and pulled him in, the pistol inches from the fishmonger's eye. "Where are they?"

Horace stared beyond the slaver to Maggie. Agony twisted her face. A moment ago, she had been so beautiful, her eyes sparkling over news of the birth. He felt the throbbing pain from his burns and saw the ashes of his shack, the box, and the twisted braid of his mother's hair that had always offered him a tiny piece of comfort during the cold hard days. "Go to hell," said Horace.

"You took my money," said Hickox. "That was a promise."

"Money?" Maggie turned to Horace.

"I never promised you nothing," Horace said. "You burned up my home. Almost killed me. Way I see it, *you* owe *me*."

"This is a waste," said McCooke. "She had the baby. They might be running now."

Horace's angry gaze fell on the doctor, who swallowed hard.

"You hold them," said Hickox to the doctor. "I'll search upstairs."

Maggie seemed as if she was trying to speak, but no words came forth.

Hickox exploded out of the kitchen and ran up the servants' stairs.

On the second floor, Joe had heard the shot and the scream, and sprang from the divan. Helen and Elymas were on their feet in almost the same instant, while Imari stayed in bed cradling Margaret.

"Miss Maggie!" shouted Joe. He ran to the hallway. As heavy steps thundered up the back staircase, he flew down the front stairs. A thump shook the front door and he saw the brute Swift trying to break in. He turned and swung past the library where Galway's bell rang unanswered. In the kitchen, Joe knocked into McCooke, who staggered, the gun still pointing at Maggie and Horace.

"Run," urged Maggie. Before the doctor could swing the weapon in Joe's direction, the boy careened out the door.

Maggie charged the doctor and reached for the musket. Instantly, he brought the weapon down on her injured hand. She crumpled in pain. Horace sprang toward McCooke, but felt the musket shoved hard against his ribs, and contracted.

"Nigger, get back!" screamed the doctor, fear elevating his voice, his body shaking.

Rubbing his side, Horace mumbled, "You gonna pay for that." He wrapped his arm around Maggie's shoulders. "I swear I never told."

"Course you didn't," she said. "Sorry I got you into problems."

In the upstairs hallway, Hickox heard the wail of the infant and burst into the room. There was his most valued prize, the slave who had killed his partner. Imari tried to calm the crying baby and turned away from him. Mr. Galway's young wife moved in front of the mother and child, shielding the two. Elymas came around the bed, ready to fight, the fresh scar shining near his mouth.

Hickox shoved the white woman to the floor and trained the gun on the slave woman. "They're both dead if you come any closer," he said. That stopped the man.

The slave catcher heard the front door slam open as if a battering ram had been applied. He called over his shoulder, "Upstairs, Mr. Swift." He took the group in with the greedy eyes of an experienced man stealer and smiled in sweet satisfaction. "And bring the chains."

Swift and Hickox, guns ready, led the captives and Helen down the front staircase. Elymas's elbows were pulled back tight with a rope. His feet were shackled. A single chain joined husband and wife from neck to neck. Imari's collar was attached with a formidable lock. A set of manacles weighted down her wrists. The chains clinked and bounced against her thin blue nightdress as she held Margaret to her chest.

"You have no right to invade my house," said Augustin, ghastly white and clinging to the library door, hands shaking, his broken leg dangling uselessly.

"You are the man in the wrong, Mr. Galway," replied Hickox. "Harboring escaped slaves is a crime. I'll see you in jail, sir."

"Slaves? I did no such thing. Who are these people?" asked Augustin, as he dragged a small chair over and maneuvered himself onto it.

"Pretending ignorance?" said Hickox. He turned to Swift. "Let no one move while I deal with the niggers in the kitchen."

"Don't you touch Maggie!" yelled Augustin.

Hickox burst through the swinging door. The doctor still had the gun pointed at the two as they sat at the table. Horace held a bloody cloth between his first two fingers and was trying to tie up Maggie's wound.

"It is about time," McCooke said. "I'm a doctor, not a prison guard."

"Where is the boy?" demanded Hickox.

"He almost knocked me out as he escaped," said the doctor. "These two made to run off with him, but you were not a match for me, eh?"

Hickox slid his hand into his jacket and produced a heavy leather pouch. The familiar clink of gold drew Horace's eye.

"I should deduct the cost of the boy." Hickox handed the pouch to the doctor in exchange for the gun. "But very well done, Doctor. I didn't think you'd come through."

The doctor held the pouch in his trembling hand, then tucked it into an interior pocket of his closely cut jacket. It produced a noticeable bulge. "Well, I must be going." He edged to the door and paused for a moment. "Is the infant . . . uninjured?" he asked, turning back to Hickox.

"Why do you care, you skunk?" said Maggie.

"The infant is *my* concern, Doctor. My investment, my reward," said Hickox. "Good day."

The doctor's eyes dropped and without glancing at anyone, he picked up his medical bag and retreated out the back. Rain started to fall and he scanned the sky before ducking away.

"I'm feeling generous," Hickox said to Horace. "You get to walk away right now and not face charges for helping to harbor runaways. But remember, the terrible luck that you've been having will continue, if you persist."

Horace stood. "I'm free?"

"You're getting out." Hickox raised his gun. "So, get out."

Horace hesitated, turning to Maggie. She nodded and he slipped out the door.

"Now, my dear," said Hickox, "shall we all go to the court and see what charges they bring against you."

"Charges? I got shot in my own home. You steal them people, and I get charged?"

Hickox motioned for her to stand. "If you ever want to see *those people* again, you'll shut up and go help Mr. Galway."

"Oh, *I* gotta be quiet," she said as she stood. "I see." She moved past Hickox, a bloody rag dangling from her left hand. "*I* get shot and *I* gotta be quiet." She went through the door, letting it swing back toward Hickox.

In the hallway, she rushed toward Imari. Swift stepped in between them.

"You can't take that baby," insisted Maggie. "She was born on free soil. She ain't no slave." She turned to Augustin, who was looking pale and miserable as he sat on the chair in the doorway to the library. "This is it," she said intently. "What I talked about. You gotta do something."

Hickox stalked up behind them.

Augustin, his face red and glistening from pain, raised a quaking hand. "Maggie, who are these people?"

Maggie leveled her eyes on him. "They's the ones he was looking for, remember that slave notice?"

Augustin appeared uncertain for a moment.

"Yes, you remember," she said. "And remember I said you gotta do just what I say?"

Augustin's eyes focused on the young man standing in chains in his hallway. Shock and pain crossed his face. Suddenly animated, he turned to Hickox. "I'll buy them from you. All of them. Name your price."

Hickox stared at him coldly. "The man is not mine to sell. He belongs to Arnold Barnwell, so he may be had, but right now he must be seen by Judge Hayden. The boy? Well, he is not here, so I might be willing to sell him to you and be glad to never have to lay eyes on his mangy head. The baby? Is she a slave or is she free? Also a matter for the judge. But the woman. No sir. She will be tried in New Jersey for the murder of Mr. Colby." He turned to Imari. "And she will be hanged. By. The. Neck."

"Don't let this happen," said Helen, looking at her husband, her voice sharp, her eyes desperate.

"Any price, Mr. Hickox. All of them. Name it," said Augustin, his voice hoarse and weak. All eyes shifted to Hickox.

"She murdered a white man," Hickox said, his body rigid, face red. "That cannot stand. There will be justice. And let it be swift."

"I didn't mean to kill him," cried Imari.

"Quiet," said Hickox, striking her across the mouth. The sounds of metal clanking against metal filled the hall. Elymas surged toward Hickox. Swift yanked on Elymas's neck chain, choking him back.

Hickox pointed his gun at Elymas's head. "Mr. Swift, get the prisoners outside."

Maggie removed her knit shawl and gave it to Imari, who wrapped it around the baby. "We gonna help," said Maggie.

Hickox turned to her. "There is nothing you can do." He nodded to Augustin and left with Imari carrying the infant, blood seeping from her lips, Elymas behind her. Both upright and silent as they passed into the cold rain. Margaret's plaintive cries grew fainter as they drew farther away.

Maggie, Helen, and Augustin were left in the hallway.

"You must fix this," said Helen, moving to her husband and grabbing his hand. "We cannot lose them."

"Of course, you're right," he said. "We need help. My dear, get Alvan Stewart out of that abolition meeting. He must, no matter what, meet us at Judge Hayden's office."

Helen threw a cloak around her shoulders and ran out the door.

"Promise," said Augustin, turning to Maggie, "to get me to that courthouse."

She hesitated, eyes dropping to the broken leg and the bandages she had put on the day before. Was this right? she wondered. She thought about the poor baby and the awful noise of the shackles and the intensity of Hickox's anger. No. Augustin had to go. No other voice would be heard. A shudder raced through the man. She put her hand softly on his knee. He needed his rest, but the new fire in his eyes couldn't be denied.

It would be hard on him, that was certain, but not as hard as explaining to God that he had done nothing. I'll be right at his side if anything goes wrong, she thought. I'll pack a few things. Opium and some brandy. When we get back, I'll get some icy water from Ballou Creek and give him a cold bath and bring that heat down. He's strong. A man like that. No broken leg could stop him from his duty and he knows it.

"I will," she said, finally.

"What happened to your hand?" he asked.

"It ain't nothing. You ready for this?"

He nodded.

"You just wait. I'll get the horse hitched up." It's only a few blocks, she thought as she hurried to the back. After thirty years, that was not too far to go for redemption.

Horace kept his eyes on the blond head of Dr. McCooke, who had just disappeared onto Jay Street, moving swiftly and with purpose. His first step, Horace imagined, would be liquor. From there he might be going toward Bagg's Square and the hotels, or perhaps to the ticket office at the canal building. If he made it that far, he might leave Utica by packet, or even a freighter . . . *if*. Horace knew that the doctor could not stay in the city now. The things Maggie had said he'd done? No one would ever allow him inside their home to see their wives—not rich, not poor. Besides, what about that gal and her baby? They were in the hands of Satan because of him. He gets on the next boat and steps off somewhere else, clean. Who would ever punish a worm like him? He had to be stopped before he wrecked someone else's life.

Horace rubbed his rib cage where the doctor had struck him. He shivered and turned his collar up against the rain.

He knew the city better than that soft, weak white man. Jay Street dead-ended at the Bleecker basin. From there the doctor would have to go back to John Street and swing over to Genesee to get to the canal building. Horace knew a faster way, by sneaking by the Exchange Building. He could beat him to the Genesee Street Bridge and keep a look out from there.

He started to run across Bleecker Street, but a disturbance at the Presbyterian church caught his eye. An angry crowd had gathered and several men were scaling tall ladders that had been moved against the building. He had no time for any white men's nonsense. The idea that the doctor might get away boiled Horace's belly. Into that stew, he heaped his lost fish and his relationship with Mr. Galway, which was ruined, along with his reputation with his black customers. And the box. Coins and papers might be replaced, but no one could clip a new braid of hair from his mother's head. She had been sleeping in her grave for two decades. The only part of her he had left was gone.

He raced to the basin. Within moments, he was over the canal and took a good position under an awning across Liberty Street. He was breathing heavily, but tried to appear unruffled. He pulled his slouchy hat over his face and peeked out from under the brim.

In front of Horace, two white men, one tall and burly, the other deeply sunburned, confronted a small group of neatly dressed young men, a mix of both white and black. The burly fellow produced a basket and led the sunburned one into pelting the group with eggs. Clearly the force of their attack worked, as the lads broke into a run and passed Horace's position, turning at Whitesboro Street. The sky began to pour down a torrent of rain. People ran for cover and Horace found himself joined under the awning by the two who had been the cause of the mischief.

The burly man focused on him. "You one of them ab-o-litionists?" he asked, his hand in the basket.

Despite his bandages, Horace pulled back his coat, revealing his favorite fish-gutting knife, a sturdy specimen sharpened to perfection, with a solid antler handle that he'd mounted himself. "Chase them boys if you gotta chase someone," he murmured, pulling out the knife.

The men backed away into the downpour. Just as they did, the doctor appeared, complete with his medical bag, at the foot of the Genesee Street Bridge. He stopped for a moment and dug into his hip pocket. Horace squinted, trying to see if the man was removing the leather purse with the reward money. McCooke pulled out a flask and took a long drink from it. He raised the container, as if saluting the god of rain. After another sip, the doctor nodded with satisfaction and tucked it back into his pocket.

Resentment burned in Horace's chest. On a day like this one—with that family probably in chains—how could the man who had handed them over to the slavers be happy?

Hate filled the fishmonger with power. He surged toward the doctor and in a few steps the two were face-to-face. Horace's blade was buried in the doctor's side.

As McCooke slumped, Horace withdrew the knife and wrapped his arm around him, guiding the unsteady man to a corner of the bridge. With all his strength, he pulled the doctor down to the towpath and threw him onto the dusty gravel.

Blood began to stain the doctor's fine wool coat. The prone man tried to sit up, but could only lift his head. The wind shifted, cooling his face.

The doctor felt confused. The black man who stood over him was talking to him, but it was like his ears were stuffed with cotton. He felt something moving around inside his clothing. The villain had his hand in his jacket. After the Negro extracted something from an inner pocket—something very important, the doctor thought, but couldn't quite remember what—he felt himself grabbed under the arms and dragged. A large pile of rope appeared next to him and as McCooke studied it with interest, he heard the man say something else and understood that he was being left alone. Good, he thought, I'm too tired to deal with this nigger right now. He touched his side, looking for the flask, but instead felt a warm wetness. When he looked at his fingers, they were bright red. How strange, he thought. But he couldn't quite sort out what was happening. I must be drunk. His thoughts drifted off to his father's plantation on the very day young McCooke headed off to medical school. Father's face shone with pride. Mother hung on to him and sobbed as if she were sending him to Hades to seek out Dr. Faustus. He went to pat her back, but couldn't feel his hand. Sleep, sleep, he thought, and closed his eyes.

Once Horace had the leather purse, he quickly leaped back up to Genesee Street, leaving the doctor to his fate. As he sped away he tapped the bulge in his coat, once again hearing the familiar guilty clink of gold coins.

CHAPTER THIRTY-NINE

MAGGIE EMERGED FROM the house and splashed through the back-yard toward the barn.

"Sister Maggie," Sylvanus called. Joe ran ahead of him and caught up with her.

"They took Momma and Poppa. We gotta save them."

Sylvanus approached. "I can take the boy to Oriskany. We must keep him safe."

"We will," said Maggie.

"But what about Momma and Poppa?"

"We're gonna help them," she said, turning to the boy. "And you got a job to do."

Maggie hurried past them to the barn, but the moment her hand made contact with the heavy wooden door, she cried out.

Sylvanus stepped in front of her and swung both doors open.

"Mr. Sylvanus, go get Mr. Augustin ready to move. He's gotta come down to the court." She leaned in. "He ain't in good shape. You gotta help him."

"Why we need him?" said Joe. "He slow. We got this white man. Ain't one good as another?"

Sylvanus laughed in spite of himself.

"Hitch up that horse," said Maggie sharply.

Joe got the horse out of its stall and began backing it between the shaft rails of the cart.

"I shall see to Mr. Galway," said Sylvanus. "But," and he pulled Maggie outside of the barn, "we must shield the boy from those villains."

"I still need him," she said, worry bedeviling her face. "And I need you too. I got an idea that's gonna keep him outta the way. It's our only real chance."

Sylvanus nodded. "I am with thee to the end of it." He went into the house.

The boy pulled the horse and cart toward the front.

Maggie paced next to him. "Listen here, Joe. I got something important for you to do. We ain't gonna get you caught by that slaver. If you show up at the judge's, you're gonna get grabbed."

"But we gotta save Momma and Poppa," said Joe.

"We will. But you got a special job. You gotta get us help." Maggie pulled the boy close and quietly explained.

Helen ran quickly down Bleecker Street, weaving easily between stopped carriages and bickering men. She was not the only lady out on this wet day; she was, however, the only one without a hat and with tendrils of her hair loose and dripping wet.

How she might get Stewart to help, she did not know. Ahead, a cluster of angry men moved down the center of the street. She could not see over their heads, so she bent and then noticed, among the knees and britches and boots, a pair of her own shoes and the blue nightdress that she had given to Imari. The dress had a fresh bloodstain on its hem. This horrible march is killing her, she thought.

As if set on fire, Helen surged deep into the circle just as an egg struck Elymas's face. She heard Hickox yell, "These niggers are my prisoners!" and order the crowd back. A man with a bloated red face and blond hair hovered near Imari's ear shouting hateful words at her. Helen seized his waistcoat and, with a burst of strength, pulled him so off balance that he tumbled to the paving stones. A pair of hands, attached to a gruff-looking stranger with tobacco stains browning his white beard, pushed her to the ground. Several men stomped across her dress, covering it with muddy footprints. She rose and dove back into the center of the mob.

"In the name of God, stop!" she shouted. "Are you not Christians?"

"Quiet, you whore," snarled the tobacco-stained man.

"She is someone's sister, someone's daughter." She slapped away his silencing hand. "Would you want your child treated this way?"

The man looked at her with a curious expression. "They's escaped slaves and we's bringing them to jail."

This gave the crowd more energy.

"They broke the law!" yelled a young man.

"These are human beings you attack," she said to him. "Not animals." Helen's eyes met Imari's and read her fear. "Look. She's holding an innocent babe, alive less than a day. Can't you hear it cry? Think of your own babies and their mothers."

"She isn't MY mother," said a man dressed for shopwork, his apron covering his chest, his hair neatly parted.

"You, sir," she pointed at him, "should be ashamed of yourself. Think of your own wife. Imagine your family dragged through the streets."

The anger dropped from his face and he stopped moving as the knot around the captives continued to keep pace with Swift and Hickox.

A musket blast boomed and a shower of sparks shook everyone. Helen ducked low, tasting sulfur and feeling her eardrums pound. Onlookers stumbled away from Swift, who held a smoking musket, its muzzle pointing to the sky.

"Clear out!" he shouted.

"You're impeding sworn deputies from carrying out their duty!" Hickox yelled.

Both slavers had their backs to the captives.

Imari signaled to Helen. "Take her," she whispered, pushing tiny Margaret into Helen's arms. "And run."

Helen fumbled with the baby, almost losing her grip. A swift kick hit the back of her knees. She fell toward the unforgiving stones, twisting as she went and landing hard on her shoulder, Margaret pressed to her chest. Hickox loomed over her.

"If that brat is dead, you owe me seventy-five dollars." He reached in to take the infant.

Elymas, his arms still pinned, kicked at Hickox. Swift whirled around and cracked Elymas in the ribs with the butt of his gun, sending him sprawling to the road. Swift pulled out his lash and delivered a direct strike to Elymas's leg. The unmistakable crack of the whip sent more people skittering out of the way.

Still on the cold ground, Helen tried to soothe the infant.

"You've lost," said Hickox, hovering over her. "That baby is my property."

"No," she cried as he tried to part her arms.

Frustrated, he turned to Imari. "Take the baby. These are the last minutes you have with it."

"Do it," said Elymas from the ground.

Imari gently lifted Margaret from Helen's arms and hugged the child to her chest, adjusting the damp shawl as best she could.

"Move," demanded Hickox, as he hoisted Elymas to his feet. The group trailed on, leaving Helen on the cold pavement stones.

Pryce raced down the stairs of the Bleecker Street Presbyterian Church. He was just noticing the rain when the blast of a gunshot broke through the gloom. He ducked reflexively, thinking that if men were firing guns at each other, his mission to board up the windows at Alvan Stewart's house might already be too late.

As he ran, he noticed people scattering away from the gunshot. At the center of the scramble, he saw the slave catchers and the runaway female. A whip cracked and more of the mob backed away from the Southerners. The slave woman plucked a bundle from the arms of a prone figure in a filthy dress. Pryce ran toward the commotion. If only there were some way to stop this, he thought. All at once, he realized that the woman on the ground was Helen. As the crowd cleared, he brought her to her feet, wrapping a protective arm around her.

She looked up and the light of recognition crossed her face. "Save them."

"How?" he asked. "It's too late."

"Get Mr. Stewart. We have to bring him to Judge Hayden's office."

"But what about you?"

Helen pulled away. "Where is he?"

"The convention was attacked," said Pryce. "He's worried the mob'll burn down his house."

"He's their only chance," she said, panic edging into her voice. "Bring me to him."

"This way," he said, and they hurried inside the church.

Imari's legs felt weak and she was still in pain from giving birth. Her breasts ached as they swelled with milk. She could feel that her thighs were slick with moisture and looked down to see a wide red mark staining her muddy nightdress. She imagined her insides falling to the ground as Hickox prodded her forward, hurrying her with a jab of his gun. Crisp air blew across her bare calves and raindrops splashed into pools between the paving stones, wetting her ankles.

Margaret felt heavy in her arms. She tried to cradle the baby, but the irons were there and she was afraid that the girl would feel the cold hardness of them. She was such a tiny thing. These might be the last hours of her poor little life. Out in the freezing heartless world so early, before she even got a chance to fatten up, it would be murder and it would be the slave catchers' fault. But God never seemed to stop men like Hickox. At least Joe is safe, she thought. The one right thing I done was to get him outta the plantation. What Master Arnold had done? Well, it certainly gave them the push they needed to get out. Hopefully the boy had forgotten all about it.

"Hurry up," said Hickox.

He be nervous, she thought. As she looked around, she noticed that a black man hauling a wheelbarrow through the streets had stopped and stood watching. Across the road, standing on a porch, she saw a woman in a servant's uniform pause. They each deliberately met her eye and seemed to be trying to tell her something. Be strong, maybe. Or, I'm sorry. Whatever it was, she did not feel so completely alone. Some of them may have been slaves too. If any of them made a move to help her, they too would feel the lash. It didn't matter. Slave or free, the whip did not care who was who.

Elymas limped beside her, his shoulder touching hers. She glanced at him. He nodded and, despite everything, managed a private look that was so tender it wrenched her heart. Had running been wrong? She thought back through their final months. Every part of her body said go, but they had lingered.

Then came that sticky hot day when Missus Bea had saved her from Master Arnold's lust. It was a Friday, just one more day until she would see Elymas. On Saturday night, he always arrived at their cabin like a cool breeze. After Missus Bea stopped her son, she took Imari to her bedroom. It was as if the attack had never happened. Imari combed out her mistress's hair and straightened her vanity table. She brought up supper and was taking the dishes away when Missus Bea said to go. Don't come back until Monday morning, she said. Nobody needed to tell Imari more than once to take a rest.

She got back to the cabin and found Joe curled up under the table. When she asked him what had happened, he covered his head. That's when she saw blood on his britches. After pulling him from under the table, she searched his limbs for a cut or whip mark. At first he was like a rag doll, letting her move him without resistance. But when she tried to check his backside, he fought her. It took question after question to finally hear what had happened.

Later that night, she told Elymas and he was so angry and frustrated that he howled with rage and bashed his forehead into the wall of their cabin. They decided to run.

Margaret started to whimper. Imari raised her and kissed her. Miss Helen said Margaret wasn't a slave. Miss Maggie too. But what did they know about the way the white men acted? To think of her baby being sold on the block. How could God let it happen? *Take me instead,* she prayed. *Even if I gotta hang, please, God, save my baby.*

Just then Elymas, as if he had been reading her mind, cooed at Margaret and made a kissing noise. Imari met his eye and knew that she had no say in her daughter's life any more than she'd had with poor lost Jimmy. She brought one hand to her heart and tapped it. Pulling the shawl over Margaret, she savored her last moments with the infant as she breathed and moved against her chest.

"We tried," Elymas said, his voice tight.

"But our Joe be free," she murmured.

"Our Joe be free," he repeated.

Maggie drove the cart to the corner of Catherine and Genesee, across the street from Judge Hayden's office. The four-story redbrick building was neither simple nor fancy, but had mystifying angular designs above each window that seemed like tricky little maps trying to pull the unwary off their path. Just like the law, she thought. It could be twisted to suit powerful men's purposes. The actions of the runaways would never be considered lawful in a place like this. Self-defense was good enough for the whites, but she knew it would never be considered good enough for slaves or even free blacks.

She snapped the reins and the horse jerked forward. Nothing else could be done, except to keep herself near and be ready for anything. The cart came to a stop. She looked back at Augustin, wrapped in blankets and propped up against the side of the cart. His leg was on pillows and Mr. Sylvanus helped to hold it still. She shook her head. The old fool was in no condition for a fight.

Sylvanus hopped down from the back of the cart just as Pryce and Stewart arrived, both a bit short of breath. Helen was with them, circles of red on her cheeks. Maggie noticed her mistress's bright eyes track the young man as he followed Mr. Stewart to assist Augustin.

"Wait." Augustin gestured toward the lawyer. "Mr. Stewart, there is something you must know." Stewart drew close and Augustin glanced resentfully at Pryce and Sylvanus. "Excuse me, Mr. Anwell, please. It's a private matter. You too, Quaker."

Both stepped away. Augustin leaned heavily on Stewart, who wrapped his arm around the man, almost lifting him off his feet as they eased toward the building.

"Miss Helen," called Maggie, "I need you to steady me." Helen came over and offered up her hand. Maggie moved slowly from the cart's riding seat to the footrest and down to the ground. I'm tired, she thought, turning her eyes to the young Mrs. Galway. "They's things that's gonna be talked about." Maggie paused and sighed. "I don't know what's gonna happen, but . . ."

"None of us can undo what's been done," Helen said, blinking hard. "The truth is, I've failed them. Failed everyone. Even my Christian duty. How will Imari . . . How will she get clear of Mr. Hickox?" She tried to dry her face with her sleeves.

"Maybe God's not done with us." Maggie squeezed Helen's hand.

"Here they come," said Pryce.

The two women peered up Genesee and saw the dreadful approach. Imari and Elymas in chains, the innocent babe wailing. A crowd of on-lookers trailed behind, some looking as if they were part of a funeral procession, others, red-faced and fists waving, seeming ready for a hanging.

"No!" yelled Maggie, as she tried to run toward them, her feet slipping on the wet paving stones. She crashed to the ground. "I gotta get them the warm things." She slipped as she tried to rise. "They're all three soaked through."

Helen took Maggie's elbow, calling to Pryce: "Get the blankets out of the cart." He brought them over. "Help Maggie," she said as she took a blanket from his arms.

She ran up the street to Imari and wrapped a salmon-colored blanket around her shoulders, bringing the corner over Margaret's head. Imari shivered and Helen wrapped her arm around the captive's waist.

"Stay away," ordered Swift. He pointed his rifle at her. Helen ignored him.

"They've *lost* the game," said Hickox. "Let her."

Swift stepped back, his weapon still at the ready. Helen fell into step.

"I thank you," whispered Imari. "Sorry I brung you all this trouble."

"You brought me no trouble," said Helen, her voice wavering. "I'm so sorry."

As they arrived at Judge Hayden's building, Hickox leaned in, an expression of excited energy on his face. "Look upon this murderess for the last time." He pulled back and scanned the group that had followed them. "This nigger killed my partner." He pointed to Imari. An astonished hush grew over the assembled onlookers. His voice grew louder with each sentence. "A man of the law. Killed in *cold* blood. I'll see to it that she hangs!"

Some of the crowd roared their approval.

Stewart motioned to Sylvanus. "Take Mr. Galway inside—quickly." The lawyer pushed his way through the knot of men. "Mr. Hickox," he cried, arm extended, finger pointing at the slaver, "I represent these people. I'll not have you stir up the specter of Judge Lynch."

"It'll be done according to law," called Hickox, pointing skyward. "But it will be done."

"She killed a white man," said someone in a tailored broad coat. "We want justice."

"You ain't nothing but trouble, Stewart," called a pimply man.

"We must get them inside," said Helen to Stewart.

Hickox smiled and nudged Swift. "Tarry a moment to enjoy this. Everyone is moving toward their proper place. The disorder of the world is being defeated."

Joe worked his way across Elizabeth Street. His challenge was to not be noticed. But unlike the other time when he'd been walking on his own, today a bustle of men crowded the streets. He decided to look like a boy with a message and trotted at an easy pace, weaving in and out, shouting, "Excuse me, sir!"

After six blocks, he turned onto a short alley and recognized he was in the right area—Post Street. He saw none of the troublesome whites. Instead, black women and children went about their business as if there were nothing extraordinary going on.

Maggie had told him to ask around for the schoolmaster. If there was anyone in the neighborhood who could help, it would be him.

A lady, so bent over that her back was at the same angle as the street and who carried a bucket of apples, tottered by him.

"You know where Schoolmaster Freeman be at?" he said.

"Your momma never taught you to ask nice?" she responded, her head raised. She studied him with one bluish eye and another that looked more like fried egg white.

Pressure built in his chest. Didn't she know that his parents were in trouble? He took a deep breath. "Sorry, ma'am. I gotta find Schoolmaster. Where he be? Please?"

She laid her bucket to the side and put a wrinkled finger to her lip. "School got called off on account of the danger. So he's most likely to home. Come on, son. Liddy gonna show you the way." She picked up her bucket and rattled slowly down the street rocking from side to side as if her hips were frozen and she needed her whole body to move each leg.

Joe grabbed the bucket from her.

"Boy," she said, "what you doing?"

"Helping you."

"Well ain't that nice. Ain't nobody falling over theyselves to help old Liddy."

"You a slave?" asked Joe.

"Where you get that notion?"

"Sorry."

Liddy looked at him with her one good eye. "This be New York State, boy. Ain't nobody a slave in eight years now." She stopped in front of a whitewashed clapboard building. "As I recollect, Freeman's up there, second floor." She ran her tongue over her gums, lingering on the one front tooth she had left. "If I was you, I'd keep my questioning down. Especially 'bout slaves and such." She turned back and proceeded across the street. "Think he knowed a slave when he see one, huh."

Joe ran up the staircase and knocked on the door. A well-dressed boy appeared. He was Joe's age, with spectacles and a book in his hand. The boy's face looked more like Joe's own than anybody he had seen in Utica. He stood still for a moment, stunned. They could be kin, yet the boy's clothing and demeanor were vastly different.

"Miss Maggie told me get Schoolmaster Freeman," Joe said finally.

"Come in." The boy led him into the parlor filled with what Joe thought of as too much furniture for a black family. He could see several tables, chairs with fabric on them, and rugs. No one had rugs but the whites.

Schoolmaster Freeman sat talking to Horace, who quickly stood and turned away wiping his cheeks.

"You gotta help us," Joe said, running to them. "Miss Maggie sent me," he added, as if the cook's name was a magic key that unlocked people. He now had their attention and explained her plan.

Freeman looked grave and nodded. "Give me at least a half an hour," he said as he grabbed his coat. "Keep yourself safe, you hear me?" He took a deep breath and let it out in a sigh. "Your mother, father, and baby sister, is that right?"

"Yes, mister."

The muscles on Freeman's jaw tensed. "Miss Maggie is with them?"

"Yes, she be there. She ain't gonna leave."

"One half hour. Don't warn them. Keep out of sight."

Joe certainly understood the man, but promised nothing. Once on the street, he heard a horn blowing a prolonged note from the window above him. Gooseflesh rose on his arms. It was exactly the sound he had heard when they fought their way out of the cart of the long-faced man in New Jersey. Everyone on the street looked up to the second floor. Joe did not linger. He headed back downtown to find his family.

CHAPTER FORTY

JUDGE CHESTER HAYDEN'S office-cum-court contained two desks. The clerk, Pearly Doyle, was a thin man straight as a knife blade who might be said to worship the goddess of good order, Eunomia; his desk was neat and precise. Judge Hayden's oak desk was massive; Eris, goddess of discord, ruled over the jumble of papers and stacks of books. It was Doyle's job to keep the judge's desk clear, but even Sisyphus occasionally must have had to dig in his heels, let the rock press against his back, and rest.

Shouts and the thumps on the plank sidewalk broke the silence in the court. The clerk stood looking from the judge to the door.

Suddenly, Sylvanus pushed inside, helping Augustin. Doyle scrambled forward, arms out in front of him as if to prevent further intrusions. Instead both doors crashed wide open and Alvan Stewart, the slavers, and their captives, followed by several other disheveled people, surged in.

"Bar the door, Doyle!" shouted the lawyer, as angry cries of *"She killed a white man!"* and *"Hang her!"* rose from the street. The clerk slammed the doors and fitted an iron bar across them.

"What kind of mess is this?" Doyle demanded, tugging at his drab waistcoat, as if he might at least restore order to his clothing.

Stewart was about to answer when Hickox marched across the room toward Judge Hayden, who looked stern and somber.

"Your Honor . . ." Hickox began.

But Hayden waved a silencing hand and leaned over the desk to address Augustin, who was coming forward with the baker's help. "Galway, we missed you. You should have seen the precious look of impotent rage when Mr. Stewart here saw us reclaim the church from that vile assembly of abolitionists." Hayden chuckled as he smirked at Alvan Stewart like a hunter, his prey finally in his sights. "I thought our 'peace man' might just commit an act of violence." The judge's smile drained away as Augustin drew closer and he saw the man's unhealthy blue pallor and weakened condition. "Sorry to hear about your accident," he said. "Matteson took your place on the Committee of 25."

"Forgive me for missing the event, Your Honor," said Augustin with a gravelly voice.

"Nonsense. But it's queer to see you here, considering your injury."

"It could not be helped," said Augustin. "Mr. Stewart is here at my request."

"Really? Of course, one is free to be represented by whomever one chooses." Hayden's gaze swept over the strange assemblage of people. "*This* should be interesting."

"Excuse me, Your Honor," said Hickox, nodding respectfully. "These runaway slaves are my captives and I need a court order to transport them back to Virginia." He handed the judge a set of papers.

"Your Honor, these people are not property," said Stewart. "Each has a rightful claim to freedom."

"Sit down, Mr. Stewart," said the judge, taking the papers.

"You all heard him, be seated. You," Doyle indicated the slavers, "to the left, and the rest of you on the benches." After one more tug on his waistcoat, he returned to his desk.

Swift pointed his rifle at Imari and Elymas, motioning them over to Hickox's side of the courtroom. Sylvanus guided Augustin to a captain's chair at the defendant's table and eased him down. Maggie came to his side and shifted his leg so that it could be elevated on a second chair. He groaned in pain and took quick shallow breaths.

"You hurting?" she whispered.

"My leg. It's burning. It needs air." Augustin began to tear at the bandages.

Maggie reached out, covering his hand with hers. "Don't you go ripping that off. We're gonna get a proper doctor to look you over—when we get done with this here."

Helen joined them just as the cook's fingers intertwined with his, gently pulling it away from the bandages. The wrappings, however, had parted and Helen gasped. The leg—red and brown—looked like a piece of liver. "My heavens," she said quietly. "This looks . . . unwell." She met Augustin's eye. "No wonder you're in pain. Maggie, can this really wait?"

"I don't know," said the cook, peering at the injury. She lowered her voice. "Them people ain't got no chance without him. But this here leg is bad."

"I won't leave," said Augustin. "Don't make me try. Promise," he demanded, gripping Maggie's arm.

Maggie turned to Helen, fear in her eyes.

"I promise you," said Helen to Augustin. She nodded at Maggie. "I make the promise."

Maggie nodded, seeming relieved.

Augustin began muttering, "*God, hide not Thy face from me in the day when I am in trouble. For my days pass away like smoke, like an evening shadow, like withered grass . . .*"

Judge Hayden settled back in his chair and examined the slavers' papers. He knew that, as always, truth would need to be separated from fiction. He prided himself that his role in Utica was to be that sieve. The judge shifted his gaze to the prosecutor's table.

"Doyle," he roared, "are you getting sloppy in your old age?"

Doyle stood and put his hands on his hips, as if to dare the judge to show him one error.

"The musket. Secure the musket, man." Hayden pointed at Swift.

The clerk's shoulders slumped. "Forgive me, Your Honor." He strode over to Swift, hands out. The slave catcher looked uneasy. A momentary standoff was broken with a nodded permission from Hickox, who also turned over his own guns.

Pryce joined Stewart at the defendant's table. "He's the judge from the Committee of 25," he whispered. "He hates you, does he not?"

Stewart reflected for a moment. "He might hate me, but he loves the law."

Baby Margaret began to fuss.

"Take the infant out of here," said Hayden.

Helen rose and went to Imari's side. "There is still a chance," she whispered into Imari's ear as she took the baby.

"Joe got a chance," Imari said. "Elymas got a chance. Margaret got a chance. But back on the plantation, I done prayed to God to save my family. I forgot to say nothing about me. So you got to promise me to see this baby through."

"We will," said Helen, lowering her eyes. After a moment's hesitation, she stepped toward the street door.

"That baby's status must be determined by Your Honor," said Hickox, leaping to his feet. "Before someone runs off with it."

Hayden peered over his spectacles. "Very well. Stop right there, young lady. You may sit with the child, but keep it quiet."

"Yes, Judge," said Helen, returning to Imari's side. "I think she's just hungry." She handed the baby back to Imari, who shielded herself with the blanket and began to nurse. Helen sat next to them while Swift maneuvered himself to be between the two women and the door.

The judge turned to Hickox. "You're the slave catcher, correct?"

"Your Honor, I am an officer of the law in Virginia."

"And here in Utica, you're nothing but a problem," said Hayden. "But problems and difficulties crawl into this court and the law sees that justice marches out. Now, as I understand it, these three are slaves from—"

"Your Honor, referring to them as slaves is prejudicial," said Stewart. "Each one has a claim to freedom."

"Noted," said the judge with sarcasm. He picked up Hickox's handbill. "These are the Negroes who *may have* escaped from the Barnwell Plantation?"

"There's a boy too," said Hickox. "He slipped away, but I purchased him from the Barnwells along with the mother and the unborn baby."

"That baby appears to have been born," said Hayden. Hickox was about to object when the judge silenced him with a look. "That is what babies do. They get born. And that means its status has changed. How shall we proceed? Why not from largest," he pointed to Elymas, "to smallest?" He was clearly pleased with himself and his role in the momentous happenings of the day. The traitors at the abolition convention had been stopped and now a complicated slave case bloomed before him with the lead conspirator, Alvan Stewart, at his mercy. The judge would show the scoundrel what the law meant in a free society. It was a victorious day and he would not let anything ruin it. "So," he said, turning to Elymas, "you ran away?"

"Don't answer that," injected Stewart. "He was illegally sold and purchased, and therefore had the right as a free man to walk away from his enslavers."

"Judge . . . Your Honor," Maggie said, pushing herself to her feet, "I gotta talk to you."

"Do not interrupt the business of the court," snarled Hayden.

"But I know about this here business," said Maggie. Then, as an afterthought, "I'm sorry, Your Honor."

He leaned over the desk toward her. "The truth is, you're not really sorry at all, are you? Now, sit down."

Maggie, cheeks burning with anger, sank to her seat.

"That's better."

The judge addressed Stewart. Maggie looked around her—suddenly exhausted. Her injured hand throbbed and the lack of sleep muddled her mind. She heard the judge's sharp tone when he talked to Mr. Stewart and she noticed a satisfied smile on Hickox's face.

No, she thought. Enough. He ain't winning again. She pushed herself to her feet and stood upright before the judge. "Elymas is *my* boy," she said firmly, her voice rattling around the room. Her eyes flashed to Helen, who sat frozen and pale. "My own boy," she continued, finally speaking the words she had not allowed herself for three decades. She covered her face in shame. God made His rules for a reason, she thought. You break them, you pay. "And I let him go. I shoulda fought," she said, looking heavenward. "God forgive me, I shoulda died."

Hickox was on his feet. "She can't testify," he barked. "She harbored these runaways. She'll say anything."

"Quiet," said Judge Hayden. "Do you think I'm incapable of sorting out what is important in my own court?"

"No, Your Honor," said Hickox, clenching his jaw and staring hard at Maggie.

"So, let us get to the truth." Hayden pointed at the cook. "You won't be sworn in in this courtroom. But as quick as you can, tell me what you have to tell me. Keep in mind, if I find you've been telling tales, you will sit in a jail cell for contempt and you'll have harmed the people you mean to protect."

"Only thing I got is God's honest truth."

"Proceed."

"Judge, sir," Maggie began, her voice shaky. She pointed to Elymas.

"This here man is my son. I was born a slave in Utica and lived in the Galway house all my life. In 1805, Thomas Galway took me from Utica to Virginia. I was already carrying the baby when we started," she said, purposely avoiding Augustin's eyes. "I got put down in a slave quarters to be sold. Well, babies got they own time and God got his time, and it don't always match with our time, do it?" She looked at Imari, who nodded gravely.

Maggie went to Elymas and let her finger touch the indentation between his eyes. "My God, you're my boy. My lost boy." She put her arm around his shoulders, drawing him close. The feel of the ropes that secured his arms was like a knife through the heart. She squeezed him and whispered, "I'm sorry." The solid truth of his muscles and the relief and dread on his face brought her right back to that awful time thirty years before. In the courtroom, looking into the eyes of her grown son, she felt again the terrible emptiness. "Hickox gotta wait," she said, speaking to Elymas. "I got scared we both gonna get sold separate. So I did something. Only thing I could do. You know what I'm talking about?"

"Sir Judge, Your Honor," said Elymas, "I got something to show you."

"A paper?" asked Hayden.

"No, Judge." Elymas looked down. "My wife there seen a paper back home, but we ain't got it. This here be something just as good." He lifted his right foot and nodded solemnly to Maggie. Their eyes locked for a moment before she kneeled to remove his shoe.

"I'll not look at his foot," said Hickox.

Elymas held up his scarred sole. The judge squinted behind his spectacles, finally leaving his desk. He bent low and inspected a series of dark scratches.

"What am I looking at?" he asked. "Is that U-T-I-C-A?"

Helen's mouth dropped open in shock.

Maggie nodded at her. "I just knew we was gonna get separated." She looked back to Elymas. "So I done cut your foot with a little knife and rubbed soot into them wounds. You was so tiny. And you cried like a brass band." She took Elymas's face in her hands. "I ached for you. It was like I got split open and half a me dragged off with Satan."

"Judge, that can't be used," said Hickox.

"You weren't even a week old," said Maggie.

Elymas swallowed hard. "Master James told me he got me cheap 'cause a them there cuts. Damaged goods, he said." He turned to the judge. "I don't think Master James bothered to try and read it. I couldn't. Not till my wife found them papers about me. Then she done figured out what it say."

Maggie rested her head on his knee.

Judge Hayden let his fingers cross the length of his chin as he slowly returned to his place. He settled himself and crossed his hands, fingers tapping on the desk. As the silence filled the room, Maggie looked up. The spectators studied him as if fearful that the judge might ignore all that had passed.

Finally, he spoke: "I agree that the scar has some kind of weight—unusual as it is." He focused on Maggie. "But this sounds like a tale to me. Why would Thomas Galway risk breaking the law to take you there? And if he did, why weren't *you* sold too?"

"Since I ain't supposed to say nothing about no white man," Maggie said, turning to Augustin, "I guess I can't tell." Their eyes met.

"My father took her there," Augustin said loudly, attempting to stand. Stewart held his arm. "In 1805, he took her to Richmond. I followed them. I knew of the sale of the infant—and consented." He wobbled, falling back into the chair.

"Were you aware that what your father did was against the law?" asked Hayden. "No one could sell a slave outside of New York State after 1799."

"The hearing is about the status of these people," said Stewart, "not Galway's actions."

"Silence!" shouted the judge. "Mr. Galway, if you have something to say, say it. There will be no tomorrows for the truth."

Augustin clutched the lawyer's arm. "Your Honor," he said, his voice full of emotion, "I admit that I knew the baby should have been free. And—" He hesitated and looked at Elymas. "And that he is . . . *my son*." His head dropped. "After the baby was taken, Maggie begged me to let Father sell her too, so that they'd be together." He looked up at her. "I was selfish, I suppose." He shook his head, his face crimson. He met Maggie's eye. "Hickox wanted you both. But he was so business-like about it. To him you were nothing. To me you were—everything. I couldn't let Father do it. I loved you."

Augustin took in a sustaining breath before speaking directly to Judge Hayden. "I knew Father was wrong. I knew he was breaking the law by selling her after emancipation." He turned back to Maggie. "While you were downstairs in that awful place, I threatened to kill myself if he sold you. But selling the baby was the price." He leaned back, seeming to shrink before their eyes. He wiped a ragged handkerchief across his brow. "Father said I would forget. Said that if people ever found out about the baby, I would be turned out—without family or name. He was going to disinherit me. Where could she and I have gone? Live in a slum in New York City?" He dropped his hands to his lap. "But the old man was stricken by the whole affair," Augustin resumed, his voice pleading. "I said that selling the baby and bringing you back would raise fewer questions. He looked at me with disgust. He left me in New York City, but what I had done ate away at him. I think it killed him."

"You thought it wouldn't touch you and you could just forget," said Maggie, shaking her head. "You've been drunk ever since."

"Well there it is," said Hayden slowly. "Truth."

Truth, thought Helen, stunned and blinking, as if all those around her were speaking in a different tongue. How could she not have noticed? She felt small, like an uncomprehending half-wit. She leaned into Imari. "Is that why you were in our shed?"

"Yes," Imari whispered. "The man who done help me in Frankfort give me the address. I know that shed be on Galway's property. I wasn't gonna go nowhere till Elymas caught up. I had to lie."

"What other proof have you," asked Hayden, "that this man is the infant in question?"

"Nothing, Judge," Augustin said, short of breath.

"You admit that you fathered a child with this woman and that your father, Thomas Galway, took her to Virginia and sold her infant son?"

"I do, Your Honor. Heaven forgive me."

Helen's hands started shaking. The sleeping baby in Imari's lap was her husband's granddaughter—Maggie's too.

"And you knew of a sale of a male infant to Abel Hickox here?" said Hayden.

Augustin nodded.

"Mr. Hickox, do you admit to buying a male infant from Mr. Thomas Galway in 1805 for the Barnwell family?"

"I bought and sold many slaves for the Barnwells. You can't expect me to remember each and every one."

"Then why'd you come to see Mr. Augustin the other day?" shouted Maggie, scrambling to her feet. "Why'd you leave off that there slave notice?"

"Silence," said the judge. "I'll not warn you again." He squinted at Maggie. "I've heard enough." He addressed Elymas: "You, boy, are free."

A gasp of relief passed through the court. Maggie sank to the bench behind Elymas and laid her forehead against his shoulder. Helen grabbed Imari's hand. They sat together, praying.

"If Mr. Galway would like to compensate the Barnwells for their original investment, then we shall be done with you."

"I will pay them the seventy-five dollars," said Augustin.

"Judge," said Hickox, "this is outrageous. There is no legal basis for your decision. Besides that, for thirty years that man has eaten and been clothed by the good charity of the Barnwell family."

"You're all wrong about what's right!" shouted Maggie, sitting up and pointing at Hickox.

"I told you to stay quiet, woman," said Hayden. "Now, step outside or I swear I will send all of these people away."

Helen watched Maggie start to speak, but it was as if the fight had suddenly left her. After patting Elymas and kissing Imari's head, the cook moved slowly to the entranceway. Doyle lifted the bar. After taking one more look at Elymas and Imari, she left and closed the door.

"Now," said Hayden. "for the woman . . ."

"Your Honor," Stewart cut in, "now that you've made your decision, Mr. Hickox should remove this free man's chains."

"Mr. Stewart," said the judge, "do not interrupt my train of thought for a mere comfort. A few more minutes won't matter. Where was I?"

"The status of the woman," said Stewart, his face reddening.

"Oh, yes. Is there a question of her origins?"

"No, Your Honor," said Hickox. "Born a slave, of a slave."

The words hammered into Helen. They took away all hope. *Born a slave, of a slave.* Perpetual—unending. How could heaven allow it?

"But she is the mother of the baby who was born in New York State," said Stewart, "where no one has been born a slave since the enactment of the Gradual Emancipation Act."

Imari brought her hand up to her heart and tapped it three times.

"Not so quick, Mr. Stewart," said Hayden. "A slave who arrives in New York with her master will remain a slave for nine months, if they stay. Before that time, if they go back to their home, then that slave is still a slave. As for runaways, their residence, no matter how long, never becomes legal because they are considered stolen property. So the mother is still a slave."

Both Imari and Helen cried out, "No!"

"I will have order," said Hayden sternly. "On to the baby. My understanding is that if a pregnant slave is in New York State with her legal master, then the fetus is considered a slave."

"Her daddy be free," insisted Imari, "so she be free."

"That does not follow the law," said Hayden. "There is no way to know if this man is indeed her father." Imari started to object, but Hayden cut her off: "Do not give me oaths about parentage because it is of no consequence. You are considered to be a possession of the Barnwell Plantation. You have stolen yourself and that baby is considered stolen property as well. My decision is that you and she are the property of Mr. Hickox, who has presented proper and lawful proof of your sale."

Imari's head dropped, her cheek touching little Margaret.

"Judge, mercy," pleaded Helen. "Don't send Mr. Galway's granddaughter into slavery."

"I'll buy them," said Augustin, his voice choked. "Name your price."

Judge Hayden looked at Hickox, his eyes sharp. "Do you still want the infant now? Or are you willing to sell?"

"One thousand dollars for her," Hickox squinted, a smile on his lips, "and another thousand for the missing boy. I sell both, or neither."

"Agreed," said Augustin, swabbing the sweat from his face. "We can go to the bank after the proceedings. How much for the woman?"

Hickox glared at Imari. "No sale. She is wanted in the state of New Jersey for the murder of my partner, Mr. Colby. She will pay for her crime when she hangs."

Imari turned to Helen, her eyes wide with fear.

Helen, illness rising to her throat, put her arm around the woman's shoulders.

"Judge Hayden," said Stewart, "what proof do we have besides his word?"

"Here," said Hickox, handing several pages to the judge. "This is a copy of the arrest warrant and a signed affidavit by the town's sheriff, who witnessed the murder. He was in the woods at the time because of an armed rebellion by the Negroes of Hightstown."

Hayden looked over the paper. "This is properly done. I have no choice but to release her to your custody, Mr. Hickox." He addressed Imari: "You will be taken to New Jersey to stand trial for murder."

Helen closed her eyes, unable to believe what had transpired.

Hickox leaned toward her. "Look upon this murderess for the last time."

"You're a beast," said Helen, voice trembling.

Imari evened out her breathing. She sat erect, the infant in her arms.

"The *law* always has the final say," said the judge, and banged his gavel on the desk.

"You be a good girl and grow up strong, like your daddy," Imari murmured to Margaret. Then, looking at Helen, she held the baby out to her. Helen shook her head, but Imari pushed the infant into her arms. "Take her." She held Helen's eyes. "Keep her safe."

Helen nodded, trying to hold back her tears.

Just then the street door burst open and another authority took charge.

CHAPTER FORTY-ONE

WHEN MAGGIE STEPPED OUT of the courtroom and into the street, she looked around, recognizing nothing.

Joe, Horace, and Schoolmaster Freeman approached her on the sidewalk.

Lingering nearby on busy Genesee Street were four wagons harnessed to four different horses. The schoolmaster's wife and two black couples stood on the sidewalk. All three women appeared to be holding a swaddled baby. Freeman's boy was brushing down one of the horses, trying to look like this was a regular task. A nervous energy animated their faces.

"Where Momma and Poppa?" asked Joe, pulling on Maggie's arm.

"Your daddy's gonna be free." Maggie looked up to Horace and Freeman. "I don't know about the others, or Joe neither. We gotta get them outta there 'cause that devil still wants to take 'em to hell." Maggie took a step toward the men, but she suddenly felt weak and stumbled.

Horace grabbed her in his arms. "You about to drop," he said.

"Just let me sit a minute," said Maggie, and both men helped her to the corner of a water trough.

Horace sat beside her. "You got shot. You ain't got no sleep," he said, speaking softly and putting his arm around her. "You best stay out here."

"No," she said, studying him closely. "They's my family in there."

"Family?" said Horace. "Real and true family?"

Maggie nodded. Horace returned her gesture.

"What that mean?" asked Joe.

"Elymas is my son. That makes you my one true grandson, that's what."

"Miss Maggie, I knew you were like me," said Joe with vindication.

Maggie touched his cheek. "Call me Grandma."

Horace looked at Freeman. "This gonna work?" His knee bounced nervously.

"It's gonna work," said Maggie, stilling his leg, "'cause it's gotta work."

"Come on, Grandma," said the boy, running toward the door.

Maggie and Horace picked themselves up and followed him.

When the court doors burst open Helen swung around in time to see Joe, Horace, and Maggie rush in. In confusion, she pulled the infant to her chest and backed away from the commotion.

"You can't come in here," cried the clerk, running from his desk to meet Horace, who pushed him to the floor.

"Stay still, Mr. Doyle," said Horace. "It don't gotta go bad for you."

Swift jumped up, already pulling out his whip. He snapped his wrist and the knot on the end of the long leather strap crackled through the air until it bit into Maggie's shoulder. She cried out in pain.

Augustin, forgetting about his broken leg, rose and lurched toward Maggie. His scream of agony was cut short when he collapsed into a heap.

Stewart shouted, "Mr. Galway!" and rushed to the stricken man's side. Maggie, despite the blood streaming from her shoulder, quickly came to Augustin's aid. Together they flipped him onto his back.

Elymas turned to Helen. "Get the baby outta here!"

Hickox jerked the chain that connected Imari and Elymas. The both fell toward him. Imari clawed at the manacle around her neck.

Judge Hayden shouted for order, but his words disappeared into the chaos.

The next thing Helen knew, Pryce was by her side. She said, "We must get Margaret out of here," forcing herself to move. They stumbled toward the door. Swift loomed up in front of them. Pryce shoved the man, but the brute's strong legs kept him stable. Swift punched Pryce in the jaw, dropping him to his knees. The slaver readied himself to use his whip again when Pryce sprang up and drove his shoulder into the man's stomach, doubling him over and shoving him to the floor with a thud.

Sylvanus dashed around the benches and threw himself onto Swift's back.

"You have to go!" shouted Pryce at Helen.

"Help my husband," she said to him. They locked eyes for a moment. She saw his determination. She turned and rushed out of the court.

"Swift," called Hickox, "get up, you fool." But the other slave catcher was immobile.

Hickox climbed onto the judge's desk, gripping Imari's chain.

"This is for Colby!" he shouted, and hoisted her up. She hung, shuddering, hands at her neck, legs kicking.

Elymas tried to shoulder Hickox off the desk, but his arms remained pinned behind his back. Horace charged forward and, with a few deft slashes of his gutting knife, cut away the ropes that restrained Elymas.

Arms finally free, Elymas lunged forward and hauled the slaver down. Imari's body dropped to the floor, motionless. Joe crawled to her and lifted her head. "Momma," he cried. But she did not move.

Elymas stood over Hickox. His arm rose and the chain that the slaver had been holding like a leash whistled through the air, smashing into Hickox's face. He grunted and raised his arms. Blood flowed from a deep gash. Elymas swung again and again; each stroke bit into flesh. Tears and spit and streaks of the slaver's blood ran down Elymas's face as he wielded the chain.

It was not until Joe screamed "Poppa!" that he stopped. Shaking himself, he scooped up his wife's body.

"This way," said Horace, pulling on Elymas's arm and running toward the door.

Outside, Helen stammered, "I think the others are coming," to the bespectacled black man who rushed to her.

Freeman guided Helen and the baby to the bed of a wagon and helped her get under its cover. "One of the ladies brought some cow's milk for the baby," he said, pointing to a small bowl covered with a white cloth. "Stay hidden."

Helen felt the baby squirming and pulled back the knitted shawl. Margaret cried in fear. How had she not heard the infant's distress? Imari's eyes had been so pleading, the message clear—make certain that this child lives free. Helen lay on her side and circled herself around the infant. A lullaby of her mother's came to her and she started singing quietly into Margaret's ear. She wet her finger with milk and brought it to the child's lips. The baby started to suckle. Helen felt the intensity of the infant's hunger and her fierce will to live.

Shouts moved in the direction of the shrouded wagon. It seemed as if the fight had spilled into the street. The wagon's tarp was heaved up. Elymas and Horace held Imari's limp body. The two men placed the woman into the wagon, the awful chains still around her neck and hands. Horace boosted Elymas inside.

Helen heard someone shout "Now!" and Horace ran to the front of the wagon, hopping onto the seat and slapping the reins, jerking the cart into motion.

An out-of-breath voice came from the driver's seat: "Go to Oriskany. I know a man." And she understood that Sylvanus was there to help guide them to safety.

"Where's Joe?" Helen called to the front. She saw a hand grasp at the tailboard. Joe pulled himself inside.

"We got four horses. Each going in a different direction," the boy said. His excitement faded as he looked at his mother's body. "She dead?" he asked, his voice quavering.

Elymas had his wife's hand in his. "I don't know," he said.

"Take the baby," Helen said to Joe. She crawled over to the still form and brought her ear to the woman's mouth, but there was no sound. "Imari," she said. She remembered that she had a small mirror and dug into her pocket. She held it next to Imari's lips. The tiniest circle of fog appeared on the shiny surface. "She's alive."

Joe bent low, put his face into his sister's wrapping, and sobbed. Relief swept across Elymas's face.

Helen lowered herself to Imari's ear. "Stay with us," she begged. "You're safe."

Just then, two musket blasts thundered outside and one tore a hole into the wagon's tarp. Horace shouted and slapped the reins against the horse's flanks. As they moved faster, Elymas tumbled onto the wagon's bed, blood staining his white shirt.

C HAPTER FORTY-TWO

ON THURSDAY, OCTOBER 22, Utica awoke to a swirl of rumors, accusations, and denunciations. Some facts were undeniable: the abolition meeting had been disrupted, the conventioneers dispersed.

The Bleecker Street Presbyterian Church had been left in a shambles, causing the poor Reverend Hopkins to almost regret his decision to allow the abolitionists access.

Armed men protecting Alvan Stewart's home had driven off a group of torch-carrying rioters.

The furniture and printing equipment of the abolitionist newspaper, the *Standard and Democrat*, had been thrown out the second-story window onto Whitesboro Street, only slightly delaying the paper's ability to report on the convention.

Dr. Corliss McCooke had been found murdered on the towpath. Some thought, after he had been seen at midday partaking in the free grog at King's Victualing House and getting his flask filled from the proprietor's special stock, that perhaps the good doctor might have been inebriated and gotten himself into a drunken brawl with a ruffian working on the canal. Others whispered that perhaps an aggrieved husband might have finally given the doctor his due.

Tongues wagged about a violent group of runaway slaves that, aided by inhabitants of Post Street, had apparently escaped from Virginian law officers. One of the officers clung to his life after a horrible beating. Judge Chester Hayden's office had been torn apart in the struggle. Hayden's longtime clerk had been manhandled and the judge himself was said to be in bed recovering from the attack.

More details spread around Post Street, as those who participated in the rescue described the desperate struggle in the judge's office. Some who had seen the fugitives forced through the streets advocated finding the slavers and turning the lash on them. Schoolmaster Freeman planned to use this opportunity to organize the community into a vigilance committee—one that would be ready to aid runaways—like the one that Mr. Ruggles of New York City had proposed to him before the convention had been disrupted.

By far the most shocking development was that the well-known financier Augustin Galway had suffered some kind of seizure, perhaps a heart problem, and had died suddenly. Many could not understand what he had been doing in Judge Hayden's office with the runaways. People speculated that it must have had something to do with the Colonization Society and the Committee of 25, but the judge would not elaborate. Most curious was that the entire matter did not seem to be undergoing much official examination.

Maggie sat on her bed as morning light peeked over the sloping eastern hills. No fire warmed the kitchen. Instead of breakfast smells, the sulfurous odor of burned black powder lingered. Her injured pinkie throbbed. The stained rags she had used to tie up her gunshot wound still lay about. Under clean bandages, the whip mark on her shoulder stung. Mr. Pryce had helped her pick out the threads of her tattered dress that had embedded themselves in the cut. In return, she had inspected his injured jaw, pronouncing it unbroken, but badly bruised. Now, to even try to lift her arms to draw water for coffee was impossible.

She had been going over the string of events that had led her to gain and lose a family, all within a few days. The vision of Elymas removing Imari's lifeless body from the courthouse circled about in her brain and intensified the ache in her chest. And poor Augustin. By the time she had gotten to his side and helped turn him onto his back, his eyes were wild with fear. As the battle to free Imari and Elymas swirled around them, Maggie had covered him with her body, her head above his face. His lips moved. She brought her ear to them. He mumbled "shadow" and "smoke" and "failed."

"You done good," she told him. "In the end, you done what you had to."

"Too late," he said.

"Never too late to do the right thing." She gently kissed the side of his face.

Augustin squeezed her hand, then suddenly went slack. She saw his eyes roll back and go still.

At Judge Hayden's office there had been nothing to do but let Mr. Pryce summon Mr. Hollister of Williams & Hollister Grocers to provide a casket and to bring Augustin home, where Maggie could help the men wash and dress him for the last time. After they had finished, they arranged Augustin's body in the coffin. The men carried him into the front parlor so that the city might be able to come and look upon him before his burial. Once the grocer and the young man left, Maggie retreated to her room and wept.

She looked into the light of the new day and fell back onto the bed, pulling a blanket over her face, eventually surrendering and letting sleep overtake her.

During the disruption of the New York Anti-Slavery Society convention, Gerrit Smith, a wealthy man who had previously devoted his time and money to the colonization cause and who came to the event at Reverend Green's urging, became so angered at the abrogation of the rights of assembly and free speech that he invited the delegates to continue their discussions in his hometown of Peterboro, thirty miles away.

Hundreds of men made the journey in the pouring rain. Carts were hired, horses saddled, canalboats filled, and many, like Pryce Anwell, went on foot in the black of night over rolling hills.

By the time Pryce arrived in the morning, the meeting was about to resume. He sat among hundreds of men, both white and black, in the Peterboro Presbyterian Church. At the lectern on the raised chancel, Alvan Stewart stood with a gavel in his hand ready to begin the proceedings. Stewart raised his arm and it was as if each man held his breath waiting for the pound of the walnut on the slate stopper to start the convention afresh.

The men knew that once the gavel fell, it would be their mission to ready themselves to fight against slavery as if it were their own families they had to save. Stewart swung his arm and struck the slate. Pryce Anwell understood his own path was now set toward justice.

* * *

Twenty-five miles away in Oriskany, in the windowless root cellar of Sylvanus's Quaker friends, Imari lay unconscious.

Helen helped the Quaker's wife wash Imari's battered body, and wept over the dark bruises that circled her neck. The ordeal of child-birth and her capture would have been too much for most, but Helen knew Imari was strong. A trusted doctor held Imari's wrist, counting the beats of her heart. But to Helen, the poor woman looked thin and bloodless.

"Her pulse has strengthened," the doctor said. "That is a hopeful sign."

Elymas lay on the next cot. The doctor removed the shot from his shoulder and sewed up the whip cut on his leg. He had stood the pain bravely, but lost a lot of blood. The doctor insisted that there was good reason to hope.

The Oriskany Quaker, Brother Hughes, told Sylvanus he feared that their arrival, and all the additional people around the farm, might draw the attention of anyone searching for the runaways. "We must be pru-dent," he said. "You must leave, or risk exposure."

Helen reluctantly agreed, but made the farmer promise to write to Sylvanus with any news.

At dawn, she fed baby Margaret fresh cow's milk and rocked her until the infant slept, only then reluctantly releasing her into Joe's arms. She felt a connection with the child that pulled at her heart and had to turn away quickly, lest she be unable to go. She said goodbye to Horace and kissed Imari's forehead. She leaned over the sleeping figure of Ely-mas and touched his warm arm. With tears streaming down her face, she allowed herself to be led away.

Sylvanus drove the wagon back to Utica. During the silent trip, Helen's mind was filled with painful fantasies. If only she had been the one shot. Elymas deserved to live with his family in peace and freedom. Why should she, a sheltered girl, have been spared? Even after the wedding and the trip to New York, she had only understood a small slice of life's truths. She was amazed that so many different people seemed ready to help escaping slaves, no matter what the personal consequences. Per-haps it was just that Sylvanus had many friends among the Quakers. But even the blacksmith, who had arrived in the dark of night, asked no questions as he removed the chains from the two still bodies. There seemed to be a group of people she had never noticed before—those who followed their own principles instead of the law. Her understanding of the arrangement of the world had been turned upside down.

She had assumed somehow that everyone pretty much believed the same things. Good people obeyed the law and bad people did not. Good people were loved by God and bad people were punished. Life could be unduly harsh and sometimes capricious. But how was it part of God's plan to enslave an entire race of people?

As the cart bumped along the road, Helen felt as if she were covered by layers of earth. What had been going on between Augustin and Maggie seemed beyond comprehension. It was difficult enough trying to picture her husband as a young man. But how had he entangled himself with a black servant? No—not a servant, a slave—*his* slave. Maggie was not like any slave Miss Manahan had described. Then again, neither was Imari, nor for that matter Elymas. All she saw in them was a family that had risked their lives for freedom. Miss Manahan taught that Negroes were better off as slaves, and Helen had believed that, until she met Imari.

She focused back to the source of her extreme discomfort. She was baffled and disquieted that Augustin had found Maggie attractive. She imagined them moving about in the house. His father in the library. His mother . . . well, she knew about Maggie's mother, she'd died by then, but when had Augustin lost his mother? She did not even know. She forced her mind back to her question. How had Augustin come to love a slave? He said in court, for everyone to hear, that he loved her. He had never spoken those words to Helen.

If she could come to look upon Maggie and Imari as people for whom she had run risks and lied, as people she enjoyed talking and listening to, how could she deny that Augustin might have felt the same way?

Did she think of the two women as less than herself? It seemed natural to do so, something accepted, like breathing air. She thought perhaps whites were born with that opinion of themselves.

Helen suddenly realized that Maggie's relationship with Augustin was much more equal than her own. *He loved her.* He could not bear to part with her. He had disobeyed his own father and demanded she be brought back home.

It was Maggie's dark skin that made the affair so difficult for her to accept. In New York City, she had seen Augustin in flirtatious conversations with various ladies. She had burned with jealousy. It wasn't hard to imagine one of them, in her finery and with her sophistication, winning his heart. At that time, she had not felt superior, but awkward, and childlike. But they were white and Maggie was black. And that changed everything.

If Maggie had been white . . . well, if she had been white she would not have been a slave. If she and Augustin had committed an indiscretion, they would have married. That would have made Maggie the first Mrs. Galway. In a very real sense, Maggie *was* the first Mrs. Galway, because she had given him a son. Helen smiled bitterly. Did poor dead Emma Galway ever know? She was certain that the lady did not.

Helen realized that it was time to disregard her many incorrect assumptions and to simply accept the facts. She was jealous of Maggie's ease with Augustin and knew she herself would never have that ease with him. But most importantly, Helen did not—and never would—love her husband. She loved Pryce, but a relationship with him could not be right in the eyes of God.

The sun was high in the sky as she approached her home, still so unfamiliar and strange to her. The curtains were closed. She looked down at her muddy gray school frock. As she approached the front door, her stomach tightened, and in a moment of weakness she veered off, heading instead around to the back.

She had expected to find Maggie in the kitchen, or at least for the stove to be hot. The small bedroom was open and Helen saw her on the bed, under the blanket, her snores filling the room. The poor woman certainly deserved some rest.

A stack of kindling stood near the stove, so Helen decided to make a fire and cook some food and coffee for everyone. She closed the bedroom door and moved about the kitchen, quietly tidying and putting things to rights. The sight of Maggie's blood on the floor and table upset her, but she pulled on an apron and erased the evidence. It took a long while for the thick iron to get hot enough to boil water, but Helen saw why Maggie so loved the stove. It was more contained than an open hearth and did away with the risk of catching one's clothing on fire to fry a few eggs. Helen put some ham aside for Maggie and then

loaded a tray with plates, cups, food, and coffee for Augustin and herself. She thought they would eat together in the library.

It was vital that he listen to her. After all the events of the past few
weeks, she didn't know if their marriage could be saved. With no idea
what to say to her husband and a conviction to tell the truth, she picked
up the tray and pushed through into the front hall.

She noticed that the parlor door was open and peeked in. The furniture had been rearranged, and toward the front window a large box sat
on wooden sawhorses. She stepped to the threshold. The tray slipped
from her hands, crashing to the floor. Her knees went weak and she
crumpled amid the broken china.

CHAPTER FORTY-THREE

CLOTHED HEAD TO TOE IN BLACK, Helen spent the next few days receiving mourners. While many people may not have known that Augustin Galway had remarried, now that he was dead, she had become the most famous widow in Utica. Not only did members of the Committee of 25 and many of the city's bankers, politicians, and businessmen come by to show their respect; mothers brought eligible sons; widowers hinted at their need for a young wife; and a few men of less-than-respectable circumstances arrived slick with charm.

Everyone assumed that Mr. Galway, an only child who was himself never blessed with children, must have bequeathed to his widow access not only to the revenue from his investments, but also control over his properties. They believed that Mrs. Galway would not be expected to survive on the normal dower's share—by law, only the interest on the income from a mere one-third of his land. Mrs. Galway, it was supposed, would have much more money at her disposal. When word spread that the well-known portraitist Anson Dickinson had taken the time to sketch Mr. Galway in the casket, the notion of the widow's wealth had been cemented.

Helen kept thinking that everything had turned to dust. Her duties as Augustin's wife had been to produce a child and keep her aging husband happy and heathy. She had failed. If only she had been more forceful when she saw the extent of the dreadful infection on his leg. That it had been gangrenous was perfectly clear now. This must have taken such a toll on his strength that his heart simply could not endure the stress.

And there was still no word from Sylvanus's friend about the runaways. Uncertainty filled Helen's hours.

Toward the end of the final day, as the parade of visitors slowed, she retreated to the library, leaving the door ajar so that Maggie could summon her. Despite the cook's injuries, together they had cleaned up the evidence of Augustin's illness. They had found a surprising number of empty bottles under the sofa, presumably shoved there by Dr. Mc-Cooke. Maggie had cursed his name when she discovered the cache, but quickly took it back, in respect for the dead. All liquors were removed and the daybed pushed back into the hall closet. And though they aired it out, the library still held the scent of tobacco. At least the room was a quiet retreat and Helen decided to look among the books for something to distract her. She found herself opening William Godwin's book *Enquiry Concerning Political Justice and its Influence on Morals and Happiness*. The title seemed to discuss many of the questions that she needed answered. A nearby cough made her jump and she snapped the book closed.

"You might find—"

"Pryce . . . I mean, Mr. Anwell. You startled me."

"Sorry," he said, "I didn't mean to sneak up. It's just that seeing you there with a book in your hand—I didn't want to break your concentration."

"I'm neglecting my duties by being in here."

"You've been so crowded by mourners that I didn't get the chance to tell you how sorry I am about Mr. Galway," said Pryce, looking at his shoes. "Terribly sorry."

"Thank you," she responded quietly, then turned to replace the volume on the shelf.

"You might find his wife's book more interesting," said Pryce. "*A Vindication of the Rights of Woman* by Mary Wollstonecraft."

"The rights of women?" Helen studied him. "Do you find that subject interesting?"

"Well, it's flipped more than a few powdered wigs," he said. "I'll find a copy for you."

"Thank you. I suppose I must go back into the parlor—"

"Wait a moment." He touched her hand.

Her breath caught. Silence overtook them until Helen focused on him, her eyes soft. "You can't be in here alone with me." She stepped toward the door.

"I don't care what people think," he said, holding on to her. "These last few days have altered me."

She bowed her head, no longer knowing what to believe. But the trembling young man's presence ignited a deep earthly longing.

"I don't just mean . . . what happened." He squeezed her hand and stared deeply into her eyes. "I so admire what you did for that poor woman. I mean, I never paid much attention to it—I mean slavery. What did it have to do with me, after all? But that's blind and cowardly. I could have done so much more."

"I did very little," Helen said, fighting down tears.

"You were magnificent. If I get another chance I'll try to be as brave as you."

"I only pray that she and her husband are still alive."

"It's up to God, not us." Pryce flipped Helen's hand over and stared at her palm. "I'm sorry if I've compromised you, but I can't apologize about my feelings."

She became aware of her heartbeat, so strong it alarmed her. She feared letting herself go unchecked. "What . . . are those feelings?" she whispered.

"For these last nights, I've stared at the sky. I thought of our few hours together. And I realized that I might lose you." Pryce cleared his throat. "You're everything to me." He brought her hand to his cheek. "I love you. I can't let you go. I said before that I'd be with you no matter what. I want to marry you, make things right."

There it was, the new life, full, young, and bursting with possibilities.

"I want to," Helen said. "But I can't imagine what's to come. It's all shadows. Nothing is as I assumed it to be."

He drew her hand to his mouth and kissed it. She moved closer and once again their lips touched. It felt so right, as if the past with Augustin had loosened its talons, grown wings, and struck out for the blue sky.

Alvan Stewart knocked and entered the room. Helen and Pryce pulled apart.

"Excuse me," he said, shock showing on his face. "Forgive me. I came in because I have news."

"About Imari and Elymas?" Helen said.

"I'm afraid not. But it seems," said Stewart, opening the door wide, "that there is a will."

Miss Manahan entered in her best black crepe dress, stopping for a moment to study the room, eyes lingering on the wall of books before her gaze focused on Pryce. He exchanged a sly glance with Helen.

"The bear has returned," he whispered before stepping away.

Miss Manahan raised her hand, revealing a substantial-looking document.

Helen remained still.

"This is the will I negotiated with your *husband* before the wedding." Again her eyes fell on Pryce. "It's private."

"Mr. Anwell," said Helen, "would you please call in Maggie."

"A servant?" asked the lady, one eyebrow elevated and lips pursed.

"She deserves to hear this," Helen replied.

Pryce left. Helen invited Stewart and the schoolteacher to sit on the sofa. She took the chair in which Augustin had spent his final days. She pressed her back into it and caught the scent of his hair oil. After three deep breaths, she touched a handkerchief to the corner of each eye. Miss Manahan was the past, one to which she would never return. But what place would Helen fill now? She looked around the room. There were hundreds of books just an arm's reach away, each filled with ideas, discoveries, and experiences. And there was a man who said he loved her, and she most assuredly loved him.

A knock came at the door. Helen called, "Enter," and suddenly felt more in control of herself and her future than she had since leaving the Female Institute.

Maggie arrived, also dressed in black, with the exception of her crisp white apron. Her injured shoulder and arm hung in front of her, supported by a black sling. Stewart stood and Helen indicated that Maggie should take his place on the couch. Pryce waited in the doorway.

The big lawyer put out his hand and the schoolteacher reluctantly handed him the document. He studied it for a moment. "Maggie, you have been left a substantial sum to do with as you please."

The cook's head bent and she quickly dabbed away tears.

"Mrs. Galway, you have been left the stewardship of Mr. Galway's entire estate."

"Stewardship? What does that mean?" asked Helen.

"It is yours," said the lawyer, "since there is no recognized legal heir." He coughed.

Maggie's eyes flashed to Helen, who nodded in comprehension.

"Sell it," said Helen.

"You can't," cried Miss Manahan.

"Can't I?" Helen asked Stewart.

"You can."

"What will people think?" said Miss Manahan.

"I don't care," said Helen. She addressed the lawyer: "Sell the businesses. Keep the house?" She glanced at Maggie, who nodded. "Let me know what you need from me." She rose from the chair. "Thank you all. I'd like to be alone."

The schoolteacher stood, huffing. "He's not even buried yet."

"Miss Manahan," said Helen, going to her and taking her hand, "I want to thank you for all you've done for me and for your girls. I won't forget the school and you when all of this is settled."

The older woman brightened considerably. "You were always one of my favorites."

Stewart offered the lady his arm, which she graciously accepted and floated out. Maggie, shaking her head, followed the pair.

Pryce lingered. "I hope you don't think that I asked for your hand for financial gain."

"You have disturbed my peace since the moment you called to me from that canalboat," Helen said.

"It wasn't my intention to bring you to sin."

"Let me finish." She drifted to the window and looked out onto Bleecker Street. "My life has always seemed small. I wanted to obey God and my elders, follow the rules, and be petted and praised for it." She chuckled. "But you've helped me realize that's not enough. At first, I was flattered by your attention, thrilled even. Part of me thought you were just an academic boy who knew too much about the stars, but nothing about how difficult life is. You were honest, terribly so. While I squeezed myself into a lie."

"I can leave if you want," said Pryce, swallowing hard.

"Leave?" She turned to him. "I love you. I can't imagine going forward without you. I need you and that makes me a sinner. But I know now that I have to be true to my own self." She took his hands in hers. "I hope that you still want to help me grow. And that I can help you—always."

"Does this mean you'll marry me?"

"Does your offer still stand?"

"Of course it does."

"Then I say yes," she laughed. Suddenly, her fear about the future vanished. What was to come was still mysterious, but he was a yellow to complement her blue. With Pryce, she could be honest, equal, part of a true partnership.

He pulled her to him and they wrapped their arms around each other.

"Let it be soon," said Pryce.

"Yes," sighed Helen, already feeling at home within his embrace.

C HAPTER FORTY-FOUR

HELEN LOOKED UP from the box she was filling with books destined for Miss Manahan's Female Institute. Maggie approached holding a package wrapped in paper and tied with twine.

"That artist fellow you hired, Mr. Dickinson, dropped this by," said Maggie, placing the small rectangular object on the desk. They both looked at it, arms at their sides, as if waiting for the other to make a move.

"I feel like I've already forgotten him, just a little," said Helen. "If I close my eyes I can see his form, but his face is indistinct."

"I ain't thinking about him at the end. I never used to let myself remember none a them old days. But now I'm thinking on it. Mr. Augustin and me played all the time when we was kids." Maggie smiled. "Later things got more . . . well." Helen looked away. "Oh, sorry. It ain't proper to talk about him like that."

Helen brightened. "I'm done trying to figure out what's proper." She came around the desk. "Shall we open it?"

Maggie produced a small knife and sliced through the twine. Helen unfolded the paper. Inside sat a green velvet-covered box. She opened it and there staring up at them was a small wood-framed image of Augustin.

"It's not him," said Helen. "His face is too smooth."

"It's him," said Maggie. "Him—without the care on his soul." They stood still.

"Do you want it?" asked Helen quietly.

"I ain't putting it in my room, if that's what you're asking."

"I have an idea." Helen carried the painting out into the hallway and held it near Emma Galway's portrait. "I think it's the *proper* thing."

Maggie went into the kitchen and returned with a hammer and nail. After they decided exactly where to place the painting, she banged in the nail. Both stood back to appraise their work.

"He loved her," said Maggie. "They's together up in the cemetery too."

"It's only right," said Helen.

"He wasn't a bad man, just weak," said Maggie, dabbing her eyes with a kerchief. "I'm glad he got to make good in the end. And that what happened ain't no big secret no more."

Helen put her arm around Maggie's waist.

The cook shook her head. "I can't believe that I told him not to marry you." She touched Helen's cheek. "So young. I said you was gonna be frivolous. But he didn't want to listen. He wanted a baby boy so bad. Well, he got one. Too bad he ain't around to see how it feels." Maggie studied Helen, then nodded. "Life ain't no clear path. You gotta be the one who decides things. The preacher says you gotta do this. The law says you gotta do that. Sometimes the heart says something that sounds crazy to the whole world, but you go and do it. No matter how clean they are on the outside, ain't nobody live perfect." She paused. "You love him, that boy?"

"Yes," Helen said. "We're going to be married. But Augustin," she turned to the painting, "he's been gone just two weeks. People will talk. It's not proper."

Maggie growled, "Let me tell you what ain't proper. Not grabbing love and holding tight, no matter what. That ain't proper—since you ask me."

Helen took her hands. "Your opinion means so much to me."

Just then, two shadows appeared at the front door and commenced knocking. Helen held Maggie's eye for a moment before answering the summons.

Pryce and Sylvanus stood at the threshold.

"Mr. Sylvanus," said Helen, her voice strangely high, "what brings you?"

"'Tis a letter," said Sylvanus, holding up a sealed envelope.

"From my people?" asked Maggie anxiously.

"It's addressed to you both," said Pryce.

Helen took the letter. Their names were spelled out in a shaky hand. She opened it. "It's from Imari." She began to read aloud.

November 4, 1835

Dear Miss Helen and Miss Maggie,

We writing to thank you both for the help you rendered us in our hour of need. We all alive and healing thanks to this here Quaker and his wife, Brother and Sister Hughes.

We so sorry that Mr. Galway got killed. It just about breaks my heart. Horace done told me that he a good man. And Elymas say that he forgive his father because he done the right thing in the end.

Elymas be healing. He wants to help around here, but mostly his right arm don't want to work. Doctor says he ain't going to use it much again. I hope that doctor be wrong and healing time be all he need.

Baby Margaret be getting fat and healthy. And Sister H. got Joe busy learning to copy out his letters and numbers. He really want to help his poppa, but Sister say he got to learn.

I be back on my feet, but still very sore. The doctor says I almost lost my voice and ain't never going to talk normal again. That's God's will I guess. I knew Elymas be getting better when he said my scratchy squeaky old voice sound like cooing doves to him.

We be missing Maggie and her cooking and trading stories all night. To be true, we all missing everything about Maggie. Elymas especially want to get to know his true momma. But that devil Hickox ain't never going to give up on trying to find me. We hear that he be heading back to Virginia, but that ain't far enough for my comfort.

We staying put for now, but our eyes be looking north. I knew you would all be troubled if you don't hear from us. Please send our thanks to Mr. Stewart. And to Mr. Sylvanus. And to that young fellow. Joe told me there be a lot more people who did all sorts of things to win us our freedom. We thank them all.

Former obedient servant, now free,
Imari

Post Script: Miss Helen, I just got to add one little bit. What you did for us give me something I ain't never had too much of and that be hope. All them other people who help us on the way north knew what they be doing. They had their whys all worked out before we got there. But Miss Helen, you done it cause you got a good solid heart. You a precious thing. Life got a way of changing us, but don't you let it.

CHAPTER FORTY-FIVE

TWO WEEKS LATER, on a warm November day, Pryce and Horace loaded Maggie's trunk onto the cart outside the Galway house. Her belongings slid next to a carton of her favorite iron fry pans. Sturdy wooden containers held a brand-new set of dishes packed individually in crumpled pages of the *Oneida Whig*, flatware, tea service, linens, and bolts of pretty cotton cloth. Half a dozen smoked hams and other food supplies and dry goods filled out the bed. Horace placed a small package of his own new clothing next to the trunk. He and Pryce threw an oilcloth over the load and tightened the ropes that secured the baggage.

Maggie and Helen sat on the back porch watching them work.

"You got it tied down good?" Maggie called to Horace.

"Yes ma'am," he said, approaching the two women.

"'Cause if I find nothing but broken china, you gonna hear about it."

"We got us a long journey ahead," said Horace, smiling and putting one foot up on the edge of the stair, "so you best spread out your compliments so I don't go getting too proud."

Maggie returned his smile and leaned her rocking chair forward to kiss him.

"You're blushing like a bride," said Helen.

"I got a right, don't you think?"

Helen laughed.

Maggie pushed back in her chair. "Give us a minute, will you?"

Horace winked and waved to Pryce. "Let me show you what's what in that barn." They moved away.

Maggie grabbed Helen's hand. "Don't stay too long here," she said.

"I won't. After we get married, I'll close the house up. There's nothing for me here. Pryce doesn't want to go back to Little Falls. Maybe we'll head west and figure out if my Uncle Bill is still alive."

"I ain't got the words to say what I want," said Maggie. "You just kept on surprising me. I ain't never gonna underestimate you again."

Helen squeezed her hand. "You're a wonder." She wiped away a tear. "You have to make sure to write me. I want to know everything."

"How can I write you if you hauling yourselves out to the wilderness?"

Just then Sylvanus came up the driveway. He rushed to the wagon, stopped, and held on to the sideboard, out of breath.

"Why you running, Baker?" called Horace as he and Pryce came out of the barn. Sylvanus held up his hand, signaling that he couldn't yet talk.

Next, Alvan Stewart came up the driveway. "I told him he didn't have to hurry."

Helen and Maggie joined him.

"Mr. Stewart, may we use your office to forward our letters?" asked Helen. "There are so many unknowns, but we all promise to keep you informed about our whereabouts."

"I expect nothing less," he said. "After all, I will have to know where to send money. And there's Elymas's third of the estate."

"We ain't likely to lose track a that," said Maggie. She held out her hand. Stewart took it in both of his. "Thank you, Mr. Stewart, for all you done. God bless you and keep you strong. All them people down south need you."

"I can but try," said the lawyer.

"Maggie, you must promise me to take care of them," said Helen, walking to her cart.

"Don't you think that's my plan?" Maggie replied, slipping her arm around Helen's shoulders.

"You have some pretty good plans," said Helen, smiling weakly. "I can't believe I won't see you again."

"Now, nobody says that. Could be they're gonna get sick to death a me being in their business. You would too, probably. You can always visit. And don't worry about nothing. You get married and go on that honeymoon and you work on bringing a baby into this world."

Helen felt the blush come up her neck. They held each other. Both women had tears in their eyes when they finally broke apart.

"Here," said Sylvanus, handing Maggie a small wooden bowl covered by a white cloth. "Thy bread starter, as promised."

"I'm gonna take good care of it." Maggie climbed up to the driver's seat. Horace joined her and after a short silent standoff, she took the reins and slapped the horse into motion.

The group watched them go. Pryce put his arm around Helen.

As the cart turned toward Oriskany, Helen realized that three generations were finally going to be together and heading toward their own destinies, free of the dreadful institution that had enslaved them all.

She took a deep breath. She'd never felt so light in her life.

The End

Acknowledgments

This novel has been a Kaylie Jones Book from conception to publication. In 2010, Kaylie saw the writer inside of me and set about nurturing and pushing and insisting that I keep on putting words into sentences. Her steadfast support for this project made me believe that a novel was within my reach. She has my undying gratitude for helping me rebloom into an author.

And thank you, David Black, for helping me see through the mountain of raw material I was uncovering and zero in on the central moral question of this work.

All my love and thanks to my husband, Charles Petzold, writer extraordinaire, whose work ethic I mirrored and whose advice I (mostly) followed. His support, knowledge, and attention to detail have been the foundation for my leap into the historical research that led to this book and so much more. His love has sustained me.

Sincere thanks to my amazing friends and fellow writers who read early versions and helped me down the path toward publication: Shakoure Char, Tina Barry, Mary Horgan, Faye Coleman, Heather Bryant, Robert Strickstein, Sharon Robustelli, Jean Ende, Stacey Lender, Ruth Bonapace, Monique Antoinette Lewis, Barbara J. Taylor, Nina Solomon, Don DiNicola, Petina Cole, Robert C. Strickstein, and Priscilla Tucker at the St. Paul Community Baptist Church. I cannot understate the help from fellow writers at the 2016 retreat in San Miguel de Allende, Mexico: Stacy Kaplan, J. Patrick Redmond, Terri Taylor, Theasa Tuohy, and Janine Veto.

Thank you to Laurie Lowenstein for her invaluable advice and support. Thanks to Trena Keating for her smart suggestions and help.

My deep thanks to the people at Akashic Books and Kaylie Jones Books, especially Johnny Temple.

Others who were of great help in this research include Dr. Milton Sernett, professor emeritus of African American history, Syracuse University; Reverend Robert and Deborah Williams, formerly of Hope

Chapel A.M.E. Zion Church, Utica; James Vaughan of Incarcerated Flavors; Dr. Jan DeAmicis, Mary Hayes Gordon, Jean Davis—whose ancestors were formerly enslaved in Oneida County—and all of the Oneida County Freedom Trail Commission; Dr. Kathryn M. Silva, chair of the Department of Humanities at Claflin University; Deitra Harvey, former president of the NAACP, Utica/Oneida County; David Mathis, longtime member of Hope Chapel A.M.E. Zion Church; Mayor Robert Palmieri of Utica; John H. Johnsen, provost, Utica College; the Other Side and their volunteers; Kim and Orrin Domenico; Alison Sinnott, who lets me sleep at her house during all my research trips; Nick Sheldon, who helps keep me fed and entertained; and Susan and Roger Smith for their years of cheerleading. I'm sorry that Roger won't be there in the front row for the publication party.

I want to thank Tom and Gay Ingegneri, owners of the Cranbury Inn Restaurant in New Jersey for the amazing tour of their historic building that was most likely part of the Underground Railroad.

I send much gratitude to Brian Howard, director of the Oneida County Historical Center, and to the dedicated staff and knowledgeable volunteers. So many librarians have helped along the way, including those at the New York Public Library, the Schomburg Center for Research in Black Culture, the New York State Library and Archives, the Fenimore Art Museum Research Library, Utica Public Library, the New-York Historical Society, Shenandoah County Library, the Library of Virginia, James Madison University libraries, Cornell University libraries, as well as the following institutions: Utica College, Bank of Utica, George Washington's Mount Vernon, the Metropolitan Museum of Art, the Farmers' Museum, the National Museum of African American History and Culture, Fulton Postcards, and the Library of Congress's Born in Slavery: Slave Narratives from the Federal Writers' Project.

In 2007, I began searching for the word *Utica* in the index of every book I saw about the Underground Railroad and African American history. I was convinced that the city of my youth must have been part of the great struggle to abolish slavery. Unfortunately, I was never taught anything about that in the school system. Finally, in one book, I found a reference to the 1835 Utica anti-abolition riot. *The Third Mrs. Galway* is one of a group of projects that resulted from that piece of historical information.

Most of the characters in the novel are my own inventions, but some are based on real people: Alvan Stewart, Esq., president of the New York Anti-Slavery Society; Gerrit Smith, who started as a leader of the American Colonization Society but went on to become the second president of the New York Anti-Slavery Society and was one of the "secret six" who funded John Brown's attack on Harpers Ferry; Congressman Samuel Beardsley, who had a fine political career and who went on to serve on the New York State Supreme Court; Reverend Beriah Green, who was fired from Western Reserve College because of his strident abolitionism and came to Oneida County to be the president of the Oneida Institute of Science and Technology and a radicalizing force in central New York; Reverend Joshua Danforth, the main traveling agent for the American Colonization Society; and Judge Chester Hayden, first judge of the Utica Court of Common Pleas, who ran the proceedings in the real-life case of Harry Bird and George, two men escaping from slavery who became the focus of the successful 1836 Utica rescue. This story is the subject of my upcoming nonfiction book. Hayden moved to Cleveland and went on to help found the Poland Law College, which later became the Ohio State and Union Law College. There are other names I used because I liked the sound of them but know nothing about the real people: Miss Manahan, Sheriff Osborn, Williams & Hollister, Charles Dupre, David Rees, Josiah Tripp, Reverend Quarters, Reverend Asa Hopkins, and others.

Some of the dialogue in the Colonization Society's meeting scene, in the New York Anti-Slavery Society convention scene, and in the court scene is either quoted or suggested from writings or contemporary newspaper reports of actual speeches.

Other real people who traveled to Utica for the convention are: Lewis Tappan, a wealthy silk merchant and founder of the American Anti-Slavery Society and a major funder and organizer for the defense of the *Amistad* captives; David Ruggles, an African American abolitionist who ran the first black-owned bookstore in New York City, edited the abolition newspaper the *Mirror of Liberty*, and was the subject of an attempted kidnapping by men trying to silence his voice by selling him into slavery; and James W. Higgins, an abolitionist and grocer who, with Ruggles, founded the New York City Committee of Vigilance and worked with others at the Dey Street Church to help people escaping slavery. Their dialogue is my own invention.

Imari's lullaby was suggested by an old song with an unprintable name from the book *The American Songbag* by Carl Sandburg (New York: Harcourt, Brace and Company, 1927, p. 455). Sandburg wrote, "Margaret Johnson of Augusta, Georgia, heard her mother sing this, year on year, as the mother had learned it from the singing, year on year, of a Negro woman who comforted children with it. The source of its language may be French, Creole, Cherokee, or mixed."

In the comet-viewing scene at the park, some of Pryce's dialogue was suggested by the wonderful book *Views of the Architecture of the Heavens: In a Series of Letters to a Lady* by John Pringle Nichol (Edinburgh: William Tait, 1837).

I do quote a few of Shakespeare's words and there are snippets from the King James Bible repeated by Augustin Galway. Hickox's musing on chaos was suggested by Ovid's *Metamorphoses*.

The poem by Anacreon, the lyric poet of Ionia, is taken from the chapter on female influence in the book *A Voice to Youth: Addressed to Young Men and Young Ladies* by Reverend J. M. Austin (Utica: Grosh and Hutchinson, 1838).

The poem about comets that Pryce quotes was published in the *Railroad Advocate* (Rogersville, Tennessee) on February 2, 1832.

The map in the front of the book is adapted from one published in the *The Pioneers of Utica* by Moses Mears Bagg (Utica: Curtis & Childs, 1877). The outline of the Ballou Creek is from the 1939 map called "Historical Map of Utica in 1839," drawn by L.W. Devereax, published to commemorate the one hundredth anniversary of the Savings Bank of Utica.

CPSIA information can be obtained
at www.ICGtesting.com
Printed in the USA
JSHW020424110821
17751JS00005B/5